Cora Pooler

Enjoy Dottie Rexford

Dottie Rexford

WESTBOW·
PRESS
A DIVISION OF THOMAS NELSON
& ZONDERVAN

Scripture taken from the Holy Bible, NEW INTERNATIONAL VERSION®.
Copyright © 1973, 1978, 1984 by Biblica, Inc. All rights reserved worldwide.
Used by permission. NEW INTERNATIONAL VERSION® and NIV® are
registered trademarks of Biblica, Inc. Use of either trademark for the offering
of goods or services requires the prior written consent of Biblica US, Inc.

Scripture taken from the King James Version of the Bible.

WestBow Press books may be ordered through booksellers or by contacting:

WestBow Press
A Division of Thomas Nelson & Zondervan
1663 Liberty Drive
Bloomington, IN 47403
www.westbowpress.com
1 (866) 928-1240

Because of the dynamic nature of the Internet, any web addresses or
links contained in this book may have changed since publication and
may no longer be valid. The views expressed in this work are solely those
of the author and do not necessarily reflect the views of the publisher,
and the publisher hereby disclaims any responsibility for them.

Any people depicted in stock imagery provided by Thinkstock are models,
and such images are being used for illustrative purposes only.
Certain stock imagery © Thinkstock.

ISBN: 978-1-4908-2937-1 (sc)
ISBN: 978-1-4908-2938-8 (e)

Library of Congress Control Number: 2014904332

Printed in the United States of America.

WestBow Press rev. date: 4/9/2014

This Book is Dedicated to:

Anne and Kenny
Linda and Rusty
Abbey and Scott
Betsy and Scott
Connor
Kathryn
Jacob

Appreciation

I thank God for creating man. There sits waiting within each of us the wondrous being He fashioned us to be. And over that perfect person we are clothed with experiences, good and bad, past and present, our own and the effect of those with us now and those who came before us. Each person I see brings thought and knowledge to my mind and my heart. Fodder for writing. Understanding. Growth.

There are, also, so many to be thanked for the loyalty, kindness, patience and joy they have brought into my life. They are a legion too large to be counted. They have made it easier for me to write. Here I can name only a few, but you are all precious to me. Carolyn Burke, LaPearl Haynes, Maria Mattias, and Virginia Brown, who taught me the value of loving and everlasting friendship. William Tapply, my mentor, a gifted writer who magnified for me the wonder of putting words on paper. My writing colleagues in Sinclairville, New York and Sebring/Avon Park/Lake Wales, Florida, the writing groups, that read, listened and encouraged. Tracy Higley, who saw something in my work and gave me reason to persevere. Larry Bolling, who was faithful to read my scribbling and was sensitive and honest in his critique. Christine Yarbour and Mary Bailey for their expertise and patience with this fumbling, inept computer user. My family, special, loved and needed. And so many more.

Thank You.

Chapter One

As I drove down the narrow roads of crumbled gravel and dirt pressed firm, roads unlined with white paint, their borders free from stretching poles and hanging wires, there came a trembling within me, a reaching back to a different way of life, a life I'd left, a life that had been denied to me. I had been banished, labeled a sinner, counted as unworthy for salvation. Shunned.

Now, twenty years later, I was home, back again, in Amish country. Stark white houses. Barns, bigger and stronger than the houses. Corn bins, nearly empty, winter feeding done. Clotheslines, empty this Sabbath day. No children outside playing … or weeding or feeding the chickens or taking water to male workers in the fields. No men … sleeves rolled up, warm weather straw hats firm on heads, muscles bulging, faces sweating … walking behind plows, harnessing horses, pounding nails or throwing manure onto wagon beds. I had come on the day of worship. They would all be together … men, women, and children. The whole community celebrating in the way it deemed right.

I passed the house that was their church on this Sunday. Parked on both sides of the dirt driveway were their buggies, all alike, as if they had stood before a mirror and dressed themselves in mourning black, unadorned, each the same as the other. Tables and benches filled the side yard. For this day the sun shone warm through clouds as wispy and white as an old lady's hair. And so, they would eat outside basking in the sweet scented heat of God's radiant star.

I wanted to stop. I wanted to watch them pour from the house, perch on the benches … graceful black crows feeding. The married men first; the unmarried, next. Then the women. In that same order. All as it was when I was there, a part of it. Simple. Ordered. Known.

I didn't stop. It would hurt too much. Not to be acknowledged. Not to be welcomed. Not to be seen. Oh, God, not to *be*.

I drove on, this day's house of worship disappearing behind me. On either side of the road were great fields of buttercups and daisies.

Gently touched by a soft wind, they rolled in waves of yellow and white splendor. I slowed and opened my windows, let their beauty fill my eyes, the scent of earth and grass and flora pleasure my nose, soak into my skin. Weaving through those fields there is a stream, Wander Creek. It is bordered with scruffy bushes and stunted trees. I pulled my car to the side of the road, turned off the engine, and looked to the field on my right. Yielding to the sway and hue of flowers, remembering, I let my thoughts drift.

I heard the voices of the small ones … from so many years ago.

"Cora, wait." Little legs, too short to match the stride of an older sister, struggled to keep up with me, twelve years older and cognizant of time restrictions.

I laughed and slowed a bit. "No time to tarry," I called back. "Da will want his supper on time, and remember, we're Maem's helpers. She needs your flowers to make the table pretty for Da."

"I have the yellow ones," Lily said, close by my side, one hand clutching my skirt.

"Buttercups," I said. "Maem will be proud you found so many."

I've got the white ones," Violet shouted behind us. "But not so many."

"Daisies," I said. "And Maem will love them."

"I'm not hungry, and I don't want to go home. I'd rather wade in the water," Lily said.

I smiled. "I know. And roll in the grass. And make daisy chains. And run in circles. Spin so fast your skirt swirls way out far. And sing, sing, sing."

"I like you to tell stories, too." Violet said, reaching us and grabbing my hand.

"I know," I repeated, squeezing her fingers. "Let's run. All together."

"All the sisters," Lily laughed. And we ran.

So many memories, I thought as I sat in the car. I could see them, the twins. My little sisters. I born early in my parents' marriage; they, born late. And in between us, four brothers: George, Harry, Sampson, and Willie. I had helped my mother diaper, feed and bathe the boys. I'd taught them to count and told them stories. I sang to them. I helped sew their clothes and I sneaked cookies to them when they forgot little boy rules and Da was harsh with them. I lay with them, after dark, in their beds, and when Da's snores could be heard, when we knew he was sleeping, I helped them learn to correctly speak the English words taught in our Amish school, words that were so hard for young Pennsylvania Dutch tongues to maneuver. I watched them grow and take on chores, learn to sit quiet at the dinner table, not wiggle during long church sermons, and to never, ever, question authority. I was another maem for them ... though less and less as they became more and more Da's sons and helpers. But love as binding as ours was not forgotten, and always there was the special smile, the touch, the *look* that kept us close. That was then. I didn't know what was now. It had been so long since I had touched them, seen them. There was only remembrance. And a longing.

My thoughts went to the girls, Violet and Lily. Lily, no longer there, and Violet, older. Thirty-six. Beyond marriage age. I wondered if, indeed, she had married. When I left their world, the twins were just reaching that magical age of courting, learning and testing a kind of love that binds one with another in the way of none other. And now I, too, was twenty years older. Forty-eight. And I had no husband. No children.

I got out of the car and stood by it for a time, looking over the flowers to the creek, remembering other times ... remembering when I was child, playing with Aaron, stealing time, he and I, to crouch behind the shrubs and the trees and throw sticks and stones into the creek, and, sometimes, to pull off our shoes and socks and splash in the water. I was so careful to hold my skirt high, just enough, not to be showing too much, but enough to keep it dry, so Da wouldn't know. Aaron didn't care. He got enormously wet. His father was dead, and his mother too tired to notice. It wasn't often I saw Aaron. He lived down the road from us, and as his mother struggled to keep their small farm producing enough for their needs, she needed his help, all his hours. He was a good son, even unto the courting years. Because he was the only male at his farm, nearly all the chores fell onto him. They left little time and energy for wooing buggy rides and young man dreams.

In those years, the courting years, I wished he would see me as female. I wished he would drive me home after the Sunday night sings. But he didn't. I was just a friend ... a good friend. For a long time.

Until one day he saw me different and I was more than a friend. Much more. For a while. Until he looked at me with the eyes of his mother and turned away. We were just friends, again.

Then came my unacceptable deed. By proclamation of the Bishop, I became nothing, a shunned person, invisible. I wondered if after I left, Aaron ever thought of me. I wondered if he believed I was evil. I wondered if he had found time to get himself a wife.

Bending, I broke the stems of several ditch buttercups and daisies and took them with me into the car. I laid them on the seat beside me. Fragrant reminders of tender moments.

I started the car and drove again, windows still open, sun on my face. Past the fields of flowers the road rose and fell taking me through a path of gentle hills. It was good to see cattle released from winter's holding barns, feeding on the lush, spring-watered pasture grass. I passed acres of plowed land, rich, brown furrows opened for seed. I went by huge workhorses, standing majestic in barnyards; their heady odor mingling with the aroma of trampled soil and old, musty hay. I paused the car for a moment, drank in the sights and the smells, and I remembered without thinking. A part of me surfacing, uncalled, instinctive, returning to roots.

Troubled and, at the same time, pleasured, I made the car move forward, slowly. It was as if I were suspended in time.

Aaron's house came into view. I went by at that same crawling pace. There was no way to know who or how many lived there now. The house doors were closed; the porch and yard, empty. Only the barn across the road and its surroundings showed signs of life. I smiled, reflecting. Of course, for there was the symbol, the barn, that depicted the heart of Amish living ... hard work and discipline. Machines and their parts needed for plowing and planting and harvesting were scattered around the building. Through the barn's great open doorway, I could see harnesses and tools, implements and all kinds of farm paraphernalia scattered on the muddy barn floor and leaning against the board walls, waiting for calloused hands to render them useful. Old rubber boots; work gloves; wide-brimmed straw hats, tattered and sweat stained, scattered among the litter tugged at my heart, effected nostalgic tears.

A lone cat, probably a mouser, ran out of the barn, followed by a tabby, then a gray and white who looked like our old Mamma Cat made a pet by the twins, though Da never knew.

All this I saw in those few fleeting moments that seemed hours in my soul.

Driving on, I came to the wooden plank bridge built over Wander Creek, the half-way point between Aaron's house and mine. I shuddered and stopped the car. Inside my head, inside my ears, I could see and hear little Lily looking over the bridge railing.

"Look, Cora. I see fish down there."

"I don't think so," I said. "This isn't a fishing creek. It's a water-the-cows creek."

"What about the horses?" she asked.

"Them, too," I answered.

"And the goats?"

"And the goats." I took her hand to lead her away.

"Wait, Cora." She pulled her hand away. "What about the sheep?"

"Okay, the sheep, too. And the pigs and the rabbits and the grasshoppers and every animal and bug you can think of. But now it's time to go home and help Maem and Violet make supper."

"I don't want to go home," Lily said, making a face. "I like it here … and I like being alone with you … without Violet." Bending, she picked up a stone and held it up. She grinned. "It's a wishing stone, Cora."

"There's no such thing," I said and reached for her hand, again.

"There is too," Lily said, stepping away from me. "Rachel told me in school. If you throw a wishing stone in the creek, you get whatever you ask for."

"Rachel has too much foolishness in her head. If you send a wish on a stone into the creek, it will simply drown," I said, wishing that wasn't so. I'd like throw a whole mountain of pebbles and make my life different, bigger. I pushed that aside. I had all I needed. My life was secure.

"I don't like you, Cora," Lily said, pouting.

"Yes, you do. You love me." I smiled at her.

"Maybe." She took my hand. "But I'm going to save this stone."

Her voice was gone. I lay my head on the steering wheel and cried.

Beyond the next bend was home. I didn't think I could bear that sight yet … my home that wasn't mine anymore. I lifted my head, backed the car over the road to Aaron's house and turned around in his driveway. I went back past the fields and the trees and the Sunday church house. I kept going, twisting and turning for miles through the back roads, until I reached Wander Lane, the village that, if I had continued forward from the house where I'd grown up, was only a mile. Too many memories, painful memories. My whole being was filled with them. It would not hold any more this day.

I drove to a motel at the edge of the village. It had not been there twenty years ago. Some things change. Others don't. I went into my room, pulled a book and snacks from my bag, and, hiding from thought, replenishing, read the rest of the day away.

That night, as I lay in bed, I spoke to Jesus. *Dear Lord, You lay a yearning on my heart, and so, I came to the place of my beginning. I did not know it would be so hard. The land was as before, so beautiful. And the clouds. Oh, Lord, the clouds. A new miracle every day. I remember lying in those fields, a twin on either side, watching the clouds move, change. Ever making new pictures in the sky ... maidens with long, flowing hair; butterflies with wings that changed to flying birds; racing pigs with stretching noses. Imagined creatures flowing from fertile fantasies. Magical gifts from you, God. They were lazy times, rare and treasured, before our world morphed frigid and solid. Before we grew up. I want to see them again: Violet, George and Willie, Harry and Sampson. My mother. Da. But, I'm afraid. I'm afraid my heart will tear into two different pieces ... and I will not know which to choose, where I belong, where it is right for me to be. I fear my beloved siblings, all grown will know only rules, and will know You, dear Jesus, only in recited prayers and as a maker of rules, stern and strict. I could not stay today. I could not knock on that familiar front door. My heart was, is, overwhelmed by that which is no longer known, by that which might be discovered, by my innards turning, roiling, roaring. I could not stay. Forgive my lack of strength and trust. Guide me to remember You are always there. Tomorrow, I'll go home tomorrow. I pray it will be good.*

Chapter Two

Sleep came late, so I didn't leave my room until the sun was high in the sky. I had done much thinking during those wakeful hours and decided the best time to confront my family was at their supper meal, and so, I had several hours to explore the village. Before I went out to find food, a combination of breakfast and lunch for my hungry belly, I made my bed and neatened my room ... residual Amish training.

Wander Lane is small. Initially it had been only a lane, but gradually streets had sprouted and spread from the main street; however, as I walked the sidewalk, the village's simple, welcoming ambience, the rugged storefronts, the colorful displays, flowers everywhere, were there as before. It pleasured me to see several new businesses; a quilt shop, an Amish bakery adjacent to an Amish restaurant, and a shop displaying crafted items. Nearly all the old businesses were still active. As I caught sight of *Harriet's Homemade Soups and Hearty Sandwiches*, the old, familiar diner sparked images of Lily and Violet and me, laughing and breathing heavy, egg filled baskets swinging on our arms, spilling through the diner's door.

"Watch those children, Cora. Those chickens of yours don't make iron coated eggs."

"Promise them a licorice stick," I said, "and they'll be extra careful."

Harriet laughed and gave the girls three sticks each. "Give the extras to your brothers."

She said it every time. And every time she would make the girls sit on the floor for a bit and get their breath back. *"You girls are too little to be running the whole way down that big hill of yours. You oughta take the buggy, Cora."*

"It's only a mile," I protested.

"Yah, but them legs is short," she said, shaking her head, pointing at the twins.

I smiled as I remembered. This would be a good eatery in which to dine on this day. Lingering memories, ghosts of family love roamed as shadows in my head. I pushed open the same old door, windows still streaked, and checked out the menu tacked crooked on a board near the counter along with a messy plethora of finger-smudged announcements and aged advertisements.

Harriet was still there. Older, much older, her humped back, bent and curving, and wrinkles weaving patterns across her face and down her sagging neck. Lips pursed tight, she nodded when she saw me. Then, winked.

"Been a long time," she said.

"Yes," I whispered, trembling. She was someone who knew the past that had been given me.

"You stayin'?"

"I don't know."

"Hear you're shunned."

I nodded.

"Well, ain't no shunnin' done in here." Harriet pulled a chair from the table near the window. "I remember you. You're a good girl. Ain't nobody that don't make mistakes. So you just set yourself right down here. I may not be Amish, but I know their cookin' and I got some right good chicken out there in the kitchen just waitin' to be et. And you look hungry enough to do just that." She looked hard at me, then grinned. "Sit. We gotta put some meat on them bones."

Overcome by her acceptance, I bowed my head and fought back tears.

"Come on, girl," she said, gently touching my sleeve. "Everything ends. Even rumor loses its power."

Her hand was light on my arm. I could feel the cold of her fingers, slender bones spread fragile, through my blouse. As she bent closer to me and guided me to the chair, the sweet, delicate scent of old age drifted from her skin. I sat and she left me to see to the kitchen. I saw, in my mind, young Amish girls working under her direction, fixing the recipes she'd gleaned from all the years she'd lived near and observed the ladies in dark colored apparel.

My lunch, when it came, was good Amish fare … gravied chicken over thick, buttery biscuits, and then, oh, blessed Harriet, fresh apple pie heaped with ice cream. I ate it all. With a tall glass of cider. And, for a moment, as I pulled at my tightening waistband, wished my bulging body wore ample Amish skirts. Then I stopped that desire, dropped my hands in my lap. Black skirts could hide layers of good eating, but they could not hide the layers of guilt and regret that lay stacked on my heart.

As I dug in my purse for dollars, Harriet dropped into the chair across from me.

"Don't be gettin' old, honey. The bones just don't quit their achin'," she said, shaking her head, "and they don't bend so good, neither." Her head jerked a little; the cords in her neck tightened. A small moan escaped her lips. Then she smiled, so briefly. "A body gets used to it after a while. And, you," she admonished, "put that money away. Ain't no good here."

"A tip?" I asked, clutching the dollars in my hand. "For the girls in the back."

"Well, maybe. But that's all. Next time you can pay."

"Harriet?" I looked into her eyes. So much was stored behind them, a lifetime of watching and hearing the heart of a town. She didn't flinch; she met my stare. "Harriet, do you know?"

"I know," Harriet said, softly. "Most of it."

"The little girl?"

"Not so little now."

"Do you know where she is?"

"Maybe."

"Will you tell me?"

"Might not be best."

Pushing with one hand on the table; the other on her chair, Harriet struggled to heft herself up. Her face showed pain. I hurried to help her. Once upright, she lifted her hand to my cheek.

"Don't make trouble for yourself," she said, her voice low and tired. "Make peace with your family if you can. That's all. Been too many years. Can't never bring nothin' back the same as it was."

"Harriet?" I whispered in her ear, her face so close to mine.

"Yes, child."

"Do you believe in God?"

"Yes, child."

"In Jesus?"

"If I have nothing else, I have Him. He's all I need. Now, go." She pushed against me.

"Do you talk to Him?" I said, resisting her touch.

"Always."

"He's why it's so hard to come back."

"I know."

"I'm afraid I'll lose Him."

"Won't happen, child. He'll cling tight. Just keep on a-talkin' to Him."

I kissed her cheek, so thin and fine was her skin that my lips sank into the crinkled silk of it, and then, I let her go.

It was too soon to climb the hill to home. The men, Da, would still be working in the fields; and Maem, in the kitchen peeling and stirring, happy in her work, preparing supper. I wanted them to be there all at one time. Shunned, I feared their response, but I hungered to see them. My family. All there, but one. Lily. Her body dead to them. Different from me. For them, it was my soul that was dead.

It was Olivia, a villager, who carried the burden of my secret, who knew where to find me. She was the one who told me of the terrible tragedy. She was the one who wrote the letter that told of the drowning. Lily was found in a full watered deep hole, floating in Wander Creek. Yesterday, as I drove, I remembered a smiling child holding buttercups and merrily wading in shallow water. Today, as I walked the streets of Wander Lane, I remembered that same child, grown to a young woman, not seen in death by me, but in my mind's sharp eye, her eyes were closed forever; her body, pale and shriveled, lost, gone to another world. They called it an accident, so she could reap the rewards of salvation. I hoped that was so.

I was grateful to Olivia. We were not exactly friends. Instead, we were the keepers of a time that was shared by only two others, and now, only one other. And, as I said, Olivia was the one who searched for me and found me, who wrote the dreadful letter that told of Lily's death. There was no letter from the brethren. For them, I was dead, too. Guaranteed to spend eternity in Hell.

I didn't go to the funeral. Lily would be laid out in our living room all the hours of day and night. Someone would always be by her coffin to accept the stolid grief of the mourners. Inside my head, I could see it; inside my heart, I could feel it. But the door would not be opened to me, and the fields to the high place where she would be buried gave me no place to hide and watch, no sacred ground on which to spill my tears. I did go back to Wander Lane, to be as close to my sister as circumstance allowed. Olivia took me into her house, and when the hour came for Lily to be carried to her grave, she held me while I cried. I longed for her arms to be the arms of my mother. So much did I ache on that day.

Back again, so many years later, I walked the sidewalks, passing the shops, remembering. There were ladies in Kate's beauty salon, hair being soaped and cut and blown and ironed to curling, pulled up and swirled into soft mounds of beauty. Touching my own, short now, not knotted and twisted and hid under a *kapp*, a happy, free feeling flashed through my heart.

I moved on, feeding my eyes and my heart with the old and new wonders. Colorful, intricately patterned quilts displayed in enticing manner, grabbing the eye, filled the show window of the new quilt shop. Peering through the glass, I saw an Amish woman, her back to me, stacking bolts of flowered fabric onto a shelf. When she turned, I saw it was Hattie Shackleton, a dear friend from long ago school years. Excited to see her, I made to go into the store, and then stopped. It wasn't for me to put upon her a difficult choice ... perhaps, not difficult, but sad. Hattie knew the rules. She was an Amish woman. She would not break them.

Next to her shop was the old grocery. Still shabby, its window was plastered with posters and flyers, and through the glass, I could see shelves stuffed with items for eating and cleaning and splashing one's home with funny, little trinkets. I went in and bought a packet of gum. The young English boy at the counter didn't recognize me as a former Amish girl. How could he? He had not yet been born when I was driven from town. He had never seen me in high-necked, long-skirted dress. It was good not to be known that way. It was good to watch eyes look upon my face and not turn away.

There was a street dividing the grocery from the next shop. I stood at its corner and thought should I go down it? It was the street on which Olivia lived. Hers was the first house from the corner. It stood hidden behind the grocery. Turning my head, just a little, I could see the edge of her front yard. She had planted a border of dark blue, almost purple, pansies along the sidewalk. I closed my eyes and lowered my head. *Dear Jesus, please guide me. I'm not ready to see her.* He gave me the strength to move on. Looking straight ahead, not turning, I crossed the street.

There were too many hours before I should go up the hill and find my family at supper. It seemed as if, in the growing panic of my heart, the hours would not pass. But though I felt rooted in a single moment in time, it was not really so. Time is finite. It lives each single second, every one the same length as another, leaves and moves on to the next. And so, the minutes ticked by, and it came time for me to gather my strength and make the trek up the hill. I walked the mile to my parents' house.

It seemed right. I had left their home by foot. It was appropriate that I come back the same way. Neither looking right nor left … nor back … I kept my eyes focused on my feet, watching them move me forward to a place I feared, but so yearned to be part of again.

I came to a spot where a jagged edge of dirt spilled onto the gravel. I stopped. Almost hidden under pebbles and clumps of dry earth, a crushed frog lay dead. I looked at him a long time, then, stepping over him, put my foot on Pooler property and began the walk up the driveway to my home. *Oh, God, be with me.*

Step followed step. My eyes wouldn't lift from my feet moving slowly, reluctantly over the packed dirt. My mind could not push them to go faster. I was afraid. If they did not take me to the front door, there would be no hurt. But neither would there be acceptance nor welcome. Without confrontation there would be no resolution, and I would never know if my twenty years of shunned absence had mellowed their hearts or if they could take me, again, into their lives.

I gritted my teeth and made my feet function as feet should do. One long step. Then another. When they reached the path that left the driveway and led to the house, they paused. Keep going, feet. Keep going. From the corners of my eyes I could see the impatiens Maem planted fresh every spring, fragile pink and white blossoms spread thick along the pathway. I swallowed and pulled in my cheeks. Maem. Inside memories of gentle touch and kindness, soft laughter and soothing words, swam through my body, delicious and warm. My whole being ached to hold her.

My feet came to the front porch stairs and stopped. Squinting down at them, I willed them to go up and walk across the broom swept floor.

I lifted my eyes.

The front door was before me. Solid white, washed spotless. The doorknob, polished, unblemished. Amish clean. I was home.

I didn't knock. This was the house of my family, my childhood home. Mine. I slid my fingers over the knob, tightened them around it, turned it and pushed.

Maem was the first to see me. As she drew in a gasping breath, her mouth opened. Her hands flew up covering it, pushing against the pulsing emotions I knew were raging within wanting to release in a wail of surprise and joy. For a moment, the others, busy eating, did not see her shock, and I had that brief time to record them, forever, in the deep recesses of my mind and heart.

Da saw me next or, perhaps, it was all of them. At the same time. A frozen moment. Their faces, blank, stunned. Then Da's chair crashed as he pushed it too fast, too hard, and it fell loud onto the floor. And their faces, released by the sudden sharp noise, showed shock and fright and joy all mixed together.

Maem dropped her hands and reached to me with arms stretched to their limits. Da said nothing, but strode, forceful and swift, over the kitchen floor, under the wide arch, across the living room, and to the door where I stood, still on the porch side, so frightened, so wanting.

And he closed the door, quietly, resolutely, against me.

And they were gone from my sight.

I waited. I heard his footsteps take him back to the kitchen. I thought I heard my maem's tears. I'm not sure. For the world was still. It had stopped, and I stood in a place of nothing. Empty of all. Until my heart started beating again. And its thud was so loud I could not have heard tears or shouts … or the sorrowful pleading from my own soul.

My feet became soldiers again, and, this time, marched away from the battle. They carried me, wounded, down the road of retreat.

I went down the first hill, moving fast, and then stopping, bending, lifting my arms, dropping my head in my hands, pushing them tight against my face, and rocking … rocking, rocking. And finally, depleted, I lowered my arms and began walking again.

Night was dropping its first layer of dark. I could feel its shadow encompass me, grow heavier with each added tier. When the dark was so dense I could not see through it, the many past times I had walked this road in the night, times stored deep in my head, came forth and guided me to stay on the road and not stumble.

I reached the place where the road turned and the hill lifted a little, a respite from dark, for from there the glowing lights of Wander Lane illumined the night. I stopped and looked down at them. And I remembered.

It was on this hill, on a night such as this, dark and somber, I had stopped, rested a moment, got my bearings, tried to think rationally, and then, holding my thickly blanketed bundle tight against my chest, my sight impaired by a thick, impeding darkness, I sent a hurried prayer to God and continued my laborious trek down the hill. My feet stumbled on the dark graveled road, and I moved quickly … step, step, step … in a fast, awkward dance striving to keep my balance. Pressing my lips in a tight grim smile, I nodded my head. I was still upright.

"We'll make it, Sweetie, we'll make it," I whispered into the night. There were no stars to guide me. A menacing mass of charcoal gray clouds hung heavy over the fields and trees and road. I was grateful for the occasional bursts of cold wind. Though they whipped my skirt sharp against my legs, the surges of blowing air parted the threatening clouds and hollowed space for slivers of soft glowing moonlight to slip through and give me solid glimpses of the shadows and shapes around me.

The way to the small village seemed far to me that night. So many times I had walked this road with my baskets of eggs, baked goods and, sometimes, vegetables, hoping to sell fresh edibles to the English grocer. Knowing the quality of Amish fare, he usually bought all I could carry. But those were trips made in daylight with the sky bright above me and the road easily seen. Happy trips. Profitable trips. Joyfully singing, arms bent, body swaying, I would walk home, triumphant, with empty baskets swinging from wrist to elbow. That night, as I left the village and returned home, my arms would hang sad, heavy though my load was gone.

In the dusky gloom it was hard to keep my bearings. Placing my feet quickly and carefully, I willed myself forward into the dark. I walked by instinct and memory. And need.

"Shall I sing to you, little girl?" I crooned, holding black images at bay. "Did her songs reach into your ears as you lay in her? Do you know her voice? Does it ring clear and true?" I kept my words soft as I walked. "Will you miss her? Will you remember?" Even in these sleeping hours, I was afraid someone might find me, that there might be others stirring in the dark air around me ... stroking a calving cow, walking off a bad dream, seeking a touch from a stealthy lover. Someone who might hear the rustle of my skirts or feel the swing of my hips moving the air. Someone who might smell my fear. I could not be seen. I could not be found. It would be the same as death.

The road leveled for a bit, then rose. The baby stirred in my arms as I walked to the top of the incline. Heaving a sigh of relief, I looked down at the glow of lampposts circling my destination. The light illuminated the streets and scarce shops of the small village with a soft yellow haze. I stopped and shifted the bundle in my arms. Lifting a corner of the protecting blanket, I bent my head and gently kissed the baby's tiny exposed cheek. Quickly I covered it again. The breeze was too cool; my burden, too precious. I stood there a bit, knowing the danger of prolonging the time of my journey, but dreading its end.

"Oh, sweet baby," I whispered, "what are we doing? Oh, baby, why did we come?" There was no choice, I thought. *God, where are You? Why do You not give me another way?*

I walked again. One step. Then another. I felt tears everywhere inside my body. It was almost over. The physical task. But the deed, the harrowing thing to be done, would go on forever ... would never leave me.

Looking down at the bundle in my arms, I spoke so softly, so gently. "I'm going to give you a name, sweet child. Before I leave you, before I go forever to not see you, I'm going to look full in your face and remember you every day of my life. Annabelle. You are Annabelle. No matter what they call you later, you always will be Annabelle."

I held the baby tight to my heart and walked down into the village.

Drawing myself back to the present, I looked down at the village. Dark. Only the light from the lamps on their posts casting murky shadows revealed the shapes below me. But the eyes inside my mind, the eyes that looked deep within and saw clear images of long ago, spread the village before me and showed me all that had happened on that fateful night. The memories were there. I stood and watched and remembered.

I had known exactly where to go. The path behind the grocer's would take me to the little white house with green shutters and a huge front porch sprinkled with rich colored rockers ... colonial blue, mossy green, dark purple, mustard yellow. It was the house where the Englisher lived. Olivia Martin. I had seen her many times. From a distance. When she came with her briefcase and visited the little girl, Amy Stoll. Poor Amy had been born sickly and couldn't breathe without a machine. Never was I close enough to Olivia to speak with her, but I had seen her going in and out of Amy's house, checking to be sure she was all right. I had watched her stop by a child playing in the yard and then bend and pat the child's head with gentle fingers. And from my porch I'd seen Olivia kneel and listen, face to face, to a little one straining to make her Amish words understood. I'd seen Olivia laugh and bounce a ball back to a rambunctious bare-foot young boy, body stopped rigid, his lips pulled back, frightened because he had thrown wildly and the ball had landed against her legs. So I knew Olivia was good, and I knew Olivia loved children. Watching her, I had seen no slippage of manner that would show otherwise, and when Nathan, Amy's father and Maem's brother, spoke of her, rarely as was his way, his words were respectful, touched with admiration ... grateful words. I would trust her. I knew she would do nothing less than be helpful to me.

Olivia's house was dark. I looked to the sky. It must be near midnight. Olivia would be sleeping. It did not not matter. I could not wait. I would wake her. There was no time to waste. I had to be back home before the sun started to rise.

Before I walked up the steps to the front door, I gently cradled the baby in my arms. My body swayed slowly, a soothing ancient rocking instinctive to all women. Unfolding a corner of the blanket that covered the child, I ran my fingers over her soft cheeks and lips, and kissed the baby's forehead.

"Remember you're Amish, sweet baby, sweet Annabelle," I whispered. "Push these words deep into your heart, understand them in your soul, let them melt there and stay a sweet puddle of love and remembrance. You are Amish of the Old Order. All the way back to the days when the oldest of us joined together and began the path that led, finally, to you. You have been wanted and loved since the beginning of time and it will be forever so. You'll always be part of my heart. Keep these words, Annabelle, in the inmost part of your soul. As you grow and wonder, look deep to the feel of their love. As they flow through you and fill you with an inner instinctive remembering of the one who bore you and the beauty of whom you are, remember their meaning. Oh, sweet Annabelle, I don't know what else to do."

I went up the steps and crossed the porch. Her front door was painted a deep mossy green. In the center was a large glass oval swirled with patterns of gold. I took the knocker in my hand and let it drop swift and hard to a mighty and resounding clang.

I remember listening, straining to hear footsteps on the other side of the door. The air was cooling and I worried the baby's blanket wasn't thick enough to warm new blood, to keep it flowing steady beneath infant skin. Turning my back against the stammering push of wavering wind, I nestled the child closer to my body.

It seemed I waited forever. Ignoring my training of patience and gentleness, I slammed the knocker against the door again and again. And, finally, a voice spoke through the wood.

"Who is it?" Her voice spoke tentatively. I could hear its tremble.

"Cora Pooler," I answered. "Nathan Stoll's cousin."

"What do you want?"

"I need your help."

"Come to the window so I can see you."

I stepped across the porch to the large front window. It was curtained too thick to see through the glass. I could sense Olivia standing behind it, confused, her mind still dulled with the residue of sleep, sifting the situation, sorting options.

The cold was beginning to seep through my clothing. Gently rocking, moving to stir my own cooling blood, I pulled my cloak over the baby to give her another layer of heat.

The curtain moved. I saw Olivia's face, a part of it, her head tilted so only her eyes showed. She looked frightened. I understood. It was late. The village was empty of persons that could see and protect. Sighing, I bent my head and closed my eyes. They were so weary. My back and my legs ached; the baby was growing uncomfortably heavy. For a moment, a floating second of barren space, a pleasant dreamlike vision of open blue sky, empty of all clouds, whispered through my heart and head, a brief respite of burden gone. Then, in that inner place where need separates from reality, inside my head, I saw myself drop gently onto the floorboards, the child cuddled close against my body, and the porch was our welcoming bed. It was a welcoming, peaceful vision. Not real.

Lifting my head, I knew I couldn't go there. Not yet. There were too many who needed me aware ... functional. Smiling ruefully, I opened my eyes. That's what good Amish women were. Functional. Always there to do what was needed. What others needed.

"What's in your bundle?"

I saw her face, the whole of it pushed through the edge of the curtain. Now fully awake, there was strength mixed within her apprehension.

"A baby," I said.

"Show me."

Slanting Annabelle toward the window, I lifted a corner of her blanket. I shuddered. Her face was so red. "Please, can we come in?"

Her face disappeared. Seconds later I heard the scrape of door against frame, and my feet moved quickly across the porch to the door.

"Hurry," she said, tugging at my arm. "Get the baby in. It's cold out there. Too cold, far too cold."

"She's all right," I said, clutching the child closer, defending the depth of my care, my choices.

"No, no, the baby needs to be warmed," she said. She pushed me away from the door and closed it. Pointing to the living room, she motioned me to a cushioned rocker. "Sit there. I'll turn up the thermostat."

Although the room seemed comfortably warm, as I stepped over the register it was gratifying to feel the toasty swoosh of air lift my skirts and run the length of my legs. Throwing a quick prayer of remorse to Jesus for undeserved pleasure, I thought of Bishop Herrfort. If he knew my delight in that heat wasted moment, the lines of his mouth surely would pull tighter than usual, and his shoulders jerk stiff. Dutifully, humbly, I brought myself back to the concerns of little Annabelle.

"Is the baby yours?" Olivia asked as she quietly slid into the floral fabriced chair across from me. For a moment she lowered her eyes and gazed at the floor as if not ready, not wanting, to take the burden of knowing my story. Then clasping her hands tightly together on her lap, she bent forward, lifted her eyes, and gazed, intently, into my own. "Is the baby yours?" she asked again.

"I can't keep her," I answered.

Olivia tilted her head and bit her lower lip. "How old is he?"

"She," I said. "Annabelle." A little angry, I wondered why she had not heard me say, *I can't keep her. Her.*

"I see," Olivia said, nodding her head. A half smile ... wistful, almost sad ... surfaced briefly on her lips. "She. A little girl." There was a pause. "And you can't keep her." It was a statement, not a question. I kept silent. "And her father? What does he say?"

"He doesn't know."

"And your mother ... the child's grandmother?"

"No one knows." I felt my cheeks blush, and I bowed my head. "The skirts of an Amish can hide many pounds."

"They need to know." She waited. It seemed she wanted to give me thinking time. I did not need it. After a bit, she nodded again. "I see."

"I've seen you with the children," I said. "You're good with them. I need you to be good with this child."

"And I have seen you with Aaron," she said, quickly. "And he is a good man. I have seen him look at you. He would be a good father."

"He isn't the father."

"Are you sure?" she asked.

"I'm sure," I whispered, relenting, fatigue taking the strength needed for anger.

"A baby is a precious thing to give away."

My eyes traveled down to the child folded sweet in my arms. Bending my head to draw in her scent, I looked at her, soaked her being into myself, for a long, saturating moment, and then closed my eyes.

"Cora?"

I heard her. She wanted too much.

"Who is the father?"

"I don't know."

"He has a right to know. You can't give away this baby without him knowing. He has a heart, too. This is not a choice you should make for him."

"I heard that anyone, even me, could bring a baby to you and you would take it, no questions asked, and you would find it a home." I heard myself beg and was not ashamed ... only frightened.

"You heard wrong. I can't do that. It's not within my province. If I took this baby, I would have to report it to my supervisor. If I did not, I would lose my job."

"Babies are more important than jobs," I said. Her face showed agreement, but she was a woman alone. She needed her job. Perhaps I could not trust her to keep silent. Perhaps I had no choice.

"I'm not sure this is best for Annabelle," Olivia said, stressing the baby's name, making me hear it, making me know the magnitude of it, making me know it was Annabelle. A person. "Just as you've seen me, I've seen you with children. Oh, Cora, you would be a wonderful mother to this child, this little Annabelle."

"I can't keep her," I repeated.

"Again, I ask you, who is the father?"

"I told you. I don't know." And that was truth.

"How can you not know?"

"I didn't see his face."

"You were raped?" Though she spoke firm, her voice was gentle.

"It was rape." What else could I say? I didn't know who the father was.

"You should report this."

"I can't."

"Let me." She lifted her arms, hands clenched in tight fists, moving in syncopation with her words.

"No!"

Sighing, Olivia leaned back in her chair. "You make it so hard. How can I help you?"

"You can take the baby."

"Annabelle." She said the name slowly, deliberately.

"The baby." I didn't want to say her name. It was special. Beautiful. My mother had shown us …Lily and Violet and me, Corabelle …how precious and meaningful a name could be. Flowers, our names were the flowers she loved. The bishop was not happy our names were not Martha or Lydia or Esther, but he allowed it. I don't know why, but he did. And now there was Annabelle, a name like the sound of bells ringing. I could not say it without tears. It was enough that the feel of her was breaking my heart.

"When was she born?" Olivia's voice was low. I could hear her yearning to comfort.

"Between the breaking fast meal and noon of this day that is ending."

"Was your mother not home? Or your father?"

"Maem was; Da was in the fields. The pains came and we had plans to tell Maem when they came that Martha Beachy needed us. She's old. We clean her house and, sometimes, cook for her. She has no children, no family, so it's not unusual for us to take a day and do for her."

"We? Us?"

"My sisters and me. I think of us as one. They know."

"Have you told them the father's name?"

Anger was back. I knew I shouldn't show that in my words, even more, I should not feel that in my heart. But I did and I couldn't stop the words from spilling my rage. "I told you. I don't know who he is. Why do you keep asking?"

"Because I think you're not telling me the truth." Her voice was steady. It brooked no nonsense.

"Amish do not lie." My words, too, did not waver.

"Amish are human," she said.

Sighing, I rubbed my free hand over my cheek. "If you won't take the baby, where shall I leave her?"

"At the sheriff's station," Olivia said, firmly. But I heard a quaking beneath her words. "There is no other warm place."

"I can't do that."

"They won't ask questions. And it's apparent that's what you want."

Trembling, I pressed my lips together. "The sheriff would go to the Bishop."

"Maybe not," she said. "Their directive is to simply take the baby, ask no questions, seek no answers. Pass no judgment." She shook her head. "Perhaps you'll see no one. Perhaps you can slip the baby through the door before anyone sees you."

"You say they won't judge, but you are judging me."

"I'm trying not to. But it's so hard to watch this."

"The sheriff will know the baby is Amish," I said, smoothing my hand over the child's quilt. "Her blanket is handsewn. He won't understand and will do the wrong thing. You must understand. The sheriff and Bishop Herrfort have an agreement. If there is a situation involving the Amish, the sheriff goes to the Bishop and Bishop Herrfort takes care of the problem. It usually works out fine. Not this time. This time it would be different."

"I can't help you. I wish I could," Olivia said. "Take the child home. Go to your bishop. Ask for forgiveness."

"I did nothing wrong." *God forgive me for questioning the Amish rules, The Ordnung, but my heart says this child was given by You. I will not ask for forgiveness for my part in this child's life. I will not.*

"Then take her home," Olivia said. "Work it out."

"I can't. Not many of us are strong enough to challenge the Bishop. Maybe none of us are. It's too painful, too shameful to resist the Amish way. It's easier to obey and more honorable to accept the wisdom of him who has been chosen by God to lead."

"Yet you came here."

Dropping my head, seeing the child, thinking of Violet and Lily, regretting the omission of truth, the disrespect to my parents, I answered, "I did come to you for help. And yes, I have sinned. But, in this, I know no other way. It must be kept secret. Please help me."

"I can't help you. I can't be part of this."

Looking at her, I saw a yearning in her face, heard a waver in her voice. She had aged in these moments, and I saw what she would look like as an old woman. If she could reach deep into her heart, I knew she would help me. She would be good to Annabelle. She just needed a push.

"Would you like to hold her?" I watched her face pale, her hand cover her mouth. She shook her head, no. There was no more I could do. I asked for a drink of water. She got up quickly and left the room to get it for me. I stood, kissed the child, little Annabelle, laid her in Olivia's pretty, soft cushioned chair and left.

A distant roll of thunder woke me from reverie. Closing my eyes, I swallowed and forced memory to slide back into my heart. It had left me numb. I couldn't let myself feel its touch on my soul any longer.

All thought quieted, I walked down the hill to my motel room.

Chapter Three

T he rain poured thick all the next day. Wrapped in a blanket, I sat
by my room's single murky window and read the hours away.
In my hands, soothing my mind, was a restful book paged
with easy conflict and predictable resolution, an armistice for my brain.
While I read, I fed from the calorie laden snacks and warm soda stuffed
in my suitcase. By nightfall my valise was empty of goodies, and I had
disappeared into a carbohydrate-sugar induced dreamless slumber.

I woke late the next morning, groggy from too much sleep. My
sheets were crumpled and damp, binding my body in a prison of
malicious fabric. Struggling to pull the sheets from under and around
me, I felt a moment of panic and just gave up and cried. It didn't help.
*Okay, Jesus, if you've got angels all around me, please tell them to let me
loose.* And I think He did. At the very least, the thought of Him calmed
and sunnied me, and, almost relaxed, I rolled my body and freed my
arms. Then lying back on the crushed sheets, I closed my eyes and blew
air through my lips. *Thank you, Jesus. Now what?*

But I knew. There would be no more waiting. No more
procrastination. This was the day I would confront Olivia. This was the
day that would bring denouement and reveal the impact of my terrible
sin. Not wanting to lose the fragile strength of my determination, I
hurried to dress, skipped the lure of the coffee machine, and ordered
my mind to stay focused on that day's mission.

The day was beautiful; the earth, washed clean. I stood a moment at
the door's opening and marveled at the clarity of God's creation …
the sharp edged leaves, the clear line of branches, the fullness of clouds
drifting, merging, reshaping, parting … and I wished my mind could
stay so. Patterned. Purposed. Pure.

I walked to the turn at the corner that would take me to Olivia's
house. Stopping there, I could feel the beat of my heart, the tremble in
my legs. This was different from walking to the home of my parents,

equal in trepidation, but at their house, deep in my soul, I knew I might be so unwelcomed as to become invisible. Here, at Olivia's, I could be taken in and filled with the knowing of Anabelle's fate. Here there was hope ... perhaps.

When I'd last seen Olivia, there had been no talk of the baby's whereabouts or well-being. From the time I opened Olivia's letter telling of Lily's death and rushed to her house until the day I left that place, numb and unable to feel, every piece of my being focused on my dead sister, Lily ...my need to see her, to watch over her body, to walk with my family over the fields and up the hill to the farm's highest spot where the grass was thick and the flowers were high ... and a hole waited. Even though I knew I could not partake of those moments, I ached to burrow in the air-dried scent of Amish sheets, to sink my head in a soft known pillow and quietly weep forbidden tears. And I longed to grasp Violet's hand behind our skirts, giving her comfort, sharing the sorrowful emotions Amish faces were not allowed to express. But I couldn't do that. I didn't belong there anymore. And there was already too much grief walking up that hill. Hearts were heavy enough without the added weight of a shunned sister walking in shame behind the burying procession. So I stayed with Olivia, and she held me while I cried unsanctioned tears in her house. And she listened when the tears were spent, when tender, loving memories of Lily and Violet and me, three entwined sisters, spilled soft from my lips. It was a time to coat grief with tender nostalgia; there was no room for words of sin or shame or shunning. Neither of us spoke Annabelle's name the whole of that time. But, sometimes, as I thought of Lily, I thought of her, too. She would have been five. No longer a baby. A little girl.

Now lowering my head, asking Jesus for strength, making my feet move, I went forward slowly up the sidewalk to Olivia's house. Deep blue pansies lined the path where I walked, and when I lifted my eyes, I saw the varied hues of painted rockers on the porch. And I knew Olivia still lived there.

The front door was the same as I'd seen when I'd knocked the first time. A welcoming mossy green with an oval glass of shining golden swirls. Standing before it, I remembered and dread crept over me. What if she would not tell me?

Grasping the knocker, I let it drop gently.

An old woman answered the door. Her body, bent and slight, leaned on a simple wood-polished cane. Her pale face was wrinkled; her dark rimmed eyes, lashless and sunken. Even so changed, I knew it was Olivia. Tilting her head, she smiled at me, and reaching, I touched, gently stroked, the gay flowered turban that covered her head.

"I love you," I whispered.

"I know," she said, her voice soft, her eyes filling with tears.

We went into the living room. I sat in the cushioned rocker, and she sat in the pretty flowered chair across from me. I nodded my head, and she smiled.

I looked at her for a long time. She waited.

"When I went back into the world after Lily died," I said, "I went into a church. It was so different from benches lined up in a house. The first thing I saw were men and women sitting together. And then all the colors … the clothes and the glass pictures in the windows, the bright painted banners on the walls. And the flowers. I thought why would there be flowers in a church? How could you focus on the Bishop …the minister …with all those beautiful colors surrounding you?" Pausing, I thought back to that time and was there again. "There were candles on a little table in front of us. A young boy in a robe came down the center aisle and lit them. There was music and a man at the front, not the minister, read from the English Bible, briefly, but with power. The people were quiet. Some of them watched him, their faces so peaceful and some sat with their heads bowed. My heart filled with the magic of it. And I thought, how can this not be sinful?"

I looked at Olivia. "Then the minister came forward. He gave plates to some men and a *woman* who came from the seats where we sat. They went down the aisles and people put money in the plates and while they took them back to the minister, everyone stood and sang. A short hymn. The minister took the plates and lifted them high and prayed and near the end of his prayer *everyone* spoke with him … the same words. Then we sat and he spoke. Words to Jesus first, then words Jesus had used to teach. There were no man made rules spoken. There was love and praise and thanksgiving and wisdom in the words he told. He held a Bible in his hand and glancing at it, again and again, he spoke. He told a story of a blind man. Healed. And he said we could be healed of our blindness, but he didn't mean our eyes. And then he was done. We sang again and it was over. All of it was over. It was only an hour and it was done."

I sat back in my chair and smiled. "Only an hour, Olivia. My back didn't ache and my mind was full. Amazing."

Olivia smiled back. "No hurry to find a seat with a wall behind it to lean on?"

"Nope," I laughed, "every bench ... pew ... had a back."

"Why are you here?" Olivia asked, gently.

"I need to know where Annabelle is."

"I see," Olivia whispered.

"You took her to the sheriff."

"I did." She lowered her eyes, and I knew she did not want to speak of that time.

"I have wondered all these years. She would be a young woman now. Marriage age ... and then some. Perhaps, even now, with children."

Olivia said nothing.

"She was bundled in Amish cloth when I brought her to you, wrapped in an old Amish quilt. You took her that way to the sheriff?"

"I did. But he didn't take the baby." Her voice seemed far away. "He left the baby with me."

"Why?"

"He thought I would know what to do with her."

"What did you do?"

"I took her to my supervisor. That was what I was supposed to do. Cora, I was alone. I needed my job."

"She was a baby. I thought you would take care of her ... maybe keep her. You were so good with children."

Olivia bowed her head toward her hands clasped tightly in her lap. "I couldn't," she said. I could barely hear her.

"The sheriff told Bishop Herrfort."

"I know," Olivia whispered.

"Someone had seen me," I said. "A boy. An English boy. A teenager. Up to no good that night. Prowling in the woods. His father found him in the morning ... drunk ...and he took him to the sheriff to scare the daylights and the excitement of drink out of his son. And the boy told the sheriff what he had seen ... a black skirted Amish woman hurrying down the hill with a bundle in her arms."

"I know," Olivia said, softly.

"And the sheriff put two and two together and went to the bishop."

"Yes."

"And the bishop went investigating. No one knew anything. But my mother knew. How could she not? She never said anything to me or Lily or Violet. But she knew. Maybe not, at first; maybe not that it was a baby. But she knew something was terribly wrong. *She was a mother.* And when the bishop came questioning, I could not put her in a place of the temptation to lie. She was strong in her faith, but she was a mother. How could she choose between God and her children? But if forced I knew she would choose God. She is Amish. She would do what the Bishop said was right. Neither could I burden my sisters. So I confessed there was a baby, that I had taken her and left her with you. When he asked who else knew, I said no one. He asked if I was sure. I said yes. He said lying was a sin. I said I had not lied, and, thus, at that moment, I did sin, and the guilt was heavy. But I did not know what else to do. He asked who the father was. I said I didn't know. He did not mention rape. He did not ask further." I shook my head. "Even a bishop can have cowardly moments."

"Cora." Olivia reached and gently rubbed my arm. "You don't have to tell me all this. There is too much hurt in your voice. I already know. Let it be."

"He proclaimed my sin before everyone at the next Sunday meeting," I said, ignoring her. "He said I had abandoned my baby and would not declare the father. He set a shunning." I drew in a deep breath of air and let it out slowly. "My mother asked the bishop to let her get the baby and bring her back into our family. He refused."

"Cora," Olivia said, tenderly, "it was so long ago."

"No, it was yesterday. I was broken. I could not bring more shame to my family. I left."

Drawing back into her chair, Olivia raised her hands to her mouth and spoke through her fingers, "If I had it to do over, I would keep the child."

"You did what you had to. I forgave you a long time ago. You were so kind to me when Lily died. I love you, Olivia."

"I love you, too. My heart has ached for you, Olivia said, patting her chest. You came to be my own child ... here in my heart."

I looked at her and prayed God would bless and watch over her. He had made our minimal time together deep and rich and everlasting.

"What did you tell the sheriff?"

"Nothing." She hesitated. "Only that a baby was left on my porch. I wanted to say more."

"What more?"

"That you were raped. It wasn't right that I couldn't tell him."

"It was my choice." Bowing my head, I spoke softly. "It would have shamed my community."

"I know. But there should have been justice. What happened was evil. Wrong. It needed to be stopped."

Sighing, I bit my lower lip and raised my head. I did not know what to say.

"It's over. It's done. We need to forget," she said.

Tilting my head slightly, it had grown so heavy, I looked onto her face. "The sheriff knew she was an Amish baby," I said.

"Her wrappings," Olivia agreed. "The quilt. The work of Amish hands."

"When he gave the baby back to you, he should have been done with it. He should not have gone to the Bishop. His work ended when he laid the baby in your arms."

Olivia nodded.

I leaned forward. "Where is she now?"

"Annabelle?" Her shoulders drooped.

"Of course, Annabelle. Where is she now?" I repeated.

"I can't tell you."

"But you know." It was a statement, not a question. And I wanted an answer. I deserved an answer.

"Are you thinking of coming back?" Olivia asked. She leaned forward in her chair, tilted her head as if pondering that possibility.

"Tell me," I said, ignoring her question. I would not let her change the direction of my thought.

"I can't," she said again, her lips trembling.

Pushing myself tight against the rocker, I straightened my back, put my arms firm against the chair's armrests, and stared into her eyes.

Looking back at me, her eyes seemed to swell with sorrowful liquid. "It would do no good."

"It would do *me* good."

"How? She's not a baby anymore. She's grown, an adult. She has a life. Don't mess it up."

"*Is she Amish?*"

"Why is that important? Are *you* Amish now?"

It felt as if the air had left my body, as if it sank into itself. "I don't know," I whispered, "but I promised Annabelle. I slipped the words into her heart, the commemoration that she was born Amish. It would honor her mother that she stay so."

"But you didn't," Olivia said. "You left the Order."

"No. It wasn't my choice. I couldn't stay."

"But you could have. You could have accepted the shunning period, asked for forgiveness, and repented. You would have been welcomed back."

"There was more. Things I couldn't change."

"What things?"

"Please," I said. "Please, where is she?"

"Are you staying?" She asked, not answering, her words coming with a gentle firmness into my ears.

"I don't know. Could I belong again? I don't know." My hands clenched, pressing my fingers to hurt.

"You're different now. English. It would be hard."

"I am both. Amish and English. Neither. In the middle."

"You've made your way in the English world. Are you happy there?'

Opening my hands, lifting them, rubbing them hard against my cheeks, feeling myself real, I struggled to tell who I was. "I've worked hard. It's not easy to have an Amish heart in an English world. They are so bright, so schooled. When I walked into that world in my dark green skirt and black *kapp*, there were not many places that welcomed me. I didn't fit. Even when I spent my few dollars on a short skirt and clingy sweater, and cut my hair … and oh, the tears that ran from my eyes when I saw it fall to the floor … even then with my kapp hidden in a dark corner of the closet section allotted me at the shelter, even then when the outside of me looked like an Englisher, the Amish inside showed through and I was still different. My speech was a bit tilted. I didn't laugh at jokes I didn't understand or were sprinkled with unseemly words. I didn't talk of frivolous things or speak cruel words. When I tried to find work, I didn't know how to fill out the applications. The words on the paper were foreign and I had to ask their meaning. It shamed me. They wanted to know too much. But I needed the dollars to live, so I answered the questions and took the only job offered. I put hamburgers together and poured french fries into little paper cones. I did it well and I didn't complain and through the years the Amish grew fainter and fainter and I became higher and higher in authority at my job until they couldn't see the Amish in me anymore. It puzzled me because I became one of a herd just as I had been in The Order. Only the strangest thing happened. Once I adjusted to being one of them, I started to stretch. And no one stopped me. I found a mentor. And he helped me. I read and I studied and I went to movies and wore colors in all different styles and slept at unheard of hours and I dated men. Men who wore shirts of plaids and stripes and many colors and they wore no suspenders to hold up their pants. And no one condemned me."

Olivia smiled. "Are you an Englisher now?"

Laughing, I said, "I still don't find obscene jokes funny." And then, serious again, I said, "I don't know. I know though I seemed to be one of them, I realized each one of us is different from another. Do you see? The thoughts in my head are my own. The feelings in my body come only from my own heart. Can you see? I am myself. There is no one like *me*. I don't have to be a carbon copy of any one of my English sisters. When it came to me that I was free to be the creature God created unique among all, it was like I could fly, soar, see everything beneath me. Every person. Every building. Every tree. Every thought. Every feeling. Nothing was hidden. It was all there to take in and savor. And I did just that."

"And your family? What about them?"

Pressing my lips together, I felt my eyes fill. I strained forward in my chair and willing Olivia to hear my struggle, spoke, "There is no perfection. Not in this world. I miss them. There is always a price to be paid. I am different now, wholly me, but still needing their substance, longing to sink into their vine and drink the sap of my inheritance. I want them back. I want them both. I want to be me and I want to have them.

"Oh, Cora." Olivia shook her head and sighed. "Oh, Cora."

"I'm not sure who I am. Maybe both. Maybe English *and* Amish. Maybe only one. But whatever this woman is, she knows it is time to discover which side she is on, where she belongs."

Olivia reached and patted my knee, then nodding agreement, she sighed, relaxed and slid back tight against her chair.

"There is more," I said, softly.

She leaned forward in her chair and looked at me.

"I have learned that I, Cora Pooler, can talk to God ... even though I'm shunned, He will listen."

Olivia did not make a comment. I couldn't tell what she was thinking. I watched her face until she seemed to realize my discontent with her silence and then she spoke. "I only want your tranquility, answers to your dilemmas ... and I do rejoice in your growth."

A peace settled over the room.

For a while we sat in a comfortable quiet, enjoying the simple and complete solace of the respect and acceptance of two people with a deep affection for one another, even while my mind, separated from the opposing peace in my heart, played its own private war. Oddly, it was all right. This house was a safe place to be.

"Annabelle is Amish," Olivia said, breaking the silence. "She was placed in a family of the Old Order."

With her unexpected and startling words, the part of my mind delving into my soul, the quest to find my own center stopped cold. I lifted my arms as if to grasp her words and hold them in my hands. "Is she here?"

"I can't tell you more."

"Is she here in Wander Lane? In the Community?"

"I can't tell you," she repeated.

"Please. Can I find her? See her? Is she near?" I made my words speak loud, insistent.

Silent, Olivia's eyes stayed on my face. I could see the yearning in hers, in the lean of her body.

"Please," I pleaded, again.

Gently shaking her head, no, a mist of sadness and regret enshrouded her being, and I knew she would tell me no more. Not on this day.

The sharp sound of the knocker falling on the front door stopped our words.

"It's my hospice aide," Olivia said. "She comes every morning."

"I see," I said, softly. And I did see. I had seen at the door ... the turban, the sunken eyes, the polished cane. Olivia was ill. Very ill. Touching the cross strung round my neck, I thanked God for bringing me home while I still could be with her. And I left her in the care of her helper.

Chapter Four

Head slumped heavy, walking down Olivia's front path, down the sidewalk, across the road and into the park, I bore the weariness of a heart drained dry. Olivia was dying. She would not tell me the place where Annabelle lived. I didn't know if I was Amish or English. My father had shut his door against me.

For a long time I sat in the park, my eyes cast down, mindlessly watching my hands lying limp and still in my lap. Then I heard a bird chirp. I felt the sun warm on my shoulders. I smelled fresh mowed grass. And I looked up. Across the street, people were moving, laughing, chatting, admonishing children, walking with purpose, sauntering aimlessly, alone, together, walking in and out of shops, glancing in windows … living.

Okay, God. I see. Olivia has help. Annabelle is Amish. My father is near. And I have You. Help me listen, God. Help me hear You. Guide me. Help me see more. For Your compassion is great and Your love endures forever.

And I did realize it is good to know God. To know him however troubled I might be, however lost, however doubting, for He sends a bird to chirp, and if I am not too stubborn, to full of myself to listen, or if I refuse to find a selfish pleasure in the self-pity of undeserved misfortune, then I will hear His song and I can grab onto those notes, play them, sing them, in the recesses of my heart. And then will I rest in the quiet of His love.

Feeling hungry, I sought out a shop that would offer me food. I stopped before Wagler's Authentic Amish Bakery and gazed upon its luring pie filled window … cherry, apple, peach … their juices overflowing onto thick, flaky crust. And there lined up right in front of the fruit pies were my favorite … three luscious open faced pies, three rich creamy brown sugar and molasses pies that caused my mouth to moisten in anticipation of the sweet smooth slide of shoofly pie through my lips, down my throat, and into my stomach.

Pushing the bakery door open, the scent of soft heated butter, cinnamon and nutmeg … that pungent aroma of pastry spices … took me back to Maem's kitchen. Flour, sifted fine, layering aprons and polished wooden floors, cheeks and hands, and the old, scarred table where crusts were rolled and cookie shapes cut. Where children were helpers, rolling and shaping, and eating the cinnamon-sugared scraps sculpted and baked just the right size for little hands.

Before me on the front counter of Wagler's Bakery, stacked high on a tray were the enormous buggy wheel sized donuts remembered from youth. I grinned. One of those shared donuts sated the appetites of three sisters …Lily, Violet and me, while the boys could each eat a whole one and then pretend their bellies weren't full and they could eat more. We knew better. One of those donuts was all anyone could eat. But, oh, they did make our tummies happy.

"Could I buy just a slice?' I asked, pointing at the pies.

The young Amish girl behind the counter smiled. "If you eat just a slice, you'll want the whole pie."

"It would be good," I said, smiling back and patting my stomach, "but, too much."

"Okay. I can't sell you a slice, but I can give you a sample. "Which pie would you like?"

"The shoofly," I said without hesitation.

"Ah, good choice. My maem made it herself," She lifted a pie from beneath the counter. There were slices already gone from it. "Samples," she said, cutting a piece and laying it on a napkin. "Most buy a whole pie after they taste it."

I bit into the creamy goodness and my mouth was pleased. "I'll be back for a whole another day," I said, sliding a bill on the counter.

"No, no, no," she said, laughing. "This is for you. Free. So you'll want more."

"Oh, I do. I'll be back. And the money is for you."

She bent her head and said softly, "*Danki.*"

"*Gott es mitt du,*" I said, gently. God be with you. I don't know if she heard.

Outside, I leaned against the door. My legs were trembling. A shudder ran through me. I wanted to go back into the shop and speak some more with the young Amish girl, listen to her Pennsylvania Dutch cadence. I wanted to look at her stiff black kapp, reach and touch its strings, pull them a little. Tell her I was Amish, too. But I couldn't. It would be a lie. And a thought traveled through my mind. *It does not have to be a lie. You could tell the truth. They would forgive you and take you back.* And they would. But only if I confessed my transgressions to the Bishop and proclaimed them before the assembly of the community. And I had done nothing wrong. The lies were to protect those I loved. There was nothing else I could do. *It was so long ago.* And it was. But a lie, a sin, doesn't fade with age. It is neither forgiven nor forgotten until it has been repented according to the directives in the Amish Ordinance Letter. But, for me, it is the Bible, the Word of God that is my place of hope and knowledge now, not the Ordinance Letter, not the Ordnung. I turned from the door and not taking notice of the shops and their names, walked down the sidewalk. My thoughts were too big to consider the store displays or signage that I passed.

"Sorry," a little boy shouted, startling me out of reverie. "My truck got away. Be careful. Don't step on it."

Looking down I saw a tiny pick-up truck rolling toward my feet; and directly behind the vehicle, a child running to catch it.

"Don't squish it," he said.

"I won't," I said, jumping aside. Just in time.

"Sorry, lady," he said scooping it up, not stopping his run.

I watched him, scooting down the sidewalk, pushing the truck to roll fast, running to catch it, swoop it up and push it again. No mother in sight. I smiled. For him that was a lucky thing.

Interrupted from my musings, I glanced at the window beside me. Hattie's Quilt Shoppe. Hattie Shackleton. My old school friend. Yesterday looking through the window, seeing her at work in her store, I'd thought it kinder not to force a choice from her … she could either welcome me or honor an old, old shunning. I'd turned away because I knew she could not disobey the Bishop, but now I was not so sure, while, at the same time, deep in my soul, I knew the shunning would be as binding to her as it was twenty years ago. But so badly did I wanted it to be different, I let myself think that it might be so. She had been a loving girl. Surely, she would be a loving woman.

I opened the shop's door. It caused a melodious tinkling from an attached series of bells. I smiled. Only a thoughtful woman, a forgiving woman, would greet her customers in such a pleasurable way. It must be so.

She glanced at me and smiled. There seemed to be no recognition.

"Hattie?" Tilting my head, I looked onto her face. She wore plain, gold rimmed spectacles and through the glass I could see wrinkles fanning out at the edges of her eyes. Her cheeks, still flushed with girlish pink, were fuller than I remembered. The line of her jaw, softer. There was a gentle sag in her neck. But she was Hattie. No doubt it was Hattie. I longed to reach and enfold her close to my heart. She was my youth. I wanted to draw it inside me, plant it firm. To be back there again. With the Amish. As it had been. A Shunning never having happened. No lies said. No child abandoned.

I could tell she really did not know it was I. "Hattie?" I said again. I watched her smile politely, then her lips slowly parted and the smile faded. The pink in her cheeks darkened, spread. She lifted one hand to cover her mouth, put the other over her heart.

"Yes, Hattie. It's me. Cora Pooler. From school." I said the words softly. Tentatively. And I waited. And I hoped.

She stood awhile, not moving. Then she leaned over the counter, picked up a bolt of material, yellow flowers dancing on grass green fabric, took it to a nearby shelf and stacked it.

"Hattie," I said, "we were friends. Please, won't you talk to me?"

Twisting her head, she looked at me. There was no emotion showing on her face, but her eyes were full and her skin was mottled.

"Hattie," I said again, this time not a question, but a plea I knew would not be answered.

Back straight, wordless, she turned and walked to the back of the store. There was a door there. She went through it and closed it behind her.

I'd had enough of this day. All I wanted was food and bed ... food to satisfy the emptiness of my body; bed, to satisfy the weariness of my soul. I thought it a good thing to buy a cache of non-nutritious, mouth-watering snacks, then munch and walk my way back to the motel and sleep the afternoon away.

As I approached the grocery, I looked up at the clouds and marveled at the mass of thick white mounds filling the sky, and at that moment, the sun broke through their cover hitting my eyes with a blinding glare. Dropping my eyes quickly, turning my head sharply, I found myself looking at a large poster in the grocery display window. I moved closer to it. Not thinking, only knowing the placard took my memory back to a time of intense pleasure, I reached my hand to touch it and was surprised when my skin felt the cold, harsh barrier of glass. It brought me back to reason. Of course, the poster was on the other side of the window. I pressed both hands against the glass, leaning into it to read the enticing words … again and again.

ANNUAL AMISH PUBLIC AUCTION
SAT., JUNE 24 at 10:00 AM
LOCATION: COUNTY FAIRGROUNDS

QUILTS
CATTLE; HORSES
FARM EQUIPMENT; BUGGIES
TOOLS
SHEDS
HOUSEHOLD ITEMS
BAKED GOODS, BARBEQUE, CANNED FOODS
HANDCRAFTED ITEMS
WOODEN TOYS
MISC. ITEMS
LUNCH AND SNACKS AVAILABLE

All money received will be allocated to the Amish Medical Fund to pay any outstanding or future medical bills.
SEE YOU THERE!

Chapter Five

The asphalt cover on the road leading to the fairgrounds ended at the edge of the final half mile mark. From there the road was dirt and dust rose thick and high from the weight of English cars and the brisk turn of Amish buggy wheels. English and Amish, alike, touted this yearly auction as a day to be celebrated, each according to the way of his own culture. This would be the first social event I would attend as one no longer considered Amish, one not sure if she was yet English.

As I drove my car onto the side of the road earmarked for gas driven vehicles, I thought of all the years I had sat in a weaving buggy stuffed full with laughing family anxious to join the throng of dark clothed bodies calling out hurried greetings and comments to neighbors and friends as we scurried about setting up tents and displays.

I parked in a row near the back of a field already harvested once and now growing new clover. I hoped the grass blades would bounce back soft and high not damaged by the heft of steel and rubber crushing them that day.

Walking across the road and passing the black buggies lined precisely, one next to another, I glanced at the sleek, buggy horses tethered on a long fence pole set a distance from the buggies. I couldn't resist. Quietly, not wanting to startle them, I walked down the line in front of the horses running my hand over their muzzles, down their necks, placing my palm under their mouths, feeling the warmth of their breath on my fingers. When I reached the end I went around the post and circled my arm around the neck of a great, tawny beauty. He lowered his head and I moved close against him and rubbing my face against the silky thread of his mane, I soaked in the rich, musky scent of horse.

A young Amish boy, nearly a man, a brush in his hand, came up beside me and began grooming the horse. I knew he would say nothing. There would be no words of admonishment said. But I knew he was telling me, by his actions, he wanted me to leave. I sighed, smoothed my hand over the length of the horse one last time and stepped away.

"He's beautiful," I said.

The Amish boy nodded and kept on brushing. I wanted to touch him, to pat his arm, to tell him it was okay to smile at me, to say words to me, but I just nodded back and went on my way.

The grass under my feet was still spongy soft near the area where the horses were hitched. By noon that same grass would be hard packed, trampled by English youngsters sneaking past the watchful eyes of protecting Amish boys to get a closer look at the ponies. The horses were skittish around the unfamiliar rhythm, accent and volume of the English youngsters, those young boys let loose by their parents to make merry this day. Wary, the animals snorted and stomped, causing the children to laugh, the grass to flatten and the Amish to sometimes wonder at the English discipline, and, sometimes, to chortle, and remember their own youthful moments of forbidden revelry.

I moved onto the path that took me to the grounds of the auction. Before me was a great, moving mass of men and women and children. Every age represented from … newborn to aged. I drank in the whole of it. All the varying paced motion of bodies going from tent to tent, from one display to another, from the barns to the cattle arena. Laughing, talking. Friendly arm punches exchanged. Hands shaken. Backs clapped. Greetings shouted. Feet moving with purpose. Feet pausing to let words be shared. Babies crying. Children darting in and out of small groups of assembled bodies, splitting them, bumping them, slipping away before hands grabbed and stilled them. Men arguing. Women exchanging news. A loose chicken here and there. Cattle pulled from stanchion to arena. Candy and ice cream dropped and scooped up by mothers before children could reclaim their goodies and stuff them in their mouths. I looked and I marveled. There is nothing new under the sun. (NIV, Ecclesiastes 1:9) And it seemed that everything that ever was or will be was happening, all at one time, right before my eyes.

"Cora Pooler."

I heard my name. There was a moment of good feeling that filled every cell of my body. Someone here knew me. Knew my name and was not ashamed to speak it. I turned to see the face of the one who spoke. And I knew the face.

"Lowell Parker," I said, stoically.

"*Sheriff* Lowell Parker," he said. There was a smile on his face. Smug. My cells no longer felt good.

"I was in your office," I said, "just two days ago."

"I know."

"Your car was outside. Your hat hung on the post. Obviously you were there."

He raised his eyebrows. Shrugged one shoulder. "And?"

"Why wouldn't you see me?"

"Got nothin' to say to you."

"But I have something to say to you."

"More like you got somethin' to ask me?"

And I lifted *my* eyebrows. "And?"

"Girl, I got no answers."

"I don't believe you."

He grinned, lifted his forefinger, touched to it his forehead in a salute and walked away. "Be seein' you one of these days," he called over his shoulder. "Call and make an appointment." He stopped a moment, turned his head to me, nodded twice. "That's the proper way to do things."

I stood and watched him disappear into the crowd. He had answers. And I would get them.

Scanning the crowd, I looked to find others I might know. As I searched, remnants of memories took me back to other Amish auctions I had lived. The underlying significance of the obvious differences between English and Amish had not stood out so clearly then. I had not paid attention to the English men and women staying together so much … walking beside each other sitting at the food tents next to each other, touching, holding hands, even pressing light kisses on each other's cheeks or lips, sometimes separating for a time but returning to be coupled again. Not so, the Amish. The men and women stayed separate from each other. Even the boy children stayed with the father; the girl children, with the mother or sister siblings. And neither had I considered the differences in the manner of dress as being of particular import. But now, looking at the horde of swarming persons I was about to join, I saw the Amish as a great flock of dark feathered blackbirds blending together as one, a chorus; and the English, a bevy of cardinals, canaries, bluejays, pheasants, peacocks and parrots, each singing his own song in his own costume ... individuals. I had not thought about it then. Gave it no meaning. It was what it was. And now I had been both ... blackbird and peacock. There was a difference. While the Amish person seemed to hide himself in a cloak encompassing all, the English inclined to step apart from one another in dress. How could I then be of both worlds? How could I blend into both? How could I have it all? It troubled me. But this was a time for pleasure, for joy. A time to savor that which I had left and could now be a part of again ... at least for a moment. I swallowed my pondering and put it to rest in my mind until a fitting time would come to digest it.

I moved forward into the multitude, and I did see familiar faces. Some changed only a little; some changed so much I barely knew them ... especially young faces matured beyond my apperception. Twenty years is a long time. Where the jawlines of those touching old age, those who had been so well known in my heart were firm and sharp edged when I left, now they curved soft and yowled, the aging women's chins softly furred. Where once brown or blond or auburn hair was hidden under *kapps* starched stiff, wisps of grey and white now leaked from the edges of those constraining covers. Eye lids drooped. Cheeks crinkled and sagged. Waists were fuller. Backs that were straight, now bent. Feet moved slower, steps were shorter. But still there was joy in their faces, peace in the sway of their bodies. If they were allowed to receive me, or forgot I was shunned, I knew they would welcome me and encompass me within the confines of their souls, and then I, too, would have peace and joy.

I realized there were some who knew me. Most, I am sure, did not. My hair was different ... and visible. No kapp. I had legs that showed, and below my neck, just a little, was skin, uncovered skin. Tiny loops of gold hung from my ears and a whisper of foundation lay on my face. But there were no stares, no gasps at my presence, no eyes that lingered on my face or body. No acceptance. No facial rejection. Amish do not show emotion in public. And I was too long gone to read the trace of a tremble, or see the hint of pause.

And then I saw Violet. She was walking with Maem. Straight towards me. The outside of my body froze while inside my blood rushed fierce and I felt my cheeks color red.

Maem kept her face down. Her hand held Violet's in a tight grip. Maem did not look at me as she passed by; she did not look at the daughter whom she must have missed, and now with me before her, must ache to touch. Violet, too, appeared not to look, but as she went by, not turning her face, her eyes moved to see me. She winked and looked down. I followed her eyes and saw a bit of paper drop to the ground.

Assuming concerned Amish eyes had witnessed the nonexistent reunion between maem and me, and even knowing they would not tattle if an untoward meeting had taken place, I chose not to take the chance of revealing Violet's disregard for the penalty of my disobedience. She was young, at least in the recesses of remembrance, and I didn't know her status among the less judicious of our community. Among Amish, as with all groups of women, there are those who are not prudent in the stories they relay to others. I did not want Violet to be admonished for my transgression. So I moved my shoe over the paper while watching them walk away from me. When I felt it was safe, I let my purse slide off my shoulder onto the ground as if accidentally, then bending to pick it up, I slid my foot off the paper and, unobtrusively, lifted it up with my purse. Holding it in my fist, I sauntered over to the display of quilts, and while it seemed I was examining an intricate design, managed to open the paper. It was a note. Apparently written quickly, the words were scrawled and hard to read. My hands were shaking. I had to read it twice.

Go into the porta-potty marked out of order. Lock it behind you. Wait there. When you hear five knocks open it up. It'll be me. It mite take awhile.

The porta-pottys were lined up at the back edge of the fairgrounds behind the cow barns near the auction arena. The cows weren't due to be sold until afternoon, so there were not many men and boys gathered at that area yet. A young Amish girl with two smaller girls, black *kapped* and barefoot, passed me as I stood by the out of order facility. I smiled at them. They smiled back, sweet and shy. They went about their business, and I quickly ducked into the nonfunctional outhouse, closed the door, locked it and covered my nose with both hands.

Every minute I waited in that odorous spot seemed an eternity. I thought I would either lose my breath and die of suffocation or breathe and die from my innards splashing out a torrent of vomit. Neither happened. I simply stood and suffered and prayed for Violet to hurry and make her escape.

Five short knocks. And suddenly the smell was not of my foremost awareness. Violet was on the other side of that door. I rushed to slip the bolt.

She came in quickly. I pulled the door shut. "Lock it." Her words were urgent in my ears. I could feel the tremble of her body; she was so close. I held her, put my hand on her face, spread my fingers over the span of her cheek and the cave of her eye, felt the flutter of her lashes. There was not enough space to step away to see the whole of her, so I slid my hand over her face, traced her ear with one finger, then glided my hand to cradle her head, while I held her tight with the other.

"I have to get back," she said, hugging me briefly. "We have to be quick."

I nodded. Though I knew she lived in a world where physical affection was rarely given, I ached for her to hold me tighter. Even so my eyes were full with the joy of the moment and, equally, the sorrow of knowing its brevity.

"Do you still know Yoder's maple shack?" she said.

"In the woods," I said, nodding again.

"It's safe there. The season for sugaring is over."

Again, I nodded.

"Go there Tuesday. The women will be quilting at Lydia Eicher's house and I can pretend an ailment so I don't have to go there with Maem."

"I'll be there."

"Right after the noon meal. And its clean-up."

"I'll go early," I said. "I'll not waste a minute."

She squeezed me, then drew her head back. She was smiling. "I love you, Cora Pooler. I always have done." She slid the bolt, and before opening the door, her smile gone, looked in my eyes. "I'm so sorry. I should have been stronger that day." And then, quickly, she was gone.

Later as I walked the grounds savoring the art of bright colored and familiar patterned quilts, sliding my fingers over smooth, sanded and shellacked toys, relishing the aroma of sweet doughnuts and fresh bread, I thought of those precious moments with which God had gifted me ... that time with Violet. She had changed; she was older. She was the same; she was my sister. The feel of her body as I held her was slight, as delicate as it was twenty years ago. But my fingers had traced a cheek less soft than before, dryer, tighter, and the skin at the edge of her eye sagged under my touch. Putting aside the regret of missing the passage of girl ripened to woman, I thought, instead, of the beauty of her smile, the blessing of her presence, and, again, reveled in the wonders of being back home.

I stopped by the pastry tent and bought a huge oatmeal-raisin cookie. Finding a bench nearby, I sat and munched on the sweet. Relaxing against the rough wooden seat, I looked out at the noisy, moving, auction-loving revelers. A deep swell of happiness charged through my body. I be could part of this dark clad swarm of Amish if I so chose. If I *could* choose. If I could release the secrets and lies to the Bishop. If I could disappear into the rules of the Ordnung. If I could deny that Jesus, through faith, had secured my place in His Kingdom. If I could accept I must keep working at earning salvation day after day by doing good works. Then it could be mine. I could be Amish again. If I could deny who I had become and go back to whom I had been.

A little girl in a billowing dark blue skirt, ankles and feet dust dirty and bare, ran giggling past me, a huge, fat donut in her hands. Behind her an older girl ran to catch her. She was not laughing. But I did. It was the way of life … little ones delighting in antagonizing older siblings.

My eyes followed the big sister outdistancing the younger, grabbing her up, and carrying her away. Still watching, I heard a shout near the cowbarn. The cattle auction was about to begin. I turned my head in that direction, and as I did, I saw Aaron.

His back was to me. His clothes were the same as the others he stood with. The same cut of cloth. The same color. The same heavy black shoes. The same straw hat. The same suspenders buttoned at the waist of his pants. But I knew it was he. I knew the lean of his body. The swing of his head and the tilt of his hat. So many times I had seen one hand slide and rest in the opening between his shirt and trousers. And I knew the common width of space between one foot planted firm in the dirt to the other. I knew it was Aaron.

He slapped his hand against the back of the man standing next to him, a parting gesture, and then turned. I saw his face. He was laughing.

He walked away from the group, a smile still staying on his lips. And he walked towards me ... towards a woman with hair that flowed free, hair that touched her shoulders ... uncovered hair, streaked with grey. A woman in the clothes of an Engisher. But when his eyes fell upon that woman, me, the woman he had not seen for twenty years, I could tell from the sharp, swift jerk of his chin, the almost unperceivable stumble in his gait, that he knew it was me. A curtain fell over his face. No more smile. No sign of recognition. No path to the thoughts that were behind that cover. But I knew. He had recognized me.

I waited. I watched.

His eyes never waivered. For the length of his trek from his friends to the bench, he looked upon my presence. When he got so close he would nearly run into me, he turned slightly and walked past me as if I were not there.

Chapter Six

The stars still shown in the sky as I drove down the path that led to the maple grove, the mass of stately sugar maples tucked within the oaks and spiny locusts and spindly furs. It was a clear night; the stars flashed bright, one then another, sending unknown messages into the heavens. It was a night you didn't need to think about God. He was just there. Within and without. I could almost touch him, feel His pleasure in the beauty He created, hear Him singing His joy.

I couldn't sleep this night. I lay in my bed thinking the words I would say to Violet, the questions I would ask. I thought, how should I say them? How would she hear them? I revised and revised, even knowing when the time came to say the words, they would be gone and each moment would bring new words, words that would be right for that precise piece of time.

Finally, knowing there would be no sleep, I dressed and drove to the sugar shack. It would be hours before the noon meal would be done and the clean-up finished. But I would be safe in the woods. No one would see me drive down the path in the dark. No one would see my car hidden in the trees. All would be sleeping, replenishing their bodies for the next day's work. And before they woke, the stars' sparkle would be fading under the faint rising rays of the sun. I spread a blanket on the ground and waited to watch that poignant, shifting work of art.

"Cora!"

I woke quickly, aware, at once, of the rich scent of earth and pine, the pressure of stone and wood pieces against my back and legs, the flash of sun through the trees, the song of birds and the rustle of forest animals. I had slept the morning away and my sister had come.

"Violet!" I sat up and saw her. And the world sang all around me.

She stood looking down at me. Her face was empty. I could not read her eyes. She reached her hand to me. "Can I help you up?"

"Sit," I said, patting a spot on the blanket.

"No, come sit with me. There are chairs in the sugar shack."

"It's so beautiful out here," I said. "Come, sit here. Please."

"I don't want to be found."

"I don't want that either, but if there are roamers in the woods, they will see my car. It's a chance we have to take."

"I don't want them to see *me*," Violet said, stepping back, looking down the path. "They know your car." She smiled, wistfully. "You've been seen driving the roads, watching them. If they see your car, they'll think you're walking in the woods. They'll leave *you* alone. If they see me, they'll tell."

"You're right," I said, standing, brushing at my clothes to clean them of the bits of loose earth and dry leaf fragments that had drifted onto me by early morning breezes. "If they see you, they will speak to you, reprimand you. You'll confess and they'll forgive. But for me, it will be as it was at the auction … they look. They stare. Their tongues say no words to me, but their eyes speak loud, 'don't touch her, don't speak to her … she's evil, doomed for eternal Hell.'"

"You're bitter," Violet said, gently. "It's your good they are thinking of."

"My *good*?"

"Yes. We all want you back. Confessed and forgiven. We want you Amish, again. I want you Amish, again. Can you not see that?"

Inside my head misty clouds moved, shading my thoughts with confusion. I wanted to believe her words. But I wasn't sure. I knew the shunning could cease. I knew if I repented and returned to the Amish way of living with all the rules obeyed, I would be accepted into the community as one of them. Amish. But would it be *Cora* they would accept, *me*, the heart and soul that had grown and learned something new and wonderful? Would they let me have *my* Jesus? Would they let me speak of Him?"

"You would be so welcomed." Violet said, but still she didn't reach to touch me.

"I know," I said, softly, "but the price would be so great."

"What price?"

"Freedom."

"Are you so free now, Cora? I don't think so. Can you have peace living so far from The Order? Can you kneel by Maem's bed in the night and wipe the tears of children lost from her cheeks? Can you make Da smile at the shoofly pies you can not bake? Can you hold you brothers' babies or run by the creek, pick flowers with their children?"

"*Stop*"

"Whisper secrets to me from the bed next to mine?"

Pressing my hands against my face, rubbing my fingers hard against my forehead, I shook my head. Then I lowered my arms, stood straight, and looked at her. "No, it's a prison you're asking me to seek. And the sad thing is I am standing outside that jail, wanting so badly to get in. *For a visit.* And you won't let me in."

"Come," she said. "I can't stay too long."

I followed her into the sugar shack. Straining, she pushed open the door. A sweet, mapley scent of boiling syrup lingered in the air. It smelled of old days I had known.

Still we had not hugged. I stepped to move closer.

"Wait." She held out her arm. "I want to look at you." She bit her bottom lip and tilted her head. Her eyes roved over my body. "You look thin in your English clothes. They cling. The Bishop would be disappointed. They give you too much shape." For a moment a smile whispered across her lips. "I might like to try them on." Then it was gone. She shook her head slightly. "It would shame me to be seen in them."

"You've changed, too" I said. "You're stronger."

She looked down at her body and smiled. "I'm older. The body grows muscles from work."

"No," I said. "Not your body. Your words. Your demeanor. You're not a little girl anymore."

"Of course not, little girls have dreams not secrets. They pretend to be mothers and keepers of the house. Not keepers of secrets."

"Sometimes, Violet, dreams are too small, too fragile to hold beautiful in your hand. But everything doesn't need to be held with strength," I said, longing to find her gentle spot, the Violet of old.

"I have to be strong."

"Sometimes, there's happiness to be found in a vulnerable heart."

"I'm the only sister left. *I have to be strong.*"

"I still live."

Violet said nothing.

"Am I as dead?"

"You know the Amish rules," she said, leaning her head forward. In the dim light, I thought I saw a shadow of yearning show briefly on her face. I reached forward to touch her. She stepped back.

The want for the now to be the same as the old was too much; the weight inside, too great to hold more. I sat down on an old stained and scarred chair near the opened door. There were no windows in the room. The only light came through the door. It wasn't sufficient for me to see Violet clearly. "Tell me about you," I said, thinking to move from troubling words of dispute. "The good things. The farm. The neighbors. You're cooking. Do you still let the water boil 'til it is gone and the potatoes burn?" I said, smiling.

"I'm the same. except for the empty hole where sisters used to live."

I sighed, looked down at my hands and waited for her to say more.

She dragged a chair across the room and set it in the daylight that came through the door. Looking up, I could have reached and took her hand. We were so closely seated our knees nearly touched. She said nothing.

"You're stronger," I repeated.

"I am," she said. "I'm here. It wasn't easy to come."

"No," I agreed. "I knew it wouldn't be. But I thought you would be kinder … softer."

"How so? I approached you." Her back stiffen even straighter in her chair. *"I'm talking to you.* How is that not kind?"

"You haven't touched me. Neither have you hugged me well. You, my little sister. Violet. The little girl who, laughing, ran through the fields clasping my hand and rolled in the grass, arms tight around me, the little girl who brought Maem buttercups and daisies for the table." I paused. "I see no joy in your face."

"I never married," Violet said.

"Because you were the only girl child left to help Maem?"

"Mostly." She lowered her head, closed her eyes.

"Why else?" I lay my hand on her lap. I could not deny the need I felt from her. And she did not push it away.

Hands still clasped, so close to mine on her knee, she opened her eyes and looked into mine. Hers were wet. "I was afraid."

"Of what, dear child?"

"That I would be punished. That I would bear a child deformed. Or a child perfect and one day he would be found missing … or taken … or dead in the creek."

"Oh Violet, you have done nothing wrong. God would not punish you."

"I lied, same as you." She raised her hands and covered her mouth. Eyes closed, she lifted her head as if seeking a way to reach God. I sat silent, knowing her guilt ... and mine ... and not knowing how to help her. Or me.

"I love you, Violet," I whispered.

"Have you been gone so long you've forgotten the Amish ways?" she said, lowering her face to see me, dropping her hands, putting them over my hand as it rested in her lap. She leaned towards me. "I am so afraid I will go to Hell. I have sinned, but if I tell, if I confess before the brethren, they will know the whole of the story. I say I am strong, but I'm not strong enough for that."

"Do you know where the child is?"

"Annabelle?"

"Yes."

"She would be twenty now. I think of her often."

"Do you know where she is?" I repeated, softly.

"No." She leaned back in her chair and I took my hand from her lap. We sat for awhile. No words. Then a soft voice ... "I love you, too, Cora."

Chapter Seven

"You need to take the auction sign off your board," I said.

Harriet smiled. "Nah. I'll just leave it up there. For next year. It's all the same. Mebbe the date changes a little. But ain't nobody gonna notice that." She gave a little cackle and grinned wider. "Ain't probably nobody even gonna *look* at that poster … 'cept mebbe the out-a-towners. That old auction rolls around every year. Same time. Same place. Same bodies walkin' its dirt. They don't need no reminding."

"The auction makes a lot of money for the Amish," I said.

"Goes for a good cause." Bobbing her head, Harriet pressed her lips together and raised her chin. "Yep, it does. The Amish don't buy no health insurance, but they don't toss out their doctor bills neither. And they gotta find some way to get those dollars. Their stuff's good. Ain't nobody gettin' gyped." She pulled herself out of her chair. "I'm gonna go get you a piece of fresh shoofly pie. Made it myself this morning. And don't you be takin' your purse out. It's on the house."

I shook my head. "You spoil me."

"Gotta spoil somebody." She squeezed my shoulder, pushed one hand hard against her back and walked towards the kitchen.

Sliding back into my chair and folding my arms across my chest, I thought about the afternoon. After giving Violet plenty of time to walk back to her home and with feelings of our meeting unsettled in my mind, I had driven slowly from the maple grove towards Wander Lane. A shaking started in my legs traveling upwards and across my body, through my stomach to my heart and into my arms. Fearful, I stopped the car at the Wander Creek bridge near Maem and Da's house, my old home, and concentrated on making myself calm by thinking good thoughts of my days lived there. And I prayed. And I envisioned scenarios of me, now, with my family at the supper table, all of them talking to me, touching me, laughing with me. As if I never had been gone.

When I'd been there awhile and the pounding in my chest had ceased, I opened my eyes and saw two Amish boys, feet bare and heads straw-hatted, running down the road, zig-zagging, giggling and pushing at each other. One of them fell into the ditch; the other toppled on top of him. They scrambled out laughing, holding long strands of ditch grass in their hands. I watched them smooth the blades, then put them to their lips to make whistles, their mouths blowing air through the grass. Then running again, they passed my car, waving and grinning at me. I waved back and thought of the days I had gone up and down this road without seeing any cars driving or parked upon it. But to these boys my car was not an anomaly. Even the Amish world was not able to keep itself from blending, even in small measure, with the English. And I wondered what Bishop Herrfort thought of that.

I had also noticed the pockets of the Amish boys were bulging. Possibly with apples. Probably with apples stolen from one of their Maem's larders. And the thought of juicy, plump apples made my mouth hunger. Harriet's good food came to mind. And that's how I came to be at her table.

I saw her coming back to the table, holding the pie. My mouth filled with the moisture of anticipation. She lay the pie before me, and looking down at it, I saw there were two forks. I looked up at her and winked.

"Guess I cut the piece too big for one," she said.

"Guess so," I agreed.

We ate. We enjoyed.

Sated, I leaned back in my chair. "Harriet?"

She cocked her head, waiting for my question. I wasn't sure how to direct it. Harriet probably knew ninety percent of what went on in the village and in the Amish community. But to share that knowledge was not a given. She was a shrewd lady. Beneath the wrinkled skin and age-shrunk and scarred bones beat a judicious and compassionate heart, a humble heart. She did not need accolades to coat her worth. She was good with God; no one else's judgment held sway. I chose to be direct.

"Why has Violet never married?' I asked.

"Why haven't you?"

"I nearly have. Twice," I answered.

"And?"

Her voice was solemn. I knew if any information about Violet would be forthcoming from her reservoir of gleaned awareness, I would have to prove myself worthy, so I swallowed pride and fear and revealed private, personal, guarded pieces of my soul.

"I have been in love, Harriet. Deeply so." I didn't look at her as I spoke. I kept my eyes on the plates, focused on the bits of crust still on them. It was less painful to remember, to share, if shards of reality, snippets of tangible substance tempered the visions, the sensations, that slipped in and out, shifting, drifting in vaporous memory.

"Two men," I said, reluctantly, but deliberately, unclothing my heart. "Good men. I think they loved me. I'm not sure. In the beginning … with both of them … there was joy. Almost the same as that found in prayer. But, unfortunately, not as lasting. Doubts came. Not about them. About me. It was the sin thing. My sin. I know Jesus forgives. And I'm so grateful for that. But I never confessed, so how can there be repentance? You see, there is still that old Amish holdover. Sometimes it encompasses me so tightly, I feel I will never break free. It tarnished the love. My doubts. My fears. My inadequacies. They grow and devour the joy." I stopped my speaking. There was more. The secret I kept hidden from myself. The one to which I could never give words. For then it would be real and I could never again hide from it.

I felt Harriet's eyes on me. I raised my face. On hers was a radiant compassion. "There is more," I said. She stayed very still, didn't move. "But I can't say it. My heart will not let me."

"There was a time," Harriet said softly, "when Violet went to the Sunday night singings. It was after Lily was planted under the flowers. Then she stopped goin'."

"Why?"

"I dunno, girl. I dunno."

"Who was it? Who took her to the singings?"

"Dunno that either."

"But you suspect who it was?"

"Mebbe." She paused, closed her eyes. Sighing, she scrunched her face and I knew she was done telling of Lily. Her reminiscing had gone to another place. "Sometimes," she continued, "when my legs ain't achin' too much, I take myself up to the top of that hill where they put Lily into the ground. She was a frisky one, that girl. Don't like to think of her all packed away tight in a box. So what I do …"

She looked at me, stern. "And don't you be laughin', girl. I dig under the spot where she is. Not deep. These old hands ain't strong enough for that. But I dig plenty far down to make sure there's ample dirt to cover the flowers." Her voice was cracking. She stopped and swallowed. Tears caught in the crevices of her wrinkles.

"What flowers?" I asked.

"I take 'em up with me. Bought flowers. The kind all full and dewy. Lots of pretty colors. Feisty flowers. Like her. Make you smile. But anyway, I put 'em down over the grave, and I cover 'em with dirt and press down hard so's they'll sink down deep and mebbe they'll get close enough she can smell 'em through the wood." Harriet folded her arms over her chest, squeezed them hard against her body, and rocked … just a little. As I watched her, I thought, in her heart, she was holding Lily tight against herself.

"I'm not laughing," I said, softly.

"Seems wrong a young'un like her layin' there in the ground, rotting, and this old buzzard sits here talkin' to you. Old body wizened, useless, still here. Don't make no sense."

"Never useless, Harriet. Never useless."

Leaving Harriet's restaurant, I thought how little we know of the wisdom and love the world carries hidden in the hearts of so many unheralded, simple persons. We comprehend a little of it, but if we dig, an abundance of new insight and appreciation, awe, is ours. Harriet had brought a measure of that to me.

It was time to go home. To my temporary motel home. I was tired. And even with a pie filled stomach, I was hungry. For nutritious fare. An Apple. A banana. A prepackaged, mostly lettuce, salad. The grocery was near. Filled with all the good stuff my craving body sought. Resolutely, I strode towards the store and as I came near it, out walked Lowell Parker. *Sheriff* Lowell Parker. Hands holding food filled plastic bags.

"Ah," I said to him. "I see you have killed a tree."

He looked down at his bags, lifted his head and smiled. "Only one … but, tell you what, I'll plant another in its place. Just for you."

"Thank you."

"Nice day, Miss Used To Be Amish, don't you think? No rain. Lots of sun," he said, tilting his head, raising one eyebrow. "Still full of questions?"

"Still full."

"Stop by the office. Any time."

"I'll do that, Mr. Perhaps To Be One Day Unelected Sheriff."

He grinned, saluted and walked away.

Shaking my head, I thought he was one big-headed man. And unless it was to his advantage, I knew it would be hard to break through his tough, arrogant skin to get the answers that would satisfy my hunger.

Chapter Eight

"Jared? It's me."

"Hey, Cora. What's up?"

"I need more time," I said into the phone, and I heard him grunt even before my last word was finished.

"His majesty won't like that," he said.

"Let me talk to him."

"Not here. The busy man is out on a jaunt. Business, you know."

"Where?" This time I heard him snicker.

"Well, it's not actually a jaunt. It's more like an encounter."

"Can I reach him?"

"Well, actually he's at the White Inn with the latest bimbo."

"Jared, don't joke." I knew he was trying to irritate me, and it was working.

"Maybe she's not a bimbo, but she sure is hot."

"Jared!"

"Don't get your gray matter all warped up. You're still the love of his life."

"Jared, he's your boss, too. And if you remember, I am a bit higher on the ladder than you. So what I want you to do is pull out your little pink pad, put it in front of you, pick up your pencil and write these words...*Daniel, Call me, Cora.* Got that, Jared?"

"How much time off you gonna ask for?"

I sighed. I really didn't know and it really was not Jared's business.

"Hey," he said and I sensed his impatience. "He's gonna wanna know."

"I'll tell him when he calls."

"Cora, Cora ... full of secrets. Anyway, you should know, he's missing you. But, also, as we all know, that man's not the waiting kind. And looking around this office I see lots of bimbos."

"You know, Jared, you're right. I am full of secrets. And I'm going to share two of them with you. Number one: I have a couple weeks of useable vacation sitting on the books just waiting there for me to use.

Number two: Daniel, who is *not* a bimbo seeking vulture, and I have not been a couple for a long time. Oh, my mistake. You already know that. It's impossible to keep secrets from you. If I were an unpleasant person, I might even call you Dumbo Ears. "

"Don't be nasty, Cora. And of course, as *you* should know, you're little secrets aren't very interesting anyway. They're in and out of my head like a bullet through a poor man's dog-eared shirt."

"Just give him the note, Jared."

"You could email him."

"Good-bye, Jared."

"He still likes you." He sing-songed into the phone.

I snapped my phone shut, wishing I had brought my computer with me. But just for a moment. I really did not want my work following me. Not on this trip.

Looking around my motel room, I thought, how dismal. But it was affordable. At least for now. Only if I stayed too much longer, I would have to pack up my clothes and maybe borrow a blanket … and pillow from here … and set up shop in the sugar shack. "Don't worry," I said, punching the pillow. "You're safe. I don't steal and I don't homestead on other people's property. Remember, I was an Amish girl once and some morals stick." I punched it again. And again. Hard. Harder. "I hate you, pillow." And all of a sudden I found myself crying. *If I could, God, I would be swearing right now … not Your name, but really ugly words. The worst I've ever heard. Loud as I can. But I guess the residual Amish in me won't let me do that. And the Amish don't whine, either, and here I am bawling my head off, so I guess I'm not so Amish, after all. But, God, I don't know what to do. I'm running out of money and I haven't found out much at all. I don't know where Annabelle is and I don't know where I want to be.*

The phone rang. I breathed deep and wiped my nose with my sleeve. Daniel's name was on the screen. I breathed even deeper.

"Daniel?" I said, answering the call, forcing my voice not to gulp a telling sob.

"Are you all right?"

"Yes."

"Jared called me and said you needed to talk with me."

"I left a message for you. Jared implied you were too busy for me to call you."

"Cora, you know you can call me anytime."

"He said you were with a bimbo." I tried not to sound whiney.

Daniel laughed. "I was having lunch with the mayor and the director of the Chamber of Commerce. Still am. And you've seen those guys. Not too bimboey."

"You can call me later, if you want. I can wait."

"No, no. I just came into the lobby. I can see them from here. They're fine."

"I need more time," I said.

"How much?"

"I'm not sure. It could be a lot. I don't seem to be making much headway."

"We miss you. *I* miss you." He paused and I waited. "The work load's heavy right now, but I think we can handle it and I know some people I can bring in to help out … older, retired staff. They know their stuff, so take all the time you need."

"You won't fire me?" I said, half seriously.

He laughed, again. "I won't fire you … Cora?"

"Yes."

He was silent for a moment, then spoke in a hushed voice. "How are you fixed for money?"

"I'm okay," I said thinking, the prideful ex-Amish girl just told another lie.

"You'll keep in touch?" Daniel said.

"I'll keep in touch."

"Cora?"

"Yes."

"It was good to hear your voice." And he was gone.

"Okay, pillow, we're all right now and for a couple more weeks, but then the salary is gone. And I just might have to steal you and find us a bridge to sleep under. Who knows?"

Seeking respite from all the questions I couldn't answer, the problems my raging brain could not sort and solve, I curled up on the bed, brought the battered pillow close to my chest, and sought a hiding place in slumber. Before sleep came, I prayed.

Dear Lord, I'm in a place of turmoil. My heart and mind struggle seeking to find solutions. Money will dry up soon. I don't know how to find Annabelle. And, God, I want to be Amish and English. Both. Can You make that happen? Can I be both? I cannot turn from You. I cannot keep Your name from flowing out my lips. I cannot take man's law, The Ordinance Letter, as my source of wisdom and love. I don't believe it is what I do that saves my soul. It is my belief that Jesus is my Lord and Savior that leads me to Your heart. And He is there for everybody, not just the Amish. It's Your Word I live. I cannot deny my salvation, Your eternal love. When I took you into my heart, when Your words were inscribed there forever, You promised You would guide me, counsel me, watch over me. I ask for that now. I ask for what I know You have already given me and my heart battles to accept. Please forgive my lack of trust. Open my eyes, my ears, and my heart to Your Word. Oh, Lord, you are my God, first and foremost in my heart ...but I want my family, too. And I don't believe the Amish, my earthly family, would allow me to confess, repent and then stay with them, if I speak and live believing as I do ... and I can't change that. Hear my prayer, Oh God. Help me.

I did not sleep long. There were still several hours before the evening meal. I smoothed the bed and fluffed the pillow.

"No need for you just yet," I said to the pillow as I ran my hands over my clothes, and shook my hair into place. "Stay there all soft and puffy and hope I won't ever be demanding you to leave your dingy home and roam unknown journeys with me."

Grabbing my purse, I slid into my shoes, waved good-bye to my pillow and left the room. I knew where I was going. I had known since I opened my eyes. The nap had been refreshing and my first thought on waking was of Sheriff Parker.

I walked instead of taking the car. The sheriff's station, attached to the back of the Village Hall, was not far from the motel. The Village Hall, itself, was a stately building. Not large, but demanding respect. I walked around to the back. As I turned the corner, the smooth, swept sidewalk altered into a surface eroded from neglect and mistreatment. Parked in a haphazard fashion in front of the station door were two sheriff vehicles. They needed washing. So did the rain streaked concrete walls of the station, so different from the august, sand-blasted bricks of the Village Hall's face. I squeezed around the cars and went into the building.

Directly in front of me on clean white walls were two large paintings, reproductions of Van Gogh's *Starry Night* and *Sunflowers*. Between them was a closed door.

"Have to have something to keep me awake and cheerful."

I looked to the left. A uniformed woman, thirtyish, grinned at me from her desk. A vase of pink and red carnations and several photo frames, pictures facing her, shared space with neatly stacked files and papers and a child's handcrafted brightly painted pinch pot filled with pens and pencils. I looked at her and smiled.

"Fact is, I have to have lots of somethings," she said, pointing at the pretties on her desk.

I smiled and gazed around the room. I saw books and boxes neatly stacked on shelves. The tops of file cabinets were empty. Electronic equipment was meticulously aligned, ready for action, on tables on either side of the women's desk. In the corner to my right were several padded straight chairs placed in a semi-circle around a table holding neat piles of magazines, a boxed checker game, and a deck of cards. On the walls behind that area were colorful paintings of cats and dogs and jungle animals.

"Some people don't like people, so I give them animals," the woman said, watching me. "Everybody likes animals. Well, almost everybody. We do get the occasional visitor who is more interested in things other than animals." She winked. "Especially the guys that come as forced visitors."

I walked over to the desk. "You do like it neat," I said.

"I do."

"Is Sheriff Parker in?"

"He is."

"Can I see him?"

"Now that I can't tell you … not until I ask him." She smiled at me, friendly, but I sensed a hint of caution, a trace of evaluation. "Sometimes a body can see him, sometimes they can't. Now, you tell me who you are and what you want to see him about."

"Can I just tell you who I am and let the what I want go?"

"Sure," she said, picking up a pencil, tapping it on the pad in front of her. She waited a moment, watching me. "But there's not a whole lot of chance he'll see you if I don't give him more than that."

Let's try it. My name is Cora Pooler." I waited to see if there was a reaction. There was. Just slight, but there. I knew she wouldn't ask. I relented. "I am relative of the local Amish Pooler family."

"The shunned one," she said.

I nodded. "I'm surprised you remember. You're so young."

I don't remember," she said. "Not much, anyway. But you kind of are the talk of the town now." She paused, still looking directly at me. "Don't let it bother you," she continued. "People always talk when something new comes along. But it doesn't last long. Something newer always takes their attention away. We folks are a fickle bunch. Good thing, too. Nobody's under the spotlight too long that way." She tapped the pencil a few more times, then nodded. "You wait here. I'm going to go in and tell the sheriff you want to see him."

I knew there were machines at the ready to contact the sheriff from her desk, but, obviously she had more to tell him than just that I was here to see him. I sensed this was an astute, perceptive woman who knew the pulse of the village well, and was, also, cognizant of which gossip-gleaned information would be appropriate to share with the sheriff.

I stood by her desk and waited. Wanting to know her name, I looked for a name plate. There was none. I considered going behind her desk to look at her photographs, but she had not invited me to do that, so I couldn't. A blue glazed dog, surely molded by a child, then shaped and cooked in a school kiln, sat on one corner of her working area. Reaching across a pile of papers, I stroked its shiny, cool surface.

"My son made that. He'll be in first grade next fall." She put her hand on my arm.

"I'm sorry, I should not have touched it," I said, blushing.

"Oh, no," she said, "it's strong."

"It wasn't mine to handle."

"A mother is always happy to see her child's work admired." She slipped around the desk and sat. "The sheriff's ready for you. Through the Van Gogh's," she said, pointing. "First door on the left. Just walk in."

"Thank you." She hadn't told me her name, so I couldn't say it. I thought it must be difficult to think you must keep your name a secret. Perhaps, I thought as I walked to the sheriff's office, she felt it safer that thugs and such didn't know it.

"Oh my," I said, opening the sheriff's door.

He looked up, his face grim. "What?"

"I think you need to bring your desk lady in here," I said looking around. The room was a mess.

"Tilly?"

"She didn't tell me her name."

"She doesn't like it. Come in. Sit. I'll be right with you."

There were two chairs positioned in front of his desk, but there was no place to sit. They were covered with papers. As was the floor. His desk. Shelves. Cabinets. Anywhere there was space, there was stuff.

"Did she wish you luck?" he muttered, still absorbed with the file in front of him.

"No."

"Must be she thinks you're tough," he said. He glanced up, looked at me, then down at his work again. "Sit," he mumbled into his papers.

"What?" I said.

He looked up, glaring. "I said, sit."

"Where?"

"Where do you think?" he said, pointing, his voice rising. "See. Two chairs. Pick one."

"I can't."

He threw up his arms, dropped his hands hard on his desk. "Okay, then stand."

"The chairs are full," I said.

Rolling his chair back with a quick jerk, he got up, picked up the stack of papers from one chair, laid it on the other, and stomped back to his desk.

"Now," he said. "Let's hear the questions."

I sat down and smoothed my skirt. "Thank you," I said, quietly.

"Okay," he said, his voice lower. "I've gotta lot of work, not much time. We'll take as much time as you need, but, remember, I'm on the tax payers' dollar and they get a bit perturbed when their money's wasted. Okay?"

I nodded and looked at him. He had aged in the last twenty years. A little less hair, a little more belly, a lot more wrinkles. He would be older now than the permissible retirement age. Not by much. So it was by choice he worked. Apparently, though tired and grouchy on this day, he enjoyed his job ... or needed the money. Twenty years ago he had seemed much older that I, but as we get older, age differences shrink. He would probably one day be a crusty old man, but now his testy manner was no more than an irritant to me.

"Well?" he said.

"I'm not sure where to start."

"Start with the baby. That's why you're here, isn't it?"

"It is." I took a deep breath. "Do you know where she is?"

"How would I know that?"

"Do you?"

"If you remember, I never had the baby. Olivia kept her ...took her to Services."

"Why ... why didn't you take her? That's what Olivia wanted you to do. And you knew she was an Amish baby. She was wrapped in Amish clothing. And you would not have had to deal with her ... that tiny, little baby. You and the Bishop worked hand in hand when it was an Amish matter. You could have just given her back to him ... let him take over. I didn't want that. I didn't want him to go snooping around to find someone to punish. So, that's why I left her with Olivia. To keep the Bishop out of it. If it had worked out as I planned neither you nor the Bishop would be involved. If Olivia kept the baby with her, I could have gone back and no one would have known there had been a child born that day." I could hear my voice growing louder. "I didn't think she would really take the baby to you. Though I know now, it would have been impossible for her to keep the baby, but on that night that's what I hoped for ..."

"And that's what would have happened if someone hadn't seen you that night," the sheriff interrupted. "I wanted no part of that mess, but there was no choice after that kid told what he saw."

"But why?" I asked, still puzzled. "You and Bishop Herrfort were friends. You took every Amish problem to him. Why did you not take this situation to him right away? As soon as you knew there was a baby abandoned, an Amish baby, why didn't you go to him? What did it matter to you? I just don't understand. Forgive the expression, but always, in every instance I knew of that involved one of the brethren, you ran to the Bishop and tattled."

"I told you. I didn't want to get involved," he said, squirming in his chair. I could see anger growing. "And what difference does it make to you?"

"It doesn't ring true. It is not like you," I said, leaning forward. "You like to be in the middle of things. And it, also, seems strange to me that you didn't give the baby to my maem, when she made that request. There has to be a reason."

Ignoring my confusion, he didn't give an explanation to my question. "The baby was already with Olivia."

"But nothing had been finalized. It would have been easy to give the baby to my maem. She would have cherished that wee one and raised her as one of her own children."

"Some things are best resolved simple and quick." He leaned back in his chair as if to be done with me. But I wasn't done. Not yet.

"Was it not a crime for me to walk away from the child?"

"No. Babies are abandoned at police stations, hospitals, wherever … no questions asked."

"Were you not supposed to discover the name of the father?"

"Me? No. I left that up to the Bishop." He paused, then said quietly, "You know, I'm sorry for what happened to you. I know everything's not rosy in The Order, but it was better that I didn't get involved with it. There wasn't much I could do and some things are best left with the Bishop."

"Do you know who the father was?"

"No."

"Did you ask the Bishop if he knew?"

"No, but I don't think he did."

I pressed my fingers hard into the sides of my face, rubbed them up and down, then bent even closer to the sheriff. "The Bishop knows everything," I said. My forehead furrowed with intensity, I stared at him. "And I think you know the name, too."

The sheriff plucked a toothpick from the mess on his desk, put it in his mouth and chewed on it. I watched him and I waited. His eyes were hard as he looked at me. "You tell me," he said. "You should know who the father is."

"I don't know," I said, slumping back in my chair.

"You were raped?"

I said nothing.

"If you don't make a charge, nothing can be done. And you didn't accuse anyone back then. So I'm assuming you do know who the father is."

"When you came with your accusations and your *witness*, my world stopped. All that was asked of the women was, *is the baby yours*? I told them, yes, it was me that took the baby to Olivia. When I wouldn't answer more questions, when I wouldn't repent, they shunned me. They never asked who the father was."

This time, it was the sheriff who was silent.

"Doesn't this seem odd to you?"

"Listen," he said, motioning at his desk. "I've got a lot of stuff here that needs doing. I don't think we've got anything more to say about this."

"I want to talk about my sister. Her dying."

"You want to talk about your sister, then you come in when I'm not so busy."

"When would that be?"

"I dunno. Guess you'll just have to take your chances."

Outside the station, my backside pressed hard against the station's cement wall, and holding my arms tight over my stomach, I bent and swallowed, willing myself not to vomit. Through the whirling in my head, I heard the crunch of tires near me, a car's engine stop, a door slam, and then the touch of a hand on my arm.

"You okay, ma'm."

I straightened and stood very still until my head cleared, then I looked at the officer standing beside me. He was so young. So awkward in his stance. But his face was kind. And the strength of his touch calmed me.

"Ma'am?"

I nodded and smiled. "I'm fine." I stepped away from him. "Thank you." I squeezed his arm, turned and, back straight, walked away.

Chapter Nine

I spent the next few days in my motel room ... reading, mostly sleeping. When I was hungry I drove to a nearby village and ate in its small diner. Sometimes, I would go the grocery there and buy food I could take back to the motel and keep on my dresser until I needed to fill my stomach. When the doubts, the unanswered questions, the yearning to know where Annabelle was, and why Lily died, became too big, too painful, I shut them out of my head, and when I couldn't do that, I took a pill from the drugstore bottle that promised respite from the worries of the world ... a pill that promised sleep. And I slept and I slept and I slept.

And then one morning I woke with magnificent music soaring in my head. And strewn within the powerful, heart-filling notes were melodious, potent words of and from God. Celestial hymns. Glorious songs of adoration. Choruses of love to Him, and from Him, words of truth. *I love you beyond measure. I will show you a path when you think there is none. And when you think there is no one, I am there.* And the mighty and marvelous music roared strong and majestic within my head. Enthralling. Compelling. Joyful. And the inner strength that comes from God's joy, came to me.

When the music faded and only a remnant was left as a reminder, I opened my eyes and there was clarity. All around me the things of this world were sharp-edged and full of color. It was good to be awake.

I dressed quickly, readied my room for the day, opened my door and, for a long moment, stood and treasured the enchanting sweep of hills and trees and sky. God's work. Then thanking Him, I started the walk to Main Street. I knew exactly where I should go.

I turned the corner to Olivia's house. Seeing the need for her pansies to be weeded, I cleaned them out as I worked my way up her path. I noticed, too, her porch chairs were rain- streaked and thought before I left, I should wash them.

Dianna, Olivia's hospice helper, answered my knock.

"Shh," she said softly. "She's sleeping. Her bath and breakfast wore her out."

"I'll come back later," I whispered.

Dianna smiled. "You can talk a little louder than that. Come on in." She took my arm and guided me through the door. "Why don't you sit and rest awhile. She'll wake soon. It's just a little nap she's taking."

I smiled back. She was older than I. "I don't think I need a little morning rest. Not yet, anyway. Maybe, in a few years." Dianna put her hand over her mouth and raised her eyebrows. Through her fingers, I could see her lips pulled down in a grimace. The cords in her neck were taut. Thinking I had embarrassed her, I quickly changed the subject. "You know what I would like to do? If you would tell me where I can find a cloth and a bucket, I would enjoy washing Olivia's porch chairs." She gave me a doutful look. "No, seriously," I said, "I really would like to do it. Olivia has been so good to me; I'd like to do something for her. And besides, this old Amish trained body needs something productive to do while I wait."

"Are you sure?"

"I'm sure. It would pleasure me if you would do me that favor," I said, laying my hand on her arm. The emotional and physical fatigue from gratifying the needs of a frail and dying woman showed on her face. "And why don't you take a little break?"

"Oh, I can't do that. This is my job. I get paid to do for her. And mostly, she might need me."

"Okay, then why don't you come out on the porch ... we can hear her from there ... and tell me how she's been doing. I haven't been here for a while and I really need to know."

Still reluctant, Dianna looked towards the parlor where Olivia rested on the couch. "I don't know," she said, rubbing her hands together.

"I think she needs me," I said, "and I need her. And I can't know how to respond to her unless I know how she is. And, Dianna, she needs you too ... strong and rested. Let me help."

"I guess it's all right. We'll leave the door open so we can hear her," Dianna said.

"Okay," I said. And so while Dianna rocked and appraised me of Olivia's recent condition and activities, I washed Olivia's rain-streaked chairs and made them bright colored again.

"I think I heard her." Dianna jerked upright in her chair and looked toward the door.

I smiled. "You were sleeping."

She turned to me. "Did you hear her?"

"Just some sleepy noises," I said from the chair next to her. I had finished cleaning all the chairs but the one she sat in, and so I was sitting, rocking, and enjoying the day's beauty. "Why don't you check on her and I'll finishing washing your chair."

Spry for a woman almost old, she rose quickly and without pausing to give her bones time to adjust from their relatively long sit, headed for the door.

I finished the last chair, wrung out the rag, dumped the water over the porch railing and left the bucket by the front door. Then head bowed, I stood by the door for a moment, emptied my soul from all human thought and feeling and rested in God's Spirit. And in that celestial space of stillness, I soaked in, again, the replenishment of strength and wisdom that only He can give.

"Dianna?" I called, stepping into the house. The parlor was empty.

"We're here. Just had to wash up a little, get ready for lunch." Dianna led Olivia in. My friend's face seemed thinner; the dark under her eyes, deeper. Her step, aided by a carved wooden, stained, and polished cane, was slower than when I last saw her. Then she smiled. It was a smile of recognition and pleasure. I nodded and smiled back at her, returning the joy.

"It is so good to see you," I said moving towards her. She shook her head, "Yes," and reached out to me. I took her hand into my own and with my other, palmed her cheek. She shut her eyes and leaned into it. We stood there, a moment, treasuring our special connection.

"I'll leave you two to talk and when lunch is ready, I'll come get you," Dianna said softly, apologetically. "If you need me, call."

"Dianna tells me you will be staying to eat with us," Olivia said, breaking away from me.

"If it pleases you," I said.

"It pleases me." She pointed her cane to the parlor. "Come sit."

As was our way, we sat across from one another: I, in a cushioned rocker; she, in a pretty flowered stuffed chair.

"Tell me if you tire," I said.

"I'm not a china cup," she said, sitting straight. "I'm more a thick, sturdy mug."

I laughed.

"And my mind continues to work on all cylinders."

"I believe that."

"I don't have a lot of time left. You can see that. The disease is moving quickly now. I have Dianna in the mornings, and I appreciate and enjoy that. But too few hours are allowed her. Yet I do feel I am safe here alone. I have this thing around my neck." She put her fingers on the chain that lay there. "If I push its button, it sends a signal that I need help." She shook her head. "How things have changed in the years I have lived. This mechanism appears to be a good thing," she said, rubbing the chain through her fingers, "though I wish I didn't need it." She looked into my eyes. "I have no one left in my family. I have friends, good friends. They come. They visit me. And they love me. But the bulk of my present life is a morning Hospice aide and lonely afternoons and evenings." She paused and drew in a deep breath. "Though I want you to know I have known Dianna many years and I love her dearly."

I watched and I could see the concentrated effort sustaining her determination to make her position clear, her struggle … and I wanted to end it, to stop her. It was hard to watch. But I couldn't disrespect her desire, her *need*, to speak these words from her heart, words that ached to be said.

"And my future," she continued, "is respite care in a hospital Hospice unit. I want you to think about that as you consider who you are … English or Amish. There are certain ways of living the Amish have kept that we English have lost." She paused, breathed deep. "You see, if I were Amish, someone would be caring for me. Family, if I had that. If not, friends. Neighbors. Community. Doing the task without thought or question. Doing it because it needed to be done. And doing it with love." She leaned back in her chair and closed her eyes.

I waited, straining to hear her fading voice.

"The English will visit. They will love me. But they will not ask me to die in their homes.

I sat silent, knowing her words were true.

"I've thought about this," she said. She sat up. Looked at me intently. "There is going to be a time, soon, when I will need more help. And I don't want to live in a little room in a home of many old women."

"Assisted living," I said, naming it for her.

"Assisted living," she agreed. She folded her hands on her lap, leaned forward. "I don't want it. I don't want it," she repeated, softly. "I don't need it yet. I may have times, many times, of feeling the isolation that comes from living alone, but there is still much I can do for myself."

"I know that is so," I said softly.

"And I do know there will be a time when even assisted living will not be an option. And that's all right. For then, I will go into Hospice respite care and that will be good. I look forward to a painless time, a quiet time, a time to be with God, to prepare, with Him, my eternal future. It will be good," she repeated.

And I could tell from the serene haze of peace that lay over her face as she spoke of her God, she was not afraid. Death, for her, would simply be a wonderful transformation.

"So, like I said," she continued, "I've been giving much thought as to how I can stay in my own house … for awhile. And I think I know how to make that happen. Only you would have to agree."

"Tell me," I said, gently.

"You're very dear to me and I would never impose upon your generosity …," she paused and lifted her hands to her face, rubbed her cheeks.

"It's you who have been generous to me," I said, bending toward her. "You know, I will help you."

"How long will you be here … in Wander Lane?"

"I'm not sure," I said, thinking there were so many things I needed to know and days were passing without revelation. How could I know how long it would take?

"I would like you to live here … with me." When I moved to speak, she put her hand out. "Wait. Not to take care of me. But just to be here … in and out. Living your life as you please. Your things strewn about. Books you are reading, sweaters and half-eaten snacks, crummy plates and empty glasses, your shoes spread out by the door. Your voice. Your scent tinting the air. Just knowing there is someone leaving her print in my space would be a comfort, would give me a sense of shared life. Before it's done."

I bent my head and closed my eyes. *I will show you a path when you think there is none.*

Later, after Dianna had cleaned the kitchen and left and Olivia went to her bed to rest, I left and thought it would be good to walk a bit before going back to the motel. It was a beautiful day, the heat of the sun tempered and made pleasurable by the drift of clouds riddling the sun's ray and by a soft breeze fanning the air. I ambled down Olivia's street savoring the scents and colors of the flowers and bushes and trees and fresh-mown grass spread over Olivia's neighboring lawns. Soon I would enjoy that splendor every day. I had a place to live. There was laughter in my heart.

I went up one side of the street and down the other. When I was directly across from Olivia's house, I stopped and looked and soaked in the knowing that soon I could sit in one of those bright painted rockers whenever and for as long as I wanted. One day, I thought, I'll sit in the blue chair; another day, in the green; and then, one day, in the deep rosy hue of a marvelous, rich pink. Waving "goodbye" to Olivia's … and my … home, I continued my trek to Main Street. There I turned and took myself to Harriet's Soup and Sandwich Shop. Feeling triumphant, I elected to treat my exuberant self to a million delicious calories … a great, huge nutty brownie heaped with ice cream and drizzled thick with dark, rich chocolate.

Bailey, Harriet's Olivia's veteran waitress and favored niece, met me at the door.

"Boy, am I glad to see you. Slow time is rotten time. No customers," Bailey said. "I'm all caught up on work. Everything's polished and filled. And still, I gotta look busy. If I don't Harriet will find some atrocious job for me to do. That woman, Old Auntie, don't like no laziness," Lucy said. She shrugged and her face scrunched unpleasantly.

"But you love her," I said, laughing.

"Maybe," she conceded. "Okay, sometimes." She waved her hand over the room. "Where do you want to sit? You've got your pick. Ain't nobody else here."

"I choose there," I said, pointing to a table near the front windows.

"You want coffee? Menu?" she asked, following me to the table I'd chosen.

"Nope," I said, sitting. "Just a big, fat, juicy brownie filled with nuts and covered with mounds of succulent vanilla ice-cream, and then I want tons of heavy warm fudgy chocolate poured all over the top of it."

"Your whole body ain't big enough to hold all that ... and I suppose you want a heap of whipped cream on top of the chocolate?" she said. And when I nodded, she added, "And how about a cherry right smack at the highest peak of the sundae ... which would most like be just about touching the ceiling?"

"Sounds perfect."

As she turned and started walking to the kitchen, I called after her, "And if Harriet's in the kitchen, would you ask her to come out and say 'hello'?"

"Sure thing. If'n she's done telling everybody in there how they should be doing everything better. Faster. Cleaner. Cheaper."

"Hear you might be moving into Olivia Olmstead's place," Harriet said, sliding a heaping sundae before me.

Startled, I looked up from the book I'd taken from my purse. "How did you know?"

"Dianna Holmes told me. She said Olivia was gonna ask you the next time she talked with you and since you stopped by today, Dianna figgered she asked you today. Did she?"

"She did."

"And you said?"

"Yes ... aren't you going to sit with me?" I pointed at the table. "I see two spoons."

"So when's it gonna happen?" Harriet asked, dropping into the chair across from me, nodding towards the ice cream. "Ain't no way you gonna get that all et up by yourself."

"You're right about the sundae. I'm not so sure about the moving," I said, smiling. "Maybe a few days. Probably not much longer than that. She wants to paint the guest room, get some new pillows ... stuff like that."

"That's silly, wasting her days on foolishness when she ain't got many left. But, I guess when you know the good Lord's comin,' you mite just as well pick out them things to do that give you pleasure." She spooned a heaping mound of the sundae into her mouth, grinned and wiped drips of ice cream and chocolate from her chin. "Sometimes it looks so good, I forgit how small my mouth is."

"I know," I said, taking a big bite for myself.

"So, how's your search goin'?" Harriet put her spoon down and leaned back in her chair, her eyes looking straight at me.

"Not well." I said, staring back at her. "But you could help me. You could tell me where Annabelle is."

"Mebbe I could, but it wouldn't be right. And mebbe I couldn't. Mebbe I'm not sure."

Sighing, I put my spoon down, too.

"Tell me, Cora, exactly why were you shunned?" Shifting in her chair, a fleeting look of pain crossing her face, she pushed her hand hard against her back, but the tone of her voice stayed gentle. "I remember you tellin' some of it before, but I felt in my bones, there was more to it than you said."

"The reasons Bishop Herrfort gave me were that I'd had a baby without having a husband and that I'd abandoned the baby and refused to confess and repent," I answered, quickly. I hoped not too sharply. "But the real reason was when he asked me who else knew, I said 'no one'. He didn't believe me." He was angry I wouldn't tell. I guess shunning me wasn't enough. He wanted my, accomplices', as perceived by him, punished, too."

"Didn't he ask you who the father was?"

"No."

"Don't you find that strange?"

"Yes."

"Who is the father, Cora?"

"You tell me, Harriet," I said, anger growing fierce within me. She was going to a place I didn't want to go. There were secrets in my heart that stayed raw and were better not riled. "You're the keeper of everyone's business. You tell me."

"I do know a lot; I hear a lot," Harriet said, softly. She reached across the table and patted my hand. "But I never tell what would hurt a body."

Immediately the anger stopped, replaced with remorse. "I'm sorry," I whispered. "I didn't mean it."

"But it's true. I am the keeper of everybody's business. The keeper. The protector. The filter. I'm not thinkin' that's such a bad thing. Storin' people's hearts with honor and respect is an okay thing to do. And I do understand hurtin' souls."

I looked at her and nodded. "I trust you," I said. We sat for a moment, quiet, waiting. "I don't know who the father is."

I saw surprise, then awareness, sadness spread over her face. "Rape," She stated.

"I would call it that."

"Did you tell the Bishop?" she asked, rubbing the top of my hand with her fingers.

"No."

"Why not?"

"I didn't want him seeking ... or questioning ... or punishing."

Harriet's sigh was deep. She put her elbows on the table and dropped her head into her hands.

I bent my head and asked God for strength.

"Sometimes," Harriet said, words muffled through her hands, "there's just too much hurt in this world."

"I'm all right," I said.

"I know that." She lifted her head, lay her hands in her lap. "This ole head of mine is all mixed up. It just don't know what to tell you."

"Tell me where Annabelle is," I said, quickly, sharply.

"Can't do that," she said, shaking her head.

"I know she's in an Amish home," I said, remembering Olivia's disclosure.

"Then you know she's bein' kept good."

"Maybe."

"Let it be."

"I can't."

"Here, put this in your mouth. It tastes better'n words," Harriet said, lifting my spoon, filling it with ice cream and stretching it to me. "Get it et before it's all turned to a puddle."

So I did.

Later that evening as dusk was settling over the land, I drove up the hill into Amish country. I stopped near the top of the hill, near my family's home, near the big tree where I had, as a young Amish maiden, legs folded and back solid against its rough and spongy bark, found a place of solace under its abundant and thick leaved branches. It was there, with the whole of the valley and fields and far off forest spread before me, I had dreamed and, sometimes, empty of all earthly desires, simply *felt*.

I got out of my car and stood beside that tree and watched the final shadows of dark drop from the sky, through the trees, over the cattle in pastures, and into the second growth of high grass waiting for the next cutting and drying and storing for the coming cattle's winter feed. As I stood I remembered those times of a young girl dreaming, and the times when Maem, off to a day of communal canning or quilting or cleaning the homes of infirm brethren, would leave me in charge of the twins, little toddlers, and we would go to the tree. I remember Lily and Violet rolling and running haphazardly in the grass, blowing dandelion seeds to cover our spot with a lacy, white curtain, stomping in puddles where the rain had found dents in the earth to fill, pushing their feet to the bottoms of those tiny pools and squishing their toes in the mud. Sometimes, under that tree, I had held them, told them little stories and lulled them to nap … stories of little girls finding lost kittens, cuddling them and making them purr … stories of little girls surprising their maems with floors swept, wee loaves of bread baked, and beds made without wrinkles … stories of little girls building snowmen that reached to the sky, hollyhock dolls that talked, groundhogs that took them into their underground homes and gave them cider.

Turning from the tree, I saw the light from the oil lamps in my family's home shining through their windows into the dark. *Oh Lord, I would be so honored if they could see Your light shine through me. If they could listen to the words that tell the their many good deeds will not guarantee their place in heaven, will not make You love them more. If only they could understand their good deeds should be an outpouring of glory to You because they love You. Oh, Lord, please give me a way to be among them, to proclaim, by action and words, the love and the joy, the promises, you have seared on my heart … for eternity.*

I walked slowly across the grass to my car and drove back to the motel.

Chapter Ten

Bored and feeling confined by the thick fall of rain pummeling the motel's thin walls, I considered alleviating the mundane state of my being by closing my curtains against the dreary view, turning the radio's volume high, gathering my snacks in a pile and losing myself in the pages of a gory whodunit. There was a stack of them stashed in a corner under the open pole holding my hangered clothes. I plowed through them, found a couple that looked readable, puffed my pillows, sat against them, legs straight out on the bed and scanned their first pages. Ate a bag of chips and drank a cola. Squirmed on the bed and tried to get comfortable. Didn't work. Tedious words; lumpy bed. So I dropped the books, wiggled some more, turned off the radio and turned on the television. Worse. I opened the curtains, shut down the television, ate a chalky, powered packaged donut and slumped on the bed, thinking, "what shall I do?" And it came to me that I had not yet gone to the Amish craft store. A little rain, or a lot, was manageable. I wouldn't disappear, become a puddle … or melt. So, that's what I did that day … explored.

By the time I had piled the books back in their corner, lined up my snacks in a drawer and smoothed my bed, thunder had rolled in and was pounding the roof. Worse was the lightening that preceded each rumbling blast. I had never liked thunder and lightning. When I was little, as I sat trembling on the couch, shoes on my feet ready to escape, whether night or day … where I would go, I didn't not know. Maem told my brothers and me, rain was a blessing. It washed the earth; it fed the plants and trees and flowers with nurturing water. So rain was to be treasured; we should be grateful. There was nothing to fear. Even so, I noted her pale face and shaking hands as she pulled us from our beds or called us from our tasks and gathered us in the parlor to wait out the storm. And a measure of terror stayed with me … not a lot, but enough.

Desperate enough to squash the debilitating drain of ennui, I walked out into the rain to combat and conquer the storm. It was awful.

Even though I had armed myself with an umbrella, the weapon was useless. It whipped in the wind and within seconds folded itself inside out. Worthless. The rain hit my hair, my face, my body with merciless, inconsiderate force. There was no way I could defeat this miserable enemy. Except by running to my car, jumping in and making it my war tank and then, rolling it down the road and into town. The victor. Me. The storm could not stop me. I smiled and went about my business.

It was really hard to see, but not impossible. They were not individual drops that fell from the sky, they were sheets of thick, streaking water splashing my windshield. And I was the champion as I rolled into the parking space in front of the Amish Craft Store. The foe was defeated. *If you could see me, Maem, you would be proud.* Fantasy over, I hurried out of the car and into the store.

As I walked through the door the strong, masculine aroma of leather encompassed me. It was wonderful; it was home. It was Da polishing harnesses. It was Willie, sitting in the barn on a raining day rubbing reins supple and bridles to shine. It was soaking in that heady scent and running my hands over the smooth sheen of leather on belts and wallets and purses and horses' strapping in Gideon Wagler's workshop. It was wonderful; it was home.

There were more than just leather products in the store. There were embroidered works, sewn articles, paintings, wooden creations, even little trinkets for decoration or play. It was a store that encouraged beholding, browsing and buying.

"If you need me to help, I'll be by the counter," said a voice behind me.

I looked up from the child's coloring book I was holding and saw a face that was familiar and dear to me. "Ruth," I said.

The young Amish girl smiled, shyly, at me. "No. She is my mother."

I looked at her face. A little more square. The nose, a bit longer. But it was Ruth's face. The Ruth I had quilted with … laughed with, chatted. But Ruth would be older now. Like me. And, to me, this was Ruth, come back as her daughter.

"I knew your maem a long time ago," I said.

Still smiling, she bent her head a little. "She made the book you're holding. There's an Englisher who prints them, but she drew the pictures."

"She always did well at drawing," I said. I didn't tell her my name or how I knew her maem. And she didn't ask. She was Amish. It would be rude.

As I turned from the girl to wander the shop, I heard the store's front door bang. I looked and there saw Aaron stepping into the store.

He saw me. And he stopped.

I took a step towards him.

He turned his head and moved away. I watched him go to the back shelves and wall where the bridles lay and the harnesses hung. He moved his hand over their leather, stroking it, leaning his head into its rich, clean odor.

I waited a moment, then put the coloring book on the counter. "Please save it for me," I said, and then I turned and walked back to where Aaron was.

"Aaron?" I said, and unable to resist, I touched the back of his arm. I felt his muscles tighten, but he did not turn. He kept his back to me.

"Aaron," I said again, stronger, and this time I grabbed his arm and shook it.

He turned, lips tight together, eyes boring into mine.

"Cora Pooler, hear me, you're not here to me. I can't see you." His words came rigid through his teeth.

"Yes, Aaron, you can," I said, smiling ruefully.

"No, you're invisible."

"Right," I agreed, sad, shaking my head. "I am invisible. To you, Amish man, I am invisible. But I can talk, Aaron. Can you hear me?"

"No."

"And I can remember. Can you remember? The last time I saw you when I was still in Amish clothes? On your porch? When I walked to your house to say good-by."

His lips stayed pressed together; there was no telling thought or feeling on his face.

"When you saw me you turned your back. Do you remember?"

"Yes." His eyes cut sharp into mine.

"I waved good-by to you. To your back."

"And now you are dead," he said.

"No, not yet. Not until I have some answers. Do you know the answers? We were friends, Aaron. *Friends.* Even more. Do you know who among your black- suited friends is a raper. How about that? Can you answer that?"

He looked at me for a long moment. I couldn't read what was behind his face. Then he turned and left. I watched him, hoping he would look back, knowing he would not. And he did not.

Later, hungry, not so much for food, but for the comfort a donut brings, I went to Harriet's.

"No donuts," she said to my inquiry. "Shoofly pie'll have to do. An' I reckon, there's nobody that don't feel better then after a good, big helpin' of brown sugar and molasses."

"Then you had better bring me the biggest piece you have."

"You got the whole pie sorrows?" she asked.

"Almost."

"You jest set and wait. I'm gonna bring the biggest piece you ever seen." And she did. With two forks.

We ate the whole thing. It didn't take long.

Pushing the empty plate aside, Harriet dropped her arms on the table and nodded. "Good. One of the best I ever made."

"They're all the best," I said, smiling.

"Feel better?"

"My stomach does."

"Okay, then let's work on the rest of you. What's goin' on?"

"I saw Aaron," I said, tracing my finger over the markings etched into the wooden table. "At the craft store. He was back by the harnesses." I pulled my fingers away from the crevices and laid my hands in my lap. "He saw me when he came in … but he walked by me."

"He didn't speak to you?" Harriet asked, gently.

"Not then."

"Later?"

"Uh huh."

"Well, glory be." Harriet wrinkled up her face. "Whole sentences … or just a grunt or two?"

"Words. Real words."

"How'd ya manage that. He don't break many rules, and even at the best times, there's not too many words comin' out'a his mouth."

"I grabbed his arm and shook it." I smiled. "He didn't like that."

"I reckon not."

Remembering his face, my smile faded, then was gone. I bent my head. "He said he couldn't see me. I was dead … and I am … to him. To Maem, Da. The whole Amish community."

"He don't bend. Not that one. Never did."

"He's Bishop Herrfort's nephew," I said.

"I know. Mebbe it's in the blood. Except, honey, it's in all of 'em. Ain't none of 'em gonna forgive you lessin' you repent." She leaned forward, her hands folded tightly on the table. "Mebbe it's not so good for you to be back here."

"There are things I need to know.'

"Things important enough to git your heart broke?"

"It is already broken." I fisted my hands and struck them on the table. "I need to fix it with answers."

Harriet sighed. "Mebbe you do."

"Can you help me?"

"I'm not sure, but I'll try."

"Where is Annabelle?"

"I'll say this fur ya. You come right to the point." She shook her head. "I'm not so sure it's the right thing to tell ya, Cora. She's got a good life goin'. You wanna ruin that?"

"Of course not."

"Let it go."

Harriet looked straight into my eyes and I knew she meant it. And, maybe, it might be the best thing to do. But if you let a hurt lie festering in your heart, and I did that for twenty years, it doesn't always sit silent and, sometimes, its ring is so loud it covers all else that dwells within. And I knew Harriet wasn't ready to give more news of Annabelle. I would have to wait. And the Amish had taught me well to wait ... and wait ... and wait. And not to ask questions. Well, I had waited and I would again. But never would I stop asking questions.

"Then tell me about Lily," I said.

"What about Lily?"

"What was she like? Before she died, what was she like?"

"You wouldn't of knowed her. The spark was gone. No more runnin' down that hill or laughin' at jokes and words that weren't really funny. No more talkin'. Quiet. Polite. Helpful. Couldn't tell her much from Violet. Ceptin' she was sadder. Sun just gone right outta her." Harriet shook her head. "Don't know what your Ma thought, but most 'em thought Lily'd just growed up."

"Did she go to the Sunday night singings?"

"I heared she did. It's funny ...there were two of 'em sparkin' her. Jacob Mueller and, believe it or not, Aaron. Least that was the rumor."

"Where do you hear all that stuff?"

"Oh, here and there. Even the black skirts like to chatter."

"And I don't believe it about Aaron," I said. "He was way too old to be smitten by her."

"Men's a funny breed."

"Not Aaron. Not that funny. But Jacob, he's a real possibility."

"He's Herrfort's nephew, too. Just like Aaron.," Harriet said.

"I didn't know that," I said, sitting straighter.

"Oh yeah. Old Bishop Herrfort. Only son. Three sisters ... Honor, Hester, and Hannah. No brothers. Well, thinkin' on it, I guess there was another son. But he disappeared. Shortly after he was born. Born here in Wander Lane. Don't know what happened. He was born, then was gone. Happened sometimes in those days. He was the youngest one. All the rest were born before they came here."

"They weren't among the first comers?" I asked, leaning closer.

"Nope, they came a mite later. I remember the whole lot of 'em sashaying into Wander Lane. All packed in with their stuff in a couple of wagons. The old man, their Pa, bought a big parcel of land ... the Bishop has it all now. Girls got married and shuffled off onto their husbands farms. Hannah married a Mueller. Hester married Aaron's pa. And Honor, you ain't gonna believe who she hitched up with. Anyway, the old man was a hard worker. Harsh. Mean. He was out there pushin' those kids to work like growed up men. It was harder for Hannah and Honor. They were built little and meek, scared to death of their Pa." Harriet paused and grinned. "Hester, now there's another story. That one was feisty, stood right up to the old man. I think he liked it; used to favor her. Little treats. Brother Bishop never liked her much. But listen to this one, when Hester married Aaron's Pa, she hounded and bossed that man 'till poor old Lester couldn't stand it anymore and he took off runnin' before Aaron was even borned. Never heard from agin. Left his name and nothin' else. Yoder. Hester must a wore away all his courage. That ole Hester, she had him chained tight with her clackin' mouth. But he got away."

"I never heard about that," I said. Aaron never spoke of his Da. And Hester kept pretty much to herself. Although she helped when she was aware of a need, it was done with a somewhat resentful manner. She didn't mingle much with the other women, neither quilting nor canning, when they grouped and made such tasks a social pleasantry.

"You Amish don't talk much about the leavers," Harriet said and I smiled at the note of bafflement in her voice. The English seemed to mull over the past, reliving, wondering, reviving events long over.

"Poor Aaron," I said, shaking my head. "His mother was always after him with one job or another. He ended up running the farm by himself."

"I will say this for the Bishop," Harriet said. "He watched out for Aaron much as he could. Used to see him buying little goodies next door, sticking 'em in his pocket so nobody see'd. Balloons. Little red rubber bouncy balls. Suckers. Never had kids of his own … or a wife, so's those kids, Aaron and Jacob, were like his'n. There's good in everybody, Cora. Even the Bishop."

"He hid it well," I said, lifting my eyebrows. "I don't know about Jacob, but I never saw him do anything for Aaron."

"You wouldn't of. Any good traits that man's got, and he ain't got many, he does a good job keepin' 'em secret. Anyway, Aaron's his favorite. Jacob's too feisty, don't listen, gets in too much trouble. And worst of all, stands up to the Bishop. He don't like that."

"And Jacob and Aaron were both sparking Lily?" I asked.

"Seems that way. I dunno if your Maem knew, but if she did, she would have been mighty worried. That Jacob is bad news."

"Then maybe Aaron was just trying to protect Lily from him. He would do that. He liked the twins, thought they were fun."

"Mebbe." Harriet tilted her head and frowned. "But I wouldn't bet on it."

"You said Honor married strange," I said, thinking to move from talking of Aaron.

"Lordy, yes. Honor, the oldest sister. Pretty too. The Amish sure wanted to share their buggies with her on a Sunday night. Seems like they weren't excitin' enuff for her. She was wantin' bigger fish. Didn't stay long in the Community after she growed up. They don't talk about her. Got herself shunned, gone and forgotten."

"Why was she shunned?" I asked. *Like me*, I thought.

"Married an Englisher."

"Who?"

"Sheriff Lowell Parker."

I drew in my breath. "He doesn't have a wife."

"Nope, he doesn't. She died. Young. Or mebbe run off. Anyway no wee ones."

So Sheriff Parker is Bishop Herrfort's brother-in-law."

You got it."

"And Jacob's uncle."

"Yep."

"And Aaron's."

"You got it agin."

I shook my head, trying to digest all this information.

"You know, Harriet, maybe we should let all this simmer for awhile and eat another slice of pie."

"Good thinkin'," Harriet said, laughing.

That evening in the soft slide of dusk, I drove back to the motel and parked my car at the back of the lot. As I got out of my vehicle I saw a mass of color on the platform that ran the length of the building. Walking closer, the form took shape and a pleasing tremor went through me as I distinguished the glorious reds and pinks and whites of full blown, grand, and regal roses. Baskets of them sat snuggled together by the front of my door. Their fragrance encompassed me as I stepped up the stair to the landing and passed through the opening in the wrought iron railing. Clasping my hand tight against my chest, I reveled in the beauty of the flowers.

There was a white card nestled among the petals. I took it and read it. There was only one word. *Daniel.* And I smiled.

Then reaching across the flowers to unlock the door, I saw a bit of tattered paper taped onto it. I pulled it from the wood and unfolded it. Even before I read the words, I recognized the remembered script from long ago.

Come to the shack. After the Thursday noon meal
I have a surprise for you.

Overjoyed I read the note again ... and again. Violet. I would see her again.

Chapter Eleven

The day were long as I waited for Thursday. I felt myself stalled, still torn and ignorant of the place that should hold my name as a citizen. I was like a plant not knowing from which window to drink in the sun. A surprise from Violet. A flower from Daniel. Dear God, if Solomon ripped me in two, could the Amish and English each have a functioning piece? Would my soul then be satisfied? Happy, at peace? And I knew it would be so. For I loved both worlds. In our desires we are not always rational. Hearts can dream and paint beautiful pictures, but heads know the practical and mine would not let me ignore there was only one right choice ... Amish or English. But it would not tell me which one it should be.

Finally with pleasuring anticipation, I called Daniel and thanked him for the roses. His answering words, amicable and welcoming, spread warmth through my ears and into the whole of my body.

"Cora," He said, and I envisioned the smile that came with that word. "I needed a break and I can't think of one that could be better than talking with you."

We chatted a little. Weather and work. Then when I told him I was not ready to come back to work and I didn't not know how long I would still be at Wander Lane, although he was concerned about the length of my stay, he assured me it was not primarily my workload that worried him. He had sufficient temporary staffers he could call. It was my wellbeing ... in my heart and with my purse. I promised him if there was a need for either to be filled, I would call him. He made me swear to it and I laughed.

"You're Amish," he said, "and the Amish never break a promise."

"Ah, but I am English, too," I replied, "and they have been known to do such."

"But not you," he chuckled. "I have complete confidence in you."

"I'm not sure you should," I said, seriously.

"But you will try?" he said.

"Yes, I will try," I agreed.

We talked a bit more. Weather and work. And when the call was done, my heart was lighter. Yet there was a mite of guilt, for I knew I would not keep my promise. I would never ask him for money or help with the needs of my heart. At least, that was my thought then.

Thursday came. I woke early. I took a long shower, dressed, fussed with my hair, and straightened my room. Then, as I did every morning, I studied scripture, recited and prayed psalms, sang hymns to God, thanked Him, talked with Him, and asked for His guidance throughout the hours before me. Yet it seemed the clock did not move. There were hours to fill before the passing of the noon meal, hours before I could seek more answers from Violet.

Picking up a book, thinking to lose myself in the plights of characters not real, an image of Olivia passed through my mind. So engrossed with myself, I had neglected our friendship and I realized how much I missed her company and her wisdom. This would be a good time to see her. Also, it would be a good time to see how preparations for my stay there were progressing. So that's what I did. I went there.

As I was parking my car in front of Olivia's house, Dianna pulled up behind me. I saw, as I waited for her at the edge of the sidewalk, that she seemed to be agitated.

"Is something wrong?" she asked, hurrying to reach me.

"I don't think so," I said, concerned by her demeanor. "Why would you think so?"

"It's unusual for you to come so early. I thought, maybe Olivia had called you. That maybe she was in trouble."

"No. She didn't call. I haven't seen her for awhile and I am kind of at loose ends. Nervous. Edgy, I think is the word. I just need something, someplace, *someone* to ease the thumps in my heart."

Dianna smiled. "Well I'm glad it's only your heart thumping. I was afraid you heard from Olivia … that she needed help." She paused and bit her lip. Then smiled. Taking my arm, she led me up the cement path. "Come on. Let's go in. She's probably still sleeping but she should wake up soon. She'll be happy to see you."

Confused, I stopped and pulling my arm from her, questioned her. "If Olivia needed help, why would she call me? Though I would go immediately to her, wouldn't she call you or press her button first?"

"I don't know. That's what she's been told to do. But if she thinks she has reached her end and only hours ... or minutes ... are left, she'll call you. She loves you, you know. Yet I can feel a sense of regret when she talks about you, maybe an incompleteness. Something." She looked at me with a puzzled expression. "She doesn't tell me what it is, but I know there's a history with the two of you, a kind of bonding."

"There is," I said, as we walked up the steps to the porch. "Twice she has been my strength in circumstances so painful and so lonely for me. She is my soul friend ... even more, my soul mother."

"Sit down," Dianna said, pointing to a porch rocker. "We still have a few moments."

"I think you have bad news for me," I said, apprehensively, seeing a flash of pathos cross her face.

"I do." She folded her hands in her lap and pushing her foot against the floorboards set her porch chair to rock in gentle movement. "You haven't been here for several days and I don't say that to admonish you, but to prepare you for what you're about to see." Her voice cracked a little. "There's been a sudden and radical change in Olivia."

I waited.

"I don't think she has much time left." Her words were gentle, but firm. "And I think she wants time with you. She mentions your name often. Not as complaining. More as reflective. Almost as if dreaming."

Covering my face with my hands, I pondered the meaning of what she had said. There was guilt swimming in my head. And fear. I had been negligent in the amount of my visits and shameful in my selfish desires to press a dying woman for information. And still, disgracefully, though I wanted her to live not only because I loved her, I wanted her to live so she could tell me more. Sadly, I dropped my hands and looked at Dianna, hoping my love for Olivia was greater than my self-seeking motives. "Days?" I asked. "Does she have only days?"

"That might be so," she said, then hesitated, her eyes looking beyond me. Then she spoke, again, with hopeful voice. "But I think longer ... a bit longer."

I waited a time, thinking. "It's time for me to live here," I said softly. "There has been enough renovation. Pretty walls and curtains really don't matter. It's faces and hearts that need to be seen and shared. Sometimes when unsaid words linger in the air waiting for an appropriate time to be said, that time never comes and those words never land on ears that should hear them. Unfinished business. I don't want that to be Olivia's legacy to me or my gift to her."

"You're right," Dianna said. "Time doesn't wait. One second can rob a body of what they know and shift the patterns of what we thought was solid." She shook her head. "One second. One second and life is changed. And Olivia shouldn't be alone any more. Not even for one little minute."

"No," I said, bending forward, searching Dianna's face, then dropping my head, shaking it slowly, "she shouldn't."

"Yet I feel something isn't right with you. I hear a 'but' in your voice."

"Yes," I said. "Regretfully, but importantly, there is a "but" in my words." Reaching out, I laid my hand on Dianna's. "This is it. There's something I have do this afternoon. It's something I can't ignore or postpone. I know the many hours you work, many unpaid, and I know I am asking much, but I have to ask if you would stay with Olivia this afternoon?"

"That's not such a big thing to ask. Of course I'll stay with her. And gladly."

"Thank you," I said, squeezing her hand.

"You know I love her, too," Dianna said, wiping her eyes. "We can share the hours ... we both can take care of her."

"We can," I agreed.

"It will work," Dianna agreed, returning the pressure of my hand with her own.

After lunch, I drove past my family's home and turned onto the dirt path half way between their house and Aaron's. Rows of knee-high corn stalks just beginning to tassel bordered the trail on either side. Filling the spaces between the stalks were spreading mounds of lush green bean plants. I lowered the car window to take in the fragrance of earth and the vegetation that grew on it. Reaching the end of the fields, I drove into the woods and followed the path to the sugar shack.

As I had passed my old home, I'd seen my family's black buggy parked near the back door. Harnessed to it, was a svelte strong- looking retired racehorse. Stepping his feet in a rhythmic dance, he thrust his body against the restricting harness and shaking his head, his dark mane gracefully swinging with the motion, resisted the restraining bridal reins holding him to the hitching post. His hide shone silky in the rays of the sun and I had slowed to admire the ripple of his muscles as he fought to be free. I wondered if Violet was going to drive the buggy to the shack. I hoped, if she was, she would be strong enough to handle the feisty animal. She had walked to our previous meeting. It was a long stretch. If she were going by foot, she should have left by the time I drove by her house. If so, I thought, then, perhaps I would see her on the road. It could be Maem had not left yet for her outing. That would be good. Maem was a seasoned buggy driver and had plenteous experience with spirited steeds.

I hadn't met Violet on the path to the sugar shack. When I reached the building, I got out of the car, peeked in the little syrup house and drew the lingering maple scent into my being. I hadn't been there long when I saw dust rising through the trees.

Once I saw her, maneuvering the buggy with confident and capable hands through the maple grove and into the space trampled clear for the sugaring, I could see she was a skilled driver. It was hard to embrace and accept the many learning years she had lived while I was gone. The girl of sixteen was now a woman of thirty-six. But not yet that old in my heart.

As she came closer, I saw she was carrying a large parcel. As she drew even nearer, I saw the bundle was slung in a wide strip of fabric wrapped tightly around her. An image of Annabelle held tight in my arms flashed through my thoughts … and was gone. This could not be Annabelle. How could such a thought grip me? Annabelle was a grown woman now. And the bundle could not be Violet's baby. She had never married. Then I thought, what did that matter? Annabelle came into this world without a wedded Maem. Perhaps Violet really was holding a baby. Her's. Perhaps she had confessed and was forgiven. How wonderful that would be. And how fleeting those thoughts. They were as brief as the time it took a fast moving horse to rush up beside me.

"Hold the horse's bridle," Violet called out to me, as she cradled the bundle and jumped from the buggy. "Tie him to the post near the shack. And keep the reins slack enough so he can graze."

I did as she told me. The horse snorted and tossed his head, pulled at the tough leather straps. But I'd had experience, too and it felt good to measure his strength and match it with my own cunning and assurance.

"See," I called back to Violet. "There is a bit of Amish left in me."

"There's a bag and a blanket in the buggy. Bring them over to the tree," she called back. "Spread the quilt. I need the bag."

"Are your arms broken? Come help me." I heard her laugh as I dug into the back of the buggy for the blanket and satchel.

"My arms are too full," she said. "Hurry. Come see what I've got."

I turned and considered the radiance that showed on her face, the smile that was more than just common. I walked towards her and as I got closer, she held out the bundle, now unwrapped, free from its bindings.

"Look," she said.

I stopped. Tilting my head forward I looked and saw and breathed in the wonder of the gift in Violet's hands. It was as I'd wished-for … a wee child. A baby.

"Is she yours?" I whispered. "Can I hold her?"

"She is not," Violet laughed. "And yes, you can hold her."

I dropped the blanket and bundle and taking the child from Violet's arms, held her close to my heart. I looked at Violet and tears were in her eyes, too. For a moment, the shadow of Annabelle hung over us both. Then I lowered my eyes to delight in the baby, so full and soft in my arms. Bending my head, I lifted her enough for hers to reach my cheek, then, closing my eyes, I touched my lips to her skin, and knew, again, the feel of a baby, the love it inspired that none other can bring.

"She's Willie's," Violet said. "His granddaughter … and you are her great-auntie."

"How can that be? Can he be so old? Willie. A *dawdi*? A grandpa?." I ran my fingers, so gently, over the baby's head.

"He is that old, Cora," Violet said, smiling, sliding her arm around me. "Time didn't sit still while you were gone. We all got older. Wrinkles and sags … happenings and wisdom. They all came … in varying measures to all of us. Except Lily."

"Except Lily," I agreed and turning my head to rest on hers, I spoke into her hair, "Time can bring hard spells that seem endless, but God tempers them with good." I pushed my head tighter against hers. "The baby. She gentles you. I don't see any harshness in you this day. God packs so many wonders in one little child … so many pleasures."

"He does," Violet said, moving away from me. She picked up the blanket and stretched it under the full leafed branches of an old maple tree. "We can sit here," she said. "Where the sun won't hit the little one's eyes."

"What is her name?" I asked, sitting carefully, not wanting to wake the child.

"Alice. After our own *mommi*, Da's Maem."

"She sleeps a lot."

"She's little," Violet laughed. That's what babies do. They sleep. And drink. Wait until she wakes. For sure you'll hear some loud noises then. She's a bottle baby. Her maem, and that would be Lucy, has some feeding problems. Anyway, you'll be hearing the strength of Alice's lungs as soon as hunger hits her tummy."

"I'm amazed she slept in the buggy. Doesn't the jostling and flying dust bother her?"

"It doesn't. Oddly enough, it quiets her. That's why I have the buggy. She can be a fussy one and Maem was afraid she would miss her mother and cry. So she left me the buggy thinking, if need be, I could take Alice for a little jaunt to soothe her."

"Where is Maem ... and Lucy?"

"You would never believe. Lydia Lambright, Amy Stoll's daughter in law, had triplets. So all the ladies decided to take a day and clean her house, wash her clothes and can up jars of beef and vegetable stew for her. And for sure, they will bake plenty of bread for her larder. So Lucy went with Maem. Lucy's not getting much sleep and figured a break would refresh her ... and I'm pretty good with little ones. Susanna Beachy picked them up in her buggy. They'll be gone the afternoon."

"Lucy sounds pampered." As the critical words fell through my lips, guilt flashed fast across my brain and I knew there was, alongside the Amish, a measure of the English.

"She's young," Violet said, lifting her eyebrows.

Not feeling too great a remorse for my words, I shrugged. Time was passing and I had not yet asked pertinent questions. Yet I relished the talk of my family.

"And Amy Stoll? Grandma of triplets? Astounding," I said, choosing to hear more of the family history I had not lived, remembering Olivia visiting our cousin, Amy, checking her and the electric powered machine that kept her alive. "I thought when she was eighteen, the Bishop wouldn't permit electricity in their house anymore. Did she get better?"

"Pretty much. But, you're right, the Bishop made them get rid of the machine. So Amy got hooked up with the Mennonites since they're okay with electricity. And, thanks be to God, as she got older, she got better, got married to an older widower with three children, who became her children … a son and two daughters. The son got married … to an Amish girl. The son came back, went before the Bishop, repented his Mennonite ways, was baptized Amish, and, oh, did the Community rejoice. Then he took over his Amy's grandpa's farm and they had triplets."

"Okay," I said, shaking my head and wondering how I ever would keep all that straight. "Now tell me, who did Willie marry?"

"You're never going to believe this, either" she said, chuckling. "Remember Hattie Shackleton?"

"Hattie from school? Hattie with the quilt shoppe?"

"That's the one. Only she is Hattie Pooler now."

"She married Willie?" In my head, I saw her turning away from me in the quilt shop.

"She did and that makes her your sister-in-law. And mine. And it makes her Maem's daughter-in-law. And Da's, too."

Bewildered, I looked down at the baby. "Well, this is *goot*. My grandniece. And yours. Maem's great granddaughter. And Da's." I thought a moment and frowned. "And Hattie is Alice's grandmother."

Violet was practically doubled over with laughter. I didn't find it so funny.

"So Willie and Hattie have a son and they're grandparents now. Remarkable." I shook my head. "Do they have more children?"

"That's for sure," Violet said. "There are seven kids in all. Five boys. two girls. The oldest boy, married. The others, too young."

"And George?"

"Married. Since he's the oldest, he lives at our house and shares the farming with Da. He saw you, you know. The day you came to our door. Didn't say anything, but I could see the hurt and the want in the tightening of his face. He's got two boys. Three girls. None married, but one leaning towards it. We think she's going to the Sunday night sing with a Yoder boy."

"But you can't ask?"

"Nope, still against the Ordinance. Always will be. Courting news is up to them to tell when they're ready to." Violet grinned. "But we're not dumb. When she's been gone so long on a Sunday night sing, there's only one likely reason."

"I guess," I said, nodding. "And Harry?"

"Married. No children. Lives with his wife's Maem and Da. His wife, Joanna, is their only child, so Harry and his father-in-law work her Da's farm."

"And Sampson?"

"Liked cars. Turned Mennonite. Don't know where he is."

And at that moment, Baby Alice opened her eyes, looked at me, and screamed.

Instantly, I stretched my arms out to Violet. "Take her. I know nothing about babies."

"Of course you do. You practically raised Lily and me." She hesitated, then added, "And what about Annabelle?"

"I never took care of Annabelle. I gave her away."

We talked about our family and the brethren. She told of births and deaths and marriages and the many happenings stretched over the twenty years I was not there. But she did not mention Lily again.

While I listened I watched little Alice coo and kick and stretch her arms to catch shadows and sun touched leaves falling from the tree. When she got fussy, Violet gave her a bottle. She drank of the milk and fell asleep, her baby mouth still moving in the endearing motion of a sleeping wee one sucking on a nonexistent bottle.

There was a lull in Violet's recitation. It was time for me to ask questions.

"On all this day you've spoken Lily's name but twice. And then so briefly," I said.

"We don't talk of the dead. You should remember that."

Her tone had changed; the fun in it, gone.

"Do you want to hear of the night Alice was birthed?" Violet said, a touch of ice still in her words.

"No," I said, "I want to talk about Lily."

Lips pressed together, Violet said nothing.

"Why is that worse than you being here?" I asked.

"The Bishop would have me shunned for talking of the dead."

"He would shun you for speaking to me."

"You're right," she said, gathering the bottle and the baby's cleaning cloth, stuffing them in the bag. "You're right. I should go."

"Don't, don't go," I said. "I know it is risky and brave for you to be here, and I am so thankful you are. And I know it hurts to talk about Lily. But I don't know how she died … the particulars. The reason. The how. Violet, I don't know the why."

"It was long ago. For years I dreamed about her. And I know it was a sin to do that. The dead are finished with our life. But I thought and thought about her. Just like I thought about you when you left. But I don't think of her so much anymore. Or of you. At least I didn't until you came back."

"Do you wish I had not?"

"God forgive me, I do sometimes wish that."

"This is hard for you, I know," I whispered. "I don't like to see you struggle with your soul."

"Why don't you simply go to the Bishop, confess to him the truth and be Amish again?" Violet asked, patting the baby's back.

"It would hurt so many for me to tell him everything. I don't have the right to do that."

"But, if you don't, you'll spend eternity in Hell. Do you think that doesn't hurt us? Do you think Maem doesn't have tears that no one sees? Or me, do you think I don't cry in the night?"

Oh dear God. Guide me, please guide me. Give me the words.

"I can't come back. I would like to, but I can't."

"You could work hard. Salvation would be yours again."

Raising my eyes, I could see the pleading in hers. I hoped she could see the heart-sorrow in mine.

"The Bishop would welcome you back. *Everyone* would welcome you," she said.

"You think I don't have salvation now?" I asked though I knew she thought I did not. *God help me. Please, give me the words.*

"You left it behind you … when you disobeyed the Bishop and walked down the hill."

"You think Jesus removed the Holy Spirit from my heart?"

"I don't want you to burn in Hell," Violet said.

"Jesus is with me every moment of my life."

"You have to repent and *work* at it. There are rules. Do *you* not understand? Did you forget?" She had dropped the bag and was kneeling, her hands clasped together against her chest. "You *must* obey or you are lost. That's why you're shunned. It's a good thing. It makes you think about what you did. It brings guilt and sorrow to your heart. So much that you confess and are made clean again. Saved, again."

"I am saved, dear sister. Forever. Even though I am outwardly weak and my worldly flesh deceives me and sins, I have given my heart, my soul, my spirit to Jesus and He lives within me. Always. *He* has invaded *me* with Himself and that part, the part that is who He made me to be, the part that is the real me, made holy, the price of my sin paid by Jesus on the cross. I hold Him in my soul. And all the good that I do, is done with my desire to bring Him glory. Can you not see that?"

"No," she said, standing, not looking at me. "If you'll hold the baby, I'll fold the quilt and get things put in the buggy."

"Please, I need to know about Lily."

"Maybe another time. I don't know. It's wrong to meet you." She reached down and picked up Alice, held her out to me. I took her. "It is an orderly life we lead here in the community. The rules are clear. Simple. The punishments, known. Your words throw my head into confusion. It's love I have for you, but you are dead to the Amish. And I am Amish."

I stepped away from the quilt and she took it and folded it. As my eyes stayed on her, I watched her unhitch the horse, and holding the reins, climb into the buggy. She said nothing and waited for me to bring the baby to her. When I had done so, she positioned the child against her and slapped the horse to move.

Grabbing the horse's bridle, I held him as he pranced in place and shook his head.

"Let go," Violet said.

"Will I see you again?"

"I need thinking time."

I took my hand from the bridle and stepped away from the horse. Throwing his head back, he moved to the direction of Violet's pull on the reins. Watching the buggy turn and make its way through the trees to the path that took her home, I rubbed the pain in my arm where the horse had yanked it. It was less than the pain in my heart.

Chapter Twelve

Time is marked by hours, minutes and seconds of precise and unchanging duration. There is deception in that premise. The hour that should hold the predetermined length of sixty minutes or thirty-six hundred seconds can, in deed, embrace within its confines twice that number and more, or be diminished by less. As Dianna and I sat by Olivia's bedside, as she slept hour after hour, the clock measured the time incorrectly. The tally of hours she slept was greater than the clock registered. And in the intervals of communication when she woke and her whispered words dropped slowly, the hands of the clock sped fast and gave us too little time before she slept again.

"How could it happen so quickly?" I asked Dianna. She sat across the bed from me, her face drawn, her body slumped forward in the cushioned chair she had pulled from the parlor.

"It hasn't happened quickly. She's been ill a long time. You're just seeing the end of it." She rubbed the palm of her hand over one eye and down her cheek, shook her head. "It's never easy."

"Do you have family, Dianna?"

"No blood kin. But I make every person they assign to me be my family."

"Even knowing they will die before you know them well?" I asked.

"Every one of them I've known well. Not long, but well." She stroked Olivia's arm. "How long did you know Olivia before you knew her well?'

I smiled. "Not long. I'd seen her working with some Amish children. Amy Stoll was one of them. She was damaged and the county required she be monitored. And that was Olivia's job. She was good with children. I saw that. Then there was a certain circumstance when I needed her help. And she helped me. Not in the way I wanted, but in the way she thought best." Pausing, gazing upon Olivia's face, I thought of that time … wistfully, sadly. "Because of that time, I left the Amish. Twenty years ago. But you know that. While I was gone from there, from my family, from the Amish, a tragic thing happened, and my sister died. My Amish sister. And my family didn't let me know. I was dead to them. Shunned. Amish woman turned Englisher. It was Olivia that told me and Olivia that took me in and Olivia that consoled me. And it was then I learned to know her well. To love her."

Lifting my head, I looked at Dianna. She had raiseded her hands to cover her face and she was crying into them. I rose and went to her, bent and encircled her within my arms.

"Go home, Dianna. I'll stay with her. Go home and sleep."

"If she needs me?"

"I'll call."

"I don't think it will be tonight. The end. But I don't know."

"If it seems that way, I will call." I squeezed her shoulder, gently. "Go home. You need to sleep."

Sitting in the soft chair Dianna had vacated, I struggled to keep my eyes from closing in sleep. Because Olivia chilled easily, we kept the thermostat high in her bedroom and the warmth of the air crept into my eyes, tiring them, weighting my eyelids. The lure of sleep was hard to resist. So I sang. Sweet, simple and powerful hymns ... *Jesus Loves Me, Amazing Grace, How Great Thou Art.*

"I hear," Olivia murmured, her voice lying soft on the dimly lit air. "The melody. It is so lovely."

"Olivia," I said, gently, taking her hand, sliding my thumb over fragile, raised veins. Longing to send love through my touch.

"Is Dianna gone?"

I slipped from my chair and knelt beside the bed to hear her better. "Yes."

"She has been good to me."

"Yes," I whispered. "She loves you."

"Cora?"

"I'm here."

"I should have told you."

She paused and I waited, scarcely breathing, praying she would tell me what she had kept secret for so long.

"She has had a good life. Don't change it for her."

"Annabelle?"

"Yes. She is in Sugar Creek."

"Ohio?"

"Yes."

"Have you seen her? Ohio is so far from here."

"Not so far. She comes to Wander Lane. Not often. Her family is Yoder."

"Is she beautiful? In her heart, is she beautiful?"

"Yes ... sing some more ... *The Old Rugged Cross.*"

I did.

"In The Garden." There were tears on her face.

"I love you, Olivia," I said, bending my head close to hers, whispering in her ear.

She smiled and I sang.

Olivia did not die that night. She lingered for several more days. She didn't speak of Annabelle again and neither did I. We sat, Dianna and I, by her bed reading aloud, often with tears, scripture from her Bible ... its black, supple cover worn; its pages, tattered and smudged and marked by pencil and pen. And we sang from the hymnbook we found lying by her Bible; that book, too, well-used and favorite hymns, noted.

She died in her sleep. It was my wont to wake in the late night hours and slip into her room. There I would sit in the soft, parlor chair and pray with low voice. I don't know if she heard me ... she was so still, like a child waiting by the window for a parent, that parent divorced from the other, that never came. But unlike that child, her face was neither sad nor resigned. Hers was smoothed silk, rested, peaceful. That night when I came in, her face was the same. Almost. For her eyelids lay motionless, no swift flutters that told dreams of which we would never know. And the sag of her cheeks drooped lower. I put my hand over her heart, then close to her lips. One did not move in its light, delicate throb and the other, blew no breath against my palm.

I called Dianna.

"Wait," she said, "I'll be right there."

Then lowering myself into the chair by her bed, I took her hand gently into my own and whispered the psalm that had brought her much comfort in her last days ...The Lord is my Shepherd ...

When Dianna came, she sat with me.

"Yesterday morning when I was feeding her," Dianna said, her words barely sounding, "she told me Jesus came to her."

My eyes on Olivia's face, I smiled and whispered, "How wonderful."

"She said, 'Not an angel, but Jesus.'"

Gliding my hand over Olivia's arm, and rubbing lightly, back and forth, back and forth, I felt her skin slide under my fingers.

"I asked if she could see Him," Dianna said, pausing, bowing her head. "She said, 'My eyes were closed, but it was as if my heart could see Him. He was everywhere in me and, at the same time, everywhere around me. His Majesty. I was in the presence of His Majesty. I could feel nothing but love.' And I asked her if she was frightened. She said, 'Oh, no, I wanted to go with Him.' There such yearning in her words, a glow on her face … we can't be sad for her."

"No," I said. "We can't be sad for her."

On the evening before the funeral, I sat by the window of my bedroom and watched the sun spill its last brightness over the backyard. Olivia had kept that space simple … grass and trees, shrubs. There were lilac bushes at the far end of the yard, but this was not the season for them to show their rich purple blooms. So, it was green the sun lit with orange brilliance, kissed the foliage for a moment and then dropped its curtain of shadows. I watched the fading trees, the leaves grow dim, then I saw a flash of blue, barely perceptible, spring from a great maple into the darkening sky. A blue jay. A mean, feisty bird, but so beautiful. I thought of Olivia sitting in a soft slung patio chair on her back porch, binoculars at the ready, watching and waiting for the birds that lived in her small clump of trees.

Olivia's Bible lay open on my lap. Bending my head and closing my eyes, I ran my fingers over the exposed words of the apostle, John, written on the pages before me. They felt real. It was as if they flowed through my fingers and into every curve, every crevice, every cell, every secret place in my body. It was God touching me with His Word. It was dropping into His peace, His rest. It was understanding, at that moment, the connection of life with death. As I sat there, I knew, even before I had committed my spirit to God, He had known me and had watched over me, because He knew, even before I knew, that one day I would choose Him, that one day I would be His child.

Olivia's funeral was small. Except for Olivia's prior instruction that her service be of a spiritual nature, she had left the majority of programing to Harold Sweete, funeral home proprietor and director of Sweet Rest

Funeral Parlor. Though unimaginative, Harold was honorable and thorough. He had his own sense of distinction and decorum. He was consistent and predictable. He was the calm in a storm.

Dressed in a white silk blouse with her mother's pearl necklace strung round her neck, the small, round nuggets lying motionless on her chest, a single bluish- gray gem in each ear, Olivia lay in a nest of pink silk in a casket of polished mahogany. The room displaying her body was awash with deep red … rug, walls, draperies, altar cloth, lampshades. The dirge of a deep and passionate lament spread softly through the air. Baskets of pink and white carnations, vases of roses of those same colors and a pot of deep blue pansies were placed artfully about Olivia's coffin, reflecting the beauty of her being. A subdued and tastefully arranged grouping of pictures and Olivia's writings of poetry and those she wrote of a devotional nature were mounted on a white sheet of poster board hung on a wall between two draped windows. And on a small damask covered table by the entry to the viewing room, Mr. Sweete had placed a stack of elegantly scripted notices stating the particulars of Olivia's life and date of demise as a memento for the visitors. Next to them was a simple white gold-trimmed book to be signed as a record of those who came to share in the service for Olivia. Solemn, it was a room that encouraged dignified mourning.

Because Olivia's only family members, cousins, lived a good distance from Wander Lane, and, therefore, were not able to come to her funeral, Dianna and I stood by her casket greeting Olivia's friends and acquaintances. As they passed in a line, one by one, most paused where we stood, some saying a few remembering or consoling words, some hugging us, and then each would either move on to gaze at Olivia and sometimes murmur a short prayer, or would go directly to the rowed chairs and sit. In my twenty years of being shunned, I had never been to an English funeral, and I found their audible grief, their unhidden tears and their touch on my body a trifle disconcerting. The Amish do not show emotion, or hug, as a conveyance of sorrow and respect for the passing of their brethren. The measure of their grief is expressed in a handshake. And so, I desired to demonstrate my aching heart by grasping the hand of each who went by me. But not wanting to disrupt or distract the manner of English mourning, I did not.

When Pastor Black came to the podium and began his brief service with a hymn, Dianna and I left our spot by Olivia and moved to sit in the chairs reserved for us. Glancing over those who had come to give honor to Olivia, I was happy to see all chairs filled. Then lifting my eyes to peruse the overflow of mourners who stood behind the chairs and expecting to see only villagers, I was shocked to see Violet and Amy Stoll, conspicuous in their black garb, in the midst of them. And Maem. I saw Maem. She was there, too. I froze. A pounding hit my heart, rushed to my head and I felt my face grow hot.

I stood there a moment, unable to move, looking at them, until I felt the tug of Dianna's hand pulling me to sit. The hymn was done and Pastor Black, his eyes on me for one quick second, ostensibly annoyed and then, taking a second look at me, my face apparently appearing disturbed, his look changed, displayed apprehension. Pausing, he bent his body forward a little and with a tilt of his head indicated concern. Silently mouthing, 'I'm okay," he nodded his head ever so slightly and continuing the service, beseeched us all to bow our heads and pray with him. I didn't. Instead, I turned my head and looked back at my maem and my sister. Violet's head was lowered, her hands folded against her skirt. Maem was looking straight at me. I looked back at her. *Can you see the love in my face?* I willed her to hear that cry from my heart. Her face did not change. *Maem, let go of the Amish, just a bit. Show me your heart.* I longed to say the words aloud.

I can only remember bits and pieces of Pastor Black's service. It seemed long, 'though when I looked at my watch, I saw it was not. I remember sitting there, twisting my handkerchief, wanting to get up and run to the back of the room, to put my arms around Maem and bury myself in the softness of her body. I know people spoke, short testimonies, words of friendship and love and good deeds done by Olivia, but I heard none of those words. I saw lips move, but their voices were silent. My mind was concentrated only on the ones to whom I could not go … and worse, if my legs could take me there, the back that would turn and walk away from me. I was full of an aching need that surpassed all that was happening behind the podium, all the audible sobs and murmurs of grief from the mourners around me.

When the final hymn was sung, the last prayer said, the pastor gone from the altar and Mr. Sweete's directions given for the manner in which to leave and the directions to the cemetery given, I turned, again, to see them, those Amish ladies so precious to me. They were gone.

The following week, William Sweete, Harold Sweete's brother and Olivia's lawyer, called Dianna and me into his office.

"Good morning, girls," he said, nodding.

We nodded back.

"I'm sure you girls are wondering why I called you." He leaned forward and folded his hands on his desk. Nodded.

Pursing her lips, Dianna raised her eyebrows. "I'm sixty-six," she said. I said nothing.

He nodded, again. Rocked a little in his chair. "I see. Well, let's get down to business."

We both nodded.

"Olivia was a good woman." He picked up a pen and began a steady drumbeat on his desk. "She wanted you girls taken care of."

I heard Dianna mutter 'and a half, sixty-six and a half' under her breath, and attempting to suppress a nervous laugh that threatened to rise, unbidden, through my lips, I pressed my hand against my mouth.

"So, she made out a will." He glanced up, put the pen down and pulled a file from his desk drawer, and centered it, precisely, on his see-through plastic blotter. He looked at us, tilted his head and nodded. "You girls are in it."

I pressed my hand tighter. Dianna had started a tapping with her foot.

"And I'm sensing you girls aren't taking me too seriously here," Mr. Sweete, William, said. "This is business of a significant nature ... to you. If you'd rather, we could do this at another time. But I wouldn't recommend that. It's best to get matters settled in a timely manner."

"Could you stop calling us 'girls'?" Dianna said.

He frowned. "Certainly."

"I think, Mr. Sweete," I said, trying to ease the tension ... and hoping not to laugh, "we are a bit sensitive right now. We have had a few hard days. It's a little difficult to control our emotions."

"I know. It happens to me, too," William said.

"Sometimes," I said, swallowing, clarifying, and feeling guilty for disparaging a man doing his job, a man trying to empathize with two seemingly mocking women. "Sometimes," I repeated, "when a situation is too big to process in an allotted time, an excessive emotion implodes and leaves in its wake a huge cavity and sometimes, for me, filling that vacuum is a mindless giddiness that is hard to control."

"I think I can understand that. Even for lawyers emotions can be tough to keep under wraps. Reading wills is always difficult, always hard for me," William said, with a sharp, quick nod. "After all, it means someone died."

"Yes, it does," I agreed. And I knew, notwithstanding guilt and sympathy for William's struggle to maintain dignity, if we did not move on, undeserved mirth was going to conquer good intentions. Laughter was aching to burst forth. "Why don't we just get on with it?"

"A good idea," he said, nodding, taking papers out of the file and busying himself leafing through them.

"Oh, my word, he's nodding again," Dianna murmured.

I kicked her, gently, but enough for her to notice ... and understand. She made a face and pulled her leg away.

Though he was apparently absorbed in the papers, I think William must have seen my kick and her face and had finally had enough of our shenanigans, for, all of a sudden his hands stopped shuffling, and sitting back straight in his chair, he glared us.

"You know, *ladies*, and I'm well aware of your ages, I understand your nerves have taken a beating and you've let loose with the sillies, but you are adults and this is serious business. Olivia put a lot of heart and thought into this will and if you don't feel the need to be respectful to me, then do it for her. I have tried to be sensitive and kind, but I'm done with that. Now, you can either ignore what you find funny about me and act like adults or you can leave and I'll put everything in an envelope and send it to you. Your choice." He folded his hands on his desk and nodded. Neither of us laughed.

"Okay then, this is what she decided to do with her possessions." He pulled the papers closer to him. "Are you ready to listen?"

We nodded.

"Good. Now then, Olivia owned her house free and clear, and being as she was a frugal woman and wise with her dollars, she accumulated a substantial and profitable portfolio." He paused and looked at us. "Are you with me?"

I heard Dianna sigh. "He thinks we're idiots," she muttered under her breath.

"Shh," I whispered. I could see, by his frown, he was aware of Dianna's continuing annoyance.

"Shall I go on?"

"We're listening," I said, "and though we may not appear grateful, we are. Both to Olivia and to you." And, for me, it was true. I could see beneath the surface illusion of bumbling arrogance, there was a kind man, certainly a capable man, maybe, in time, a likeable man. I was not so sure Dianna was in agreement.

Since Dianna said nothing and William, apparently was waiting for more stroking, I repeated, "We're grateful."

"And you should be," he said. "I'm the one who advised her and helped her gather up this pile of resources." He took a deep breath, and then, exhaling, his face sagged, crumbled into itself. He looked at his desk and smoothed the papers with gentle touch. "You know, this is not easy for me. Like I said, Olivia was a good woman."

"I know," I said, softly. "A very good woman."

"I'm going tell you ladies something. I probably shouldn't. I know I'm not at the top of your list of appealing men … or even suitable, but I'm going tell you anyway. Olivia trusted you. She only said good things about you two. And she was a wise woman … knew people. So I'm going trust you, too."

Out of the corner of my eye, I saw Dianna bite her lip.

"A long time ago, for a little while, Olivia and I had a thing going."

"A *thing*," Dianna said. "I don't think so."

"Don't, Dianna," I said. "Listen to him."

She shrugged, but didn't say more.

"I know," William continued. "It's hard to imagine the two of us together. But we were. The do-gooder and the wimp. And it was good. Both of us could see underneath the other one. It fades you know … the pretend stuff, the survival stuff, that mask you put on that hides who you are. When two people are in sync, when somebody else can see the inside of your soul, that stuff just disappears. I'm not a bad guy, not if you've got eyes that filter the crude veneer, that arrogance I can't seem to shake off, can't recognize. But she had those eyes. She could see *me*. Would you believe we used to read poetry together? Simple stuff. Wordsworth. We both liked him. And Poe. He was mine. Her favorite was e.e.cummings. Hard to believe, isn't it? Sweet girl like her. But he was." He paused and rubbed his forehead. "It didn't last long. But it was good."

"Why did it end?" I asked, gently.

"He was married," Dianna broke in. I heard bitterness in her voice.

"I was," William said.

"To my sister. Meggie. My only family. You cheated on her. You think nobody knew about your little affair, but I did. "

"I guess I did ... cheat on her." William dropped his face into his hands. "In a sense."

"Olivia?" I said, still not believing. Not wanting to believe. She was like Amish ... faithful. Obedient to her rules.

"I forgave Olivia. From the very beginning, I forgave her." Dianna looked at me. "She was my sister's friend. A good friend. And it was my sister who wanted Olivia to get William out of the sick room once in a while. She wanted her to take him and go to a happy place where her dying didn't constantly dangle its eminent threat, where it didn't bang at his heart every minute. She wanted them to go and do the kind of things friends do." She paused and took a deep breath. But I don't think she ever knew what good friends they became. Dear God, I hope not."

"You forgave Olivia, but not William?" I said.

"Yes. Olivia was duped. She felt so sorry for him. Him, the underdog. She always championed the poor, old underdog. He probably cried and moaned," she said, squeezing her eyes shut and shook her head. "Probably even beat his chest. And probably he used his pathetic wiles and hypnotized her so she couldn't think straight. *Creep*," she said, looking at him.

I gazed at her, amazed. This was a Dianna I didn't know. But I did know sister love. I closed my eyes and sighed. I *had* known sister love. And now, in Diana, I saw it still alive for her dead sister, furiously alive, even after many years of sisters separated. And I believed it. For I had lived it. Still lived it.

"I didn't. I didn't hypnotize her. I didn't force her," William said. I watched him begging, pleading to be understood. "It just happened. We were both sad. We both loved Meggie. But this was different ... Olivia and me. I guess we were both vulnerable and saw the terrible ache in the other. But you're right, Dianna. I was the stronger and I pulled Olivia's sorrow right into my own. You have to understand. I was scared. Meggie was dying. I was afraid of being alone. What would happen to me? And I'm sorry, but much as I loved Meggie, I loved Olivia, too. In a different way. But it didn't last long. We both saw it for what it was ...just a magical interval that took us away from a cruel world for a little time."

"I don't understand," I said, shaking my head. "A magical time? For whom?"

"For him," Dianna said, interrupting, answering for William with trembling anger in her tone. "Meggie was dying. And he was playing games. With his wife. With Meggie. And she was losing. And yes, he was playing Olivia, too. Later on, I got to know her really well, William. When you wash and feed and toilet the body of an old sick woman, especially, a sweet and dignified *lady*, you get to know the real character and stuff she's made of. And Olivia was one good lady. And while poor Meggie was dying, you were off having your little fun with her. You used both of them. Just for your own selfish pleasure."

William shook his head. "Yes, that's so. But not the way you think. It wasn't a physical affair. I didn't sleep with her. Maybe I would have. But not Olivia. She wouldn't have done that. She didn't think like I did. Not in that way. It was just a friendship, a deep friendship. Too deep. And Meggie saw that. She broke it. She wouldn't hurt Meggie. Not in the physical way. Not in any way when she saw the direction it was taking."

"But you would have?" Dianna scoffed, scornfully.

"Okay," William said, "sure, I wanted to. So, I guess, biblically, on my part, it was an affair. But only of the heart … and the mind, the imagination. But never of the body."

Listening to Dianna's scathing words, I began to feel a little sympathy for William. It was time to end this, so I spoke. "We need to move on. Tell us what we need to know of the will, and then, we'll go and absorb it and decide what the next step for us is."

"Olivia left everything to Dianna, maybe retribution. I don't know," William said, his face pale, a remnant of tears clinging to his lashes. "But there are stipulations. There is to be a room for Cora and Dianna is to share the house with Cora for as long and whenever Cora chooses to. House expenses are to be Dianna's. Olivia has left plentiful resources for that. If you, Dianna, no longer want to live in the house, everything will then be Cora's. If neither of you want the house and its furnishings, they are to be sold and the money split between the two of you." He put his hands down on the paper and looked at them. His face was drawn; his eyes, weary. "Any questions?"

"No," Dianna said.

"None now," I said.

"Then we're done," William said.

I nodded. "We're done."

Driving home to Olivia's house, not yet filled with Dianna and the things she would bring to it, and exhausted, I drove up the hill and past the place I longed to call home again. And though the sun still hung high in the sky, my heart ached to light a candle, walk up the stairs, crawl into my bed, pull heavy hand sewn quilts over my body, and sleep.

I kept driving. Miles and miles. Through Amish land. Until I realized the folly of it. It was useless. A head full of dreams and a heart simply wishing would neither implement nor teach.

I drove back to my home, for now Dianna's house, at Wander Lane.

And there, slowing rocking his chair on the porch, reading a book, waiting for me, was Daniel.

"You picked the green one," I said, motioning to his chair, walking up the front porch steps.

"I did." He smiled, put his book down, rose and held out his arms.

I went into them.

Chapter Thirteen

My first job in the world of the English was with a fast food restaurant. I worked in the back slapping hamburgers onto buns and topping the meat with the varied desires of the customers …lettuce, cheese, bacon, extra ketchup, and a sundry of other concoctions …whatever instructions given the front counter workers, were passed on to me. Also, it was my job to throw frozen potato strips into hot oil, cook them crispy, drain them, cone them, and line them up in an oblong wire basket to be grabbed up by those same front workers, and stuffed into bags or plunked onto trays for the customers. It was hot, quick work, bad for my skin, but I learned to keep my face clean and lotioned. The same with my hands. My hair, shorter, stuffed into a net, felt lighter than when long, stuffed under a *kapp*. I liked that. I didn't complain when the food line was long and the manager pressed for the work to be done faster, with greater efficiency and less verbalizing. I did whatever I was told. I was used to work. It was a part of my heritage. And I learned to enjoy the freedom that came when a day of work ended. It did take awhile. Hours with no prescribed tasks and no written authority of The Ordinance to obey were strange to fill at first. But, little by little, I realized the many precious ways there were to utilize those hours, and then, they were wonderful.

Sometimes, when the order line was so long, and help too minimal, orders would back-up and I would have to run them out to customers already sent to their seats to wait for their food.

That's how I met Daniel.

He came in every day. At the same time. The busiest time. And often, he was among those who had to wait for their food to be made ready … his choices always being: chili, a small salad, and coffee. It was his way to sit and read … sometimes, a book; sometimes, papers from his briefcase. It was usually I who brought his food to him. Invariably, he smiled and thanked me. That was it. No other words. Until one day. The day I spilled the chili.

Someone had slopped soft drink onto the floor making a rather large and sticky puddle. I didn't notice it until I felt the slide of my foot on the liquid. I stopped in time to avoid major catastrophe, but a bit of chili and the top portion of coffee, dark brown and hot, dribbled over the rims of their containers into his salad and onto the tray.

"I'm so sorry," I said, sopping the dripped food with napkins, and at the same time, spreading the mess.

"Let me," he said, taking a fistful of extra napkins and swiping them over the liquefied disarray.

"No, no. It's my job."

"I can help." He continued to wipe the tray.

"Thank you."

They weren't many words, but there must be some spoken before there can be more. A lake is not filled until many drops are poured into it. The first words said opened a door. The next busy day when I put his tray of food on this table, he looked up, smiled and directed his words to my face.

"Ah, the lady with my lunch. And no chili in the salad this time," he said, tempering his words with a smile.

And this time, before leaving his table, I smiled back at him and said, "A lady learns ever to do her job more skillfully."

He nodded his head, pleasantly, and replied, "A good lesson for everyone."

I felt his eyes on me as I walked from the table. After that day, the sentences grew longer and more plenteous each time I brought him his food. And then one day, he asked me to dinner.

"At a slow food place," he joked.

"No net on my head, no odor of hamburger?" I said.

"Candles burning and wine glasses shimmering," he answered.

And that was the beginning of a new kind of relationship. He became my mentor, my friend, and then, something more … the like of which I cannot name. It was more than common friendship, or familial ties, but less than the love of marriage. He saw my hunger for knowledge and led me beyond the myriad of books I'd been reading and structured my reading on a path to the magic of literary words that spoke of beauty and truth, and informative words that fed my brain and created an appetite for more information, more comprehension. He led me to adult education classes, then college courses, still encouraging independent reading that taught me the world, that taught me the cultures of countless peoples. And then he began to narrow my academic studies to suit the needs of his business realm. He was the CEO of a massive company that developed and produced healthful, enhanced seeds for appropriate high-volume, economical and ecological growth of food in our own country and on foreign soil. His staff was large and he groomed me for a significant position in his company. I worked directly under him as a pair of additional eyes so nothing he needed to know would be left unseen. He invested a great deal in me and was always generous with time and money. I lived well, but, and I don't believe he was aware, I didn't spend recklessly nor did I save prudently. Any excess dollars were sent, anonymously through Olivia, to the children in need she found in her work as a child care advocate and to the Amish community. I didn't want him to know my funds were diminishing.

And now Daniel was here, rocking next to me. As I sat by him, I in my blue chair, he in his green, I felt a comfort in his presence, a release from the loneliness that comes when one is not wholly certain of where she belongs. There was an assurance with him that I would ever be a part of his life, always accepted, whether English or Amish, never thrown away.

"I'm glad you're here," I said.

"I miss you."

Smiling ruefully, thinking how rarely I had spoken with him in the last months, I asked, "Me, the person who sits here, or me, the person not in your office?"

"You," he answered, "the person who sits here and you, the person missing from my office."

"That's not an answer."

"You're wrong," he said, looking in my eyes. "It's a whole answer."

"I know," I said, softly, reaching, touching his arm, then bringing my hand back and resting it in my lap. Relaxing, I leaned back against my chair.

"How long will you be here?" he asked.

"I don't know."

"How is the search for the baby going?"

"She's not a baby anymore." I sighed. "I almost wish she were. That's how I remember her. Little. I just cannot picture her big."

"Are you giving up?"

I looked at him. "I know where she is."

"And?"

"And? Will I go to see her? I don't know exactly where she is. I know the state ... and the town. Sugar Creek, Ohio. Should I search that town to find her? I don't know. I would surely love to hold her in my arms again. But I wouldn't really know her. Twenty years is a long time; she was just a baby. And, for sure, she would not know me." And realizing I had lapsed into Amish speak, *for sure,* I smiled inside my head. "I just don't know."

"Is it enough to know where she is?" He was not looking at me. "Look," he said, pointing. There was a squirrel scurrying up the trunk of an old maple across the street from us. "She'd be better off scouring acorns under an oak."

"I am not sure," I said, answering his question, following his eyes to the squirrel. "Wouldn't it be nice to have your only worry a search for a nut?"

"It'd be kind of boring. And why are you not sure? It's something you've wanted for a long time. Are you frightened of what you'll find?"

"Maybe. Maybe I have made her to be something she's not. In my head. In my heart. But still there is a need in my heart to bring her home. To her real family. To where she belongs."

And where is that?" he asked, shifting in his chair, looking at me.

"Here," I said.

"With you?"

"With her family."

That's you." He turned back to sit straight in his chair.

"Partly," I said, pressing my lips together. The squirrel was gone. "Partly it is me. But there are aunts and uncles and cousins and grandparents, too."

He shook his head. I could feel the beginning of an impatience with my indecision. He crossed one leg over the other, his foot on his knee, and tapped his fingers against his shoe. "If I were a smoking man," he said, "I would enjoy a good, strong pipe right now."

"If you weren't so fond of working lungs, that would be a comforting thing. Good smell, too. Candy for your nose."

"Cora?"

"Yes."

"I ask, again. When are you leaving here?"

Pulling my arms tight around my chest, I dropped my head, then lifting it, looked across the street at the maple tree. How stately and firm it stood. Simple. Just waiting for wind or rain, the sun, night. No need to consider options, make decisions. Even so, beautiful.

"And I say, again," answering. "I don't know. Daniel, I am so confused."

"How can I help?"

"Pray for me."

"For resolution?"

"For guidance and wisdom."

He said nothing. I heard him sigh. We sat in silence for awhile. My eyes were filling. I had no answers for him. There were none inside me. None that would satisfy him … or me.

"I need to know why Lily died," I whispered, breaking the silence. He didn't respond. "I need to know it wasn't suicide. I need to know she is safe. I need to know she is with God."

"So, it's not just about Annabelle?"

"No," I agreed, my voice low.

He sat awhile longer, not speaking. I couldn't hear him move, no rocking of his chair.

"Daniel?"

Not speaking, he stood, went to the porch railing, leaned against the post supporting the porch roof. I waited.

"Am I also to understand you have not determined whether you're English or Amish?" He spoke, but he did not turn to look at me.

"I have not."

"When will that happen?"

"I don't know."

"Give me your apartment keys and I'll water your plants," he said, his back yet toward me.

"I do not have any plants."

"Then I'll feed the cat." He still did not turn.

"I don't have a cat."

"How 'bout I jiggle your toilet handle."

"That I've got," I said, smiling, "but I doubt it's needed."

"So, it's just prayer." His voice was fixed. There was no laughter in it.

"That is enough," I said.

After Daniel left, I sat for a long time gazing at the trees across the way, and then higher, thinking of God taking His hand and swiping clouds over the sky from pole to pole and the whole round width of the equator ... thin, white strips rippling over the blue ... then taking them in His hands, molding them into soft, puffy shapes ... gently blowing His breath against them, sending them over the earth, soaking them with vapor rising from the seas, pushing them over great land masses, then dropping their bounty, glorious rain, onto the maples across the street, cleaning their leaves to shine.

Then I went into the house, found a glass, globe-shaped and gleaming, and a bottle of wine, deep red and transparent, took them out to the porch, sat in the green rocker and watched for the squirrel to come back.

Chapter Fourteen

I got a call from Dianna. The meeting with William Sweete had upset her. She said it had brought back a lot of unhappy memories and she wasn't sure she wanted to keep the house.

"I'm so sorry," she said, "I know it's a place for you to live and I don't want you to feel you need to leave it because of me, but he made me remember what a rotten rat he was when Meggie was so sick ... when she *died*. It was in her house that all of it happened. I know it was. Where else would they go? And I do think he slept with her. It wasn't so bad when Olivia was sick. I never thought of those things then. Olivia is a sweetheart and I loved her. I really did. And I never blamed her for what happened. He's goooood. When he wants to, he can charm the bark off a tree. And you know what happens when a tree loses its bark. It dies. That's what charm can do."

"Oh, Dianna," I said, interrupting her rambling, "it was a long time ago and he said he didn't sleep with her and probably, they simply went for walks or to the park or maybe sat in the car and talked. I don't think Olivia would have brought him to her house, especially to be alone with him. You think about it. Wonderful as Olivia was, she was a bit of a prig."

"It's not her. It's *him*. Anyway, I can't get it out of my mind. You should understand. You have ... had ... sisters. You know what it's like to lose them."

Drawing a deep breath, exhaling slowly, I held the phone away from my ear for a moment. "Dianna, I think you need to quiet your soul, take some time and call me back."

"I didn't mean to hurt you. You know that, don't you?"

I could hear the regret in her voice.

"Don't you?" she repeated.

"Of course, I do," I said, gently. "And I know how very good you were to Olivia. And I know *you*. You're not a mean-spirited person. William just opened a very sore spot in your heart. Only it won't make you feel better to hate him. Take some time. Be good to yourself. Remember Meggie as a happy person. From all you have said about her in the past, she was."

"Yes, she was," Dianna said, and I heard her words as a bit calmer. "But I still think William's a jerk and I don't want the house ... you can have it."

"We'll talk about the house later."

"Cora?"

"Yes."

"Do you think you could start cleaning out Olivia's stuff? Her closets? And her drawers?"

"Would it make you feel better?"

"Yes."

"Then I'll do it."

"Thank you," she said with meek voice.

"You're welcome." I smiled and hung up. Sometimes, I thought, it helps, when you hurt, to become a little child again. For awhile. Dianna was entitled to her moment of reverting back to the years when it was okay to cry and have a little tantrum. And to be a little ashamed of it when it is over.

And so I began the sad task of sorting Olivia's things ... her clothes, her jewelry, her papers, records and correspondence, the secrets held in dresser drawers.

I started with her closet. It was hard touching the fabrics that had touched the line of her body, the stretch of her limbs, the move of her skin ... the aging sag of it, the ravages of a killing cancer. Fabrics that had touched the sheen of her hair. The flow of silk over her arms and shoulders. Denim against muscle and sinew. Satin, soft on her back. Unexpected lacy, black and thonged undergarments mixed in with simple white cotton briefs. Push-up bras still in their packages. Full skirts and straight skirts. Pants. Blouses. A sequined dress. A tailored black suit. Shawls. Shoes. And the scarves ... turbans of sharp and bright colors, patterns of seascapes and forests and flowers. When I touched her clothes, it was she I felt.

There was a drawer at the bottom of her dresser filled with white socks. So white they were, it was as if they soaked long in bleach and then were spread on grass under the sun to dry. And instead of sending its hot rays to stiffen the cotton, the sun had kissed them soft.

I stacked the socks, carefully, on the bed behind me, one pair upon another, until there was only a single layer left in the drawer. And when I lifted the last pair, I saw two envelopes, fragile pink in color with delicately embossed scallops on the edges of their flaps. I turned them over and saw the names written on them. Dianna on one; Cora on the other.

Overwhelmed for a moment by the unexpected sensation emanating from those envelopes … the disappearance of the here and now, and the filling of Olivia's presence in my mind and heart … I responded, automatically, by picking up my phone and calling Dianna.

"Cora?" Dianna answered.

"Yes," I said. I hesitated, not exactly sure how to tell her of the letters, not sure if it should be done on the phone.

"Cora?"

"I found something in Olivia's dresser." Instinctively I knew these letters were important, but I wasn't sure they held good words. I was fearful of their news. There might be something in my letter about Annabelle. Something bad. Something she had been afraid to tell while she was still alive.

"What?" I heard Dianna saying. "What did you find?"

"Letters." I bit my lip, lowered my head, and spoke, "One for you and one for me."

"Well, open them."

"I don't think I should. Not yours. It would seem to me they must be of a personal nature."

"Is there a letter for William?"

"No."

"I want to know what's in mine."

"I can bring it to you."

"I want to know now." Her voice was commanding, impatient. "I don't have a problem with you knowing what's in it. Just open it and read it to me."

I slid my finger carefully under the flap. The casing opened without tearing. The paper was the same delicate pink as the envelope, trimmed with the same embossed edgings.

"Are you sure you want me to read this?"

"Please," she said.

I hesitated. It seemed wrong to expose Olivia's words to anyone other than the one to whom she had written. It might be Olivia didn't want me to know what she'd written to Dianna.

"Cora!"

I heard Dianna's impatience and so I read Olivia's letter aloud to Dianna.

Dear Dianna,

You have grown dear to me, a friend. I treasure all the times we had together. You are much like your sister, Meggie. I remember her often and always with love.

I am growing weak and there are things I must tell you. Things about William Sweete and me. I write them so neither of us will be embarrassed in front of the other. And I hope you will not be uncomfortable with these written words.

I know you suspected William and I had an affair. We did not. When Meggie was so very ill, we did spend much time together. Alone. But Meggie knew. It was she who asked me to be his help, his shoulder to lean on. She could not be that person. She knew he was not brave enough to tell her his fears, his feelings. She knew when he looked at her, he saw death. She ached for him to have a measure of solace, to have someone upon whom he could spill his sorrow without shame. Someone he could trust. She loved him enough to give him that gift. She knew I could do that. She knew I would share with him, in words, the love she had for him, that I would tell him of the remembered love that swam within her soul.

I would go to Meggie each night and tell her what we did, what he said, how he was holding up. It was beautiful to see her pleasure when I told her of his love for her. She made me promise to never to tell, never to betray the confidences of his heart, the depth of his anguish. I never did, until now. You were Meggie's sister. You deserve to know.

Remember, as you read this, Meggie trusted William and me with all her heart and never questioned our faithfulness. Neither should you. We never dishonored your sister. We both loved her. Remember, too, that Meggie loved you so very much. You were a good sister to her.

I pray you will not reveal this letter to William. He is a prideful man.

Again, dear friend, thank you for the wonderful days we shared. We will share them, once more, one day in Heaven.

Love always, Olivia

"I've read it all," I said.

"It was not what I expected," Dianna said.

"What did you expect?" I asked, gently.

"I thought she would tell me William and she had an affair."

"Does it help to hear Olivia's words?"

"Yes," she whispered. "Yes. Are you sure there isn't a letter for William?"

"There were only two letters. One for you. One for me."

I waited for her reply. When there was none, I looked down at my phone. The screen was black.

Later that evening, sitting in Olivia's favorite flower patterned stuffed chair, I opened the letter Olivia had written to me. With a perplexing sense of foreboding, I took the notepaper from its envelope and unfolded it. Closing my eyes, not understanding my trepidation, I held it in my lap. Olivia had assured me Annabelle was happy and well, but she had also admonished me to stay out of her life. Surely, she had known I would do nothing to hurt the child. I blinked my eyes, the woman. Annabelle was no longer a child.

I picked the letter up and read:

My Own Dear Cora,

The first time I saw you, you were running with your brothers and Aaron in the hay fields. It was before their first cutting. The grass was high and bright green. You were coming from school. I think one of the boys must have thrown a ball into the field and you were all running to find it. You were laughing, holding onto your bonnet with one hand while the other swung your lunch bucket high. I watched your legs pump hard as they struggled with your bundling skirt. But you ran nearly as fast as the boys. And I saw Aaron find the ball and give it to you ... a trophy. Even then, not knowing you well, not seeing you often, I could see in the sweep of your bodies, a sweet connection between the two of you.

I saw you, after that, from a distance. I watched you grow, Cora. You and your brothers ... and then the twins. And even all the Amish children in your Community. It was refreshing for me to see the innocence and the joy that came from living in a loving and peaceful place ... simple and plain. Though I learned through the years that not everything in Amish Country is simple and plain.

Later when you were older and came to me with a baby in your arms, I'm afraid I acted badly and left you with a troubled heart. I should have taken the baby until a time it could be better determined where the child should be. I just didn't know what to do that night and things happened so quickly. You were there. The baby was there. And when I was out of the room, you lay the baby on a chair and left. I followed procedure and took the baby to the sheriff. He would not take her, so, the next day I took her to my supervisor. It was too fast. If you and I had time to think things through, I think I could have convinced you to take the baby to your home, to your Maem, and work it out with the Bishop. But it didn't happen that way. When it was reported to the sheriff a boy had seen an Amish woman carrying a bundle in the night, he had to act in an official manner and things got out of hand. You were shunned. The baby was put with Child Protective Services.

I remember the sadness that was in you when I wrote you Lily had died and you came to my house. Such anguish there was in your face ... and I knew it was for Lily, and, also, for the baby. Annabelle. We didn't talk about Annabelle during that visit, but I knew behind the tears for Lily were tears for Annabelle. They were both gone from your life. It was during that time I grew to know you and to love you. And I knew you felt the same for me.

I am dying, Cora. You know that. I am blessed to still be able to write ... though I do it in spurts for my strength is quickly diminishing. There are things I want to tell you. I cannot tell you the exact location of Annabelle's home. I have made that a promise to her mother, the woman who took her. It is important that no one knows. Let me explain why.

When I took Annabelle to my supervisor, Agnes Hall. I informed her the child was born Amish and the mother desired she remained so. It is unusual to place an Amish child. The Amish nearly always take care of their own. Yours was a rare situation. But sometimes the world comes together in a strange and wonderful way. And it did this time. Agnes was a woman with a bright mind and a big heart. She was remarkably aware of the happening in the nooks and crannies of the people in her area of responsibility. She could sense needs, decipher them, and think out solutions. So it ensued with Annabelle and a woman different from Annabelle's mother. That woman, an Amish woman, gave birth to a baby conceived within the bounds of her marriage. A happy marriage. The baby died. It had been delivered in the home of an Amish midwife. The midwife knew Agnes and called to her for help. Agnes, secretly and lovingly, was able to exchange Annabelle with that baby. The timing was right. And Agnes was respected by the Amish midwife as trustworthy. The only ones who knew of the switch were the mother, the midwife, Agnes and me. Annabelle went home with her new mother and she lived in that family with everyone thinking this was the baby of Abe Yoder and his wife. None of us has ever told it as otherwise ... until now. For now I'm telling you. Annabelle has had a beautiful childhood and womanhood. She doesn't know the circumstances of her birth, nor does Abe Yoder. Every person believes she is their natural daughter. Annabelle has married. She is happy. Let her be. It would serve no purpose to reveal her story. One last thing. Annabelle's new mother renamed her baby Talitha, like the child Jesus raised from the dead. I say, again, Annabelle ... Talitha ... is happy. Your baby, Annabelle, is loved by many.

I love you, Cora, as my own child. I have been blessed to know you. Souls don't die. I will be with you again.

Love, Olivia.

Chapter Fifteen

When I was little and lay wide awake in my bed long hours after I'd crawled under my blankets, Maem would come into the my room, sit on the edge of my bed and sing little songs in her soft Pennsylvania Dutch voice. Usually, the melodies lulled me to sleep, but, sometimes, they did not. On those nights she would bring me a cup of hot milk sweetened with a tablespoon of honey and she would put a hot water bottle on my stomach. The warmth of the milk and the heat on my tummy soothed my restlessness and I would drop into a peaceful sleep.

On the night I read Olivia's letters, my head would not stop repeating the words Olivia had left me. Alive in my mind in bold, black letters ... Annabelle, adopted, Yoder ... her words, her secrets, whirled and spun and reverberated against the structure of my skull. I could not sleep.

I got up and heated milk, poured a little honey in it, took my filled cup to the porch, and sipped and rocked until the magic worked and my eyes grew drowsy. Then I went back to my bed and let relaxing sleep drop its calm upon me and spread its welcomed escape within.

I woke the next morning with the words *God will show a way* shining behind my eyes, and His presence, His spirit, not seen with eyes, but *known* in my heart was powerful ... breathtaking. The wonder of realizing the loving aura of God encompassing the whole of my body, my very soul, was greater than words can tell.

I lay in my bed a long time, absorbing the joy, letting it become manageable, an entity that would carry me with clarity and wisdom through the day, an understanding that would help me see choices, discern the right path to walk.

Leaving the house, I chose that day to drive the back roads through Amish country, to take in the crux of a people that were mine, to learn them again, to soak them through my skin into my being, to be one with them, to wallow in the soul of their substance.

The air was soft and warm, the cusp of summer turning to fall. Harvest time. The colors, the smells bold and *there*, infused the world with a crisp energy. I passed corn fields with high swaying stalks heavy with hard-kernelled ears, winter fodder yet to be harvested. And other fields already cut, their thick, sharp stubbles lining the earth. I drove by a young Amish girl carrying a jar of water and I remember taking water to Da out working the land. Farther on I passed houses with rows of black pants and shirts and sharp white sheets hanging by wooden pins clipped to rope clotheslines. I stopped by a yard and watched a slender figure in dark green dress reach in her woven basket, pull out a towel, whisk it up and down to straighten the crumples, then pin it on the line and reach for another towel. More memories. Washing clothes with maem. Using the soap we had made from lye and lard. Hanging them to dry in flowing breezes, and smelling the sweet, crisp fragrance of air-dried cloth when we took them down. Thinking back to my Amish days when I smoothed my hands over soft cotton and laid the clean, dried clothing carefully into the basket, then took them into the house, all the while savoring the pleasure of a job done well, regret for the lost years loomed large.

I drove farther, and seeing a garden, stopped again. Rows of tomato plants with vines, dried and browning, spread over the ground; their fruit lay deep red and lush waiting to be picked and canned for the winter. I saw pumpkins still growing. Cucumber plants, stripped clean of the long, green vegetables; most likely already picked, pickled and jarred. Thick, green leaves covered potato mounds and I could see where carrots had been pulled. A desire tugged at me to leave my car and walk in the garden, put my hands in the soil, lift it and smell it, sift it through my fingers. Then to sit among the tomato plants, pluck the juicy red fruit and inhale the musky puff of earthly scent as the tomato's stem broke from the vine. And to pretend it all was mine. To pretend I belonged there again.

But I pushed on, over the roads, up and down the hills. I saw men in the fields. Single and in groups. Harvesting. Preparing for the cold months. Cows still in the pastures. Chewing fresh grass. Green and luxurious. Gourmet grass. Better than hay. In the distance were smears of red and orange and gold among the trees in the woods. Leaves dying early. Flashes of fall.

A young man, sleeves rolled up, straw hat pulled low over his brow, standing at the front of an empty flatbed wagon, slapped heavy black reins over his beautiful, powerful workhorse and pulled out of his barnyard driveway straight in front of me. Startled, I pushed my brakes hard.

He didn't look at me, but dipped his chin in the barest of nods as he passed me and I could sense a roguish smile behind his expressionless face. From my rearview mirror I watched him jaunt down the road, at least I believed he thought he made a frisky and debonair picture, but, to me, it was a plodding he was doing. Remembering the sweetness of adolescent Amish boys acting as grown men, I smiled.

It had been a good morning. I patted the letter in my pocket. It was time to go back to the village. I took the road that would pass Aaron's house and Da's house, the road that would go down the hill I'd walked just a few months ago ... after twenty years of not knowing the feel of that pathway under my feet.

As I drew nearer my old home, I slowed the car to a near crawl, so I could let my eyes linger, for a moment, over the house and the yard. I was surprised to see Maem outside so close to noon. For sure, Da and George and his sons would be coming soon for their midday meal. I put my foot on the brake for a moment. I considered pushing the horn, so Maem would look up. But I didn't. I had not the courage to do that for if she looked and did not acknowledge me, the hurt would be too big in my heart.

Walking from the chicken coop by the side of the barn, Maem's arms were filled with maroon and pink mums. Smiling, I remembered the clumps of flowers she planted every year near the coop so the chickens would have *a special spot of beauty, for even the fowl have eyes to be pleasured by God's creation.* Her steps were tentative as she came through the grass. She seemed so frail, so bent. As she got nearer the house, she faltered and reached out to balance herself against the ancient willow tree where our old swing still hung. Mums spilled from her arms and with her free hand she clutched at the flowers straining to keep some from falling to the ground.

I turned off the car and opened the door meaning to help her. But I didn't need to. A child, about eight or nine years old, a girl, strands of hair, bright in the sun, escaped from her *kapp* as she came out of the house and skipped across the yard to her. She carried a cane and gave it to my maem. Smiling, Maem took it, then still holding onto the tree, bent and kissed the child's head. And with a twinge of envy, a harkening back to my own childhood, I marveled at maem showing affection in a place where a passerby could see her. The little girl smiled back at maem, took her arm and led her back towards the house.

I started the car to leave. Hearing the engine, the child looked to the road. She smiled at me and waved. Maem, struggling, it seemed to stay upright, kept her head down.

I waved back and drove off.

Once back in Dianna's house, I sliced an apple, put it on a napkin and went out to the front porch to think. A gentle breeze sighed softly over my face and the shaded sun blanketed me with warmth. It was not a thought inducing atmosphere. I fell asleep.

When I woke, my head still bowed, I saw the apple slices, pulp browning, in my lap. I smiled and breathing deep, rubbed my eyes and stretched my body. The apples shivered on my skirt. I rose and laid them in a line on the porch railing. For sure, one of God's creatures would find them there and feast on them.

My stomach rumbled. I had slept too long. Wasted hours. It was not my wont to nap. Shrugging, I went into the house and readied myself to leave and find food for my hunger.

I chose to go to Harriet's restaurant. In that comforting place, Harriet's was an old and loving heart that understood the hurt of my shunning.

It was the time between lunch and dinner and there were only a few patrons in Harriet's eatery. Folding napkins around silverware, Bailey sat at a table near the door. She waved and greeted me with a smile when she saw me.

"Sit anyplace," she said, handing me a menu, not getting up. "Not too many people here, so you got lots of choices."

"Thank you," I said, taking the menu and pointing. "I think I'll sit over there in the corner."

"Good spot. Private. I'll be over in a bit to take your order." She held up a napkin. "Gotta get this done less'n the aunt yells."

"You know," I said, "I don't think I've ever heard Harriet yell at you."

Bailey looked up at me and grinned. "She does it in secret."

"I wouldn't bet on that," I said, shaking my head. "Is she here?"

"She's always here."

"If she's not busy, would you tell her I'd like to see her?"

"Sure," Bailey said, making a face. "When I'm done."

On my way to the corner table, I passed a couple finished with their meal. The older gentleman was digging in his wallet, while the lady discreetly looked in a different direction. I smiled, thinking, perhaps, from their dress and awkward maneuvers, they were in the beginnings of a potential romance. I smiled. It was a lovely thought.

He found his money, laid several bills on the table, and went to his lady to assist her in rising. I watched with pleasure. As they went by Bailey, the gentlemen looked at her. She held up a finger indicating she would be right with them. He frowned but said nothing and the couple waited, silently, at the counter while Bailey wrapped a few more knives and forks. But the old gentleman kept his eyes on Bailey and she, finally, succumbed and took his money. He eyed their table as she gave him his change and I wondered if he wanted to go to it and take his tip back.

When the couple was gone, Bailey looked at her work table strewn with napkins and cutlery and shrugged. Then looked at me.

"Might as well take your order while I'm up," she called out, walking across the room.

"Vegetable soup and rye toast," I said when she reached me.

"That's pretty dull."

"And you can tell Harriet I'm here."

"I guess."

"And you can bring me some napkins to fold while I wait."

Are you kidding? Old Auntie would kill me."

I smiled. "Just thought I would help."

"Yeah, right," Bailey said, sauntering away. "Get me in trouble." Then she turned. "Did you say vegetable or chicken noodle?"

"Vegetable," I laughed.

"Did that girl give you trouble?" Harriet asked, setting a tray with soup and bread on the table.

"No," I said, taking the bowl and plate from the tray and setting them before me. "Actually, she is pretty entertaining."

"Humph," Harriet said, sitting, "can't seem to get her trained right … you want crackers? Looks like I forgot 'em."

"No, I'm fine." I looked at her and smiled. "I'm surprised you didn't bring two spoons."

She smiled back. "That's only for desserts … later on … when I git the pie and ice cream."

Nodding, I swallowed a few spoonsful of soup, then broke a slice of the toast into pieces and sprinkled them over the soup.

"I have something I'd like to show you," I said. Looking at her, I hesitated. "I need advice."

Harriet sighed and rubbed the back of her neck. "Give me the problem."

"It's an old one," I said.

"The baby," Harriet said, gently, lowering her arm onto the table, leaning towards me.

"Yes." I folded my hands in my lap and bent nearer to her. "Olivia left me a letter."

"I see," Harriet said.

"It's in my pocket." Pressing my lips together, I sat back and looked at her.

"You want me to read it?"

"I think so."

Harriet reached out her hand. I put the letter in it.

"Are you sure?" Harriet asked, holding the envelope. "If I open it and read it, I can't unread it."

"I'm sure."

"I can't see too good, but I ain't givin' into no spectacles. Not yet anyways," Harriet said, opening the letter, holding it close to her face.

I watched Harriet read the letter. Though she glanced up from time to time, I couldn't read her thoughts; her face gave away nothing. When she was finished, she positioned the letter carefully on the table, sighed, and smoothed her hand ... slowly ... gently ... over the paper.

Then raising her face to look at mine, she closed her eyes and moved her head in a slight nodding motion. When she opened her eyes, they seemed to reflect a weary sorrow.

"Harriet?" I whispered, and wanting to join her in some way, I laid my hand on hers as it caressed the letter. Her hand, under mine, stopped. She turned it over, palm up, and grasped my hand as it lay on hers. I felt a tremble under her skin. Her fingers were so slim. Cold. Delicate. "Harriet, are you all right?"

Her lips quivered. Looking down at our hands joined together, she shook her head. "She was my friend."

"I think I knew that," I said. "There is a sameness with you and her." With tender touch I slid my free hand over her arm. "To have looked at you and Olivia with the eyes of my face, I would not have guessed that, but to see you both with the eyes of my heart, the likeness was a shining thing."

I didn't think she would ever tell you." Harriet looked down at her lap. "She sure surprised me."

"Tell me what?"

"About the baby. She was so fixed on keepin' it a secret." Harriet pulled her hands from mine and rubbed her face, then she dropped them onto the table and with resolute movement bent towards me. "She didn't want you to know."

Her words rang fierce in my ears. They hit with a knowledge that had not been mine and I felt a sense of betrayal. "*You knew.*"

Harriet nodded assent.

"She said nobody else knew. Just her and the midwife. And the new mother. And Agnes. Agnes, the facilitator of it all." I heard my voice grow bitter. "But not me. Me, she didn't tell."

"She was afraid."

"Of what? Of *me*?"

"Yes."

I saw the strength coming back in Harriet's face. I wondered if she saw the anger in mine.

"Did Olivia think I would hurt the child? The baby I loved? The baby I loved enough to give away? Did she think I would find shunning fun? That it would pleasure me to be torn from my family?" I slammed my fist on the table. There was little Amish filling my soul at that moment.

"Don't let your anger be killin' your love," Harriet said. "She didn't know you would be shunned when you left the baby. Don't be blamin' that on her. Luck wasn't with you. Somebody saw you and told. That's life. You deal with what is."

"I could have found Annabelle and brought her back and confessed and everything would have been perfect."

"You're dreamin' and you know it." Harriet sighed. I saw her face crumple and heard her voice soften. "Listen, child, Olivia did what she thought was best. And prob'ly it was best. Annabelle has a good life now. Don't spoil it for a selfish need."

"Don't you think she has a right to know who her real maem is?"

"Oh, Cora, did you think she had that right when you walked her down the hill?"

"No," I whispered.

"You did your best. So did Olivia."

"Why did she tell you?"

"It was a big secret. Too big for Olivia's heart to hold alone."

"And why did she lie to me? Why didn't she tell me that you knew what happened to Annabelle?"

"I think she thought it would hurt you to think other people knew … mostly 'cause you put that burden heavy on your heart for so long and you still carry the shame of it. And she knew what you would do and there were too many lives to hurt."

I folded my hands against my chest and bowed my head upon them.

"She was right," I said, softly into my hands.

I heard the moan of aging pain as Harriet lifted herself from her chair, and I felt frail arms come round me as she encompassed me in a circle of love. I looked up and saw the wet of her eyes matching my own.

"But, I guess she couldn't die peaceful without you knowing the truth. I guess that's mebbe why she wrote the letter," Harriet said.

I rose and held her close against me, then guided her back to her chair. As I eased her down, I could sense the weariness in her body and knew the tiring weights of life soaked through her skin all the way down to her soul.

"So many secrets," I whispered, kneeling by her chair, resting my hand on her thigh.

"And you have many," she said, patting my hand.

"I do."

"Will you tell me?"

"No," I said, rising, putting my hand on her shoulder, and I know lies, secrets, are deceitful. Told by us in order to hide a part of self we don't want known … something that shames us so much we can't bring those secrets, those lies, into the light … so well hidden as they are, so deeply entrenched, we give them power and we don't let them go and therefore, God, waiting for us to acknowledge our deceptions, will not wipe them away."

Harriet stroked my hand as it lay on her shoulder. "Go set yourself on your chair and get that soup et 'fore it gets too cold," she said, softly.

"I miss them both, Olivia and Annabelle," I said, rising, returning to my chair. "Do you know how great the pain is?"

"I do." She reached across the table and took my hand, held it tightly for a moment, then released it and eased back into her chair.

I looked at her ... her face, strained; her body, slumped. My heart beat sad, but I had to know more.

"There are two more things I need to know," I said, soberly, leaning slightly towards her.

Harriet picked up the salt shaker and tapped it lightly on the tabletop.

"Will you tell me if I ask?"

"If'en I can," Harriet said, pursing her lips; the furrows in her forehead, tightening.

"Just two," I said.

"If'en I can," Harriet repeated.

"Does anyone else know Annabelle's story ... anybody I do not already know about?"

"I won't lie to you. The answer is yes. But I won't tell you who." Her words were firm.

"How many knew?"

"Is that the second question?"

I smiled, wryly. "It's the second part of the first question."

"I guess that's fair enough." Lifting her chin, she sat straighter in her chair. The color was returning to her cheeks. "Only me and somebody else. That's all. Two of us."

I waited, hoping she would tell me more.

"That's it. I ain't tellin' you who," she said, with a sharp nod of her head. "Now, eat your soup."

"It's cold," I said. "And I've still got my other question."

"Shoot it out."

"Did Lily kill herself?"

Harriet looked away from me. She lifted her shoulders and drew in a deep breath, swooshing it out as she let her shoulders drop back down. "I don't know."

"You know something."

"You got your two questions. I ain't answering no more."

"It wasn't a question. It was a statement."

"A statement," Harriet repeated my words. She sighed. "I see."

"I am waiting for a comment," I said, hoping she would, at least, share an opinion.

"I ain't got no comment."

"But you know more than you are saying," I said, looking straight into her eyes.

"Mebbe. Mebbe not."

And then, right at that moment, to my chagrin, and, I'm sure, Harriet's relief, Bailey sauntered up to the table with a tray.

"Hey, you got more soup in there," she said, pointing at my bowl. "You gonna eat it? Or I could heat it up ... I guess."

"I don't want it."

"Up to you," Bailey said, shrugging. She started picking up the dishes.

"Take 'em to the kitchen," Harriet said, poking Bailey's arm, "and bring back a big slice of carrot cake. A huge slice. And two forks."

I looked at Harriet and smiled. It was an astute and delicious way for her to move me away from my unwelcome digging. She smiled back and we were all right again.

Sometimes, carrot cake works wonders. Sometimes, it does not. This time it did.

That night I slipped the letter under my pillow hoping it would magically cause me to dream of Annabelle ... Talitha. To dream of a baby grown to an adult with a wee one of her own, a wee Amish baby. Amish because God had made my promise to Annabelle be honored. And my Annabelle had grown up among the brethren ... her people. My people?

Trees do sing and flowers do smile. The clouds are God's chariot and the fields are jubilant.

Dreams are beautiful pictures He puts in our heads, that He sets with joy into our hearts. They are gifts that play carols in our souls. I dreamed of Annabelle that night.

Chapter Sixteen

I woke early the next morning. Happy. There was music, sweet melodic singing, spreading its songs throughout the inside of my skin; and smiles, running up and down the outside of it. It didn't matter anymore who knew where Annabelle had been all those long years. What mattered was that *I* knew. And she was content. And she was Amish. The joy of it rained off my skin. Puddling on the floor. Misting through the air. Spattering against the walls. It was too big to hold within myself. It ached to be shared.

I called Daniel.

"Daniel, it's me." It was too early. Already I was beginning to think I should not have called.

"Cora?" His voice was full of sleep. "What's wrong? Are you all right?"

"No, no, no," I said. "I am sorry. I forgot the time was so early. Go back to sleep. I can call later."

"Cora?" he repeated, "Are you all right?"

"Yes, I am all right. Better than that. I am wonderfully, beautifully, ecstatically exuberant. I know, Daniel. I *know*."

"And what is it you know, Cora?" He laughed.

"You're awake," I exclaimed, so very pleased.

"I'm awake. And what is it you know?"

"Daniel, you won't believe this. I know where Annabelle is now and I know where she has been and I know how she got there."

"So, are you coming back?"

"You mean now?"

"I mean now. You found what you sought to find, and I miss you. Very much."

"You said you had replacements for my work. Good replacements."

"I do," Daniel said. "Good replacements. For your work. But not for *you*."

"Oh," I said, walking to the window, pushing the drapes aside, absorbing his words. The sky was filling with the oranges of a new sun. "Me?"

"You," he said. "I told you, I miss you."

It seemed I could not find my words. They would not come. I held my phone in silence and waited.

"Are you there?"

"I am here," I said, softly. "I think I miss you, too."

"You think?" He said and I heard his laughter through the receiver.

"I know. I do. I miss you." The trees were black silhouettes afore the blazing sun. Their shapes, sharp and crisp-edged; their limbs reaching to the sky.

"Tell me all you've learned about Annabelle … and then pack your bags and come home."

"I can't do that … come home. There are still answers to be found. About Lily and me. How she died and who I am. But I can tell you all about Annabelle."

And I did.

When the call was done, it was still early. Annabelle lay in the center of my heart. There was a peace from the knowing she was all right, that she was a part of a loving Amish family. They would take care of her. A flash of dread zipped through my mind. Briefly, I thought of Annabelle's Yoder mother. I didn't know her given name. I wished Olivia had written it. I thought of the lies and the grief for her dead child that must lay heavy on her heart. How could an Amish wife keep such a large secret from her husband for all those years. If he knew Annabelle was not his, that his own child had died and Annabelle was given to him in his baby's stead. He would have driven his wife with the child from his home. She would have been shunned. She was a strong woman, this Amish Mother Yoder, though I knew there must have been days when the quilt loomed large, darkening her days and consuming the sleep of many dark nights. Yet she kept Annabelle, Talitha, safe and loved. May God bless her, then, now, and forever.

Not wanting to dwell on gloomy possibilities, I turned my thought to the farm I knew, that had been mine, my family's. The cows would be making their journey to the barn for the first milking. In my head, I could see Maem and George's wife, Eunice, and their older daughters, straightening bedrooms and preparing the morning meal. I, also, saw George' older sons, the morning still dusky, already in the barn with Da and George doing daybreak chores. And the little ones, maybe energized by a good night's sleep or maybe grumpy from wanting to stay in the nest of their blankets, rubbing their eyes and crawling out of bed. I watched them in my head, straightening and smoothing the covers on their small cots, struggling with skirts and pins and kapps, and then running to feed the chickens and gather the eggs. Eager to fill their hungry, empty tummies, I pictured them scurrying through the first rays of light to the kitchen, proudly presenting the eggs to Maem and helping her with the simpler kitchen chores. A family, busy with joined lives even before the sun was full in the sky.

I could not be busy with them there, but I could do an Amish thing. I could make cookies, Maem's tasty sour cream sugar cookies, the recipe of which was burned on my mind. Adding tingling expectation to the songs and smiles of my soul, I searched the cupboards and refrigerator for flour and sugar and all the good things that made Maem's cookies special ... real butter, thick sour cream, plump raisins. I found them all.

I melted. I mixed. I dropped batter onto cookie sheets. I baked.

They were perfect. Six dozen cookies sitting on waxed paper, covering the whole of the kitchen counters. What could I do with so many cookies?

I could cool them and bag them. Then what?

I sat in a corner of the kitchen in an old wooden rocker, stained and scarred with the ravages of time. I kicked off my shoes and rubbed my bare feet over the softly tufted throw rug Olivia had designed and then, constructed together with latchet hook and yarn. I contemplated the fate of six dozen fat, round cookies. Who should receive them?

I got up, grabbed a fistful of the delicacies, went back to my seat. I ate one. Two. Three. Rocking away in my chair. They were delicious.

Brushing crumbs from my jeans, I stood, went into the dining room, took Olivia's thin, delicate, rose patterned plates from her china cabinet, brought them back to the kitchen and pushing cookies closer together, made space to lay the plates on the counter. Five plates. There should have been six. A plate for each dozen of cookies. But I had eaten three cookies and the rest of that dozen I would save for later enjoyment.

Then I covered the cookied plates with plastic wrap and lined them in a row. My face wrinkled in thought, I considered who might be the first recipient of the results of my Maem's delicious formula for the tastiest cookies ever conceived.

And I knew.

Smiling, I looked out the window. Full sun. Noon. Lunch time in the English world. Lunch time in the Amish world.

There was no answer when I knocked on Aaron's door. He had no wife or woman overseeing his needs as a man, so I had not really thought the door would be opened, but it was the place to start. I picked my way through his unkempt yard, got back in my car and began my hunt to discover the field where he would be working.

I found it. He was gleaning the last of the grapes in the few rows of vines he kept at the back of his pumpkin patch. I remembered he was particular to the juice of the grapes and perhaps he could find a kind Amish maiden who would boil them with sugar and store them in jars for him to enjoy when he chose. Whatever his thoughts, I doubt they were of an older English maiden about to accost him with a plate of cookies.

I knew he had seen me. The car drove neither invisible nor quiet. He might not look, at least not obviously, but I'm sure his eyes rolled in the direction of the road. I smiled and gave my head a quick, sharp nod. He couldn't avoid me. Unless he jumped on his wagon and lashed the old, gigantic workhorse to run swift. And that was unlikely. I thought I could probably run as swift as that ancient, overfed nag.

He didn't try. He kept snipping at the grapes.

"Hi, Aaron. It's me," I said, walking up to him. I held out the plate. "I brought you a treat to go with your lunch."

I heard the thud of a lush bunch of purple concords as it dropped into his bucket. Neither looking nor saying anything, he moved on to the next vine. I stepped forward with him.

"If you talk to me, I won't tell anyone," I said, nearly bumping into him as he stopped and reached into a scanty mass of gold and copper leaves. A few of them, dead and dry, fell as his hand brushed against them. "There aren't too many grapes left. I hope you find enough for a hefty supply of juice. Before a hard frost comes."

Still he said nothing.

"We have good memories, Aaron. You and I. We were friends."

I followed him up the row and back down the next. When we came near the wagon, I stepped away from him and, deciding this would not be a productive visit, left his small vineyard and walked to my car.

Disappointed, and a little angry, I considered feeding the cookies to the horse, so I changed my direction a bit and headed that way. The ground was hard and lumpy under my feet and as I came near the wagon, I stumbled on a loose clump of dirt and fell. I sensed from the hush of Aaron's boots clomping from vine to vine and the silence of the clip of his grape shears, he was aware of my dilemma and had stopped his picking. But he didn't come to help me.

I pulled myself up and went to the wagon. I heard his step again and the click of his shears. Ignoring the horse, though he snorted and the rich earthy scent of him was pleasant, I put the plate of cookies on the flatbed and turned to go to my car.

"I put the cookies on the wagon," I called out to him, as I walked to my vehicle. "I hope you enjoy them, Aaron. And I hope you don't break the plate. It is one of Olivia's good ones."

"Are you so English you gotta eat off pretty plates now?"

I heard his words and, surprised, stopped. Biting my lower lip, I looked back at him. He was turned away from me, his head lowered, his hands searching in the vines. I waited and watched him as he reached into the leaves and pulled out a handful of grapes, looked at them and threw them to the ground. Dead fruit, I thought, already dried by the cold.

"Hey, Aaron," I called. "God made the world pretty. Why can't a plate be pretty?"

"God made plates to be useful, not to be admired."

I could hardly hear his words; they fell into the vines and the leaves and the fruit. And still he would not look at me. Defiantly, I lifted the plate of cookies off the wagon and strutted across the ground to where he was gathering his leftover crop.

"Eat one of these," I commanded. "You like them. I remember. You ate them by the dozen in Maem's kitchen. So hot they were, fresh from the oven, they near burned your fingers. Eat them and be grateful."

He said nothing. Just kept moving and picking. Plopping grapes into his bucket.

"You already talked to me," I said. "The damage is done. You sinned, Aaron. You spoke to a shunned woman." I poked at his back, so angry was I. Such an arrogant man. "Are you damned, Aaron? Are you going to hell? Am I so evil, speaking to me will determine your eternal fate?"

Finally, he turned and looked at me. "The Bishop will know I sinned. I will tell him and I will repent."

"Talk to me, Aaron," I said, gently, regretting my harsh words, remembering words should be kind and helpful, remembering the words that should seep from an Amish heart. "I've missed you. I've missed my Amish friends. My Amish life."

He said nothing.

"Aaron, please. You already have to confess your transgression, that you spoke to shunned me, to the Bishop. What difference would more words make?"

"Don't you know? I shun you to help you. You need to see your evil ways and come back to the Amish ways." He shook his head. "Why are you so stubborn?"

"Aaron, do you really want to help me?" I said, ignoring his question.

"I am helping you."

"No, I mean more than shunning and shaming. Help me know how I can make things right."

"Tell the truth. All of it."

"Do you do that, Aaron?"

"Yes."

"To me? Will you tell the truth to me?"

"I don't lie. And I will not talk more with you. It's wrong. You're a shunned woman."

I hesitated, then held out the plate of cookies. "Here, take one of these. They're good. Maem's recipe." Surprising me, he succumbed and did take a cookie. And I thought, hoped, the sweetness of it would temper his reluctance to speak with me. I wasn't sure if I should say some gentle words to encourage him, and then ask the hard question, or if I should go directly to the heart of my questions and speak right away about Lily. I chose to go lightly. Though I cared most about learning of Lily, I sensed he would be instantly done with words if I spoke of her death too soon. For sure, it was wrong to maneuver him to speak of things he would rather keep hidden, but I had to know and I knew no other way.

"Aaron, do you remember when Rufus ran off and the twins cried and cried?" I asked hoping to soften him, bolster his ego with a memory of his heroism.

"Yeah. Your old dog. I found him. Out in the woods. All scuffed up and bleeding. Thought he was done for."

"But you brought him back. And fixed him."

"Yeah, I did." He smiled and bit into his cookie.

"Do you see Maem much? I miss her," I said, softly.

"Sometimes."

"And Violet?"

"She comes in sometimes and cleans my house. Sometimes, brings her cooking ... sometimes cooks in my kitchen."

"The girls loved you when they were little. Violet would remember that and help see to your needs."

"Yeah. Those were good years. Long time ago 'though. Times are different now. We're all grown."

"We were friends. Remember?"

I saw the cords in his neck tighten. He took another cookie from the plate, broke it in two. Looked at it for a long moment, then put it back on the plate, and looked hard at me.

"I wanted to marry you," he said.

"I couldn't. I wanted to, Aaron. I really did. But I couldn't."

"Why not?"

"Your maem didn't like me."

"So?"

"I can't tell you. It's too big," I said, thinking of her hateful words and mean tricks, artfully hidden from Aaron, cleverly aimed at me. She wanted no one near Aaron but herself. I couldn't tell him that. Even dead, she was his maem.

"So *you* can't answer questions, but *I* should," Aaron said. Then he shrugged his shoulders and walked, with heavy step, towards the end of the row. His back was towards me. I couldn't see his face.

"She said she would kill herself if I married you," I called after him.

He stopped, lowered his head. He didn't turn to look at me.

"I'm sorry, Aaron, I loved you and I wanted to marry you, but I couldn't let her commit such a sin."

"She wouldn't have done that." He turned and looked at me.

I said nothing. I had told him the truth, but it had not brought me closer to him. I sighed. He would tell me nothing of Lily now. It would be useless to ask him. I looked at him with resignation and sorrow. Silently, I watched him step closer to me. I didn't like the look in his eyes.

"I will say this now and then I am done with you." He stood before me and it was not a friend staring at me. It was a man, at that moment, blind with anger.

"Aaron," I said, pleading.

He held up his hand to stop me.

"I don't know you. You're dead," he said, his lips pulled in a tight, thin line. "And your mouth spills lies."

"It does not," I said.

"You left the Amish way. The right way. You broke God's law. He'll punish you. You turned from Him. You're not His anymore."

"He is still my God, Aaron. My precious Lord and Savior. I am His," I said softly.

"*He is not.*"

"How can you be so hard? Where have you gone, Aaron. I don't know you."

He took the plate of cookies from my hand and threw it to the ground. The earth soaked in the sound of it breaking. I couldn't hear it, but I saw the shattered pieces … the flowers, the fragments of gold rim. Putting my hand over my mouth, I looked up. Aaron was gone. Back into the vineyard.

The cookies were spread on the ground. Sweet sugar cookies. Fodder for the wild ones. I picked up the pieces of Olivia's plate and took them with me to the car.

I had not asked him about Lily.

On the way home, my phone rang. My hands still trembling, my heart aching, I didn't want to answer it, but, reluctantly, I did.

"Cora, it's Harriet here. Are you far from the restaurant?"

"Harriet, what's wrong?"

"Are you near?"

"Not far. Coming down the hill into Wander Lane."

"You need to come here. Right away."

"What's wrong?" I repeated.

"Just come."

Chapter Seventeen

I t was only a mile down the hill to the village. But each yard, each foot, each inch seemed to be its own separate mile. And although the car's speedometer showed a number well above the mandated speed limit, it felt as if its wheels were running on glue.

Parking in front of the restaurant, I shuddered, dreading what waited inside the building. Through the car window, I saw Harriet waiting by the door. I got out and hurried to her.

"Harriet?" I said, as she took my arm and led me in.

"It's all right. We need to hurry. You're not gonna git much time, but I think you need to be a little prepared," she said, walking me to a corner of the kitchen. There was activity all around me, blurry, a hazy mass of movement. Swiping it all to oblivion, I focused on Harriet.

"This is what it is, Sweetie," Harriet said, facing me, placing her hands on my arms, holding them tight. Her eyes locked into mine. "I want you to listen and not be alarmed. Do you understand?"

"I'm a big girl, Harriet. I can handle whatever it is."

"Your maem is here."

I stiffened in her grasp, bent my head to her words.

"She ain't got much time. Your Da thinks she is shoppin' for material. She wants to talk with you."

I gasped.

"She's in the supply room."

I tugged at her hold. She needed to let go. Maem was in the restaurant, through the near doorway, waiting for me. But Harriet held tight.

"Wait," she said. "Your maem is frightened. This is a big thing she's doin'. Against all she's believed, all she's been taught. You be gentle. You hear? You be gentle."

I nodded. "Please, let me go."

Harriet stepped away and I went into the storage room.

There was a small window in the back of the room, smeared with the dirt and fingerprints of years. The sun barely shone through. Her back to me, Maem was looking through the glass. I think she wasn't seeing whatever distorted scene was beyond the window. Her stance was still; her back, straight. I think she was looking at visions from her heart.

"Maem," I said, tentatively, softly, just loud enough for her to hear.

She turned and looked at me. I could see the sorrow in her eyes, eyes too small to hold the tears that came from the years of missing a child ... two children ... one shunned, another dead. Then she lifted her arms around her chest, hugged herself and bowing her head, rocked her body. And I heard her sobs.

I stood for a moment unable to move, then went to her and held her, so tight did I hold her. And I rocked with her. And shed tears, joy mixed with pain, with her. For long moments. Moments that were lost years disappearing in the comfort of tangible love.

Stepping back from her, I took her face in my hands and tenderly rubbed my thumbs over her tears.

"It is so good to see you, to touch you" I said, my own eyes full as they looked into hers. "I have missed you so very much."

Maem stroked her hands over my hair, then moved them down to caress my cheeks.

"Your skin has wrinkled," she said, smiling wistfully, "but it was not an Amish sun falling on Amish fields that dried it."

"No, Maem, nor was it the English sun. Away from the Amish, most of my days have been spent in electric- lit rooms. No, Maem, It was not the sun, neither English nor Amish, 'though, sometimes, I wish it was the brilliance of that blazing star, beautiful and real, falling on grass and crops and soil, that caused the furrows in my face. But, no, Maem, it was simply the passing of years that aged me."

"Come, sit over there," Maem said, nodding towards boxes stacked on the floor. "They make good chairs for sitting."

We sat and Maem drew my hand into her lap and held it there. I could not remember a time since I was a little girl she had touched me with such affection. I drew in my breath and waited. When she took her other hand and brought it to cover ours laced together on her skirt, I looked down at our hands, then up at her face. She was looking down at them, too.

"I have always loved you," she said, looking up. "It was not my way to show my feelings with touches or words. I'm sorry for that. I hope I've learned better. How can one know love if it is not shown?"

I thought of the little girl I had seen from my car, running to Maem with a cane. And Maem, with her arm full of flowers, smiling at the little girl, bending and kissing her head.

"There are many ways to show love, Maem. And you did. I never felt unloved by you. Or Da. We were a good family ... good to each other. There was love."

"You've been close to my heart, a part of my heart, since the first moment I knew you were growing in my body. It is the same for all my children ... you, Willie, George, Samson, Harry, Violet, Lily. You're all entwined inside me. Yes, even Lily." She squeezed my hand and sighed. "I know we are to forget the dead and let them go, but I can't. I don't want to. There's a part of Lily still living within me," she said, her eyes full. "I know your pain. I know your hurt. Your loss. I felt your pain when the Bishop wouldn't let me tell you of her death, and it was an outsider that gave you the news. An Englisher. My heart was hurting at the same time yours was. I wanted to tell you. I wanted you walking, with me, up the burial hill, crying, with me, the tears we weren't allowed to show, the tears we hid in our ravaged hearts. It was wrong. If I had a chance to do it again, I would throw myself over her grave and cry my pain into every Amish ear close enough to hear." Maem paused. Lifting her hand from my mine, she pushed it against her chest. I saw her bosom heave beneath her dress.

"And if I had a chance to do it again," she said, her eyes focused on mine, "I would grab you, all those years ago, and drag you, baby and all, back up the hill and take you in and scream my rejoicing over a new life born on this earth. I would shout loud enough that every Amish brother and sister could hear my joy. "All those years. Those wasted years. So I do know your pain, dear Cora. I've felt it fierce." She pounded her fist against her heart. "It's still here."

I drew in my breath. I saw a piece of my mother I had not known.

"The pain is still here," I heard her words repeated. "But it's covered now with an awareness and gratitude for the blessings God showered upon me by putting my beloved one, my Lily, in my life to enjoy and remember, and by giving me a strong and beautiful daughter who did the right and loving thing 'though everyone condemned her for it. I am proud of you, Cora. I miss you more than I can say, but I am proud of you."

Sliding my body to the edge of the box I sat on, I took my hands from my maem's lap and lifted my arms to embrace her. She leaned her head against me and for a moment, her body, frail and dependent, nestled into mine. And for that moment, I was the mother; she, the child.

"Maem," I whispered into her hair.

She moved her head across the surface of my chest and straightened her back. Looking into her face, I could see there, the strength and wisdom of women who endured.

"Harriet said we haven't much time. Da will be thinking your task should be done. He will be wanting you to be making his supper."

"For sure, he will," she said, nodding her head. "But this may be the only time I will be free to talk with you, so we have to say all the words that need to be said. We have to say them now."

"Da will angry."

"You're right. And I will tell him I saw you and talked with you. And he'll have to decide what he does with that information."

"Will he go to Bishop Herrfort?"

"Perhaps. He is Amish. He follows the rules ... not just with his head, but with his heart, too. He's a good man. Sometimes obeying hurts him. But he does what he thinks, and for him, what he knows is right. You can't fault a man for being true to his way of life."

"Will you tell him what we say to one another?"

"I will only tell him you are well and beautiful."

"Maem," I looked at her, my eyes pleading, "you will be shunned."

"It's likely." She smiled. "It is but a little punishment for seeing you. For hearing your voice. For touching my child, and holding her, smelling her, feeling her breath whisper against my skin. When I am living as shunned and they are living as if I'm not there, I will be remembering you. And so, my child, if you have words you should say, I have the time to hear them."

"I have hard things to ask."

"Ask them," she said, and she stiffened her back even straighter.

"I need to know about Lily's death."

"I'll tell you what I can. What is it you want to know?"

"Everything. How did she die? Where did she die? Why did she die?"

"Oh, Cora." Maem's head dropped and she shook it slowly. Then she got up and went to the window, looked out through the murky glass, and shook her head again.

I knew her eyes were seeing Lily. I wanted to tell her to forget my questions. To let Lily stay safe and whole and happy in heaven. To not go back to the time of sorrow and death. Pain. Grief that is lonely and tears that go deep into the soul.

She began to speak. She didn't turn to look at me. Not then. She spoke to the pictures she saw on the other side of the glass.

"Lily died in Wander Creek. At night. Alone. Noone knew why she was there. Perhaps, sleepwalking. I would rather think, unable to sleep, she walked in the moonlight gathering the wild flowers, the buttercups and daisies the cows had missed in their search for the sweet, succulent grasses." She turned and looked at me. "I know that's probably not so, but it's what I like to think."

"What do you think really was so?" My heart was breaking from making her look deeper into her soul for the truth she was trying to hide from herself.

She bit her lip and put her hands over her face. Then she dropped her hands and stood tall.

"I think she was meeting someone. A boy. Not a good boy. She was different after you left. Angry. You can't hide that from a mother. From a father, yes. From a mother, no. There isn't much you can hide from a mother." She tilted her head and stared at me. "There isn't much you can hide from a mother," she said, again.

"What are you saying?"

"The night you left with the baby, I sensed there was something wrong. When you girls decided that midmorning to clean Mrs. Beachy's house, I didn't question or argue with you. It was a thoughtful thing to do. I knew she was gone to her cousins for some respite care, and I thought a clean house would be a good thing she would find when she got back, but the rags you brought back to our house were too clean. Wet. Soaked spotless. And your buckets scrubbed. It was your custom to bring them back here to be washed. The three of you were more tired than you should have been. So sweaty. Your faces lines with exhaustion. So pale. And Lily, wanting to sleep, not wanting supper. It wasn't right. You weren't strangers to hard work. There should have been more energy left in you."

Maem stepped from the window and I helped her to sit back on the box. She sat and wiped her eyes.

"I let her go up to bed without eating. You and Violet ate. Sparingly. After supper, I excused you from cleaning the kitchen. Da didn't think that was right, but he allowed it." She paused, clasped her hands together on her lap, leaned forward.

"Maem," I said, quietly, "do you want to stop?"

She shook her head and continued speaking.

"When we were all in bed and Da and the boys asleep, I got up and went to your room. Mothers don't sleep well when they sense their children are in trouble. I didn't carry a lamp; I knew where to step. Every board on that floor, their positions and their quirks were sealed inside my eyes. I pushed your door. It wasn't latched, and I stepped in. There was little light from the window. The clouds were thick that night, but my eyes could see shapes and, as my sight adjusted to the dark, the shapes formed familiar patterns." She paused, sighed. "So many nights, I had stood by that door, cracked open just a little, and watched my girls sleeping." She smiled. "Now there are little *kins-kind*, granddaughters, filling those beds."

"What did you see that night?"

"I went and bent over Lily. She was the one who worried me most. She had been so shaky and pale in the kitchen. When I touched her cheek, it was clammy. Then heard Violet whisper, so I went to her. *Lily is just tired*, she said. *She's having a hard time this month with the bleeding.*"

Rising and moving to the windowed wall, lined with shelving packed with rows of empty mason jars, Maem stroked their slippery glass surface.

"So clean," she said. "Shiny. Ready to be filled with good things. Do you think our hearts are like that, Cora?"

"I think there are many that are not," I said.

"So sad. Is that not so sad?"

"That's why we have Jesus," I answered, softly. "To shine hearts, wash them clean and fill them with good things ... love, comfort, peace."

"*Yeah*, yes."

"Is he in your heart, Maem?"

She turned from the mason jars and looked at me. "How else could I live?"

"What else did you see?" I asked, quietly.

"I thought I saw you in your bed by the window, so covered in quilts that your head didn't show. I started to go to you, but Violet called me to her bed. *Come sit with me, Maem. I'm having a hard time sleeping.* So I did. I went and sat on the edge of her bed and I held her hand and I asked her to tell me what had happened at the Beachy house, why you all were so weary. I sat there a while, 'till I thought she was sleeping. Then I rose to go to you again, to touch your face and ask God to watch over you this strange night. But as I bent to give Violet a blessing before I left her, I heard her whisper in my ear, *I love you, Maem, but I think I will sleep better, if you're out of the room.*"

"So you left and didn't check on me," I said.

"I did. I left the room." She put her hands over her face and rubbed her forehead, then walked over to the window, looked out. "The clouds are gathering. I think it might rain. Da's in the fields."

"If it rains, he'll work in the barn and see the buggy is gone too long to buy just a piece of fabric. Perhaps, you should go," I said.

"No. I told you I will tell him of this visit. He won't be worried if I am late." She smiled, ruefully. "Amish men don't show worry. I'm not even sure they even feel it. But he will want to know why."

"You're just feeling maudlin, Maem. He loves you and worries about you. It's sad he is not able to show you. Anyway, you still have time to change your mind. You don't *have* to tell him you saw me. You know he won't like what you say and you'll have to confess and repent if you tell."

I won't lie to him. Not about this. This I will confess to him ... that I talked with you, but I will not repent. I'll accept the shunning; it's our way. But my heart knows I am not sinning and I will not repent." Repeating her declaration, her words spoke firm. "And, maybe, I'll tell him I'm going talk with you again ... maybe I won't tell him that."

Pausing, she screwed up her face and I knew she had more to say. I waited while she pleated the front of her skirt, her fingers moving slowly and deliberately, making herself ready to speak.

"There is more to tell you."

"I'm listening."

"In the morning when Bishop Herrfort came to our house, when he declared his condemning statements, I understood why Violet didn't want me to go to your bed. You weren't there. You were off in the village giving away a baby."

'Though I knew she didn't mean to hurt me, I cringed at her words.

"What I thought was you in that bed," she continued, "was a bundle of blankets shaped like a body. And it all came together in my head. Why you all were so tired. It was because there had been a baby born at the Beachy house and that same night you, Cora, had taken that baby to the village to hide the knowledge of its birth from the community."

"You're right. There was a baby born at the Beachy house."

"There is more."

I watched her draw a deep breath, let it out slowly. I saw the struggle in her face to keep herself strong. Then, for a moment, she dropped her head into her hands and I witnessed a shudder sweep through her body. She straightened. There was resolution in her demeanor. I waited.

There is more," she repeated. "I am a mother now and I was a mother then. That morning when the Bishop came to the door and asked his questions and you admitted you were the one that walked the infant down the hill to Olivia's house and left the child there, I was stunned. And then I realized exactly what had happened."

Again, she stopped, drew in her breath. My maem was a gentle woman, but I knew the magnitude of might within her.

"I knew you were my strong child, the daughter that could take charge of a bad situation and make it bearable." She bit her lip and I watched her battle the tears that threatened to fall. She won. Her voice did not falter.

"'Though vivacious and full of life, Lily was the weak one, always succumbing to pleasure, doing before thinking. And that night, when I went into your room, she was the sick one. And Violet had said Lily was bleeding. And, oh, Cora, that morning, while Bishop Herrfort was telling us an Amish woman had been seen carrying a bundle down the road, Lily was upstairs, too sick to come down from her bed."

"And Violet, dear Violet," Maem's words were falling faster and faster, "the sweet child, the peacemaker, the fixer, was the one who tried, the best way she knew how, to keep the Bishop and me, from knowing your secrets. And then, there was you, confessing. And Violet, holding onto my skirt and crying. And even now, older and feistier, she has never told what truly happened that day. She thinks I don't know."

"And what is it you do know, Maem?" I asked, dreading her answer.

"I know that you are not Annabelle's mother."

Bending my body, I bowed my head into my hands and wept. Through the harsh, sharp memories surging, gushing through my head, I heard Maem's footsteps, and then, felt her arm slide around me, pull me to her.

"You knew," I said, cradled against the soft fabric of her dress, the familiar scent of her filling me.

"I knew," she said, softly.

I drew away from her and she sat, still holding my hand.

"Why didn't you tell Bishop Herrfort?"

"You were my children. I had to decide. You had told him you took the baby to the village. I knew you were strong and Lily was not. So, I said nothing."

"But the rules. You lied. He asked what you knew. You said you knew nothing."

"Bishop Herrfort is not God. And it is God I answer to."

"But weren't you afraid he would know you were not telling the truth? The Bishop is stern. He is smart. Discerning. If he found out, perhaps even if he perceived deception, he would admonish you before all the brothers and sisters. Weren't you afraid?" I asked again.

"Afraid of what? Of hell? Of shunning? None of the Amish, not even Herrfort, is God. Not one of them can name the place of my eternal home. God, alone, will judge me. Not them. God. He, alone, will determine my fate. And shunning is as nothing compared to protecting Lily."

All those years ago and all the years that followed, I had been wrong. On that fateful morning when I did not speak truth, when I did not tell the baby was Lily's, when I thought if Maem knew the truth, she would shun us all ... Lily, Violet, me, I was wrong. Maem would not have chosen the rules; she would have chosen her daughters. She would have chosen her God, His love. And she never did tell what she knew ... not to Bishop Herrfort, not to me or Lily or Violet, not to Da. Until now.

"You're strong," I said to her, reaching and gently touching her cheek, wiping her tears.

"Perhaps, but not strong enough to walk away from all of this. the rules, the shunning, the Way. But I wanted more for you. You were different. I didn't want you to be molded so firm you couldn't dream ... or do."

"You gave me freedom."

"I hope I did that." She tilted her head to touch mine.

"Did you ever want that dream, too?" I asked.

"Many times," she said into my hair.

"Still?"

"Occasionally."

"How can you live here with those thoughts?"

"I am Amish. Deep in my heart, I am Amish."

After Maem left, I went to a corner table and sat down. Bailey came over and asked me if I wanted anything. I shook my head, no.

"You sure. It's early, but Harriet's got the dinner stuff ready. I can get you a plate. She's got pork chops. They're good."

"Just water," I said. "I'm really not hungry."

"Suite yourself," she said, shrugging and wiping her nose with her finger. She held it up and looked at it. "Make-up. Cheap stuff. Not worth the money." Wrinkling her nose, she looked at me. "You want me to go get Harriet?"

"No."

She raised one eyebrow, tilted her head and shrugged, again. "Up to you."

Before Maem left, I had checked the dining area. There was no one in the eating room, except Bailey. No customers. No one to see Maem and me together. No one to tell the Bishop of Maem's transgression. So I walked with her through the dining room to the front door. We stood for a moment, eyes locked on each other. There were tears and small smiles. Bittersweet. Regretting the past separation had been so long; the secrets, so entrenched. Grateful to be one again, mother and daughter.

"I can't walk out with you," I said. "If a brother or sister saw us together, you would certainly be shunned."

"For sure," Maem said, drolly.

"I hope, if you tell Da where you have been this afternoon, he will let it be and neither tell the Bishop nor turn his silence on you."

"Shun me?"

"It is a harsh word."

"He will do what he thinks is right," she said squeezing my hand. "And I'll be all right with that." Maem reached with her other hand

and ran her fingers over the side of my face. Tenderly. Then she lifted her hand and stroked my hair. She smiled and I could see a touch of sadness in it.

"It nearly reached your waist," she said. "I am glad I talked with you, dear child. I am not sorry. Whatever happens, I am not sorry."

"Perhaps, again?" I said.

"Perhaps."

She opened the door and stepped into the rain. It was pouring water, swift and thick, from the sky.

"Maem," I called, stepping over the threshold, ignoring the possible consequences. "Is your buggy far? I can drive you to it."

She did not turn. I don't think she heard me. Perhaps the beat of the rain was too loud. Perhaps she was afraid if she answered, she would ask me to come back with her. 'Though she wanted me to live a life of choice, inside her heart I know she cried for me to return, in black dress, to her home. But the strength that was in me was inherited from her. Her gentle, quiet strength. She would do what she deemed right for me, her firstborn child. And so would I.

I stood by the door and watched her walk away. When I could see her no more, I found a far table and asked Bailey for water. She left to get it. I sat and waited, edgy and worried about Maem, her drive in the rain and the reception Da would give her, so I went back to the door, put my arm out into the rain and felts it cold, piercing wet. I needed to be sure she was safe.

"Come back in, Cora. Out of the rain." I heard a voice behind me, felt a hand on my arm drawing me back into the room. Harriet's voice. Harriet's hand.

"She'll be wet. I don't want her to get sick from the damp," I said, fighting tears, tears flowing upwards from my hurting heart. Tears flooding my eyes. Tired tears, worn out from so much hammering at my soul.

"Are you all right?" Harriet said, gently.

"I am joyful," I said, as the tears I struggled to keep within, escaped.

"Well, you certainly ain't lookin' that way," Harriet said, her voice firm and solid.

"Inside I am smiling. I saw Maem. I talked with her. And it was wonderful. But I have to go now," I said, struggling against Harriet's hold. "I need to make sure she got to the buggy and she is all right."

"Honey, she ain't sugar and she won't melt and besides that, she's driven that horse and buggy over roads in weather ten times worse than this."

"Probably," I said half-smiling. "But, I'll feel better if I know that, if I see the buggy wheeling down the road. I promise I'll follow her just a little way. And I'll keep hidden. She won't know."

"You takin' your car?"

"Yes."

"It's kinda hard to hide a car on a lonely, back country road. I think it's a pretty good guess she'll know you're behind her ... now git yourself over to the table and I'll bring you some food."

"I'm not hungry."

"Shoofly pie?"

"I don't think so."

"We can talk."

"I think I need to be thinking rather than talking. And I think I want to be going home."

Harriet nodded and patted me on the back.

"You be needing anything, you call. Okay?"

"Okay." I kissed her cheek, left, got in my car and went home, to Dianna's house, the house I lived in ... for now.

When I got home, I drove the car into the garage, made a cup of hot chocolate, took it, along with a thick, fuzzy blanket to huddle in, and went out to the porch. Pushing my feet in simple rhythm, I rocked in one of Dianna's inherited, colonial-hued wooden chairs while the rain poured heavy on the porch roof. Nestled in the soothing, lingering scent of Olivia buried deep in her old heavy blanket, I sealed every work Maem had said into memory. I pictured her at home, flaming the stove, cooking, sitting with the family, eating the food she had fixed. Praying first. All heads bent while Da spoke the words. And I remembered Maem's words. *I am Amish. Deep in my heart, I am Amish.*

The air grew colder; the rain, harsher. When it got too hard to deceive the damp and my bones declared it the winner, when I could no longer conquer the need for dry air, I gathered my cup and my blanket and went into the house. So weary, I determined it was time to go to bed and let sleep wash over me and erase all thought.

Before I went to my room, I took my phone from my pocket and called Daniel. He didn't answer. It was a good thing for, in my want for family, I think I would have told him I had decided. I think I would have told him I was Amish. But in that place where God dwells within, far down in the trenches of my soul, was the definite answer and I had not yet reached far enough to grab it and know it and be it. I could not truthfully echo Maem's words ... *I am Amish.*

Chapter Eighteen

The next few days, it rained. It was a drizzly rain, an energy-draining rain. I didn't know if Maem caught cold driving her buggy home in the nasty weather, but I do know, I got sick. Most likely from throwing caution and wisdom to the wind and sitting on a dank and chilly porch for too many hours, for I woke the next morning with a miserable, raspy throat, an evil stuffy nose, and a pounding head.

That morning, Dianna called me. She had a few moments to fill before leaving for work and wanted to chat. She still had not decided what she would do about the house. Retirement loomed. Not yet pressuring. But soon. She thought she might like to go traveling. If she could afford it, she thought it would be interesting to enroll in one of those retreat programs where you could go to a cabin in dense woods and, living in the midst of enlightening nature, write your memoirs. Reconsidering, she thought it might be more appealing to rove the oceans on luxury liners, choose a likely island and spend romantic months among the natives.

"I think you caught my indecisive bug," I said, as she rambled on sharing her fanciful thoughts.

"That could be," she agreed. "Only I *know* who I am."

"Do you?" I asked, unfairly resenting the implied implication that I was uncertain of who *I* was … English or Amish. And I did not want to admit, either to her or to myself, that she was right. "Then tell me," I continued, "… are you a writer or a traveler or an old home body, or an island hopper, or just a plain dreamer?"

"Dreamers aren't plain. They have beautiful thoughts of majestic wonders."

"Even serial killers?" I said, beginning to be just a trifle irritated. "They dream."

"They don't count. They're nightmarers, not dreamers."

"That's true," I said, making an effort to stay focused, "You really don't want to live in this house, do you?"

"I don't think so." There was a pause in our conversation. "Do you?"

I hesitated before answering. She was forcing my poor, aching head to think. "It has been a good place for me to find refuge. With Olivia's aura still permeating the house, it reeks of good character. And there is a glow in my heart because it was hers. But forever? No, I don't want to live here forever. Though for a while longer. Until my life is resolved." And until I am well, I thought, sniffing.

"Probably until you decide to go back to the city or choose to put on a black dress and bonnet," Dianna stated.

"Probably. And until I know Lily is safe in heaven."

"How are you going to know that?"

"I'm not sure."

"I don't like to say this," Dianna said, "but you don't seem to be making much headway in that department."

"I know that," I said, sighing.

"Maybe you should give up."

"Maybe I should take a little nap so I can think a little better," I said. She took the hint.

"Sorry. I'll talk to you when you finally get healthier and become human."

"Thank you."

"Goodbye ... and, oh, by the way, Cora, a little prayer might put you in a better mood."

I put my phone down gently. Dianna was right. I did need to pray. Sometimes, it seems the closeness to Jesus slips away. And I begin to feel empty of His peace. That's when someone's words, or some happening, or a whisper from the Holy Spirit, reminds me of my need to go to Him and listen, with my heart, to His wisdom and to feel the embrace of His love.

And, as Dianna said, I was not progressing in my quest to discover the reason for Lily's death. I knew it was judged an accident, but my mind wouldn't accept that. I couldn't explain my feelings, but whether they were from an inability to think Lily could die so young and so purposelessly, or if it was the Holy Spirit nudging me to action, I knew it was more than an unexpected or unintended happening. And I also intuited the Lily I knew, my Lily, would never have jumped in a creek and held herself down in the water long enough to stop breathing. She never would have committed suicide.

Dear Jesus, help me think straight. Please guide me to truth and give me the wisdom to know what to do with it when I find it.

I slipped down into warm sheets and pulled Olivia's purchased Amish quilts over me. Snuggled safe in squares and triangles stitched together in patterned beauty, I slept.

Waking, I sat up in bed. The room didn't spin, my body was steady, and the lamp and the brush on my dresser, the pictures on the wall, the piles of unwashed clothing on the floor were all clear and sharp-edged. It was over. I was well.

Gathering up used tissues, empty cough drop wrappers, and sticky paper plates, I went into the bathroom, tossed the gruesome garbage in the wastebasket, shed my sweat-sick night clothes, and slid my body into the tub. Gilding my body with slippery, sweet-smelling soap, I scrubbed and scrubbed 'till my skin glistened with a soft, rosy hue. Next was my hair, lank and oily and feeling as if little critters had dug tiny homes within the stringy clumps of my crummy locks. I stood in the tub and leaning my head under the shower spout, poured luxuriously scented shampoo into the soaked wet of it. I dug my fingers into the mass of suds and rubbed them round and round. And then, I stepped out of the stall wonderfully, gloriously, magnificently clean.

I dressed. I ate. I was completely me, again.

Munching toast crusts and mulling over the plans for that day, I walked to the front door and looked through the glass oval inset. Thoughts coming together, I decided it was time to address the issue of Lily and conquer it. Easy words. Difficult execution. Logically the first person to talk with should be Violet. As Lily's close sister, she would know best Lily's last days … her moods, the people she had seen, the places she had been. Hopefully, the secrets she had confided.

But I didn't know how to contact Violet. Always before she had contacted me and our last meeting had not ended in a manner that would suggest there would me more. I, also, didn't know if I would see Maem again. I hoped it would be so, but, even then, I would not be able to speak of Lily's death. Although she had gone against the Ordnung once, it would be difficult to ask her to talk of Lily again. It was against her teachings to speak of the dead and, even greater, would be the anguish such talk would bring to her heart. She had told me, with aching heart, her gut feeling was that Lily had met a boy that night. She seemed not to know more than that. And it would not be fair to ask her more, to ask her to break the silences commanded by The Way would not be easy for her.

I left the front of the house, went into the kitchen, and poured another cup of coffee. I took it into the parlor and sat in Olivia's chair, the same flowered chair she had sat in when I held Annabelle out to her. Perhaps a residue of her wisdom had soaked into its cushions and maybe, I could garner a measure of it. Wishful thinking, but it lent a measure of imagined hope. Slowly sipping my coffee, I leaned back, closed my eyes and willed my brain to concentrate.

There was the sheriff to consider. An instinctive bit of perception nagged at me. Innately, I knew he had some knowledge relating to her death. I didn't deem him a man of honesty. But still, he might offer an indicator of truth. An arrogant man, in an effort to appear more than he was, he might speak hints signifying he knew of what had truly happened to Lily. Or at least, inadvertently, drop clues.

And there was Harriet. It seemed she always knew all, the operative word being, seemed. I wasn't sure. And as I thought of Harriet, I remembered she had told me Bishop Herrfort was the sheriff's brother-in-law. And thinking back further, I remembered the many times the sheriff came into the community to speak with the bishop, usually about the *Rumspringa,* running-around, boys and their antics, but now I reasoned many of those times could have been social and gossip exchange encounters. Lily, Annabelle, and myself could have, at times, been paramount in their discussions. Perhaps it was the sheriff I should confront. He was the easiest available prospect.

I changed my clothes from soft, many times washed jeans and baggy sweater to black sharp creased dress pants, simple white tee and dark tan blazer. That day the only jewelry I wore was the gold cross ever present around my neck, a gift from Daniel, and small gold hoops in my ears ... apparel that reflected purpose, determination, no nonsense. Looking in the mirror, I stood straight, smiled and nodded. I would look pretty classy in his messy office.

Grabbing my purse, stuffing my feet into sensible clogs, I let myself out of the house and walked to the sheriff's office.

By the time I reached his building, my shoes were stained from the splash of puddles and the cling of soggy leaves that covering the sidewalk. Lamenting the tainting of my spotless appearance, I thought Lowell Parker would probably not look down that far. I wasn't so sure of his secretary. Tillie. I remembered she didn't like that name. I would avoid calling her that.

The first thing I noticed when I stepped into the station were the two large pictures between the door facing me. They had previously been marvelous Van Gogh paintings. Now the spaces were covered with great, huge posters. One, a circus; the other, Cinderella dancing in front of a lovely, pink, sparkling castle. Turning my head, I looked at Tillie.

She lifted her left eyebrow and smiled. "He didn't give me the day off for my daughter's birthday," she said. "They're deserved retribution."

"Is he in?" I asked, smiling.

"He is," she said. "you can go right in. "I'll tell him you're here … in a minute." She motioned me to go through the door.

I knew I would be in his office before she announced my presence. Sometimes, payback is pleasurable … and deserved. Nevertheless, I didn't care to be a part of it, nor did I want to antagonize the sheriff. So walking slowly to his office, I waited a moment, then knocked, lightly and briefly, on his door before I went in.

He looked up, startled. At the same moment a buzzer sounded. I had not waited long enough. He didn't respond to the noise and, appearing annoyed, looked up at me. As I had feared, Tillie's antics had compounded his natural reluctance to receive me. There was little welcome showing on his face.

"Looks like I'm still being punished for expecting certain staff people to work when they're supposed to," He said, sarcastically, glancing at the buzzer. "And what do you want?"

"Hello, Mr. Parker," I said.

"Sheriff Parker."

"*Sheriff* Parker," I agreed. "And again, I see there is no chair to sit on," I said, looking around. "Shall I empty one?"

"How long do you intend to stay?"

"Only until you answer my questions."

"No point then in dismantling my office. Leave the papers where they are, ask your questions, I'll answer them if I can, and then you can walk right back out." He shrugged and swiped his arm across the room. "Obviously, you can see I'm busy and don't have time for stuff that is over and done with."

"You mean Lily's death," I said, stacking and removing the papers strewn on the chair across from him. I placed them on his desk. "I think, probably, you have time for a citizen's legitimate concerns."

"Oh, are you a citizen now?"

"Temporarily," I said, sitting.

"Okay," he sighed. "What are your questions?"

"Who found Lily's body?" I said, matching his brevity.

"Your father," he said, and one side of his lip lifted, ever so slightly, as if he were the victor, almost pleasured, to tell me of something that would take me down a peg. And it did.

I drew in a deep breath, but said nothing.

"You didn't know that?" he asked, his face expressionless, but a shadow of satisfaction lingered.

"No," I said. "I didn't know that." Lifting my arms, I rubbed the sides of my forehead. Somehow, I had never envisioned my father finding Lily, and a picture of him pulling her from the water, looking at her face and knowing there was no life behind it, crept behind my eyes to settle in the deep recesses of my mind.

"He carried her back up to the house and sent one of boys to get the Bishop," the sheriff continued, adding to my vision.

I couldn't speak. Though he appeared smug and nonchalant, there was an undercurrent of reluctant compassion in Sheriff Parker's voice. I was grateful for that. Yet, I couldn't respond. Of course, Da would take Lily to the house, to Maem and the others and though they would not show their grief to the brethren, they would have their own moments of shared mourning. And I had not been there. To mourn with them, to wash Lily and dress her for the grave, to walk up the hill with Da and Maem and Violet and the brothers, to see the hole fill with dirt and Lily's body.

"Cora?"

I looked up.

"What else?" He was back to business.

"Did you do an investigation?"

"We asked a few questions." He sighed. "Okay, Cora, bottom line, what's the big question? What is it you really want to know?"

"Everything."

"And what is everything?"

"What time did she die? Was anyone with her? Did she have a note tucked in her dress? Who was the last to see her?" I wiped the tears on my cheeks and looked at him, defiantly. "Was there anyone who would have wanted her gone ... dead?"

"Whoa, there, Cora. Are you asking if she was killed?"

"I don't know."

"The Amish are a peaceful people, Cora. You know that. The Amish don't murder."

"The Amish are *people*. Mostly peaceful. But with every emotion every person has. How can you think there could not be anger or hate or revenge in an Amish soul. The Amish are human."

"You don't really think that. You think an Amish man could be violent enough to kill?"

"Don't you?" I threw the words back at him.

"I don't know." He laughed. "But I was being a bit factitious when I said they're a peaceful bunch. I should of said, they're mostly peaceful. So, if you're asking if she was killed, my honest answer would be ... who knows?"

"If anybody knows, it would be you."

"Or the killer. He would know." He paused. "But you don't really think she was killed, do you?"

I looked at him, a million thoughts and feeling rumbling through my head. Fear she had been murdered. Fear she had killed herself. Reluctant hope it had been murder instead of suicide for if she had killed herself, there was no hope she would be in heaven now. Guilt for thinking those thoughts. Sorrow she was gone ... dead. Regret I had not answered the Bishop's questions with the truth. If I had, she would have been shunned, but the shunning would have ended long ago. Ashamed for even considering a brother or sister of the brethren could hurt one of the their own.

"No one killed her, Cora. I've never known an Amish man to murder," the sheriff said.

Hearing a note of sympathy, perhaps a shade of condescending, but, still, an indicator he might reason with me, I bent my head, rubbed the back of my neck and tried to concentrate.

"I've heard she was seeing Jacob Yoder," I said, remembering either Harriet or Violet had mentioned him.

"All the girls were dating somebody at one time or another. And sometimes it was Jacob they were dating. Don't mean nothin'."

"But it might. She had to be out for some reason. Amish girls don't go out after dark for no reason. Unless it is Sunday night singing. And even then, it's no secret who they leave with."

"You said it yourself. The Amish are human."

"Was she dating Jacob Yoder?"

"Dunno."

"Did you question him?" Furrowing my forehead, I leaned towards him,

"No need." He picked up a pencil, started tapping on the desk blotter.

"Why no need?" I pressed my lips together, strained to hear his words.

"It would have been superfluous."

"Another big word for a small town Sheriff," I said, losing patience.

He put the pencil down, hard. I could see his endurance, like mine, had almost maxed out.

"We sheriffs are almost as bright as you Amish," he said sarcastically. His face stiffened. "I can match you word for word. Fact for fact."

Deflated, I slid back in my chair and exhaled.

"Yes, you probably can," I conceded. "And, I am sorry. I really didn't come here to antagonize you. I just need to know what happened to Lily?"

"And I've told you what I know."

"You haven't told me whether she was seeing Jacob or not ... or if they had been fighting ... or if their relationship was good. Or if there was she was someone else she was seeing."

"Now, how would I know those things?"

"You're Jacob's uncle. The bishop is your brother-in-law. And it's your custom to speak with the bishop ...often."

"You listen here now, Cora," the sheriff said. "You can question all you want. You can scream and beg and wallow in tears, but no Amish man is going to admit to murder. He'd be excommunicated, proclaimed a heathen in front of the congregation, a servant of Satan, and shunned. That man would be an outcast doomed to Hell. You think a man who would kill would put himself in a situation like that. You better believe, he would keep that secret forever."

"No, you're wrong. That man's soul would wither to a point of death or confession."

"You know, I've got a lot of paperwork sitting here. You can watch me work or you can leave. Whatever. But I'm done with your questions." He drew a sheaf of paper to him, picked up his pencil and began to write.

I waited a few minutes, then got up and walked out.

As I passed through the door to the waiting area, Tillie called out to me.

"Was he human?"

"I think you should take your pretty posters down and replace them with pictures of snakes and the devil."

I walked home, weary and defeated, convinced the sheriff knew more than he told. He had not helped me. Nor would he ever. I didn't know what to do next.

By the time I reached Olivia's house, my body ached all over. I feared the sickness was returning. My head hurt and my eyes begged to be shut. As soon as I walked in the door, I would head for the bedroom, lay down on the bed, burrow in quilts and remove myself from this world and slip into sleep.

It didn't work. My legs groaned under the covers; my exhausted head pounded with remembered words spoken in the sheriff's office. I could not rest. I knew there were pills in the bathroom cabinet that would help me sleep, but I didn't know how old they were and I didn't like to take medication. Alien to me, never used in my childhood and young adult years, rarely consumed in my English years, I didn't trust pills sold in a bottle.

Thinking of Maem, my comfort when sick, I ran a sink full of water until it was hot, then poured vinegar in it, soaked a washcloth in the mixture, laid down, placed the cloth on my head and waited for sleep. My last thought was of Maem, her hand gentle on a vinegar soaked cloth on her young daughter's feverish head, my head.

Chapter Nineteen

I slept the rest of the day and well into the night. Waking in the early morning hours, my head felt better and as I swung my legs over the mattress, I could feel their strength returned and their pain gone. I got up and roamed the house, restless and then, hungry. Taking some crackers from the kitchen, I went to the parlor window and drew the drapes open. A dim, hazy glow poured through the glass from the corner streetlamp. It shimmered the fat, lazy snowflakes dropping, floating through the near dawn air and disappearing as they hit the ground. I watched as the night faded. A rabbit scrambled across the yard, his body revealed, soft-edged and nebulous, before the sun rose bright. Smiling, I closed my eyes and saw Lily and Violet chasing rabbits in the fields. Laughing. Tumbling over each other. And then, I thought of Aaron and me walking through high grass near the road when he was young enough to spend time with me, a girl, and dropping together into the sweet smelling blades, hiding, when we heard the creak of steel-rimmed buggy wheels coming down the road. The scolding would be great for escaping chores and, worse, for flattening the forthcoming winter hay crop.

As one thought led to another, all Amish, my head grew heavy; my body, listless. I missed them. My family. My people. I filled a hot water bottle, went back to bed and put the rubber container on my stomach ... again, thinking of Maem's hands doing the same, so many years ago, when her children were little and could not sleep.

It was noon when I woke. The sun streaking bright through the curtains, I sat up, yawned, and threw the now cold water bottle on the floor. I was awake, really awake. And ready to attack the circumstances of Lily's death. The problem was, I didn't know the whereabouts of the battle or the weapons to use. Nor did I know who my general might be. Obviously, not the sheriff. And it couldn't be Maem or Violet. Hidden behind a thick steel shield of doctrine, they were not reachable. That left Harriet. She knew all things ... some true, some perceived, some rumored. If, together, she and I, perhaps we could sift the dross from the truth, and perhaps I would know the next step to take.

I dressed, put on a heavy jacket and walked to Harriet's.

"If it's lunch you're here for, it's meat loaf, mashed potatoes and green beans," Bailey said, looking at me. "If it's Harriet you want, you'll have to wait. She's cooking."

"I brought a book, so I can wait. But, I am hungry, so a glass of milk and a thick slice of meat loaf would be nice."

"No potatoes and beans?"

"No, thank you."

"Gravy on the meat?"

"No. But lots of ketchup."

"It's on the table," she said, her face wrinkling … and I heard the unspoken, *Duh.*

Smiling, I pointed at the corner table and said, "That one."

"Whichever." She shrugged and walked towards the kitchen.

As I walked by myself to the table, I passed an elderly lady lunching alone. She shook her head and held her menu out to me.

"Thank you," I said, pausing by her, "but she knows what I want."

"These young people," the old woman tisked, "they just don't have any manners. Imagine her making you take yourself to your table. Lazy, that's what they are. Lazy."

"She'll learn." Smiling, I patted her shoulder and moved on.

I sat and took a book from my purse. Eyeing the pages, I ran my fingers over the sheets. Words, all running together. No answers there. Dreams. Good endings. Problems solved. Maybe, I thought, I should write a book. Give it a good ending. Amish woman decides to live …. where?

"Cora?"

I looked up to see Harriet standing by my table.

"Sorry I can't be settin' with you now. We're a little-short handed, so I'm doin' a little cookin.' Shouldn't be long. The crowd'll start thinin' out soon."

"Can I help?" I said, standing, giving her a hug.

"You jest set there. Won't be long," she said, again. "Bailey takin' good care of ya?"

"She is." I held up my book. "I'll be okay."

As Harriet headed back to the kitchen, I saw her stop by Bailey, busy clearing a table, and whisper in her ear. Bailey looked towards me and frowned. She nodded and Harriet left her. Bailey put her tray of dirty dishes on the table and ambled over to me.

"I forgot what you wanted."

"Just a slice of meatloaf."

"Yeah, and a glass of milk."

"I thought you said you forgot," I said, unable to resist.

"Yeah, and there's the ketchup," she said, pointing. "Don't you be forgetting where it is."

She whipped her body away from me and paraded towards the kitchen.

"Don't forget your tray," I called after her … nasty, but satisfying.

She neither looked back nor picked up the tray. Just kept marching.

I tried, but I could not concentrate on my book. It was a simple story, predictable. I always carried that kind with me, so I didn't have to dwell over the words or remember them, though sometimes they carried an unexpected beauty.

Memories of Lily replayed over and over in my head. Mixed with them were images of long ago. Feelings. Yearnings. The farm. The animals. Maem's gardens. Aaron. Random thoughts. Drifting untethered. There and then gone. Replaced.

When Harriet came and sat by me, I put my book down, and looking at her, tears came from nowhere flooding my face. I couldn't stop them. I looked down at the table and through a liquid veil saw a plate filled with a mass of flavored hamburger. And a full glass of milk beside it. I hadn't seen Bailey bring it. Looking at the milk, I shook my head, slowly. A metaphor. The last word.

I did not realize I was sobbing aloud until Harriet took my arm and guided me from the table to the little storage room. She sat me down and stood by me, rubbing my back, while, my head bent into my hands, I cried and cried.

When I was done, she handed me a napkin.

"It's been too much," she said. "You needed a cry."

"You know, Harriet," I said, "the worst part is that when the thoughts whirl and jumble together in a huge, indistinguishable mass … a dark, solid, unbreachable mounding cloud, puffing out in all directions, I forget there is a way to walk through. My mind turns off what I know to be true, and reaches into itself for answers."

"And what do you know to be true?" Harriet asked, quietly.

"There is a way. I don't know why I let myself suffer, when I know it's there."

"Tell me."

Her voice was as soft as the inside of flower petals. I heard her tender tone and let it soak through my skin and slide around my soul.

"You know," I said.

She nodded.

"Tell me the word," she said. "Say it with your tongue."

"Jesus," I said and the tears came again, but this time they fell gentle. This time they were of a quiet sadness, a longing for a treasure gone.

Harriet pulled a chair tight to mine; she leaned so close I felt her breath.

"The answers are with Him," she said, rubbing my arm.

"But I think I have lost Jesus," I whispered.

"No, Honey, you ain't lost Him." Harriet slipped her arm around me and held my head against her breast. "He is right there beside you holdin' tight to your hand."

"I have forgotten how to speak to Him."

"Oh, Sweetie, His Spirit is sittin' smack in the middle of your heart just awaitin' to hear you call. You don't have to speak with words. Love is said in so many ways. Thoughts. Acts. And those powerful things that don't have no words big enough to lasso what you want to say. Your feelings. Yearnings. Reachings. That urgent agony of not being able to tell Him how big your love is. You don't have to put a rope around them things, box 'em in. You just let your mind and your heart call Him with that burning, earnest, passionate desire that longs for Him to take care of you. He knows what you need. He's hungry to hear your call. And Cora, He'll fill you up with all you really need and more."

Her words were a balm that worked its healing on my misguided thoughts. Fear and a thinking that the answers for hard, and even simple, questions, live within self builds a crumbling wall cemented with pride and foolishness. On one side of that wall lived a body, me, striving to do right through my own inadequate wherewithal; on the other side of the wall was Jesus ... ever there, waiting for me to remember from Whom my strength and wisdom comes.

"You're right," I said to Harriet. "Thank you."

"And didn't I see a plate of meatloaf sitting on your table just awaitin' to be et?" she said, patting my knee. "Come on, let's go get that crusty old meat and replace it with somethin' good."

"I like cold meatloaf," I protested, following her into the dining area.

"Well, if I set a great big slice of my famous mouth-waterin' carrot cake in front you, betcha that meatloaf won't be lookin' so tasty anymore."

I laughed and followed her to the corner table. The food was still there, drying and cold.

We both sat. I, younger and nimbler, faster than Harriet. She, older and rickety, slower than I. But as soon as her backside hit the chair bottom, her arm raised high and her fist came down fast and hard, smashing against the table.

I jumped and looked around. Embarrassed, I was relieved the dining room had emptied ... except for Bailey. Cockiness gone, she stood behind the counter, lips drawn back, neck cords tight, looking at Harriet.

"I would suggest you get yourself over here and clean up this mess. Now."

I had never seen Harriet that angry. Nor had I heard her speak so harshly. Her words had a momentary effect on Bailey, but by the time she reached our table, the swagger was back.

"Anything else you want?" She spoke the words to Harriet, but her eyes stayed on the table.

"Yes," Harriet said, wearily. "Carrot cake. A big slice ... two forks."

"Two plates?"

"No, one."

Bailey gathered the dishes from the table and we waited, without talking, until she came back with the cake and two glasses of iced tea.

"Thank you," Harriet said.

Bailey shrugged and walked away.

"I think I let my temper get away from me," Harriet said, pushing the cake closer to me. She sighed and shook her head. "And me just tellin' you about Jesus standin' tight right up next to us, always there, always knowin'. What do you think He's thinkin' about me right now?"

"He is thinking you are a dear, tired woman who, busy as she is, takes on the troubles of this silly woman and points her in the right direction. And my guess is He is understanding, even smiling and, certainly, knowing you regretted the bitter spice of your words even as they left your tongue." I paused, then said, "She did deserve a bit of a put down."

"She's not gettin' any better. And I'm not gettin' any younger, Cora. I was hopin' I could teach her to take over this place. Ain't happenin'. What do I do, Cora, what do I do?"

"Same thing you told me ... give it to Jesus."

"Eat your cake, girl." She pierced the sweet with her fork, dragged a piece of it across the plate, speared it and looked at it. Then she raised her eyes to mine. "I know you're right, but sometimes, it sure is hard."

I put my fork down and put my hands in my lap. Leaning towards her, I struggled to say the words that wanted to spill from my mouth and trigger her to respond with the knowledge I had been seeking. But she was so tired; her face, so old. I didn't want to burden her further, but my want for knowing was so great, I succumbed to it.

"Harriet?"

"Your heart is still hurtin'. I can tell," she said, her face so drawn, I felt guilty.

There are things I want to know," I said, hoping she would understand my desperation.

"'Bout Lily, ain't it?" she said, pushing crumbs over the plate. She put her fork down, wet a finger with her tongue, then ran her finger over the crumbs and lifted those stuck to it into her mouth. "I told you all I know."

"I don't think you have."

"I've told you all I *know*," she said, picking up more crumbs, "but that don't mean there ain't things I *think*."

"Tell me those."

"They say she died in the creek. Drowned. Your father found her and took her home. Someone, I don't know who, called the sheriff. That's what I *know*."

"And the rest?"

She put her hands over her face and as she leaned her head hard against them, I heard a sigh behind her fingers. Dropping her hands, blowing air out her cheeks, she looked full into my face.

"You sure you want to hear? It ain't gospel, you know."

"I know. But, maybe, we can render a measure of truth from it."

"Okay," she said, "This is what I think … from things I know and from things I heard."

I bit my lower lip and bent over the table to hear better.

"First off, ain't nobody knows for sure how Lily died. Whether it was from a loss of footin' … it was dark that night, no moon showing, clouds so thick … or whether somebody helped her fall into the water. But this is certain. Lily drowned in Wander Creek." She paused and looked at me, hesitated. I felt her struggle.

"Say the rest."

Still she said nothing. I waited. I could see there were words in her mouth that she wanted to speak, but was reluctant to let go of them. I presumed she thought they would hurt me.

"I'll say them for you," I said. "Maybe she lay in the water by choice."

"It's an ugly word," Harriet said, softly. "Suicide. But it could be."

I slid back in my chair and shook my head. "I don't think so," I said.

"If we're goin' to find truth, we have to put all the cards on the table," Harriet said. "And suicide is one of 'em."

The word had been said. Twice. Suicide. Now it was solid and my heart couldn't pretend that was an impossible supposition. I closed my eyes. *Lord, help me find truth, whatever it is, and hold me strong before it.* I opened my eyes and nodded.

"The word around town was that Lily was having her own little *Rumspringa* …"

"That couldn't be so," I interrupted. "Lily was already baptized. She would not go back to running around, *Rumspringa* was never for her. And, Harriet, she would not have done that thing, holding herself under water. That's a huge sin. Lily was a part of the church. She knew the punishment for taking life. Even her own. She wouldn't have done it."

"Oh, honey, bein' baptized don't mean you don't sin no more. Sometimes a need, or a pleasure, or a want, grows so big inside you, you can't control it. It just takes over all the rules you've been taught and you give in. You just fall right into it. We're human, Cora. We do wrong things, bad things. But God forgives."

"All my life," I said, "I have been told to take a life, to take your *own* life will lead you directly to Hell, to eternal damnation. Just like all my life I have been told that it is that same fate for an Amish person if they leave the Order. My fate, Harriet. Eternal damnation in Hell."

"Not all your life, Cora. You haven't heard that all your life. Only before you left the Amish."

"I don't want that for Lily. I don't want her burning in Hell. And I do not want to burn in Hell."

"You're not listenin' to me, Cora. Now *hear* me," she said, shaking my arm.

"It is what was driven deep into my heart."

"*Listen to me.*"

Swallowing, I held my head back and rubbed the nether part of my neck, my hand working furious and fast. Through the rushing panic inside my brain, my heart, I heard Harriet get up from her chair and come around mine.

"You can't stop what's been," she said, behind the chair, wrapping her arms around my shoulders, bending and turning her cheek to rest upon my hair. "Lily is dead. You have left the Order. Think, Cora, think. What have you learned since you left the Order? What did you learn in the English church?"

I reached my hands to hold on to the arms that encircled me. I heard her words, so soft, above me. I thought of Jesus, how near He was to me.

"Come sit," I said, my voice scarcely more than a whisper. "Your back will grow tired."

Her arms slid across my body, one tenderly slipping down my arm to hold my hand with hers, and she walked, that way, our arms stretched to stay together, to her chair and sat.

"What have you learned?" she repeated.

"I'm so tired," I said. "I can't think." And I felt Him growing closer.

"What have you learned?" she said, again.

"I have learned," I said, sweet tears forming, "I have learned Jesus forgives."

"What does He forgive?"

"All things." I could feel my body, my words, tremble. And I felt His warmth.

"What does He forgive?" she said, again.

"A soul that is hurting and longs to be with Him and makes a foolish choice. And a soul that leaves a community and finds a place where she can know Him fuller, love Him deeper."

I touched her face, grown weary for me, so beautiful in its love, and I wiped her tears. Then she reached to my face and wiped mine.

"Are you okay?" Harriet asked.

I nodded. "I need to know more. Please."

"There was an Amish boy. Jacob Yoder. Aaron's cousin. He was a wild one when he was a tad. Grown now. Don't see him much. Got himself a wife … Amish. Went to a community over in Ohio right after they took Lily up the hill. You know, we should go up there, up the hill, you and me, to the grave. Take some flowers. Recollect how she was … the special things that stick in hearts." She paused and sighed, shook her head. "Anyways, Jacob stayed there for a long time. And he come back with a wife. They got kids now. A good, big parcel of 'em …"

"Harriet," I interrupted, "how much was he seeing Lily?"

"Dunno. I think a lot. The Amish girls workin' in my kitchen joked about it. I couldn't understand most of it … don't know a lot of Pennsylvania Dutch words, but 'Jacob' and 'Lily' were a big part of their talk … and their laughter. I could pick out they were going together to the Sunday sings and I heard the word *bunndel,* bundle, and, forgive me, I figured there might be some monkey business goin' on."

"What happened? Why did she stop seeing him?"

Saying nothing, her head bent, looking down, Harriet picked at the napkin laying on the table, pleated it, over and over, with restless fingers.

"Harriet, don't drift off. Tell me what you're thinking."

"Your maem, Esther … I've known for a long time what she told you. She knew right from the day the bishop came questionin' and set your shunnin' and you took off to the English. She knew you weren't Annabelle's mama and she knew Lily was."

"How do you know that?"

"She told me."

"When?"

"A long time ago."

"She told me no one else knew." I was riddled with anger … disappointed … surprised. "Maem doesn't lie."

"Everybody lies. Might not want to. But they do. Mostly so's the person they're lying to don't hurt so much as they would if they knew the truth. Don't make no sense, maybe, but you know sometimes it's just too hard to tell the whole of a thing."

"Why are you telling me this now?"

"Because your maem thought Jacob was the father."

"She told you that?"

"She did."

"What about Jacob? Did she go to him?"

"No. He was off to Ohio almost the next day. Probably less than a month." Harriet sighed. "I don't think she would have anyway. You're maem weren't too feisty in those days. Stayed quiet, in the background. But I think the old wheels in her head were well oiled, always turning fast … but silent. It wasn't hard to her to figger out there was more than just watchin' the moon that was goin' on in the buggy after the sings."

"I guess everything changed with Annabelle's birth. And Lily wasn't the same after I left, was she?" I cringed to think of Lily lying together with Jacob, but I wasn't surprised. There had been shades of change in Lily even before I left. I smiled, ruefully. A pregnancy was a pretty dark shade.

"Not exactly. There were changes," Harriet said, her face drawing up as if in deep thought, "but don't be taken' the blame. Those girls were laughin' long before your shunnin'. The big change came after. You gone. Jacob gone. The baby gone. Lily didn't have the joy in her anymore. She'd bring me eggs, sometimes, and it looked like her arms could scarcely hold the basket. There wasn't much left of her, neither. Skinny as a rail. But quiet, always quiet. No quick steps and face looking this way and that, not anymore."

"Did she never laugh?" I asked.

"She smiled. Sweet smiles. Sad. Like an angel watching a soul, a soul circled with angle wings around. and then that soul pushed those wings away … and falls into the pit. Sometimes, her eyes, drillin' straight into mine, looked like they growed three inches. Lookin' for answers. And missin' you. Eyes so big, wantin' to be filled with yesterday."

"What about Jacob? Did she ever say anything about Jacob?"

"Nothin'." Harriet hesitated, closed her eyes, tilted her head, thinking. Then she opened her eyes and her head moved in a half-nod. "I remember one time … yes. She'd brought in some tomatoes and cukes. A gift from your maem. We were talkin', her face to the window and I saw her face light up, so I turned to see what she was lookin' at. It was Jacob ridin' by in his buggy. When I looked at her again, her face was blank, but her cheeks were red, and I remember thinkin', something was goin' on between those two. And I thought those kitchen Amish girls weren't so dumb. They knew exactly what they were gigglin' about. That was just before he turned up gone. I dunno. Maybe Lily even knew then, he'd go. Leave her. If that baby was his, he wasn't about to stick around and chance lettin' it get known."

"What do you think now?"

"I think, I *know*, Cora, the bundlin' part was real. I think Lily and Jacob had somethin' goin' on and maybe it was good, but I think, after you left, it was gone. That's when she started big time withdrawing. That's when her spirit shrunk smaller and smaller."

"But don't you think if she was sad because Jabob and she had parted ways and if she was sad I was gone ... and the baby, don't you think if it was suicide she was thinking of to end the pain, she would have done it a lot sooner? It wouldn't have taken five years to do the actual act, to jump into the water, into the deepest part of the creek, and will herself to stay under even while her body would be fighting for air. That makes no sense. Five years is a long time. By then there would have been a measure of healing. Either it was an accident ... or there had to be more."

"She told me once that Aaron was watchin' her. She was in here. At the counter, spreadin' out some potholders Esther had knit for me. That woman was always doin' those little kindhearted things. Anyhow, I think Lily meant it to sound grateful, but there was a bitterness, a bite in her voice," Harriet said, thoughtfully.

"She said Aaron? What would Aaron have to do with it?"

"I'm not sure. Maybe, nothin'. I never heard the girls in the kitchen say his name. But you know what, Cora, I'm not thinkin' it was nothin'. There was somethin' in her face ... an' when I asked her why she thought that, it was like a mighty shudder went up and down her body."

"Do you remember her exact words?"

"Kind of." Harriet said, putting a finger on the bridge of her nose and squinting. "It was pretty much like ... *Aaron watches over me. All the time. He knows everything I do* ... and I remember while she was talkin', her hands were just aflutterin' all over the counter, touchin' the toothpicks, flyers, those butterscotch candies I keep for the customers ... and the suckers for the kids." She smiled when she mentioned the children. "And those kids sure do like suckers. I let 'em take as many as they want. Some of 'em fill their little fists right up."

"Harriet! Did she say anything else?"

"Yeah, she did. I remember it. Exactly," Harriet said, back on track. *"I guess he means to keep me safe."*

"She said that? *Keep me safe?* From what? Did she say from what?"

"Nope. But I could tell she didn't like it."

"It would be akin to Aaron, the Aaron I used to know, to look out for her ... as a sister, but I wonder why he would feel the need to keep her safe. It's scary knowing now that maybe she did need somebody watching out for her."

"Maybe you should tell that to the sheriff," Harriet said.

"Mmm," I said, thinking. Should I? I thought not. "I do not think so, Harriet. I'll tell you why. All these thoughts are running through my head. And it's like they are telling me ... *wait, think this through.* I don't trust the sheriff anymore. He won't talk to me about Lily's death. And, remember, he's Jacob's uncle. And so is the bishop, who is, also, the sheriff's brother-in-law. And I think it might be that Jacob's involved in Lily's death. I don't know exactly how, but it could be bad. And remember, too, Jacob is Aaron's cousin. They could all be mixed up in this. I think, mostly, protecting Jacob."

"Cora," Harriet said, gently, reaching to stroke my arm, "do you think it might be time to let all this go? Lily's dead. There's nothin' to be gained by beatin' your head against a wall. Nobody that knows anything is gonna help you. There comes a time when you gotta admit you're beat and there ain't no way of winnin'. You do a lot of thinkin', Cora. Jest start thinkin' of good memories, all those loving moments with Lily and your family. And let the rest go."

"I'll try," I said. Another lie. I couldn't let it go. Not yet. But I still didn't know what the next step should be.

"Good girl," she said, patting my arm. And even while she said those words, the front door opened and Aaron walked in. His arms were full of little pumpkins. Setting them on the nearest table, he looked up and saw us. Quickly he turned his head away.

"Harriet?" I didn't know what to do.

"Wait here, Sweetie," Harriet said. "He's just bringin' in some punkins ... for pies."

"And Halloween decorations?" I asked, frowning.

"Yep. That too." She drew in her breath, blew it out, then shook her head, shrugged, lifted her arms and dropped them on the table.

"It's okay," she said, wearily, and rising from her chair, she paused and clutched her back for a moment, and then turned to walk towards Aaron.

"Wait," I said, grabbing her arm, stopping her. "Does he know how the pumpkins will be used?"

"I have to go pay him. You stay here," she said, again, ignoring my question. She looked at my hand on her arm, and then raised her eyes to my face. I couldn't read hers. It didn't reflect the emotions that lay beyond its blank façade. There were too many possibilities. Anger, disappointment, confusion. Sadness. Guilt.

And on my face was a plea for understanding. I didn't let go of her arm.

"Does he know the pumpkins will be cut into jack-o-lanterns?" I asked, again, each word separate and precise.

"Prob'ly."

"But, Harriet, the Amish don't celebrate ghosts and goblins. Tell him what you are going to do with the pumpkins so he knows for sure."

"Oh, Cora," Harriet said, shaking her head, "once I give him the money, the punkins are mine. It's not his business what I do with 'em."

"Would you sell a man a gun if you knew he was going to shoot someone with it?"

"It's not the same."

"It is. He's selling something that, for him, will be used in an ungodly way. He needs to know. He needs to be able to make that choice."

"Honey," Harriet said, gently, "he has been selling me punkins for years. Do you really think he don't know his punkins are carved with funny faces for Halloween?"

"Maybe he does. Anyway, he's waiting," I said, capitulating. Reluctantly, sadly, I let go of her arm. "Go take his money."

"There's still a lot of Amish in you," Harriet said, touching my cheek with tender fingers. "Stay here, I'll be back."

I didn't stay there. I followed her. I don't think she was aware of it until we were both at the pumpkin table. His eyes on Harriet, Aaron's face flashed anger. It didn't take Harriet long to realize the reason. Either she sensed my body filling the space behind her or she grasped the logical cause of Aaron's fiery reaction. An astute old lady, I think she identified the cause promptly and correctly.

Turning her face, stern and unforgiving, she stared at me for a long moment. I stared back.

"Aaron and I are havin' a personal conversation," she said, dignified, back straight, language stilted. "Would you please return to your seat."

"No," I said, "He should know."

"Humph," she said, "I've known the Amish to be stubborn ... but not often rude."

"So, maybe I'm not so Amish after all," I said.

"Maybe not."

I didn't like what was happening. I couldn't recall a time of ever coming near to a fight with Harriet. But she was wrong and I couldn't stop it. This was an Amish thing. Important. Aaron must have known Halloween with its evil spirits was not a welcome celebration for the Amish. He shouldn't have had to be reminded.

"Do your business with me, Harriet." Aaron's words rumbled harsh.

Startled, I looked at him. He was not looking at me. He had turned his back to me and spoke only to Harriet. An ache started in my heart. This was a man I had once loved. And he would not look at me. Didn't he understand, I was concerned for him ... this could bring him to be shunned.

"Aaron," Harriet said, softly, "ain't you gonna say 'hello' to Cora? She's been punished a very long time."

"She's dead. I'll be back for my money tomorrow."

"And the rest of the punkins ... the big ones?"

"Tomorrow."

"Bring them in, Aaron, bring them in now," I said. "You can pretend I'm not here. You can pretend you can't see me, you can't hear me, you can't smell me. But even pretending I don't exist, you know what I'm saying is true. The bishop would be extremely disturbed if he knew your pumpkins were turning into little, orange evil things."

Directing his words to Harriet, Aaron said, "Tell that whisp of invisible air that I remember a young girl who used to dip her fingers in mud and draw faces on those little orange things while they were still growing in the field. And tell her I remember her calling the ugliest face, *Hairy Herrfort*." And then, he stomped out.

"Is that true?" Harriet asked, peering through the glass door and watching Aaron jump on his wagon and shake the reins hard against his horse's back.

"It is ... but we were children," I defended.

"*Hairy Herrfort.*"

"Yep. Hairy Herrfort. And he was. Probably still is. Hairy all over."

Then I looked at Harriet and she looked at me and we both broke into peals of laughter.

Later walking home, kicking at wet, soggy leaves sticking to the sidewalk, and clenching my coat collar tight, then tighter, around my neck, I nursed a growing anger directed against Aaron. It seemed every disagreeable emotion that was labeled 'Aaron', tucked away and sitting dormant inside my gut waiting to be brought forth and used, in its turn, had been experienced, more than once, during the duration of our times together. As a child, I had played with him. As a young girl, I had mooned over him. As a young woman, I had loved him. As a shunned woman, I had missed him. As an English woman, I had thought about him ... albeit, less and less as time passed ... until he was, almost, forgotten. And when Daniel came into my life and filled my heart, Aaron fell so deep into the past, he no longer surfaced. Until my return to Wander Lane. And then, I discovered some not so pleasant feelings rose and invaded the lovely, nostalgic buried thoughts of old Amish recollections. Bitterness. Rejection. Anger. I wasn't dead. I was more alive than ever. And Aaron knew that!

Nevertheless, there was no hope of learning information concerning Lily's death from Aaron. He was not the path that would lead to knowing the truth of Lily's heart in her final days or to knowing the truth of Lily's demise. Not when her very presence was vile to him, an evil cast upon his being. But, for sure, he was the one who could help me. There had to be a way to get through to him.

Then I stopped, my feet mired in the damp of wet leaves. I didn't feel their cold. My face, screwed up in thought, gave visible credence to the intensity of my deliberation.

And it came to me. There was a way. A way to reach Aaron. Could I do it? With honesty ... integrity ... love? I thought ... maybe, hopefully ... I could. No, not maybe, not hopefully, but definitely I could. Emphasizing my determination, I gave a sharp nod, a hard kick to the leaves, grinned and walked on.

That night, I sat in the stillness of the parlor with the only light that of the moon filtering through Olivia's delicately patterned, sheer curtains, and I prayed. Seeking God's wisdom and guidance, I talked with the Father through Jesus for a very long time. I told Him my plans. I struggled to receive His counsel. I willed my determination to weaken, to let His Will come through. But my thoughts were so powerful, I could feel a wall, built by own desires, surround me. I knew He listened, but I am not sure I did the same.

When I went to bed, secure in His love, knowing He was always there … watching over me, waiting for me to heed His Word, before I slept, I prayed, as my personal prayer, from the words in Paul's letter to the Philippians (NIV, Philippians 1:9-11). *And this is my prayer: that my love may abound more and more in knowledge and depth of insight; so that I may be able to discern what is best and may be pure and blameless until the day of Christ, filled with the fruit of righteousness that comes through Jesus Christ … to the glory and praise of God.*

Chapter Twenty

The first thing I did the next morning was make a list. Drawing the bedroom drapes, I scarcely noticed the brilliant clarity of flora and fauna glowing under the radiant beams of sun as I briefly glanced at the wakening world on the other side of the window glass. Dropping the curtain cord, I made hasty progress to the small writing table tucked in a corner. Olivia had secreted a delicately scrolled wooden desk there as a treasured spot for writing special little notes to loved ones and jotting down fleeting words and thoughts that spoke beauty to her heart. Picking up pen and paper, I wrote with hurried hands. I did not want the energy of a full and roaring mind to weaken or the sharp, precise roll of required tasks running through my head to fade in the rush of harried activity. Too often, a mind wakes full of ideas that fall away as the patterned manner of living slips in.

The list finished, I dressed, brushed my teeth, splashed water on my face and threw some clothes and toiletries into my soft quilted overnight bag. I would not need much. I wasn't going far. Anything I might need beyond that which I had packed would be there. Scanning the room, I saw my list still on the small desk. I went to it, picked it up, and gazed at it. As I skimmed the recorded tasks, my heart slowed and whispered me to pause. Lowering my head, I waited. As the urgency faded and my body stilled, God and I came together, not with voice, but with silent words that have no form, but are filled with wonder and connection.

I was ready.

My first stop was William Sweet's law office. Although it was still early, I hoped he would be in his downstairs work rooms. I got out of my car and pausing before I stepped over the curb, looked with nostalgic pleasure at the old brick house he had purchased from old Miss Lamphere during the time I lived among the English. He had restored the first floor of the crumbling home into office space and remodeled the second floor to be his living area. Floating through my mind was the image of the aging maiden Miss. Lamphere, a teacher in the English school, white-haired and stiff-backed, turning her back on suggested retirement, living there before William bought her house. It seemed a big, majestic home for one old lady. But it suited her … soft and sweetly aging elegance. I liked her. She gave me extra pennies when I delivered eggs to her house.

"These are for you. For candy," she said, then smiled and winked. "If you want, you can share with your brothers. Sharing is a good thing." Then taking my hand, she led me along pebbled paths running through the grand patches of fragile pink and blue and violet perennials that flowed over the grass in her yard. "These are for your mother … maem," She said, reaching into the flowers and plucking a large bouquet, tucking it into my arms. Then patting my head, she smiled and I watched two little and fascinating creases sink into the thin pink of her cheeks.

Unable to resist, I lifted a finger and reached into one of those small holes.

She laughed and I blushed.

"They are dimples, dear child. Given by God to show his delight in our moments of joy."

In those days there were green vines clinging to the sides of the house. William had pulled them down, cleaned the bricks, painted the window wood white, and replaced railings with wrought iron. The look was fine and stately, but I liked the homey warmth of a house well used better.

A light came on in the lamplight fixture affixed to the frame of the front door. William Sweet was open for business. As I walked up the cobbled walk to his office, I admired the rich hues of maroon, mauve and deep pink mums lavishly planted among the bushes bordering the rough brick exterior of his house. Sliding my hand over the railing, I walked up the steps and across the small porch. Placed modishly about the wooden floor were massive black kettle shaped pots filled with hordes of mums matching those by the bushes, and a welcoming soft light glowed through the draped window at the side of the door.

Resolutely, words at the ready, I placed my hand on the doorknob. The door was still locked. I drew a deep breath and pulled the rope hanging from an antique bell attached the top of the front door. The clapper rang loud.

It didn't take long for William to open the door. I was glad. I didn't want extra moments to ponder the words I would say. I wanted them to drop swift and plain from my mouth. If I thought them too long, I might leave them lay silent in my throat.

"Cora Pooler," he said. "Come in."

"I know it's early ..." I began.

"No, no, no," William protested. "I'm open and it's always good to start the day seeing an old friend. How can I help?"

"I need to talk to you about Olivia's house," I answered, thinking I wasn't really a friend, but, for sure, I wasn't many years from old.

"Well, just come on in and sit down first," he said, smiling, pointing me to his office at the right of the foyer. "Shouldn't be too many questions about the house. The will was pretty clear and simple."

"I know what it said," I said, a bit too tersely. Lifting my hand and with one finger rubbed the spot between my eyebrows. I needed to remember none of my anxieties were his.

"Sit," William said, and ignoring my rudeness, with a tilt of his head indicated a soft, padded chair facing his desk.

He waited until I appeared comfortable and then sat down behind the desk.

"I want to release myself from the will," I said, briskly, hoping to make this visit brief and to the point.

His face expressionless, he folded his hands on his blotter and bent towards me.

"There wasn't time."

"Just when did you make this decision to void your inheritance?"

"It doesn't matter. It's what I want," I said. I waited, watched him look at me. The pencil kept moving up and down, the eraser steady in its taps. I wanted to grab it and break it.

"You need to think this through," he said, finally.

"It's what I want," I said, again, firmly. And again, I waited.

He put the pencil down and drummed his fingers on the desk.

"Do you have some kind of a form I should sign?"

"Yes."

"Then get it and I'll sign it."

"I don't want to do that."

"You're my lawyer and you have to."

"I'm not exactly your lawyer," he said, sighing. "It's Olivia I'm representing."

"Then I'm making you my lawyer and you're representing me," I said, "so please, do as I ask."

"Then if I'm your lawyer, as your lawyer I'm telling you to do some waiting and some thinking," William said.

"I can't," I said, leaning forward in my chair.

Looking hard at me, he blew air out from his cheeks, then lifted his shoulders in resignation. "There's no arguing with you, is there?"

"No."

"I'll have papers ready for you this afternoon." He stood up. "And I hope you do call Dianna to explain what you're doing. It's the right thing to do."

"I need to sign the paper now," I said, trying to keep my voice calm.

"It will take a while to get the papers ready."

"Now." Calm was gone.

"Okay, now."

William did not anger easily, but I could see I had pushed him near to the brink. It shamed me, but I didn't know another way to quickly free myself from Olivia's generosity. And if I did'nt do it now, Dianna might decide not to keep the house and lose her inheritance. And I didn't have time to explain all this to William.

He produced the proper forms. Writing rapidly, we completed filling the blank spaces. I signed them, and he said he would take care of the rest. He was gracious with his words, careful, but I could sense his displeasure.

When we were done, he walked me to the door. He nodded his head at me, but didn't shake my hand. As I walked through the front door onto the porch, he made one final attempt to reason with me.

"Are you sure?" he asked. "We can rip the papers up."

"I'm sure," I said, turning, stepping back into the foyer, and looking up into his face. "It truly is the best thing to do."

"Will you tell Dianna?"

"She's on my list," I said, nodding.

He shrugged his shoulders. "Then we're done."

"William." I put my hand, gently, on his arm. "I'm sorry. I didn't mean to be unpleasant. You're a good man. Kind." I smiled, ruefully.

"I guess I said that before. But it's true and I think I took advantage of that. I truly am sorry. It was unfair. I hope you'll not hold it against me."

He said nothing, but reached with his free hand and put it over mine.

"I truly believe Olivia would applaud what I've done," I said, squeezing his arm. "And I *know* she would understand."

"But will Dianna?" he asked after a moment.

I lowered my head, then lifted it and looked at him. "I don't know."

William reached and pushed the door further open. Before I stepped through, I looked at him. He *was* a good man. And Dianna was a good woman.

"You know, William, it might not be a bad idea for you to maybe get to know Dianna a little better."

I did call Dianna after I left William's house. Selfishly relieved when she didn't answer, I left a message. A short message ... suggesting she call William's office and that I would explain everything shortly. In a few days. Or later, I thought. When all was in place.

Two items wiped off my list.

Looking with apprehension at the next entry, I moved my eyes down the list and chose a simple task. Snacks. Simple and fast. A run into the grocery, a grabbing of favorites, and a toss of a bag into the backseat.

Done.

Next two items. Easy again. A visit to Harriet's Homemade Soups and Hearty Sandwiches and a purchase from Wagler's Authentic Amish Bakery. I chose to go to the bakery first.

Closing my eyes, I pushed the shop's door open. Smiling, I let the delicious odors of spices and sugars and simmering fruits swirl round my body and sink into my skin. And, oh, the baking of bread. Earthy yeast. Buttery crust. And cookies. Vanilla and melting chocolate.

When my nose was done, I opened my eyes. It was all there. The wonders of an Amish bakery. Cakes and pies and cookies, donuts and breads. Beautiful works from stirring hands and hot ovens. Sumptuous gifts for salivating stomachs.

"You're back. This time, a whole pie?" the girl behind the counter said, grinning.

"A whole pie," I agreed, recognizing her, spreading my arms in delight. "A great, huge, succulent, whole pie. Not just a sample today."

"And that would be shoofly?"

"And that would be shoofly," I agreed, again. "Molasses and sugar flowing over the brim. And wrapped tight so that none will escape."

"A gift?" she asked.

"A gift," I answered, "for the most wonderful man in the world ... well, maybe not quite ... but close."

"I'll put it in a box," she said, smiling.

And then I went to see Harriet.

There were a few breakfast patrons still in her dining room. The underlying sounds of murmuring voices, clinking silver touching pottery, shuffling feet, laughter gently teased a pleasant din against my ears. Spotting Harriet at a table in the corner, I walked over to her.

"You're busy," I said, glancing at her table spread with sheets of paper.

"Just makin' up some menus," she said, looking up, putting her pencil down, spreading her fingers, wiggling them. "Sit with me. These old bones need a rest." She lifted her hands and shook her head. "You'd think the little bones wouldn't ache so much as the big ones, but they do. I guess wearin' down is sumpin we all do." She grinned. "Your times acomin', Cora Pooler. Old age don't miss nobody. 'Ceptin' those already dead 'fore their time."

"Put some of your good beef stew on those menus," I said, sitting next to her, turning my body so my knees almost touched hers. "Cold enough out there for some good hearty meals."

"Winter's comin'. Not before Halloween, I hope."

"Did Aaron bring the pumpkins?"

"Not yet. Still just got the little ones. Some of the girls out in the kitchen are hollowing 'em out. Gonna stick yellow and orange mums in 'em. Decorate the place up."

"They'll be pretty."

"I reckon."

Bowing my head, pressing my lips tight, I clutched my hands together in my lap and leaned forward. I didn't know how to start. It was so important to me that she understand.

"Spit it out, girl."

I lifted my head and wet my lips. I could not think of words that would soften or lighten my decision. *Please guide me, Jesus, fill me with Your strength. Temper my words with love. Help her hear with understanding and respond with truth ... even though I might not like what she says.*

"I'm leaving here and I need your help."

"You found out how Lily died?"

"No," I whispered.

"Then why are you leavin'?"

I told her my plan and what I needed her to do. With my eyes half closed and my own face scrunched, waiting, dreading her reaction, I watched her lips draw tight over her teeth, then her mouth stretch to one side of her face causing a washboard of wrinkles to deepen over her cheek. Biting the corner of her lips, she shook her head.

"It will work," I said, reaching, taking her hands into my own. She pulled them away and sat straight.

"Have you prayed?" she asked.

"Yes," I said, quietly.

"And He approves?"

"I'm not sure," I said, even softer.

"Then this is too fast," she said, her voice breaking, old. "You need to think more."

"I have been here for months. The only thing in this mess I know for sure is Annabelle is all right. I thought that's all I came for, but it wasn't."

"You came to mourn Lily, too. To let her rest in your heart. That's not done yet."

"No, that's not done ... and I'm not sure it ever will be. But I am working at it. I pray and I think of the good memories."

Bending forward, Harriet spread her fingers over her thighs and rocked her body back and forth on the hard wooden chair.

"And you've told me you've decided who you are. You're sure you know where you belong," she said, tilting her head, scrutinizing my eyes with her own. "Are you really *sure*?"

"I think," I said, maybe sadly, certainly earnestly, "there is very little, other than God, we can be *sure* about. And I think, sometimes, in our anguished yearning, our aching hunger to please Him, we just don't stop and be quiet and listen. And we end up pleasing ourselves instead of Him. At least, that's the way it is with me. Sometimes, I have in my head a thought so strong, I think it must be from Him, and then, sometimes I *know* it's from Him. And that's when it's so simple and wonderful ... the warmth, the peace ... the fullness."

"And this thought … this plan … is it yours or is it His?"

"I think it's within His Will."

"But you're not sure?" Harriet said, her voice falling so gentle on my ears.

"Oh, God. I'm not," I said, lifting my fingers, massaging my temples. "I am so afraid I want this so desperately that I'm confusing my will with His."

"Child, you should wait."

"You think I's is wrong for me to do this?"

"There is anguish in your eyes. Shouldn't be none if it's right."

Perhaps I shouldn't have told her my plan. Maybe I should have just left town without explaining. But I needed her help, though surely I could have found a way to do what needed to be done without her. It was selfish to include her in my plan. Yet she was loyal and she loved me. She would do as I asked. And whether I asked for her help or not, she would eventually know what I was doing and if I had not told her, she would be hurt. I sighed. There were so many thoughts and so much confusion in my head. It was important that Harriet *understand*. And approve. She was so very special to me.

"You been to church?" Harriet said, breaking into my thoughts.

"I pray. I read scripture. I sing. To God. The old hymns from the English world. And the praise songs. Every day. Nearly every day. Most days."

"You been to church?" she repeated.

"No," I answered, "never in Wander Lane."

"You should go."

"I didn't think I'd be this long in Wander lane. I kept thinking it would be done … the search … and I could go home."

"I mean now. You should go now. To the church."

"I know God is with me," I said, quietly, glancing at my watch. It seemed the hours were passing so quickly. I looked at Harriet … sunken lines layered her face, and her eyes had dropped deep into the frame of it. I wanted to lean over her and kiss the two pink spots stretched tight over the edges of her cheekbones. I wish that I had.

"You need to get goin'," she said. Sighing, she nodded her head as if giving me permission.

"You look so sad," I said, running my hand up and down her arm.

"I worry. I don't think you've thought about this enough."

When I said nothing, she nodded her head again, as if accepting.

"Will you go by Sugar Creek?" she asked.

"It's on the way," I said.

"Will you stop?"

"I don't think so. I know Annabelle is safe; I think of her as happy... and I want to get to Norleen before dark."

"Then hurry on, girl. The days are short now and it's a long trip."

Shortly past noon, I drove by the turnoff that would take me to Sugar Creek. Though my heart said *turn*, I did not. Annabelle was a part of the past I could let go. She was happy. I would not mar that. I turned on the car radio, swirled through the stations until I found words that I knew, pressed the button so the music rose high and sang with it.

A little over an hour later, muting the radio, concentrating, I drove through the traffic of Cleveland, found the entry to Route 90 and drove east. I couldn't sing anymore. No matter how loud I tuned up the radio, my head kept drowning out the melodies with thoughts of Daniel. Resigned, I silenced the radio and let my mind wander.

"I like the way you think," Daniel said, peering over the précis of a meeting I had attended in his place. "Concise. Thorough. Perceptive."

"Do I get a raise?" I said, smiling.

"No, but you get an invitation to attend The Annual Seedman's Banquet."

"As a representative of the company?"

"No, as my date."

It was our first official date. We had met for lunches and dinners, explored museums, watched movies, talked for hours on the phone, but always as friends, good friends ... never as two people coupled. It changed the shades of our relationship ... soften them, veiled them with a delicate layer sweetness, colored them with anticipation, trepidation. It was a wonderful time.

Then one night, he took my hand and whispered words that tried not to hurt. He said I was elusive. He could not reach my core, the heart of whom I was, the secrets of my spirit essence.

The drifting came that descends when two yearning souls cannot meet. Yet friendship stayed ... with a tenderness that made it different, more, than most. It was love in a unique and precious form.

Passing Erie, I realized, in that hazy world of thought, I had made good time. I would be near Buffalo before dark, and, therefore, my body needing a break, I turned off the thruway and drove into Dunkirk. At the edge of that small city I remembered there was a Greek restaurant overlooking the shores of Lake Erie. Daniel and I had found the most delicious sweet potato fries there. My stomach hungered for them and I was anxious to pleasure its rumbles.

The restaurant was closed. Disappointed, I headed down Central Avenue to get back onto the thruway. Stopping for a red light, I noticed a museum on the corner to my left. My legs needed to walk, so when the light turned green, I turned onto the narrow side street by the museum. When I saw there was no parking lot behind the museum nor were there empty parking spots at the side of the road, I kept driving, thinking to backtrack to Central Avenue. The side street had taken me into a residential area. Lovely old homes, regal in their bearing, with lush greenery splashed with autumn color and with magnificently branched ancient trees, the late sun shining through the openings among the barren patches of leaves not yet dropped, bordered the road with dignified splendor.

And then I saw it. On the corner. An old and beautiful church, its steeple rising high, lifting a golden cross to the heavens for all to see and remember, for all to pause and offer a short, poignant prayer of praise and thanksgiving. The exterior of the church was of aging, blackening bricks. On the side of the building I was able to see was a line of brilliantly elongated stained-glass windows elegantly mounded at their apexes. Turning the corner, I saw at the front of the church a massive and stately stairway rising to two great polished wooden doors and at the top of them were two half-circles of brightly colored stained glass.

I wanted to go in.

On the far side of the church was an area of blacktop. Several cars were parked in its lined spaces. I pulled onto the asphalt and parked by them. Not hesitating, I got out of my car and walked to a simple white door at that side of the building. I tried the knob. It wasn't locked. Opening it, I stepped onto a small landing. At the right of it were stairs going up; at the left, were stairs going down. I could see a part of a kitchen area at the bottom of the stairs, and I could hear muffled chatter and laughter coming from beyond that space. Apparently some ladies of the church had gathered for a get-together of sorts. I was tempted to go down and take a peek, to see those English ladies enjoying their church building. But I didn't. I went up the stairs.

At the top was a carpeted hall. I followed it into a large paneled room with a round table, chaired, in the center. Scattered around the room were a couch and several chairs that looked to be soft and comfortable. Book shelves, full of all manner of reading materials lined one wall, and two closed doors were set in another. There was a great opening in the third side, the wall to my right. It led to a hall with another stairway at the end of it. The hall was bordered with a massive dark wood wall. There were doors at either end of it.

I stepped into the welcoming room before me, walked around it … read the titles of books on the shelf and ran my hand over some of the printed material, perhaps thinking I could absorb the magic of their words, then turned and slid my hand over the silk feel of the polished dark wood of the center table. I felt good in this room. I thought I might sit for a bit in one of the velvety padded chairs. The floral one, the one that brought Olivia's into my mind.

"Can I help you?" A woman stood in the doorway I had seen. A desk was behind her and a large copy machine behind that.

Her voice ran like sweet lotion over my body. I looked at her. White sugar candy hair. A cushioned tummy. Gnarled hands, hinting of long ago work, and now, seeming delicate. Feet encased in black sturdy, roomy shoes. And a smiling face.

"Can I help you?" she repeated.

"I'd like to pray," I said, softly.

She took my arm and led me … across the room, out the large opening, down the hall, through the further door, and into a red carpeted narthex.

"God bless you," she said as she led me before two beautifully carved doors. Swirls of divine images etched on ovals of beveled glass centered on each of them.

She opened them. Gently nudged me through. Closed the doors behind me and left.

Before me was a grand high-ceilinged room … a sanctuary. God's room. I walked down the middle aisle, light pouring through the stained glass windows on either side of this magnificent room. Straight ahead of me were marble columns, adorned with gold trim encasing on each side of the area on which the wood carved altar stood. In the center the ornately sculpted wooden wall behind the altar was a white curtain section upon which hung a simple … provoking … cross.

I went to the railing and prayed.

Back in my car, I drove the rest of the way to Buffalo in silence.

When I got to my condo, I sat outside in my car for awhile, not wanting to go in, wishing all this were over and I was back on the highway heading back to Wander Lane. And wondering, was this right. And, finally, resolutely, pushing that thought out of my mind. I could not live in two different places as two different people. I had chosen.

But artificial resolution does not last. *Dear Lord, stay with me. Your presence is everything. I truly need you to hold me together.*

I took my bag upstairs and went in.

The rooms were cold. Throwing my purse on the couch, dropping my bag on the floor, I turned the thermostat high and, shivering, went to the wall of windows facing Lake Erie and opened the drapes. Holding my sweater tight around me, I watched the sun sink into the lake, its last rays of deep orange spreading and disappearing into the dark water. And then, that light was gone, leaving only the glaring reflection of shore lights on the water. I closed the drapes and turned on lamps.

Hungry, I crossed the room, stepped into the kitchen, reached into a cupboard, found a tin of canned spaghetti, opened it, and ate it cold. Then, fighting the tears of fatigue and jumbled thought, I stumbled to my bedroom, pulled at the covers on my bed, crawled under them and huddled there, fully clothed, shoes still on. Though I thought my head was too full for slumber, sleep came quickly.

The next morning, I woke with majestic song spilling from heaven into my head, my heart, my soul, filling every crevice of my body. Joyful music. Devine. God rejoicing over me with singing. The peace and love of it, the enormity of its goodness exceeded all earthly rule. I lay in the throes of His ringing gift until it faded, softer, ever softer, leaving a blanket of happiness covering the whole of my body. And with the stifling chains of fatigue, gone; the energy of joy, full, I hurried to open the living room drapes and drink in the healing warmth of God's great sun, to feast on the great span of Lake Erie's waving waters, to indulge in the bounty of trees, flora, squirrels and birds. It was a gorgeous day.

Delaying the acceptance of the day's obligatory responsibilities that on the previous day were so vital to instantly accomplish, I ambled about the condo savoring the bits and pieces of décor that made it mine … that were me. Touching. Smoothing. Drawing in the scents of the home that was *mine*. Absorbing the feel of familiar air. Saturated, I stood very still and reveled in the fragments of life that had been mine.

It came time to accept, to close my eyes and feel the slide of the concrete and intangible slip from mind and body. I opened my closet and chose the clothes I would wear to face Daniel.

The drive from Buffalo to Daniel's corporate offices and surrounding seed production and research buildings located on the outskirts of Norleen was not long. When I had worked there, the ride had been a daily pleasure for me. The passage from city scurry to country peace was a genial way to begin a work day and a satisfying way to end it. Coming into the quaint little village of Norleen with its charming houses of noble character and the old style Main Street paralleled by a huge treed and benched park, always gave a burst of joy to my heart.

I drove through the village slowly, soaking in the familiar sights, smells, sounds. And when I reached Daniel's company, I drew in a deep breath and smiled. Drawing out the anticipatory pleasure of seeing him again, I walked to his building with unhurried step.

Mae Summers was at the reception desk when I entered the office area. She smiled when she saw me. It sang sweet in her face, in her eyes, in her outstretched arms.

"Cora!" She hugged me, then stepped back. "You look so good … a new suit? And you're hair! How could it grow so much in such a short time?"

"That's what hair does," I said, smiling back at her.

"Not mine. Every four weeks it gets cut into shape. Otherwise, I'd have a great, big forest growing on my head."

"I don't think so," I said, laughing. "Is Daniel in? I'm anxious to see him."

"Oh, dear. I think, maybe, you'd better go talk to Jared. He's kind of the big cheese around here these days."

Tilting my head, I lifted my eyebrows. "How's that?"

"I guess that it's more like he thinks he is. Anyway, he sure does act the part."

"And I think you're telling me that Daniel isn't here?" I said, scrunching my face.

"He's not."

"He'll be in later?"

"You mean like today?"

"I mean like today," I said, wanting to see him, disappointed he wasn't in his office right at that moment.

"He's in Africa ... you know, one of his field trips."

"For how long?" I stood by her desk watching her twisting her body with little nervous jerks, fiddling with paperclips, pulling at her hair. Obviously, though happy to see me, she wasn't sure what to do with me. I sensed something awry in this place.

"I'm not sure how long he'll be gone. Probably awhile."

"Can I call him?"

"I don't have his number."

"Why not?" I asked, hearing the hesitancy in her voice, not believing her.

"Jared keeps it kind of secret," she said, squirming. "Look, I really don't know very much. Things have gotten pretty secretive around here ... that's what it's like when he's gone."

"It never was before. And you say Jared's in charge?" I said, thinking that was certainly different.

"Not exactly ... but kind of."

"And where would I find Boss Jared. Not in Daniel's office, I hope."

"Nope," she laughed. "He's in his same old dinky one. Only he's dressed it up a little. With gold framed diplomas and certificates ... and old football trophies. Stuff like that."

"I see," I said, moving away from her desk. "Anyway, it's good to see you, Mae. And right now, I think I'll just go find Jared."

"No, wait," she said. "Let me call him first. Let him know you're here."

"No, I don't think so." I said, looking at her. "Don't call him."

"But I should," she protested. "He'll be angry."

"I'll take care of it," I said. "I mean it, Mae. Don't call him."

"Things are different here when Daniel's gone," she whispered.

"Because of Jared?"

"Not exactly," Mae said. "I don't want to get in trouble ... I really need this job."

"Okay," I said, turning back, touching her arm. "Call him."

"Thanks," she said, softly. I heard the relief in her voice.

I stood quietly by her desk while she called him. When she was done, she me motioned back to the office area.

"He said to go right in."

I nodded. Before I opened the door behind her, I turned and smiled. "I am glad to see you, Mae. You've always been a good and helpful friend and I've really appreciated that."

"You, too," she said, smiling back.

"Hello, Jared," I said, walking through his door. Mae was right. There were all kinds of ornamental paraphernalia hanging on the walls, spread out on shelves, all proclaiming Jared's lifelong achievements. From kindergarten on up. I wondered if he had stolen the clay pinch pot on his desk from his mother's home. Or the sports trophies from his older brother's cache.

Jared didn't get up from his chair.

"You're the big man now?" I said, sitting in a padded chair directly across from his desk.

"Looks that way, don't it?"

"Doesn't it," I corrected.

"You don't change much, Cora," he said, frowning.

"And you don't seem very happy to see me," I said, setting my purse by the side of my chair.

He picked up a pencil, tapped the eraser on his blotter.

"Why do men do that?" I asked.

"Do what?"

"Tap with their pencils." I leaned back in my chair, and crossed my legs.

"Women do it, too," he said, putting the pencil down.

"Not usually," I said, watching him bend forward, lean his arms on the desk and tap the fingers of one hand against the fingers of the other. He saw me looking and stopped.

"Well, are you back to stay?" Jared asked.

"Would it please you?'

Jared shrugged, picked up a roughly painted and shellacked, red and purple, crudely shaped animal figurine and moved it back and forth from one hand to another.

"That would be about second grade art class?" I remarked, indicating the lumpy statue he was holding.

"Third," he said, putting it down carefully, running his finger over its shiny back. "Did you do clay sculpture in your little Amish school?"

"We were more into reading, writing and arithmetic … and learning English."

"I thought you were more into domestic and farm stuff."

"That, too."

"Simple stuff," he remarked. "For a simple life."

"A good life," I said, and waited.

"Okay, Cora, why are you here?" Jared asked, putting his hands flat on his desk.

"I came to see Daniel," I said, keeping my body still, hands folded loosely in my lap.

"He's not here."

"Obviously." I paused. When he said nothing more, I spoke. "I'd like the phone number he's using on this trip." I didn't tell him I had the number for a certain phone Daniel kept private. I wanted to see how Jared would play this out.

I could see him forming an answer, but before his lips could shape the words, his head snapped back and his eyes concentrated on the space at the rear of me. Not moving, I focused on Jared and waited.

"I'm sorry," a voice said behind me. Cool. Clipped. Confident. "Daniel has given a strict directive that his traveling number on this trip is not to be given to anyone."

"Then call and get permission to give it to me," I said, not turning, hearing the slide of fabric snaking past me, dropping into the chair next to me and then, the swishing swing of legs crossing.

"Jared, tell her, whoever she is, we cannot do that," spoke the woman next to me.

"We can't do that, Cora," Jared said. Relieved his backup had arrived, I sensed his pleasure in relaying those affirming words to me.

"Hmm. So you must be Cora Peeler," the woman said, shifting in her chair, looking at me. "Have you come to unseat me?"

"And you are?" I questioned without answering hers.

"Marie Zelinski. Your replacement."

"My substitute," I countered.

"Perhaps."

"And I would suggest," I continued, "you give me Daniel's phone number. I guarantee, if you don't, he will be more than a little chagrined."

"Perhaps a trifle peeved, but, also, cognizant that I obey orders under all circumstances ... not a trait to be dismissed," she said. Her words rang with assurance.

Until that point, directing my words into the air, my eyes had focused on Jared. I had not looked at her. Then, shifting my body, just a little, biting the corner of my mouth, I slid my eyes up and down the whole of her. She raised one eyebrow and one side of her lips in a half-smile, a hint of disrespect, and watched while I looked.

"Do you like what you see?" she finally asked.

"You're a beautiful woman," I said. And she was. Carefully coiffed hair, a lush, dark red; a tall and slender body, long legs, shapely; quality clothes, fabrics that would feel good under stroking fingers, elegant lines. "On the outside."

"Isn't that's a bit harsh, Cora? You don't know what her strengths or values are." Jared said, his expression showing surprise. "Not too Amish. Not that statement.

"I can handle her," Marie said, waving her arm at me in dismissal.

"You're right, Jared. It was neither a kind remark nor typically Amish, and I apologize, Marie," I said, looking first at Jared and then at her. "I have no idea what you are inside."

"Probably not as beautiful as the outside," Marie responded, her confident smile spreading wider. "At least by your standards. By my own, I'm downright gorgeous. Inside and out."

Reaching for my purse, then standing, I addressed Jared, "If you're not giving me Daniel's number, there's no point in my staying."

He shrugged and said nothing. He did not rise from his chair.

"Well," Marie said, "why not take a look at my office before you leave. See if you like the changes I've made."

"I'm sure it suits you," I said.

"Come see." She said, rising and walking towards the door. "That's where I'll be when you're done talking with Jared. And you really should talk with Jared," she said without looking back.

"Okay, Jared, what do we need to talk about?" I said, sitting back down, but keeping my purse in my lap.

"Isn't it obvious?"

"No." But it was. He wanted me to tell him if I was there to reclaim my position in the company. I knew it would be helpful in his planning to have that information. Perversely, I didn't want to tell him. I sat and waited. He said nothing. Sighing, reluctantly satisfied with my little obstinate 'no', I relented.

"Yes," I said, "I do know what you're silently asking, but it really isn't fair to talk to you about my return until I talk with Daniel … which would be possible if you would give me his phone number."

"You know I can't do that."

"Why?"

"You heard what Marie … Ms. Zelinski … said."

"And I also know that was never a previous directive … at least for me. I was always given his traveling cell number."

"You're not exactly an employee here, you know."

"Of course I am." I said, putting my purse down and standing. I walked over to the window behind Jared and looked out the windows. "I was here long before you, Jared. I remember the first foundational shovel of soil that was dug out of the earth for that experimental building I'm looking at right now. And the one for this building. I helped move furniture from the Buffalo offices to this these rooms. I chose drapes and pictures … colors and fabrics. With Daniel. He has never kept anything from me."

"He didn't give you his travel number this time."

"No," I lied, "he didn't. "But I'm sure you know, if I asked, he would want you to give it to me."

"But he didn't tell me that … and if I did give it to you, I'd be in big trouble."

"From *Ms. Zelinski*?"

He hung his head and didn't say anything.

Walking quickly by him, I grabbed my purse. Wiggling my fingers at him, I walked out the door. "I'm off to see Her Highness and all the wonderful changes she has made in *my* office," I said, and like Marie, I didn't look back.

"You can have that attitude," Jared called after me. "You don't have to work with her."

I walked to the end of the hall. The door to my office was open. Stepping through, my eyes swept over shades of white and gray and black to the gloriously great and clear windows that satisfied the dimensions of one whole wall. This first moment of the glowing view of fields and pastures and trees and sky had always filled my soul with song.

"What do you think?"

My eyes moved from the window to Marie and then circled the room. The room was Marie in furniture form. In fabrics and paint. In canvases and statuettes. Sophisticated. Stylish. Pricey. Chairs with scrolls on legs and backs. White, cream and gold striped upholstery, silk pillows of those same colors. Thick white throw rugs. Little glass topped tables. Llardro figurines. Splashes of vibrant colors on canvas. Creamy white walls. But the same white drapes, full and thick fabriced, that had been hung over the windows for me, now pushed back to the sides, still hung there for her. And the desk I had chosen, Queen Anne with a large writing top. That was there, too. Not thinking, I went to it and ran my hand over its rich polished surface.

"I haven't had time to replace that old piece."

"Why would you want to? It's perfect in here," I said, glancing at her.

"I like to put my own stamp on a room."

"Well, you certainly have done that."

"Thank you," she said, her lips lifting, taunting. "Though we both know it wasn't a compliment."

I said nothing. She had done a good job with the decorating. It was beautiful. Not to my taste, but reflective of hers. As it should be. I gazed at her and wondered how important this job was to her, if she did it well, if she was enamored with Daniel … and if she feared me. And I thought, what was important to me? And it was Daniel who first came to mind. And what he wanted was to feed the world, so that was what mattered to me, too.

"You're wrong," I said, regarding her statement. "It was a compliment. Only I think you should leave the desk alone. It suits this room far better than the décor I had chosen."

She looked at me as if sizing me up. Unflinching, I met her eyes and hoped she found honesty in mine.

"I want your job," she said.

"I know."

"But I'm not you," she said, sucking in her cheeks, "and I'm sure you know how profoundly kind and capable you are regarded by everyone who works here."

"Except Jared," I said, smiling.

"Even him. You're a hard act to follow ... but I can do it."

"And you're telling me that you're going to do everything in your power to do just that," I stated, nodding my head.

"I'm going to get your job," she said. "You've been away too long."

"You're right," I said. "I have been away too long. Long enough for you to know what this company stands for. The circumstances and needs of the world keep changing, shifting, and David doesn't stand still in his work. There are too many hungry people ... and he really cares. Opportunities come, mistakes are made ... the world trembles, and he needs someone, always available, a second person who can think as he does, who can see what he sees, who can anticipate what is needed. Can you do that?"

"I've done it so far."

"And he needs someone who can hurt when another hurts, someone who can feel what another feels, *and do something about it.* Can you do that?"

"I don't know."

"Let me ask you ... why do you think David gave you permission to change this room, to make it a place comfortable for you, a retreat that reflects *you?*"

"I'm not sure."

"Think about it. I don't know you well, but I *know* Daniel. He is not a frivolous man. Every decision he makes is well thought out, purposeful, and, in the long run, kind. And, Marie, Daniel knows me. He knew before I did that I wouldn't come back here. And this," I said, lifting hands, palms up, to designate the refurbished room, is an indicator that he chose you to replace me."

"But I'm not you. I am not a gentle person."

"Nor should you be, but he must have seen something in you that revealed understanding, empathy, compassion, for his goals. I don't know what he saw because, truly, I have not seen that in you. But I do know within each of us, for some so deep it seems it can't be reached, is a sense of *right,* a measure of God's love. Apparently yours is not so deep he couldn't find it. The thing for you to do, right now, is to look into your soul and find it for yourself ... and then use it to the max."

"Do you realize," Marie said, softy, "you have admitted to me you are not coming back."

"I do," I said. "It was not my intention after discovering Daniel wasn't here, to tell anyone I would not be back. Surely, it is Daniel's right to know first. But, sometimes, circumstances are such that protocol should be broken. You needed to know. And Daniel would have done the same as I did. I trust you will tell no one else until I've had a chance to talk with him."

"Of course," she said, walking to her desk. She drew a notepad out of the top drawer and wrote on it. Holding it out to me, she said, "This is his number."

"Thank you," I said, looking at it.

"Don't you find it strange he changes his number every time he travels?"

"We all have our little quirks," I said, smiling. "Perhaps, he feels safer that way. He does, sometimes, travel in scary places."

"Yes, he does."

She came near to me, bit her lower lip and shook her head. Then holding out her hand to me, she said, "I'm glad I met you and I'm sorry I was rude."

"Sometimes, we slip … but you're sharp, you'll learn," I said, taking the offered hand in both of mine. "And I'm sorry I was jealous. It blinds the eye. You're a good lady and the more we have of those in the world, the better it will be. God bless you, Marie Zelinski."

I stopped outside Jared's door and knocked.

"Cora," he said, opening it. "I thought it might be Marie. But I guess she wouldn't have knocked."

"She'll learn too."

"You almost sound as if you like her," Jared said, screwing up his face.

"I do."

"Well, I could drop dead over that."

"Don't you?"

"Like her? Not so much I'd ask her out on a date."

"Give her time, Jared. All she needs is a little more assurance. She'll come round."

"I hope," he said, shuddering. "Any way, I hope you get back here soon."

Laughing, I pulled him into a hug. "Oh, Jared, how could I not love you?"

He tensed at my touch and I laughed a little harder. Then gently kissing his cheek, I whispered in his ear, "God be with you."

"You, too," he said awkwardly.

I backed out the door and closed it.

As I walked into the reception area, Mae Summers left her computer and phones and the myriad pieces of technological equipment I could not name, those that boggled my mind and shouted my electronic comprehension deficiencies loud in my head, and scooted towards me.

"Listen," she said, grabbing me and shoving a piece of paper into my hand. "I could lose my job if Missy Marie finds out, but I've got the number and I'm giving it to you. I don't think she knows I've even got it, but I do. Mr. Daniel gave it to me in case of a problem here in the office, but she doesn't know that. And he told me to keep it our little secret. Don't ask me why? All these funny little secrets drive me crazy." She grinned. "But it's kind of fun."

"Thank you, Mae," I said, smiling. Daniel adored Mae, and she loved playing these pseudo games. He called her a woman made of solid fluff, meringue that doesn't shrink, whipped cream you have to chew, because he knew beneath a cap of silver-blond curls and within the crux of babbling words and high-pitched giggle was a competent, well organized brain. And I knew he trusted Mae to use the number as he intended. And I didn't tell her, either, I had a number for Daniel. We all enjoy a secret or two.

"Now, give me a hug," she said, "and be on your way. I know you're a busy girl. Your condo must have a ton of dust. And your cupboards need to get filled and you probably haven't even started unpacking." Then pausing a moment, her smile disappeared and her face grew serious. "I really hope you are staying ... but if you're not, it's okay. You'll decide what's best. And whatever happens, I'll see to it that Daniel's all right."

"I know you will," I said hugging her hard. "I love you, Mae Summers."

"I love you, too. God bless you."

That night, sitting cross-legged on my bed, holding my cell in one hand and Daniel's number in the other, I contemplated the words I could say that would not hurt. But even if all the words in the dictionary were floating inside my brain, I could not seem to choose the ones that if put in the right order would not cause his heart to bleed.

Throwing the phone onto the bed, I slid my feet onto the floor and moved swiftly to the closet. Grabbing a garbage bag from the pile by the closet doors, I began stuffing it with dresses and skirts and pants and blouses. One bag, then two, then three. Then losing a battle with a chemise stuck on a hanger, the undergarment refusing to let go no matter how hard and how long I tugged at it, shook it, screamed at it, I sank to the floor, buried my head in my hands and cried.

Exhausted, I went to the window, looked out at the lights reflected on the dark water and then leaning my head against the glass, closing my eyes, so weary, I gave myself to God. And as the draining thoughts and feelings of this world left me, His peace, His Spirit within me came to be realized again. His rest. His love. I opened my eyes a looked upon the water. And smiled.

Depleted of sadness … self-pity … anger, filled with Spirit, I went to my desk and turned on my computer.

Dear Daniel,

> *If I were to open my hands to hold all the wonderful moments you've given me, they would fill to overflowing. For me, treasured memories are not sharp-edged visuals; instead, they are soft-edged images that are veiled with beautiful emotions and feelings, wonder and joy. When I think of you, it is my heart remembering the touch of your hand on my arm; the tilt of your head when you smile; the bend of your body against the side of a booth as you listen to me; the spontaneous burst of laughter; the kindness, the acceptance in your eyes; the quietness, the listening; your smile when you see me; the strength of your hugs; the swing of your body as you walk away; the joy and excitement in your voice when you tell me of your readings.*

> *So many things, I cannot number them all. Their magic will never die.*

> *I know no words that hurt are harmless no matter how they are meant. And while the words I now write may be painful for you, please know they are also painful for me.*

And remember no matter where God takes us, whether it brings elation or suffering, He make it to be good within His eternal plan and, in the end, He will disclose to us our part in that plan.

I am going back to the Amish world. Blunt words, but I know of no other way to tell you. I have wrestled with my own selfish desires even while I struggled in my prayers to hear God's directives for me. Would that I could live in both worlds, English and Amish, but in my heart I know that cannot be. I must do what my very soul demands. Dear Daniel, I truly believe God has work for me to do in the Amish community. I believe there are lessons to be taught there that I must learn and I must share. I pray I am not wrong, that my faith, my love for Him, is strong enough to hear what is right. If it is not, I pray God will increase my faith and reveal the path He laid down for me, the path He framed for me even before I drew one breath, and I pray He will lead me to it and guide my way upon it.

I will miss you and I thank God for every minute He gave me to be with you.

You will always be in my prayers. Please pray for me.

May God be with you and may He pour his blessings abundantly upon you, my dear, dear Daniel.

Love always, Cora

It was done. I hit the send key.

The phone rang in the night. Startled, not totally awake, instinctively I reached for the phone and pushed the start button.

"Are you sure this is what you want to do?"

"Daniel!" The fuzzies in my eyes left. I was awake.

"I just got a chance to read your email."

"It's the middle of the night here." My heart was beating fast.

"I know."

"But that's all right," I said, quickly, not wanting him to say he would call again later and then hang up, yet dreading to hear judgment or condemnation ... or even sadness ... in his words.

"I know," he said, this time so very softly. "Cora?"

"Yes?"

"Are you sure?"

"I think so," I said, after a pause.

"If you can't say yes, it's not a surety."

"Oh, Daniel, I'm as sure as I can be," I said, my heart hurting.

I heard his sigh whisper across the miles.

"If you really feel this is what you should do, if you really believe this is your destiny, then do it. But remember, nothing is written in stone. You can always change direction … "

"Thank you," I murmured, interrupting. Grateful. Not wanted to be persuaded to stay. And he was the only one who might be able to accomplish that.

"Like I was saying," Daniel continued and his utterance was a dirge in my ears, "humans learn from experiences, they grow, and there is no dishonoring in changing direction. Sometimes, that very action comes from wisdom gleaned from life's happenings. If you go, you don't have to stay."

"I know," I said.

"And I'm here for you. Always. Don't be ashamed or hesitant to call for help … or advice." He paused. "Or encouragement."

"Thank you." I didn't know what else I could say. More words would bring tears.

"Good luck, Cora."

Though I knew he struggled to speak firm and strong, I heard the tremor in his voice. Even so, I knew he would not ask me to stay.

"Thank you," I said, again and hoped my gratitude … and love … rang through the wires.

I went into the kitchen, picked up a spoon and dug into the shoofly pie.

Chapter Twenty-One

I left Buffalo the second week in November. There was nothing left to be done. My home was rented by another. Chosen pieces of furniture had been given to friends, the rest to a charitable entity. My clothes ... clean, folded and bagged ... were left with Mae to sort and decide which she would keep and which she would donate. All my possessions ... jewelry, curios, paintings, plants ... had been distributed to those who would value them. Legal issues, insurances and financial holdings were resolved. All I had left for myself were my car, which I would give to Harriet, and three boxes of journals and treasures I could not part with. Mae was keeping the boxes for me. "Just in case," she had said. All I took with me from my belongings were a minimal amount of clothing and a tiny crystal porcupine, Daniel's first gift to me.

As I left the city, I lifted a concerned look at the sky. It seemed to be filling with clouds hanging heavy. I shivered in anticipation of the promised cold front predicted on the early weather report. I had a full day of driving ahead of me. Snow would not be a welcome manifestation on my itinerary.

It was not long before the first heavy snowflakes floated downward through the air, plump, lacey enhancements, twirling, pirouetting, frolicking in a leisurely sparkling white dance. And that beautiful, graceful performance was totally unappreciated by me.

By the time I reached the Dunkirk thruway exit, the snow had stopped dancing and was attacking my car. My windshield wipers were racing with the flakes, now sharp round pellets, and the snow was winning. And though it was still early and I wasn't yet hungry, I thought this might be a good time to stop for lunch, and therefore, I departed the thruway and headed for the Dunkirk tollbooth.

Near the exit were several chain restaurants, but I decided I would go into the city and seek out the restaurant Daniel and I had found that served perfect sweet potato fries It was a place that held special memories for Daniel and me. So, slowly and carefully, I went through the tollbooth, drove straight for a bit, then turned onto Central Avenue, the road that would take me through Dunkirk to Lake Erie, and to perfect sweet orange fries. As I slipped and slid and strained my eyes to see through the swirling snow, it seemed to take longer than it should. When I saw the street sign for the road that would take me down Washington Avenue to the church I had visited on my way to Buffalo, I turned onto it. It took me to the church.

There were no cars parked near the building. Not a good sign if I wanted to talk with anyone, but a good sign if I wanted an easy drive into a slot in the lot. And since my want was a quiet, calming and reflective uniting with God, I was content to know there would be only myself, and, I presumed, the pastor of the church.

Thankful I had dressed in warm clothing, I pulled my hood over my head, tightened the scarf around my neck, changed my thin leather driving gloves for thick, home knit mittens, a gift from Mae, and opened my car door to the cold. I got out. It was colder than it had looked through the car windows. I stood shivering for a minute weighing the choice of a cold, wet run through the snow to the church's side door against the slipping back into the still warm cushions in my car. I chose the vision of candles and stained glass waiting to soothe me and pushed through the snow.

The side door was locked and my sneakers were soaked. Again, I had a decision to make. I could make a run to the car or I could force my cold feet around the church building, scurry up the snow covered steps and try to open those big wooden doors that logically would also be locked. Moreover, the run around the building and up the steps was much longer than the run to the car which was only a few yards from me. And sensibly, if I went to the car, I could step in the snow packed indentations I'd already made and, maybe, not get my feet much wetter.

Before I could make a rational choice, a small pickup truck rammed through the snow into the parking lot, grabbing my attention. Holding my arms tight around my body, hoping to conquer the cold and failing, I watched a bearded, bundled man park his vehicle, get out of it and stomp his way through the snow to stand by me.

"You're early," he said. "I'm sorry I wasn't here to unlock the door for you."

"Good thing I wasn't Jesus," I mumbled under my breath. As I turned my face to him, I must have looked puzzled … and I was …

for bending his face close to mine, he squinted, pursed his lips, and nodded a couple times.

"I don't think I know you," he said.

"I don't think I know you, either," I said, raising an eyebrow and shrugging.

"Well then, let's get acquainted ... inside where it's warm," he said, pulling off one glove, rummaging in his pocket, and bringing out keys.

I watched, freezing, while he fumbled with the lock and, finally, connecting, turned the key and pushed open the door.

"Ladies, first," he said, motioning me in.

Letting one last breath of air billow into the cold, I stepped, quickly and willingly, into the building.

"Brrr, this is one doozy of a storm," the old man said, trodding in close behind me. Slamming the door closed, he stretched out his hand. "Pastor Manford. But you can call me Manny."

"Cora Pooler," I said, trying to step away from him, but finding no spare room on the landing. "I'm not quite sure what I'm early for."

"Eh?"

"You said 'You're early' to me and I'm wondering, early for what?"

"Aren't you one of the ladies comin' to set up and cook? I figured you were from one the other churches comin' to help. The rest of 'em, from this church, should be here soon. This storm is gonna bring plenty poor homeless souls looking for supper and a bed."

"No," I said, "I'm not one of them. Actually, I don't live around here and ..."

"Oh, my goodness, here I thought you were one of us. Didn't notice your license plate ... probably couldn't have seen it anyway, probably covered with snow," Manny interrupted. "I apologize. You just go on downstairs and I'll get you a cup of coffee and maybe a cookie, if I can find one, and the ladies'll be here any minute. They'll fire the stove and get the stew goin' right fast. There'll be food for you directly."

As he talked, Manny pushed my hood down, *nice fur there, should of kept you cozy warm*, unwrapped my scarf and pulled my coat zipper down. Not knowing what else to do, I let him.

"Manny, I'm not homeless and I'm not poor. I came to pray," I protested when he nudged me a little towards the down steps.

"Say what?"

"I'm traveling. I'd been in your church before, so I knew it was here and I stopped to pray ..." Before I finished speaking, I heard the muffled voices of women calling out to one another on the other side of the door. Shivering, I felt the door push against us and a great swoosh of cold blow in from its narrow opening.

"Wait, wait, wait, ladies. We'll get right out of your way," Manny said, tugging my arm and waving me up the stairs. Pushing against me to make room on the stoop for the women, he followed me up a few steps, then stopped. One hand still on my arm, he fumbled in his pocket for a key, and finding it gave it to me.

"There's a light switch inside the door. Just go on in. You know where the sanctuary is?" he asked.

I nodded.

"Okay. I gotta go help the ladies set up. And I apologize again. I guess I should have realized you couldn't be too poor what with having a car, a pretty nice car at that," he said, patting my back, "and your clothes are pretty nice, too."

The sounds of the ladies stomping snow off their boots and chatting away as they went down to the kitchen reached up to my ears. Looking down I saw one round, pink faced woman turn and shout up the stairs to Pastor Manford, "Hey, Manny, Alice couldn't make it. She's sick. Don't you know, that flu bug is gettin' us all. Sorry to say, but nobody here knows how to make the bread. She's the only one with a yeast recipe stuck permanent in her head. Guess maybe though, we can make some biscuits. Don't taste as good, and don't smell as good, but they'll do. No point in runnin' to the store in that mess outside. Likely to get stuck in the snow or fall on the ice and break a leg. Don't ya know."

"I know how to make bread," I said to the Pastor.

"That Letty's a chatty one," he said.

"I can help."

"You came to pray. You just go on up. The ladies and me'll do fine," he said, dropping my arm and backing down the steps.

"Don't fall," I said, instinctively holding out my hand.

"Don't you be worried. I've lived most of my life in this here church. I could find my way up and down and all around blindfolded ... or even asleep," he chuckled.

"Just be careful." I watched him go down the stairs and disappear into the kitchen, then after a moment, I opened the unlocked the door to the social room, found the light switch, illuminated the room, crossed it and went into the sanctuary. Still as beautiful as I remembered it, as peaceful and deific as before, I slid into a pew near the back, bent my head into my hands and quieted my mind to receive God's love.

I didn't stay there long. My body and mind emptied of tension, I went back through the social room, locked the door and followed the pastor's trail into the kitchen.

The room was empty of people. Lettuce, juicy half sliced tomatoes, celery stalks and cucumbers lay abandoned on a counter. Steam rose from a large pot of water boiling on the stove. Pot holders and wet kitchen towels, some embroidered and yellowed with age, were drooped over the sink, strewn over the counters and one, lay too close to the stove burners. A large packet of hamburg, blood juices seeping through its packaging, sat open in one side of the double sink. In the other were used cutlery and coffee cups. Cupboard doors and drawers were open revealing stacks of dishes, cooking utensils and silverware. All indicators of hurried exertion, but no sign of workers.

I moved the towel away from the stove and walked over to the door that led into what seemed to be a large recreation room. There I saw the pastor and his ladies struggling with cots and sheets and blankets. A few tables had been set up, but there were more, still folded, leaning against a wall. Apparently the kitchen help had been requisitioned to assist readying the room for the homeless.

I went back into the kitchen and scoured the cupboards and refrigerator for ingredients that would come together and produce sweet, yeasty bread. I had no idea how many would find their way to the church for a warm, filling meal or a bed for sleep, but I knew the bread recipe I had used so many times for a large Amish family, if doubled, would feed an entourage.

I was running warm water out of the faucet, testing its temperature on the inside of my wrist and measuring it into a cup, when Letty, grumbling, and another lady, quiet, came into the kitchen.

"Well, what in the world are you doing here?" Letty asked, stopping inside the doorway, scowling. "I ain't never seen you before."

"I'm making bread," I said, pouring the water into a large bowl and whisking the liquid to dissolve the waiting yeast.

"Well, I hope you're using the cool-rise method or that bread won't be ready 'till doomsday."

"That's exactly what I am doing," I said, smiling. "I just hope it's enough."

"We'll probably feed twenty-five to thirty," she said. "Not more than ten will probably stay and sleep. Hard to tell. The storm's really bad. Supposed to get worse."

I poured in the warm milk I had heated on the stove and the softened butter.

"Could you hand me the flour?" I asked Letty.

"Who are you anyway?" Letty asked while the other woman brought the flour to me. "Alice always made the bread. But, of course, now she's gone and got sick and ain't none of us knowing how to do it the quick way. Besides, too many of us are sick. That miserable flu bug just won't go away. Not enough of us left to do it all ... the beds, the tables, the food. Besides I ain't made bread since bought bread started tasting better than mine. If you can believe that."

Behind her, the other woman, her strong and plain face serene, winked at me and smiled.

"You from another church?" Letty asked.

I shook my head. "No."

"Where then?"

"Just passing by and thought I might drop in and say a little prayer," I said, dumping the dough on the floured counter, kneading it. "Your sanctuary is beautiful."

"It is," the second lady said, stepping forward. "My name is Grace. And wherever you're from, I'm glad you're here."

"Me, too," I nodded, smiling, sensing a kindred aura. Her body was tall; her back, straight; her bones, solid and her demeanor spoke of elegance, graciousness.

Stepping past me, Grace went to stove and looked into the pot. "I think I'd better add some water. Looks like it's almost boiled out." Adeptly, she moved and reaching under the sink pulled out a pan and filled it from the faucet. "Probably would be a good idea, Letty, if you started slicing the celery for the salad." She took the water and poured it carefully into the pot on the stove. "It's spaghetti instead of stew tonight. Easier and faster," she said to me, "and good."

"I have to let this dough rest for twenty minutes," I said, "then I'll shape it and put it in the refrigerator for three hours. After that we can bake and it will be good and warm and smelling wonderful when your friends come in."

"Good timing," Grace said, adding, "and there's a whole bunch of chocolate chips in the cupboard. I think we'll have just enough time to make cookies. Plenty of them. Enough for leftovers to send home with the children for a nice evening snack ... and enough for the grownups, too."

For the next several hours, we worked together ... chatting, laughing and, sometimes, silent. Occasionally placating the impatient, domineering and boisterous Letty. When Manny and the third lady, Helen, were finished setting up the tables and cots in the big room, Manny went up to his office and Helen helped in the kitchen. People ... women, children, men ... started coming before the food was ready. Anticipating those early arrivals, Helen, a retired teacher, had set up a corner in the big room with blocks, dolls, toy trucks, books, paper and crayons. On a separate table, beyond the waiting cots, she had placed cards and puzzles for the adults. The children, quiet at first, then progressively louder, played in their corner, straying sometimes, curious, wanting to be with their mothers, tired. Helen seemed to know their wants and needs and, unobtrusively, kindly, kept an order in their mayhem. A few of the adults played cards and one lone man, coat still on, scarf tight around his neck, bent over the puzzle, shuffling the pieces, pushing them together to make them fit, shaking his head in frustration. But most huddled by the wall, watching and chattering. There was an air of pleasant waiting.

"Maybe, we should go out there and talk with them," I said. "They're our guests and Helen's got her hands full with the children."

"And we got our hands full in the kitchen," Letty said, spooning a mixture of noodles and sauce into several big bowls on the counter. "Told ya, not enough help today. Besides, they all know each other and they're doing fine. You can bet your booty the gossip is flowing fast and furious. And Gracie girl, you can start slicing up that bread ... it's cool enough. And you, Cora, get those salad bowls on the table." She twisted her mouth. "It sure would be easier to just put the food on the plates, let 'em sit and eat it up. This family style stuff is just too messy."

"Aye, aye, Captain," Grace said, looking at me and grinning.

When all was ready, Manny came down and helped Helen gather and lead their guests to the laden tables. Then he sat down with them, said a prayer, and began the passing of food. With the sharing of spaghetti and salad, and with the common act of slopping up sauce with chunks of bread, bodies relaxed and voices mingled. Manny told jokes, children swung their legs under the tables, men shouted comments from one table to another, and there was laughter all over the room.

Grace and I moved from table to table replacing empty bowls with those Letty refilled in the kitchen. As needed, Grace refilled glasses with milk and juice; I, cups with coffee and tea. We worked well together.

It was good. It was as if I were back in an Amish family.

Thank God for paper plates and plastic forks ... and I mean that literally," Grace said, handing me the last dirty pan. "Perhaps, someday we'll have disposal pots."

"I kind of like the feel of soapy water," I said. "It's a cozy feeling."

Grace shook her head and laughed.

Manny and Helen had left to deliver our visitors, full-bellied and laden with cookies and containers of spaghetti, back to their housing. After they had deposited them out of the cold and into welcoming warm rooms, Helen went off to her own home and Manny picked up his wife and they returned to the church to counsel and enjoy the company of the seven men who stayed overnight. Letty, complaining of back pains and swollen feet, left as soon as the eating was over. Despite her cantankerous words, she had worked hard and had proven her heart was tender and helpful. I was happy I met her and she, too, reminded me of home ... of the rich, varied personalities of the kindhearted, hardworking women in black.

"Where are you staying this night?" Grace asked." It's still snowing pretty hard."

"I know," I said. Letty had called down the stairway when she opened the outside door and told us the snow was still piling up, but Manny had swept her car and she was sure she could plow through the drifts of 'that miserable white stuff. And by the time you guys go, Harold will have your cars cleaned off and the lot cleared.' Harold, a big, strong, dear man, who would be sleeping on a cot in the church, had grabbed a shovel after dinner and was attacking the snow with furious determination.

"There are a couple motels near the thruway. Probably I'll go to one of them."

"No. I don't think so," Grace said, resolutely. "I think there's a great, big welcoming house on Leverett Street just waiting to wrap itself around you"

"Your house?" I asked, smiling.

"My house," she said, patting my back. "And before you say, 'No,' you have to understand it's a house just aching to surround you in friendly warmth."

"How could I say 'no'?"

"Another cookie?" Grace asked. "Maybe another marshmallow in your chocolate?"

"No," I said, quietly, burrowing deeper into the soft couch cushions. "This is just perfect."

We sat, relaxing, comfortable in the soft light and warmth of Graces living room.

"It's been a good day," she said.

"Rewarding."

"Yes. All to the glory of God."

"Yes," I said, "all to the glory of God."

"Are you tired?" Grace asked, putting her cup down.

"A little," I said. "In my body ... but this is good. Your house brings peace to my tired bones ... and into my head and my heart.

"I'm glad."

"Is this your husband?" I said, picking up a photograph from the small table beside me. "He has a kind face."

"It is," she said. "He's been dead for awhile. But we had a good marriage, a happy marriage, full, no regrets. I keep only the joyful memories ... the rest, except for their teaching, didn't matter. How you about you, Cora? Do you have a special person in your life, a family?"

"I did. I hope I will again."

Grace raised her eyebrows.

"I think I should explain ... I'm an Amish woman. I *was* an Amish woman." Exhaling, I closed my eyes for a brief time. I was tired and the thoughts pressing within the whole of myself were shouting to be let loose. I felt I could trust the kind, godly woman sitting across from me and relieve my deep need to tell my story with voiced words.

"I am so full of the want to be undivided, to be whole … whether it be English or Amish."

Leaning forward, Grace handed me a delicately edged cloth handkerchief.

"If you're comfortable sharing your heart," Grace said, "I'll listen with care and respect and love. And all that you say will be mine alone."

I didn't realize my eyes had shed tears. I took the handkerchief and held it to my nose. It smelled of roses, like the sweet delicate and fragile scent of old ladies. I smiled and pressed it under my eyes and against the wet on my cheeks.

"I'm shunned," I said, my voice struggling to be heard.

Grace nodded gently.

I bent my head into my hands for a moment. How fast a bond can form, I thought. Then dropped my hands and looked at her, saw a sister.

"Twenty years ago I took a baby down the hill from my home and into the village. In the middle of the night, I did that. I took her and I abandoned her. I walked away and left her."

Grace sat silent.

"Someone saw me. A boy. He saw an Amish woman holding a bundle, walking in the night and he told the sheriff. And so the crime and the criminal, though it was not truly a crime for I had left the child safe in a place where it was promised there would be no prosecution, that act, because the boy had seen me, became a known happening to the sheriff and, through him, to the Bishop. And it came to be discovered that I was the culprit. And because I didn't reveal all circumstances to the Bishop as he demanded, I was shunned. And because I knew I would not ever answer his questions, and, therefore, would remain, always, in a state of sin, a state of shunning, I left the community and moved in to the English world. Where I have been for twenty years."

"And now you want to go home?" Grace whispered.

"And now I am torn." I looked into her eyes. "I want to go home … but it is so hard to leave the English ones I love."

"And it is too hard to choose?"

"But I have chosen." The tears came again. "I have said goodbye to the English world and I am going to confess, to answer all questions asked, and be Amish again."

But it's hard," Grace said.

I nodded. "Yes, it is hard."

"And you are leaving a special someone you love?" Grace asked, softly. "A man?"

I sighed and rubbed my temples.

"You don't have to answer," Grace said, and I heard great compassion filling her words.

"I want to."

Grace leaned back against her chair, folded her hands and lay them in her lap.

"I've loved twice in my life. A woman's love for a man." I sighed, hugged my body, rocked it a little, stopped and kept my eyes on hers. For strength. And I answered her. "Yes, there is one who is English. But it's an unfulfilled love. Never spoken, but *known*. And it hurts me to leave it."

When I didn't speak more, Grace tilted her head and it seemed as if her words strained against her lips, forcing themselves to come out. I could barely hear her ask, "And the other love?"

"There was a boy. An Amish boy. Aaron. He lived next door and we played together when we were young. When we could. When there was time. Even Amish children have tasks and chores. But there was time to play, too." I smiled, remembering. "There were the fields to run in. Creeks to explore. Barns to hide in. And trees, so many trees ... I was a good climber. Even in skirts. And snow in the winter to roll in, to slide down the hills, to throw at each other. Aaron was a little older than I ... not much. When I was about twelve, I started liking him in a different way. And about that same time, he started hanging around with the other Amish boys and ignoring me. I vowed someday I would marry him."

I looked up at Grace. Her body resting against the back of her chair, her hands folded in her lap, she sat so still in what seemed a peaceful silence. Her eyes met mine and her lips curved upward.

"When I was sixteen, courting age, I went with the other girls to the Sunday Sings." Grace looked puzzled, so I explained. "It's kind of a chance for the boys to look the girls over and choose one. Except they already pretty much know who they want. Anyway, the singing's held in different houses. The boys sit on one side of the room; the girls, on the other. And afterwards, the boys ask their chosen girls if they want a ride home. Aaron asked me and I said, 'yes'. So, he drove his buggy up to the door and we took the long way home."

"A buggy ride in the moonlight," Grace said. "Romantic."

"It was. And I was smitten." I looked down at my lap, then, smiling, up at Grace. "He was, too. He really liked me."

"Did you marry him?"

"No. I would have. He asked me. But his mother didn't like me. And he lived alone with her. He said it would work out. But it wouldn't have. I'm sure she had a hard life. She didn't have a husband. He had died young. And, like I said, they lived alone. She would accept help from no one. Not from family. Not from neighbors. I could have been a big help. But she truly didn't want help of any kind. She just wanted Aaron. I don't mean to be unkind, but she was a mean woman. Both to me and every other Amish woman. I tried to overlook her harshness … her unending gossip and her malicious, hurtful conduct. But, finally, it was too much and I told Aaron I couldn't marry him."

Grace waited, quietly, for me to say more.

"I know I hurt him. And he was too prideful to beg. He was really angry with me. We didn't stay friends. It was awkward at first, but as the years passed, it grew easier."

"And then you left."

"I did. Much later."

"And now you're going back."

"Yes."

"Will you see him?"

"I already have. I've been staying in the village … for various reasons … and I've seen him, tried to talk with him. But he says I am dead. And I am. I'm shunned. Doomed to hell. At least for the Amish. And so, Aaron won't talk to me."

"Forever? Are you shunned forever?" Grace asked, her words tender. "Why would you go back?"

"My heart is Amish. And no, I don't have to be shunned forever. Not if I confess and repent and behave in the manner of a proper Amish daughter. You see, there will be a testing time before I can be accepted back into the Church. The brethren will want to take me back into the fold, and they *will* take me back … joyfully … if I demonstrate true repentance. The Amish are loving. But they are strict and I have to display obedience."

"And you are going to confess? And repent?"

"Yes. And I *will* prove to them that I am earnest and credible."

"Your answer has a firm ring to it."

"Yes."

"And a bit of defiance."

"I don't mean it to be that way."

"Will you see Aaron?"

"I hope so." Weary, I bent my head and pushed my hair away from my face. Without even touching it, I could feel the heat of anxiety-forced warmth flush my face. "He lives alone now. His mother is dead. I think ..." I said pausing, looking up at her and narrowing my eyes, "I think, when the shunning is over, he will accept me as he did before. He's Amish. And it's not Amish to be unforgiving or to hold a grudge."

Her fingers pleating her skirt into narrow folds, Grace bit her lip and leaned towards me. I could see it troubled her to think I had abandoned a child. I could tell she wanted to ask me more.

"Ask the question," I said, quietly, nodding in her direction. "I will tell you."

"The baby," she said and I could see an embarrassed flush sweep down her cheeks to her neck. I sensed she knew she was moving into a protected part of my past and that it was not her wont to pry. Instinctively, I knew she sought the secrets of my heart from a position of love.

"The baby," she repeated, "was it yours? And Aaron's?"

"No."

"But you did leave a child in a place that was not her home." She wet her lips with her tongue, then drew a deep breath. "You gave her away."

"Yes," I said, answering that question willingly, yet guarding the revelations of a community's hurt, reluctant to answer more. I had given her the most important answer. She knew the baby was not mine. That was enough.

"How painful that must have been," she said.

Her words were tender and I could tell she took no pleasure from taking me back to that place of hurt. But she had taken me there and I wanted her not to delve deeper.

"Yes," I said, softly, hoping she was done. But she wasn't.

"It was the right thing to do?" she asked, doubt in her tone.

I looked at her. Her face showed concern. There was almost a yearning, a hope, that I could explain, justify the horrendous thing

I had done. There was no vindictiveness in her utterance. I knew her heart to be caring; her motive, to be helpful, so, I would answer as kindly as I was able. I couldn't explain it all. So much of that time, so many of those happenings, belonged to the brethren ... to them only.

"And how do you think now?"

I covered my face with my hands and shook my head. She was causing me to think and perhaps that made her queries worthy of consideration. Perhaps it would do my heart well to reach into it, force what was there into clarity. Perhaps I could share a greater part of me with this new and gracious friend without betraying the secrets of others.

"How do I think now? I don't know," I said, attempting to answer her question honestly. I looked at her and spoke with an earnest attempt to illuminate the thoughts that were emerging from their storage place in my heart and were rising to fill my head. "We make choices as best we can, with good intentions, but sometimes, we make them too fast, without clear thinking. Sometimes, we don't tarry long enough to hear God's wisdom.

"The baby was a little girl ... Annabelle, renamed Talitha by the woman who took her and raised her and loved her. She's grown now. A young mother. And she's all right. Her life was good ... but there were so many lives damaged by my actions ... and the actions of my sister, Violet, the Bishop ... and the beautiful one, my sister, Lily, who was broken, so terribly broken. And the healing is not complete. The damage lingers. Perhaps, if I return and do what my family, my community, my Bishop deems to be right, perhaps that will be a soothing balm that heals the places within me that I can't see, that we can only feel. I don't know."

"Oh my," Grace said, drawing a deep breath, letting it out slowly. "I hear such turmoil in your words. Is there a way for me to help?"

"I think you have been a help. Compassionate ears pour a healing ointment over sorrow. And yours are such as given by God ... the oil of joy, His gift. He is my help. His unleaving presence sustains me. His hand upon me holds me up." Covering my face with my hands, my head bent, I couldn't stop the tears that came.

"Yet you are still so very troubled," Grace said, moving from her chair to sit near me on the couch, taking my hand in her hand, and with calming strokes rubbing her thumb over mine. "Your body is trembling."

"In the years I've lived in the English world," I said through the tears, "I have seen beauty beyond the Jesus that was painted in the words of the Bishop's sermons. I have seen Jesus doesn't care if my skirt is exactly thirteen inches from the ground or if my hair escapes from my kapp. I know He rejoices when I study His Word, when I say His Name, when I lift my arms to Him in the church pew, when I say 'Amen' loud and clear. I have felt Him when I talk to Him. I have known His power, His strength when mine was too small. I have seen Him in sunrays and rain drops. I have known the joining with the Holy Spirit when His gift of sweet tears filled my eyes as the strains of holy song ascended from my heart to Him. I am fearful, if I go back, I could lose that."

"Dear child, dear heart, that cannot happen. He has sealed you as His own."

That night, as I came from the hall bathroom, readied for sleep, I saw a note on my bed.

Fear thou not; for I am with thee:
Be not dismayed; for I am thy God:
I will strengthen thee;
Yea, I will help thee:
Yea, I will uphold thee with the right hand of my righteousness
Isaiah 41:10 KJV

Chapter Twenty-Two

Central heating is a fine English accommodation. Even old houses, such as Grace's, were blessed with that wonderful, non-chopped-stacked-dragged in chunks of wood, warmth. A flip of a switch and cold air retreated.

Rousing the next morning to the unfamiliar sounds of Grace's old house wakening ... creaking, settling, odd little scratchings ... my eyes resisted the urge to open. Snuggled within a thick downy comforter, my face was as warm as my toasty flannelled body resting inside the bed covers. Silently, warm and cozy, I thanked Grace for flicking that magical switch on the furnace.

"Mmm," I murmured aloud. It felt so good. Burrowing deeper into the soft puffy nest of slippery silk, I closed my eyes and relished those last sleepy moments of delicious comfort. And then, with great effort, I slid the comforter off and shivering in the warmth of imagined and expected cold, swung my legs over the mattress and stepped onto the floor. My feet sank into thick, spongy carpeting. Warm. It was good.

By the time I had showered and dressed, the sun had risen full and was shining through the translucent bedroom curtains. I went to the window. God had spread a heavenly glow and as the sun's bright rays fell on the earth, they sparkled it with luster. The snow flashed diamonds; the trees dropped shimmering tears. Looking across the way, I watched great mounds of snow, freed and falling, released from roofs, drop down and splash in a flurry of fluffy fragments as they hit white snowy lawns sprinkled with sun melted patches of grass.

"I slept too late," I said, walking into the kitchen.

"You slept just the right amount of time," Grace said, smiling, placing a platter of pancakes, a bottle of syrup and a bowl of strawberries, blueberries and sliced bananas on the table. "Coffee, hot chocolate, milk or juice? Maybe all four?"

I grinned. Breakfast for lunch. An English thing. Never would an Amish home serve breakfast at noon. And never would an Amish man, woman or child rise with the sun already high in the sky.

"Looks wonderful," I said. Hunger was running thick in my stomach; longing juices rose under my tongue.

"Come sit." Grace said, indicating the chair I should take.

The table was set for two.

"I hope you didn't wait to eat until I woke," I said, moving to the table, waiting for her to sit before I did.

"No, no, no. Like you, I enjoyed the unusual pleasure of sleeping longer than the stars shone in the sky."

"You slept late, too?" I laughed.

"I did. It seems to be the usual thing for me to do these days," Grace said, shaking her head. "Lately I have had such a hard time getting to sleep. I'm sure not why. Old age, I guess. But anyway, you go to bed late, you get up late. Now, sit yourself down and we can get to the task of eating."

So I did. And so did she. But first, Grace spoke a short prayer, patted my hand, forked a pancake onto my plate and passed me the syrup and fruit. We ate in a pleasant silence, too full of comfortable companionship to need the filling of space with words.

After we ate, leaving dirty dishes in the sink, Grace drove me to the church to get my car. The lot had been cleaned and the sun was melting the residue of snow the shovels had missed. How fast the weather can change, I thought. A blizzard when I went to bed. A sunny day when I woke.

"Drive carefully," Grace said, hugging me. "I've enjoyed your company so much. Will you write to me?"

"Yes. And you, to me." I smiled thinking of the note I had snuck onto her bed that morning when I went upstairs to get my things:

Dear Grace,

Thank you for your kindness. Breakfast was lovely; talking with you was wonderful. And try a hot water bottle on your tummy when you go to bed. It will help you go to sleep ...an old Amish trick.

Love and Blessings, Cora

I drove west on the lesser highway, Lake Erie on one side of me; farm land, vineyards and scattered woods, on the other. As I got closer to Erie, the spaces between houses grew smaller and the traffic, heavier. It slowed me. Looking up I saw clouds gathering, blocking the sun and lacing a veil of gloom. Contemplating possible precipitation from the darkening sky, I thought it prudent to get back on the faster road; therefore, I made my way to Highway 90. As it was a faster road, it would take less time to get home and I wanted to be in Wander Lane before deep darkness or heavy rain.

Driving through the heavier traffic, I focused on the cars and trucks zipping in and out of the thick lines of vehicles. Past Erie, the roads were less crowded and I allowed a second layer of thought to drift through the lesser need for intense concentration on driving. And thus, images wove their way through my mind … dark clothed persons, men milking cows with their hands, women hanging clothes on their front porches, young boys standing tall on open wagons holding tight rein on the strong, massive horses pulling them, children swinging metal lunch buckets as they walked to school, fat Amish donuts. And I was hungered to see them real.

As I turned south near Cleveland, sprinkles, not cold enough to freeze, pattered against my windshield. They didn't slow my drive, and though the clouds hung full, I didn't think they would let loose with a barrage of showers falling from their heavily stocked warehouses, so when I reached the turnoff to Berlin, I took it, thinking I would stop there. I hoped the treasured sights of Amish country might fill a portion of the great empty pocket in my heart, that hurting loss of heritage that haunted me. Certainly Berlin, commercialized, but still mostly authentic, would ease the pangs of immediate need.

The drive through Holmes County poured a nostalgic warmth through me. And with a voracious longing for a visual connection with my old life, I pushed my foot heavy on the gas pedal only to be slowed when I mounted a small hill and saw a horse and buggy clomping along ahead of me. I followed it. Opening my window, I ignored the cold raindrops hitting the side of my face and listened to the steady clip-clop of the horse's hoofs. It was the sound of home. And as I drove behind the buggy, ears and thoughts attuned to the harmony of Amish life, more memories assailed my mind. I heard the click of sealing lids on freshly canned jelly jars, a cow's tail swishing against the barn wall, the slide of Da's shoes on spilled grain, Maem's 'good night' murmurs … all swelling my heart with a precious longing. Just as it had been … twenty years ago. I wondered could it be again? *Should* it be again?

I shuddered and pulled off to the side of the road. Is that what I really wanted? To be Amish again. And I thought of Daniel.

A mile east of Berlin I passed the Christmas Shoppe, tiny twinkling lights showing through its windows, bright in the darkening day. Glancing at my watch, I saw the afternoon had passed to early evening. The increasing density of the rain intensified my difficulty in seeing. I drove even slower. I wanted to see it all. Every shop, restaurant, little business. I considered stopping at the Troyer Country Market. The thought of their cheeses and their pickled baby beets released a flow of saliva under my tongue. But worried about storms and time, I didn't.

Coming near to Cindy's Diner, I remembered its wonderful Amish date pudding. Slowing my car to a crawl and ignoring the plea of my stomach to stop, I stretched my neck to look in the diner's window. As I was searching signs of Amish life within, and, simultaneously, willing the steering wheel to stay straight, I saw a young Amish woman dash out of the eatery and scurry towards a horse and buggy waiting for her, just beyond me, on the side of the road. I slowed and stopped behind the buggy. The rain was falling so hard, I didn't want to hinder the driver's ability to see. Before she stepped up and pulled herself into the buggy, she glanced my way. And my heart stopped.

I pushed my way out of my car and hurried to the buggy. But before I could get there, she was already settled within it, skirts pulled safe and the uncurtained side door closed.

"Lily," I cried out. I was too late. She must have heard me, for she opened the curtain and glanced at me, her face questioning. At the same time her driver slapped the reins against the horse's back and the slick haired black beast trotted forward.

"Lily," I called again and even as I spoke her name, I knew Lily was dead and the woman surely must be Annabelle. No, not Annabelle … Talitha.

I had seen her. It could be none other. This is where Olivia said she lived. In Ohio. Berlin. And I had seen her. Lily's beautiful baby.

The image of her mother. My shoulders slumped. What should I do? Nothing. Olivia's appeal rang in my head, *Leave her alone. She is happy. Let her be.* I dropped my head and, wet and cold, walked back to my car. Standing by the car door, I watched the buggy go down the road until it disappeared.

The woman had looked so much like Lily. Her face. Her eyes. I wished I could have seen her hair. But it was hidden under the cloak that covered her *kapp*. There were no escaped strands visible. I imagined her hair blond. I wanted it to be blond. Like Lily's.

I knew I could catch up with the buggy. But my heart knew Olivia's words were wise and, besides, it was already too close to full dark and I still had far to go. Yet, I could not regret my detour. Not even if it meant I would have to travel through the blackest night and the fiercest of storms, I could not regret seeing Annabelle ... Talitha.

Wet and trembling, I climbed into my car. I drove back to the main highway and made my way through the progressively dense downpour to Wander Lane.

Finally, exhausted, I pulled into Olivia's ... Dianna's ... driveway. Though the night was gloomy and the house was dark, it felt and looked like heaven to me. A refuge. A shelter for my tired mind and body.

Taking nothing inside, I went into the house, threw my coat on a chair, went up the stairs to my ... Dianna's ... bedroom, slid my feet from my shoes, pushed the button on my CD player and climbed into crisp sheets and soft blankets. The music played soft ... *I love you, Lord.* That's all I heard. It was enough. I fell into asleep. I didn't notice until the next morning that the furnace was off and the house was cold.

Contemplating the bedroom's cold temperature, I considered a quick and immediate shower. But shedding my clothes and scrunching my shivering body, knowing that was not a prudent idea, I turned up the thermostat and crawled back into bed.

When the room was heated enough to endure, I got up and went about the business of readying myself for the day.

The rain had not stopped but, thankfully, it was merely a drizzle. Partially thawed bagel in one hand, opened umbrella in the other, I stepped out the front door and went to the car. There I juggled the bagel with the umbrella and managed to open the car door and get in.

Anxious to see if Harriet had done what I asked, I drove to her diner.

Entering the restaurant, I saw a young Amish girl, new to me, gathering used dishes and wiping tables. A second Amish girl was moving among the substantial breakfast trade refilling their coffee cups. Bailey was at the counter watching them.

"Bailey?"

"Cora Pooler," Bailey said, turning her eyes on me. "You're back."

"Is Harriet here?"

"Nope. Not yet," she said, raising one eyebrow and smirking. "She's training me to be boss lady while she's gone."

"I see," I said, nodding towards the Amish girls, "and it looks like you've got good helpers."

"I run a tight ship."

"And you've got a crew already trained to work efficiently and thoroughly."

"Maybe," Bailey said, "But I keep an eye on them. They're not perfect, you know. Maybe their mamas' taught them the workings of an Amish kitchen, but a restaurant's different. All kinds of new stuff to learn. But it shouldn't take me long to bring them up to snuff."

"Will Harriet be here soon?" I said, smiling ruefully. Maybe Bailey wasn't enthused by physical work for herself, but she surely did like to delegate tasks to others.

"Don't know. She's been feeling poorly." Then, apparently seeing my concern, said quickly, "Nothing serious. Just the flu."

"You're sure?"

"Who can be sure of anything?" she said, her eyes perusing the dining room. "Listen, I've got work to do. Those girls could move a little faster."

"Did she leave a package for me?" I asked, placing my hand on her arm.

"Not that I know of," she said, a scowl flashing over her face as she wiggled away from me. "You gonna sit and order some food or not?"

"I'm not," I said. "I'll be back later." And I left the restaurant.

Stepping over the crusty mound of dirty snow bordering the curb, I slipped and reaching out, spread my hands over the hood of my car to keep my balance.

"Treacherous landings no matter where you put your feet. Miserable winter. Made for the young. Better get yourself a cane."

Embarrassed by my awkward position, I regarded the old man shaking his own cane at me. His lean frame was tightly bundled with thick knitted hat, scarf, and mittens and his bulky black coat hung heavy and long on his body. I smiled when I saw his goulashes. Far too large for his feet, buckles undone, sides flapping, they exactly fit the caricature he appeared to be.

"You wanna go in and get a cup of coffee?" he said, motioning with his thumb at Harriet's restaurant. "I'll pay."

"Are you hitting on me?" I asked, laughing.

"You women. All alike. A man tries to be nice and what do you do? You think he wants to hop in bed with you. All it meant was a simple invitation for a simple cup of coffee," he said, shaking his head.

"Okay," I said, pushing myself away from my car. "I'll go in with you."

"Forget it," he said, flapping his hand at me. "I'll get me a decent Amish woman to drink with. No sass from them." And shaking his head and sputtering words I couldn't decipher, he walked away from me.

"Poor man," I murmured, shaking my own head and smiling as I got into my car. "He has no idea he was just talking to an Amish woman ... at least an almost Amish woman ... I think."

Although, I was anxious to talk with Harriet, my mind, heart and soul were aching to see the ground that could be mine again, so, perhaps, it was a good thing Harriet wasn't yet in her eatery. I would see her later.

Trembling, wanting to see and soak in every speck and shred of my brethren's Amish life and land, I drove my car, slowly, carefully, up the hill to Amish country.

Beautiful to my eyes were patches of pristine snow snuggled within the root crevices of the old gnarled trees that flanked the hill to my parents' house. In my mind's eye, I walked in the woods, feeling the crunch of acorns and the spongy mat of fallen pine needles under my boots. And I ran my hands over the knobby bark of the barren leaved oaks and tall, pine-coned evergreens. I saw winter coated rabbits hunched on their hind legs, still as statues staring at me, then sudden as a meteor shot from the sky dart on winged feet into the scrub. Soundlessly. And in my mind's ears, I heard birdsong, running fox feet crackle the dead ground leaves beneath them, the rustle of hawk wings, the drop of a weak branch heavy with ice.

I was nearly there. I could see the outline of my house. Mine. Soon, I prayed. I drew closer. There were clothes hanging on a line on the front porch, heavy from their washing and not able to dry in the water filled air, moving in a slow rhythm with the persistent bursts of wind. Sturdy, similar, matching Amish clothes ... solid black, deep raspberry, hunter green, navy ... rich colors, dark colors, that would not harbor pride. They would hang there until the sun stayed long enough to dry them.

I saw no one there. Neither in the yard nor by the barn. Maem would be inside baking, maybe bread ... or stew, rich with farm butchered beef and garden grown vegetables. Or she might be cleaning. George's wife and Violet helping. Da, in the barn tending animals. George, helping. The children in school or if they were too old and were finished with the studies taught there, they would be with their elders learning the skills that sustain a family.

Sighing, I remembered the rules, the Order. I had been gone too long. It would be George that was head of the house now, making decisions, albeit with Da's wisdom sought. Same with Maem. It was her time to step down, too. And seeing beyond the house was proof ... piles of lumber. Preparations for the raising of the *dawdi* house, the grandparent's house.

I saw no flowers. The soil along the pathway to the front door showed only rich brown, almost black, earth peeking through the melting snow. And the garden by the side of the house was plowed into gaping furrows of walloped soil. Those plowed rows sat strong and sturdy waiting for the distant spring planting. And deep within the cultivated furrows laid the remaining flakes of yesterday's early winter storm, captive swirls of white. And so, I looked upon Maem's garden, neat even without the bright colors of flowers and vegetable foliage. Then, smiling, I saw the remains of one broken pumpkin, pieces spread in the far corner. Perhaps left there for a forest creature seeking an easy meal.

I drove along and then, stopped by Aaron's house. Biting my lower lip and exhaling from deep within, I viewed his house with consternation. It had a shabby look. Yet, all was in order. There was no rubble, no forgotten hoes or shovels or tools laying in the yard. The porch was empty, swept clean. The windows, each curtained on one side, glared at me, straight and clean. His garden, too, like Maem's was plowed and empty, waiting for spring.

I looked at the barn across from the house. The large front doors were closed and scattered before them on grassless ground, softened by melting snow, were the large of pieces of old and beaten machinery … plows, hay rakes, manure spreader. On the far side of the barn, in a barbed section of land next to a well-stocked corn crib, several cows stretched their silky, moist muzzles pulling hay from a high piled stack, then chewing, their lower teeth moved side to side breaking the dried grass in, for me, a funny and endearing manner. So solid and stalwart were cows. Sweet, big animals, unwavering in their daily gift of milk. Gentle. I loved them. I missed them. And soon I would seek them out, slide my arm around their massive necks and stroke their scruffy, thick winter hide.

Turning my head, I looked, again, at Aaron's home. No sign there of a happy family. No clothes hanging wet in the winter cold, no footprints in the melting patches of snow, no little faces in the windows, no warping rocker on the porch. Aaron's house. Lonely and sad.

I drove on.

I passed fields of dry, yellowing cornstalks, decaying nutrients for a soil depleted. There was a lingering beauty in their starkness, a wisp of sorrow that they had been left behind from the harvesting. Urged by the influx of melting snow, the creeks were running fast. Ice covered hollows in vast flat fields glistened under the sun's rays; diminishing sprinkles of rain splashed against the melting frozen water. And where the small hills rose and rolled, short-lived streams of water rushed down their slopes and into ditches, muddying them, overflowing them, spilling their surplus onto the road. Windmills turned at varying speeds, spinning to the will of the wind. Amish countryside. Landscape of my youth.

I drove and drove and all the while, it seemed as if my heart, my head and my very soul swelled to near rupture from the wonder of it all.

And then, the twisting, turning, horse trampled roads took me to Bishop Herrfort's farm.

Heart pounding, I turned in his driveway. It took me to his barn. The building was open, and he was inside holding tight rein with one hand on a nervous, side-stepping black buggy horse while, with the other, he rubbed a thick cloth over the animal's front quarter.

As I got out of the car, I saw his wife, Martha, come out of the chicken coop set a close distance from the barn. Head down, walking briskly, she carried a heavy, metal feeding bucket towards the house.

I knew she had heard the car, but she didn't look up. Her back was bent. She looked old. It must have hurt old bones to step so quickly. I guessed she had recognized either me or the car and had chosen not to meet my eyes with hers, to avoid obeying the required ordinance to turn from me without acknowledging my presence. Neither had Bishop Herrfort given any indication that he was aware I was standing on his property. Me, Cora Pooler. A living, breathing person. Visible.

"Bishop Herrfort," I said, moving into his territory, not getting too close, as he eased his tight grip on the bridle allowing the horse to toss his head. I stepped back as the animal, mane waving, lifted his forelegs and neighed. Bishop Herrfort, concentrating on the horse, ignoring me said nothing.

"Bishop Herrfort," I said, again.

He jerked the horse's head down and pulled him into stable, closed the doorway between him and the rebellious steed, and reaching over the gate, slipped the halter from the horse's head. Throwing the rubbing rag onto a broken milk stool stuffed in a corner at the back of the barn and ignoring me, he limped past me and went through the barn door.

"Bishop Herrfort," I said a third time. "I want to confess."

He stopped. Then shifting his body from the direction of my voice and standing, his body tight, rigid, he spoke out, words loud, strong, forceful. I could not see his face; his back was to me.

"If you want to be speaking to me, put yourself in decent clothes and get rid of that evil vehicle."

He walked away and went into his house.

"Are you okay?" Harriet asked, bending over me, patting my arm as I sat in the little storeroom behind the kitchen.

She had said nothing when I stepped over the threshold into her restaurant. She had simply taken my hands into her own and held them for a bit, then had led me to the storeroom and bid me to sit.

"I'm fine," I nodded. "Please, you sit, too."

"I have the clothes for you," she said, taking a box from the shelf and setting in my lap. "Just as you wanted."

"And only Hattie knows?" I asked, rising and setting the box on the floor, then leading her to the plain, wooden chair across from me. "Please, sit, Harriet." She looked so tired, older than when I'd left.

"And your maem. She knows sumpen's going on. There weren't no way to keep it from her. You didn't tell me how long you'd be gone, but you made it clear you wanted clothes sewed and ready quick as you got back. Hattie needed help. And I trust your maem. Maybe she guessed the reason, maybe thought so, anyway. I dunno, and it might have set her hopin hard.'" Harriet pushed stray hairs from her face and rubbed a hand over one side of her face. "I didn't tell 'em the reason and they didn't ask leastways, not with words. They don't pry and they won't tell nobody what their hearts are thinkin' … hopin' and it would hurt 'em real bad if you stomp on those hopes. But you gotta be carefull. Don't be doin' this lessen' you're sure. Better to break their hearts now than whet their appetites and give 'em a little sugar with them thinkin' their gonna get more and then you grab the candy away."

"I won't." I was scared. Inside my heart was torn. *I wanted to go home.* But what if my heart was fooling me? What if I went back, confessed, rejoined the church and my head was still full of English?

"Cora?" The soft voice of Lily poured through my mind. "What if I took them both?"

"You can't. Harriet said, one. To take both would be stealing. You have to choose."

"But I like them both the same."

"Root beer or butterscotch. Either or. Or none. If you can't choose, don't take any."

"You're mean, Cora," Lily said, grabbing the butterscotch.

On the way home, she told me she had made the wrong choice and her tongue hungered to have the root beer candy drop sitting on top of it.

Harriet's voice broke into my thoughts.

"It would break your maem's heart if you went back and then left." Hattie shook her head. "I didn't want her to know. Not for sure. Not 'till it was done and you be sleepin' in her house."

Folding my hands, I brought them up under my chin.

"They sewed 'em navy, just like you wanted."

I nodded and looked at the box. Someone had colored daffodils and tulips on it.

"Not so pretty like the English dresses are."

"No, they're not," I agreed. I thought, probably, Hattie's grandchildren had been in her shop and decorated the box. Hattie's grandchildren. My grandnieces. Family.

"You gonna try one on?"

"What did maem say about it? The sewing of the dresses?" I leaned forward, moved eyes to concentrate on her face.

"Nothing. I told you; the Amish don't ask. You know that. But she's scared. Afraid to believe it." Harriet paused, scowled. "You gonna change your mind so's her worries are real?"

"I don't think so."

"You don't *think* so. What's that mean? You're maem set in that same chair you be sitt'n in now, just a tremblin', thinkin' she's so close to getting' you back. Scared. Maybe she should be."

"It isn't just my decision. It depends on what Bishop Herrfort decides. He makes the rules, not I, Cora Pooler," I said with a sharp nod.

"Ain't that where you were this mornin'?"

This was hard. Harriet was a combination of sternness and gentleness. And she was relentless.

"He won't talk to me unless I'm dressed Amish."

"And like I be askin' you before, you gonna try one of those dresses on?"

"You shouldn't have let her help. Hattie could've made them herself," I said, standing and reaching into the box. I lifted the dress. The skirts were heavy. I moved so my back was to Harriet and took off my outer clothes, lifted the dress over my head and dropped it to cover my body. Turning, I turned saw Harriet had covered her eyes.

"It's safe to look," I said, smiling wistfully.

"You said navy. So's that's what I got. Pink flowers would have prettier."

"We Amish ladies don't aim to look "pretty. God looks at the heart."

"Men look at the body. And it looks better dressed out in pink flowered silk than harsh, heavy navy," Harriet said with a sharp nod, then a sly smile and a wink.

"Bishop Herrfort requires navy ... or black, or green, or old lady maroon," I said laughing, then serious. "I have to please him. He holds my future."

"Balderdash! He'll take you back. Probably will even be glad to. He's Amish and whether I like him or not, he's got an Amish forgiving heart."

"Then maem shouldn't worry."

"She's been through a lot," Harriet said and I heard compassion in the softness of her words.

"She has," I agreed. "I pray she will let the hurt go."

"When you goin' to the Bishop?"

"Now," I said, quietly.

"Ain't no time perfect," Harriet said, sighing. "Guess this is as good as any. The old man's belly'll be stuffed to the brim with his noon vittles. They say his wife's cookin' is pretty good. I dunno. Never had it. Meat loaf's her specialy. Least that what the girls in the kitchen say. Prob'ly not as good as mine."

"Well then let's hope she made meat loaf for today's lunch," I said, smiling. "And I'm absolutely positive hers is not nearly as good as yours."

"Be careful with Herrfort. Don't be thinkin' Amish when you're talkin' to him. Keep your head thinkin' English. But keep your words soundin' Amish. Don't let him best you."

Chapter Twenty-Three

"**A**aron?"

He was in his barn spreading hay in an empty horse stall. I knew he had heard me, but he didn't stop his work. Animal heat released from the row of stanchioned cows permeated through the air and, though the big front doors were open, the building was relatively warm. Even so, a shudder ripped through my body and left me trembling. I was afraid of this man. I was afraid I had put such a thick wall of betrayal between him and me that he would not help me and I would have to go to my father. I didn't want that. I didn't want Da and Maem to hope. I didn't want them to know I was going to Bishop Herrfort until it was certain I could be accepted into the fold.

"Aaron?" I said again, still with hesitation, with dread. "Look at me. I've come to ask a favor. I need you to help me."

His hayfork stayed moving in his hands ... pushed under the hay pile, lifted tufts of the dried grass, tossed them onto the stable floor, pushed at the clumps and spread them even, then reached into the hay again ... all in the rhythm of a farmer's song.

"I want to come back."

His back yet to me, he paused.

"Aaron?"

"You want to be Amish again?" Still he did not look. Still he would not face me.

"Yes." The word came forced out of my mouth. Once said, it could not be erased. It was the true beginning of a journey that could not be stopped. A decision made solid.

"*Yes*," I said, again.

"How can I know that?"

"Aaron, I have never lied to you." I willed him to look at me, to *see* me.

"You said you would marry me."

Stunned, I looked at his figure, his back confronting me … set stiff and unyielding. He had thrown old words, unexpected words into the air to surround me and hurt me with memories of a time long before the shunning, a decade of days lived without his friendship, those days before I walked down the hill. We had been so young then. Had he never forgotten? Had rejection haunted him all these years? I had never known it was so.

You know why I couldn't marry you," I said, pleading to the face I could not see.

"You said it was my maem, but it couldn't have been that. My maem was not evil."

"She didn't like me," I said, wringing my hands. "She told you that. She told *me* that." In my frustration, I lifted my arms and shook them at him. "She told me she would make life unbearable for me. She said those very words. I couldn't live in the same house she lived in. No matter how much I loved you. For sure, I would have grown to hate that life … maybe even hate you. Have you never understood that?"

"She was my maem," he said, dropping his head.

"You're right. She was your maem," I said, gently. "I should have been kinder … more understanding. For I did love you, Aaron. With all my heart. I was wrong not to work harder at knowing your maem and I wish I had given her time to know me. I'm so sorry. And I can't tell you how much it hurt me to break our love. Please, will you forgive me? Be my friend again."

"You're sure you have chosen to return to the Amish way?"

"Yes."

"And will not stray?"

"It's for always." Again a shudder ran through my body.

"Then I'll help you," he said, laying the hayfork against the wall, pivoting slowly, then looking at me. He saw my dress, but said nothing.

"I need a horse and buggy," I said. "And to leave my car here."

Staring at the car, he frowned.

"I'm giving it to Harriet." I could see the car was a problem for him.

"How?"

"It's simple. I'll come and get it and drive it back to town. And she'll drive me back here."

"Not so simple," he said, still scowling. "Old Herrfort ain't gonna be letting you off Amish land 'til you've proved yourself worthy to be Amish."

"Can we worry about it later?" I asked, "I need to see him now." And I did. My knees were shaking and my heart pounding fast. I didn't know what to do about the car, but I did know I had to go to the bishop with a horse and buggy. And I had to go right then, immediately, while my adrenaline surged hefty and my resolve held strong. I dreaded this meeting almost more than anything I'd ever done. If I didn't see him right then, I might think myself right back into the English world. Daniel's world. And I dare not give that world, or Daniel, more than a flashing moment of thought. I had chosen and I needed to act on that choice, firm it solid, wrap it indelibly around my heart. I had promised Aaron. I was committed. And the Amish don't break their word.

Looking at me thoughtfully, Aaron tilted his head, tucked his tongue to fill the inside of his lower lip and nodded, slowly, three times. Then he hauled down a harness hanging against the barn wall and lumbered towards the horses' stalls. I stood and watched him make ready a small, frisky steed and his old black courting buggy for me to take to the Bishop, to the man who held my future.

Crawling into the buggy and settling myself firm against the backboard, Aaron pulled a heavy blanket from the floor of the buggy and tucked it firmly around me.

Before I lay the reins on the horse's back, I said 'thank you' to Aaron. He didn't reply.

Please, God, let this be the right thing.

Not to dawdle or leave time for my mind to think on what I was doing or where I was going, I drove the horse at a fast pace. It wasn't long after the time of the midday meal and I figured, on this cold and damp day, Bishop Herrfort would be working in the fair warmth of his barn. He was not. Although the doors were open wide, allowing me to see the scope of the barn, there was no sign of the bishop. Slapping the harness straps, I tendered the horse to go farther thinking I might find the Bishop in the fields beyond. I determined he was not within a mile of his house, so I went back to ask his wife his whereabouts.

When Martha Herrfort didn't answer her door in a reasonable length of time, I pounded on it harder. I needed to know where the Bishop was. I didn't want to make this trip again. And this time, thankfully she came the door quickly in response to my noisy knocking.

"I's good to see you, Mrs. Herrfort," I said pleasantly, reluctantly remembering the gracious salutation that was expected from a sister member of the faith.

"Is it you, the Pooler girl?" she asked, squinting. "No, you're not Violet. You look like her, but you're way too old. I don't understand."

Her visage was hoarier. Twenty years had deepened the lines of her face and there were more of them. They crinkled across her cheeks like the narrow pleats of a blush pink skirt and dropped down to her neck, sagging its heavy and old roughhewn skin.

"I am Cora. The oldest Pooler girl," I said, laying my hand on her arm.

"Cora?" She said, moving her arm away from me. "No, Cora is gone. A long time ago. A bad girl. The evil one touched her. She went away ... I can't talk about her."

"I came to see the Bishop. He doesn't seem to be in the barn or the fields. Could you tell me where he is?" Fearful that I had frightened her with my presence, I spoke in a gentle voice.

"Oh, no, I can't disturb him. He would be angry," she said, wringing her hands and shaking her head in short, quick motions.

"I really need to see him. It's important." I tried to keep my words calm for she seemed to be flustered. Too many years. She was already old when I left, but now it seemed she had entered the stage of revisiting the mannerisms and trepidations of the very young.

"Is he in the house?" I asked.

"Shhh. He's sleeping," she whispered. "Don't tell anyone. He keeps his naps a secret. I think he's afraid the men will think he's lazy ... or too old to watch over their sins." She giggled. "But he's really just as stern as ever. They better watch out."

"Will he wake soon?"

"I never know."

"Please can you wake him and tell him I'm here?"

"Oh, no," she said, narrowing her eyes and pursing her lips. "You'd better come back later."

"I can't do that," I said. Putting my hands together and pressing them against my chin, I leaned towards her. "Look, why don't I just go over to the table and sit there for awhile, just until he wakes."

"Oh, I don't know." She paused, seeming to bring her thought together. "I guess that would be all right."

So, I sat and waited while she puttered about kitchen.

It seemed a long time passed before I heard his shoes clattering across the next room's hardwood floors and then into the kitchen. I stood to be ready for him.

He frowned when he saw me.

"I hope I haven't come at an inconvenient time," I said. "I know you're a busy man and I'm sure your schedule is full. Yet I'm asking if you would give me a few moments of your time?" I spoke carefully, choosing my words judiciously. I didn't want him to know Martha had revealed his napping habits. It would embarrass him. Pride, I thought, 'though he never would admit to that. And raising my hand to cover my mouth, pushing my fingers tight against my mouth, hoping it looked as if I were stifling a sneeze, I smiled a bit.

"You're dressed Amish," he said, pressing his lips together, squinting as he moved his head forward and scrutinized my appearance. "Your skirt isn't long enough."

"When it was stitched, I wasn't there to be measured. It appears I am taller than the sewer guessed. The fault is mine and I'm truly sorry. I'll be sure to have it corrected."

"Thirteen inches above the ground," he said.

"Yes," I agreed. "Thirteen inches above the ground."

"The rest will do." He ran his tongue over his lips. "And the car?"

"I borrowed a horse and buggy to come here. As you wanted. The car is at Aaron's. Your nephew. I don't know how to get it back to town without driving it."

Bishop Herrfort didn't respond. His eyes stayed on me. Stern. I could see no compassion.

"You're here to confess?"

"I am."

"I'm listening."

"Aren't you going to sit?" I said, thinking an ancient one's body would surely grow weary listening to the plethora of sin about to be expunged from a storehouse of English experience. And I, not sure how long my trembling legs would hold me up, wanted to sit, too.

He folded his arms over his chest. "When I'm ready."

I bit my lip. Until he sat, sitting was not an option for me.

"You've been gone a long while."

I waited.

"Shunning isn't a punishment." He drew his eyebrows together. The furrows between them were deep. As were the wrinkles of his forehead. I remembered a long time ago a particular visit to my doctor. I was still new in the English world and all the inexperienced phenomena and some of the strange mannerisms of the English fascinated me. There was a little girl in the waiting room, sitting there while her mother was in with the doctor. The girl was about six or seven years old. She was pressing the rims of dimes into each side of her face. She had been at it the whole of the time her mother was out of the room. Curious, I asked what she was doing.

"I'm sticking dimes in my cheeks," she said, frowning as if it were totally obvious.

"But why?" I asked. The why of it was not obvious to me and it seemed very strange.

"I'm making dimples. My mother says if I had dimples I could be a celebrity. 'Cause I'm so pretty. Except I don't have dimples," she said, shaking her dark curls. "So I'm making some."

"And what does your mother say to that?"

"She says if I don't stop, the dimes are gonna go right through my brain and out the back of my head. And besides, it's not so great being a celebrity anyway. At least that's what she says. But I think she's wrong," the little girl said, shoving the dimes even harder against her skin.

"Isn't it hard to talk while you're pushing the dimes into your face?"

"Nope."

"Is your mother a celebrity?"

"Kind of. She's a weather girl. On television. I watch her," she said, getting up and walking in circles around the room. After a while she stopped in front of me. "My mother says if you dig a hole deep enough, you'll fall into China. Maybe that will happen to my dimes if I push too hard."

Back in the kitchen, I thought maybe if Bishop Herrfort pushed his fingers into the furrows on his forehead, they'd go right through his brain and the back of his head and fly into a world far beyond. And if he stayed attached to those fingers, his whole body would follow them and end up in a place we couldn't see. Gone. At least for awhile. Until I was firmly ensconced in this little Amish world near Wander Lane. Sin forgotten. Happy.

"Did you hear me?" Bishop Herrfort asked, his forefinger pointing firm, his voice rumbling thunder, his eyes flashing lightening. "Shunning is *not* a punishment. It is to save your soul, to bring you to repentance, to lead you back to the ways of the Order, the rules of the Ordinance. There is rejoicing when a sinner returns, when one of our own confesses, repents and is forgiven. When an Amish woman, you, falls into the world of the wayward English, and then, walks away from that fallen world and comes home, it's a time for celebration. "

"There is kindness in that world too, the English world," I said, softly.

Bending his head, the bishop shook it slowly. Then he sat at the table, put his forearms on it and folded his hands. His shoulders slumped and his head still moving, one side to the other, he sat silent.

"I came to confess," I said, still with quiet voice.

"Then speak," he said, waving me to sit.

"When I left … twenty years ago, no, twenty-one now … I didn't speak the whole truth. But you know that. That's why I was shunned. Partly. And because I had taken the baby and left her with Olivia. An Englisher. I guess you would think that was condemning her to Hell." His face looked up. There was an anger showing beneath its surface. "But it isn't only the Amish that are saved. You might think that, but Jesus can be in the hearts of the English, too. In the heart of anyone who believes. Wherever they live. "

"They don't follow His words. Pride. Vanity. It's in their speaking, in their clothes, their cars, their movies, their music," the Bishop said. "And they make those things, those things that have no heart, no soul … they make them into idols. Physical things that have no eyes to see or ears to hear their prayers. And sex. They show their bodies; they share bodies. To everyone. With everyone. And greed. They have to have more and more and more. Things. They think it's enough to say, 'Jesus, Jesus, Jesus' and then do whatever they think will make them feel good. Where is kindness and gentleness? Where is peace, joy? Where is love?"

"Where is it here? I don't see it in your face," I said.

"You have changed. You don't speak like an Amish woman."

His words came into my ears in tones that bespoke no anger, but the hidden sounds, the crawling undercurrent I couldn't hear, rang loud against my mind.

"I am trying to speak truth," I said. "Isn't that what the Amish do?"

"It *is* what the Amish do. So what is the truth you are here to tell me?"

"The baby wasn't mine. She was birthed by another woman. A young girl who was raped. I took her baby, to save the mother from shame, and since I couldn't keep the baby, I took her down the hill and left her, abandoned her, to the only place, yes, the only English woman I knew that was kind enough and would love the baby enough to assure her a good life."

"You didn't think the Amish would have cared for their own?"

"Not then. I didn't think so then. I could only think to hide the child. To keep everyone safe. Keep life as it was."

"And now?"

"They would have loved her. She was an Amish child. She wouldn't have been blamed for the circumstances of her birth."

"And the mother?"

"She would have been forgiven," I said, lowering my head and covering my eyes, pressing my fingers against them to hold back the tears, whispering, believing at that moment, "I was wrong."

I heard a murmur from the far side of the room. Dropping my hands and looking there, I saw Martha, by the sink, her hands clasped together, held tight against her heart. And glancing at the Bishop, I saw his face, naked and anguished.

"It is her heart," he said, rising. "It sometimes gives her pain."

I stayed in my chair and watched him move quickly across the kitchen … to her. He took her, his arm sliding gently around her waist, one hand covering her own clenched hands, and he guided her into the next room … slowly, carefully. I saw his face, bishop mask absent, as he passed me. Bent over her, looking down at her, leading her, the love shone splendid and abundant over the whole surface of his face. A shudder ran through me, an awareness. Bishop Herrfort was more than just a bishop. He was a man, a husband. The rules and regulations were a cloak of responsibility and obedience he wore over his love … for God, for Martha, for his flock.

I had been wrong about the Bishop.

When he came back into the kitchen, Amish façade returned, I looked at him differently. The crevices on either side of his mouth still pulled his lips downward in an ever present scowl and his eyes still pierced sharp, but I knew beneath that frontage, goodness pumped from his heart and colored his thoughts and decisions.

"Who was the father?" he said, not wasting time.

"I don't know."

"Who was the mother?"

"I would rather not say."

"Yet you want to be Amish," he admonished.

"Yes, I do. I am Amish." I leaned back in my chair. The wood was hard, unforgiving, against my body. My words challenged him and he took up the dare.

"It is not the want of Amish neither to lie ... nor to have secrets. We are an open people, not given to deceit," he said, raising a fist and pounding it once into the air.

"And a peaceful people," I said, mocking him, making the same gesture as his.

"I didn't mean to be defiant," Bishop Herrfort said, apparently recognizing peace was missing in the movement of his arm. "It is God who judges and it is He Who determines where and when and upon whom His wrath should be poured. Not I. I ask His forgiveness. And yours."

"And I, yours," I said, regretting my pettiness. "But don't you think every human being, English or Amish, carries some thoughts or deeds that are theirs alone, never shared?"

"I ask again, who was the mother?" he said, ignoring my question as if it had never been said.

Raising my arms and bending my face into my hands, I, silently, beseeched God to give me strength and wisdom ... to give me words of truth and compassion, words that would not dishonor a dead sister.

"It was Lily ... still a child ... confused, frightened, even terrified," I said.

"Did she know you would take the baby away?" the Bishop asked.

"I don't think so. She was beyond reason. Have you never been so overwhelmed by circumstance that you couldn't sort the real from the overpowering images in your mind or the unbearable terror and sorrow in your heart?" Lifting my arms, holding my palms up in a pleading position, I leaned over the table, reaching with my words, my yearning, to touch his emotions. "Can you not feel her horrendous pain?"

"God gives us strength to bear all things."

"Doesn't He sometimes give us that strength through others? Doesn't He sometimes call upon another of His children to give the strength and love and prayers, silent and voiced, that His child in pain, struggling, has lost and has forgotten the way to Him, the way to His help?"

"And that was you? Given strength for her? " His tone was doubtful in my ears.

"Yes, that was me. That night it was me."

"God told you to give Lily's baby away ... an Amish baby, one of our own? God told you to abandon that precious child to an Englisher, to abandon an Amish infant to eternal Hell?" He looked at me and I saw a maze of acute astonishment frozen on his face.

"I did the best I could. I prayed. I was afraid, too. Like Lily. I wanted the baby to be safe. I wanted Lily to be whole and well again ... in her body, in her heart. It's hard to be Amish. There are no bends, no soft corners of safety in the rules. They are straight and harsh. They don't hear a soul crying ... or the heart weeping. I prayed. Jesus heard me. I know that He did. Amid my doubt, the desperation, I knew His compassion. He didn't leave me in that time of great need. He knew my intention. And He knew my weakness; He knew my errors. Yet, even so, He stayed with me."

"Did He tell you to leave the Amish?"

"No, that was all my doing," I said, sighing. It seemed as if a great and heavy veil of weariness was falling over me. The remembering brought sorrow.

"You should have told the truth."

"Perhaps," I said.

"You should have told the truth," he repeated, this time firmer.

"Yes," I said, succumbing.

"You have confessed it all?"

"Yes."

"You are done with the outside world?"

"It's not all bad, you know," I said, softly.

"I've seen young Amish boys, thinking they're men ... and girls, thinking they're women, I've seen them ... they go out into that English world ...*Rumsprina* ... and it pollutes them. For the boys ... cars, fancy women. For the girls ... bright colors for their faces and figures, men in tight pants. For both, freedom. Too much freedom. It makes right choices too hard. They forget rules protect. And direct. They forget the security of family. They forget God."

"Most come back," I argued.

"You didn't. Not for many years," he said, shaking his head, drumming his fingers on the table.

"But most come back," I said, again, watching his fingers striking the table in a steady rhythm. He saw me and stopped.

"Yes, they do," he said, "but it makes the Amish life harder. They remember the easy ways, worldly ways. They're grateful for family and the peaceful, godly way of life, but when the workload gets hard, when they're tired from long days in the fields and the barns, when the snow blows cold and the roads iced and slippery and horses move slower than cars, the old memories, the easy English habits, slip into their minds and thread their way through the old ways of The Order. And there is discontent. For awhile."

"And then?"

"And then the importance of obedience seeps deeper into their hearts and they realize, *know*, that the way to eternal life is found within it. Do you understand that?" he asked, standing, pushing his hands, hard, into the small of his back, rubbing. "Do you understand the importance of obedience?"

I stood, too. And waited.

"You don't answer," he said, sitting.

"Eternal life," I said, sliding into my own chair, perching on the edge of it, "is for all who believe that Jesus is the Christ. Our Savior."

"Salvation comes to those who live a godly life, who obey the rules in all they do."

"According to the Ordinance?" I said, trying to keep defiance out of my tone and out of my heart.

"It keeps them in obedience to the ways of God."

"God?" I wondered if the Orndung with its manmade rules, thirteen inches above the ground, was part of his God, was meant to be worshipped. And I was ashamed, for I knew he was aware of the difference.

"Father, Son and Holy Spirit," he clarified.

"Yes," I said, closing my eyes, straining for words that would tell of God's wonder and unconditional love for all who loved Him. "And a stained glass window or red stained lips do not keep you from God. It's taking Him into your heart, the Holy Spirit sealing your heart for Him that takes you into the realm of His being, that brings eternal sanctuary to you ... believing what cannot be seen." Stopping my words, pausing, praying his ears would hear, I added, "And it is not works that bring you to God or bring you salvation. Works are a way to give glory to God for His gracious gift of eternal life. Those works are done from a heart that is grateful and wants to serve Him in all ways."

Quickly, unmindful of his back, Bishop Herrfort shoved his chair away from the table, its legs soundly scraping the wooden floor, and stood. Then turning from me, he walked across the kitchen and looked out the window.

"You show your ignorance, your loss of Amish doctrine," he said, not turning. Staying in my chair, resolved to listen to his words, I struggled to hear the strong, but even toned, spill of his voice. "It's foolish to believe such nonsense. You have to continually work to retain your salvation. *Faith without works is dead.* Your eternal fate, your rewards, will be determined by the substance of your obedience to the Ordnung. And I fear for you, Cora Pooler. It seems the English world has filled you with pride. I pray you are sincere in your desire to return to the Amish. Such a happening would bring joy to my heart. But it must be sincere and complete."

Pressing my lips together, clutching my hands in my lap, I bent toward the bishop, my body intent on his words, my mind searching a way to reveal the knowledge of my heart with words he would let himself hear and grasp.

"I understand what you say," I stated, pleading from my heart that he listen with his, "and this is my home ... my family. I want to come back. But I bring with me comprehensions gleaned from intermingling with those who live outside our community. There are among the English those who love God as much as we do, who have accepted God's gracious gift of His Son just as we have.

"And, yes, some of them, they who are lovers of God, are women with perfume behind their ears, lace on their underwear, colored streaks in their hair. But they love God. They show joy in their faces when they sing, when they *shout* song before their God, *our* God, when they lift their arms in praise ... and, yes, when they *dance* before Him.

"Why do you hide your joy behind a solemn face? Why don't you sing passionate praise, dance with abandonment? Celebrate with mighty sound? It is there ... in you ... the joy. I know it is." I looked at him, looked for a fissure in the stern cover of his face. I couldn't find one, but his eyes stayed on me, clear and watchful, and I knew he heard what I said.

"Before I was shunned," I continued, "I lived in a house full of love, surely shown in a quiet way, but a passionate love shouted out enhances that wonderful, gentle, quiet affection. Why can't your face reflect the enormous joy in your heart? Why can't your arms lift in holy praise to the God above? Why can't you hug your wife where all can see?" And then I began to perceive an awareness spreading from the outside edges of the bishop's face and moving inward, like two rows of dominoes falling, one on either side of his cheeks, each domino falling against the one next to it, meeting in the middle, crashing. And it was anguish that was on his face.

"Inside," he said, touching his heart, "the glory of God glows like the fiercest of fires. It fuels the highest moments of my life … and the most mundane. I don't have to twirl and shout to show God my love. He knows. He knows because I obey and I guide others to do the same."

We sat in the kitchen, quiet in our chairs, and then folding his hands as they lay on the table, Bishop Herrfort closed his eyes and bent his head so low his chin nearly touched his chest. I watched while he prayed, his words, disconnected by gentle sighs, rumbled low. When he lifted his head, I knew he was ready to speak the words that would determine my future.

"We want you back, but you have to want it, too …"

"I do," I whispered.

"… and there has to be more from you than deference to a conditioned obedience. You know the rules. But it's not enough just to know them. You must live them. And believe them. I don't know if you can do that."

I listened to his words, heard their underlay of sadness. And I wanted him to know the depth of my belief, the core of it, was the same as his.

"You believe in God … Father, Son and Holy Spirit … the Trinity," I said. "And I do, too. You believe Jesus, God, lived on earth as a man; that He bore our sins, paid our ransom, and died on the cross; that He ascended to heaven and prepared the way for us to be there with Him. That is what you believe. And I do, too."

"But you don't believe your skirt must be thirteen inches from the ground," he said, shaking his head.

"Nor do I believe that God whips out a ruler and measures that length. But I will wear a skirt thirteen inches from the ground out of respect for you," I said, resolutely, lifting my chin, perhaps, unintentionally, a prideful act. I hoped he would not interpret it to be so.

"You make light of the Ordnung?" he spoke, his words measured and careful.

"No, of course I don't." Pressing my lips together, I drew in a deep breath, let it out slowly. "I wouldn't do that. I understand it means much to you ... to Maem and Da ... to the community. It's your Bible, but it's not *the Bible*. It's not the Word of God."

"You would not obey it?" His words were stern.

"If I am to rejoin the church, I understand I would to have to obey all rules, those of the Ordnung and those of God's commandments."

"What is it that troubles you so much, that makes you so rebellious?"

"I can accept your desire for us all to live a peaceful, loving and productive life according to the directives of God. I don't understand why we all have to look alike in dress, be alike in attitude and sentiments. I don't understand why education stops at grade eight. I don't understand why our thoughts must all be the same. Surely it is good to dream and explore and taste the wonders God has spilled on others outside our community, and, possibly, in the souls of some of our own, the gifts of art and literature and music ... the gift of healing hands in an operating room, and minds that discover, hearts that teach and minister in need outside the realms of our own rich country. Why is it wrong to mingle with others and learn from them their connections with God and for us to teach and share with them the marvels of the Amish heart?"

"God tells us to separate from the world. It reeks of pride ... selfishness and self-glory. It's hard to stay humble in such surroundings as the English live in, too easy to forget God when all around you is sin, beckoning, looking so good, so easy."

"But doesn't He say that although we live in the world, we are not *of* the world. We are His. Should we not live our faith, proclaim our faith, to others? Should we not walk among nonbelievers with His light shining through us ... a lamp, a beam, a vision of hope and eternal beauty?" Even as I spoke those words, my hands clasped against my heart, a pleading soared from my soul to God, begging He open the ears of the Bishop and pour understanding, insight, into the man sitting across from me. I begged He would drop words from my lips that honored Him, brought Him glory.

"The Amish are a people determined to live a pure life, a good and godly life," the bishop said, sitting so still, his eyes, imploring, gentle upon me. "Obeying the Ordnung, our rules, keeps evil from us, keeps us clean for God. Breaking them leads to eternal damnation. That's why we shun. To teach. To bring an Amish soul back into God's good graces. That's why you were shunned, Cora Pooler. I can't stop you from coming back to this community and living, again, with your parents, nor do I want to. You are loved by us and we pray for your return to our ways."

As he paused in his speaking, I slid my trembling hands over my skirt, back and forth. I felt him gathering his next words and I was frightened. He would let me come back to live among the brethren, but his next words would tell of the conditions that would be imposed upon me. If he told me I could not speak freely of Jesus as inspired by the Spirit within me, I didn't know how I would respond. As I waited, I prayed for guidance … and strength.

"Until you have confessed and proven your adherence to the rules of this Amish community as set forth in the Ordnung, you will not be received as a member of the church. You may sit, apart from the others, at the Sunday services. You may take food from their table after the services, but you may not eat *at* the table with them. The same holds true at your home. And you may attend family gatherings, but, again, you must eat separately, alone, at a different table from theirs. You may speak with others, but your words with them are limited to necessary communication. I know you have seen others shunned and I think my words are clear, so I would expect you to adhere to the rules. Do you understand?"

I nodded.

"Periodically, you will be required to speak with the elders and deacons … and me. For confession, praying and learning. For discipline." Pausing again, the bishop pulled at his beard. He seemed to be studying me. His face was passive when he spoke further, but his words were not. "You tend to be a rebellious woman. Work on that.

It's up to you to determine the time it will take for you to be ready to rejoin the church."

"It won't take long," I said.

"Understand. Final readiness will be determined by me." His voice was firm.

"I know," I said and repeated, "It won't take long."

"Pride practiced for twenty years is not easily purged … be careful, Cora Pooler."

"The Holy Spirit lives in me. He has sealed my heart. No one can break that seal. Neither Satan nor the whole Amish community. Not even you, Bishop Herrfort."

"Think on the words I have said to you," he said, standing.

Fearing any further words I might say would cause me harm in my quest and knowing I'd made the essence of my heart clear, I stood silently and made ready to leave.

"May I say goodbye to your wife before I go?" I asked, quietly.

"She is resting," he denied.

As I walked through the back door, I heard his last words to me for that day … *I will be praying for you.*

Chapter Twenty-Four

As I drove down the dirt lane from Bishop Herrfort's home and turned onto the gravel road that would take me to Aaron's barn, Aaron's horse jerked against his harness and tightened the pressure of the leads in my hand, pulling them from me, forcing me to drop the reins. Helpless, I slid over the seat and against the side of the buggy, hitting it with a painful jolt. And with no one to guide him, the horse, twice lifting his head to the sky and lowering it in swift, sharp strokes, his mane whipping in lashing, spreading waves of silken hair, gathered speed and raced down the road. Praying he would not trip on the dragging reins, I clung to the edge of the buggy door. He stayed on the road and, after awhile, it seemed less dangerous and more exciting. Taking my hands from a clinging safety, I raised my arms and delighted in the sweet, fresh feel of moving air against my body and through my hair.

The horse took me straight to Aaron's barn. And stopped. Turning my head, I saw Aaron leaning against the closed barn door. There was a half-smile on his face.

"He always comes home," Aaron said, moving towards the buggy. "Grain time. The horse has a clock inside his belly."

"Well, I'm glad he didn't trip over the reins," I said, laughing as I jumped down from the buggy.

"Never has yet. 'Course most people have sense enough to keep a tight grip on 'em."

"I think sense might be something I'm lacking these days," I said, scrutinizing the area. Then, frowning, said, "I don't see my car."

Aaron ran his hand over the horse's back flank, then patted the animal's neck and took a firm hold of his bridle. Reaching with his free hand, he retrieved the reins lying on the ground under the horse. Giving me a quick glance, he led the horse closer to the barn, backed him up and lined the buggy next to a second, heavier one.

"Aaron, where's my car?" I asked, my eyes still combing the area surrounding the barn.

"It's all taken care of. You won't be needing it, anyways." He looked full at me. "Unless you're not staying."

"Where's my car," I repeated, scowling.

"I don't think I'm supposed to be talking to you," he said. Shrugging, he reached into the second buggy and pulled out my purse.

"You *can* talk to me ... if there are words that need to be said," I said, an unAmish anger growing inside me. "And I'm thinking you need to find the words that tell me where my car is."

"Humph. Can't think of any words that need saying," he said, grinning. Not mentioning my car, he handed me my purse. "Better be walkin' up the road to your house. Supper should be about ready."

"You're not going to drive me?" I said, looking, pointedly, at the hitched horse and buggy.

"Not this day," he said. "Probably never."

I gritted my teeth, gave him a dirty look, turned and walked away.

It was a short distance to my parents' house, but I was tired. It had been an eventful day. My poor body and mind and *feet* were exhausted. And my purse and satchel were heavy. And the road was slippery. It seemed to me Aaron could have been a bit more thoughtful, a bit more of a kind, considerate, normal Amish man and driven me home. The buggy was ready. The way was short. It couldn't possibly have interfered with his apparent, grossly important schedule. And besides, even more irritating, there was an obvious smirk trying to hide behind the deadpan mask covering his face. But I could see it and I knew Aaron was enjoying every bit of my surrender.

Actually, it didn't take me long to walk my way to Maem and Da's driveway. But once there, my feet slowed on the path to the house. I willed them to hasten; I was anxious to see them. But the anticipation of their reaction to me, shaded by the remembrance of my last stop at their door, frightened me, filled me with a trembling dread and caused my feet to drag. I didn't think I could withstand a second rejection.

It didn't happen. Maem opened the door and, without hesitation, took me in her arms. Da was behind her and although he said nothing, I saw joy in his face.

And then I realized. It was the clothes. I was dressed in Amish garb.

Later, as I lay in bed next to Violet, I thought back on that wonderful evening. There had been little talking. At least to me. While Da scurried about finding a small table and setting it in the kitchen near the family's eating area, Maem had gathered the curious young ones and explained who I was. Because it was forbidden to speak of those who were shunned and absent and as I been gone for twenty years, I was but a whispered entity secreted from their ears. All during supper, while I sat apart from them, I caught their cautious glimpses even as they tried to hide them from their hawk-eyed *dawdi*. And Da kept those piercing eyes, unobtrusively, on me, too. I did manage a wink, though, now and then, at the gaping children ... causing their lips to stretch in guilty grimace and their hands to raise to cover smiles, but, practicing the expectations of a shunned Amish woman, I said no words.

After supper while Violet, George's girls and his wife, Patsy, cleaned the kitchen, Maem took my hand and led me to the small sewing room next to her and Da's bedroom. It had been sectioned off to be their space until their *dawdi* house was built on the land near Maem's flower plot. George and Patsy now slept in Maem and Da's upstairs bedroom. So many changes. Brothers now with graying hair, with grown and almost-grown children and all, but George, married and moved away; one sister dead, the other sister, heavier in body, tiny wrinkles spread over her face; rooms, rearranged in occupancy to fit a changing family; lumber laying in the snow speckled yard, waiting to be lifted in the spring to build the *dawdi house* for Maem and Da. Maem and Da, old.

"I can't speak many words to you, Cora ... dear child, Cora," Maem whispered, placing her hand on my cheek, so gently, for a brief and wonderful moment. "You know ... only words truly needed are allowed. And, Cora, I dare not stretch them for I would do nothing that would delay your acceptance into the church. I would do nothing to keep you under the ban, dear God, to keep you damned. Yet, Cora, dear heart, I am so thankful to have you in our house again. It's enough for now ... don't let it be too long."

She clasped her hands against her heart, tilted her head and smiled. Her eyes looked deep into me, and her voice, so yearning, spoke soft, "I love you, Cora."

"I love you, Maem," I said, fighting tears. It was stupenously good to be in my house with my Maem, my family. My heart was so full, it ached. An ample and pleasant ache. How could so much love be packed in one human body? Astonishing. Magnificent.

Maem measured me for clothing ... dresses, aprons, cape, nightdress, even underwear. And a white *kapp*. I hoped one day it would come to be her time to fashion a black *kapp* ... *a* black *kapp* to be worn by a married woman ... a black *kapp* to cover the head of Violet or me. But, sadly, both of us were so old. I, forty-eight; Violet, thirty-six. And it wasn't a common occurrence for an Amish woman beyond the years of her youth to marry. But I could not let such thoughts lay trouble over our hearts that day. Those first days of return were a time too precious to stain.

Evening hours in an Amish home are scant. Amish retire early. Their first milking and animal feeding times begin before the full light of day and their subsequent hours are filled with the chores essential to maintain their simple and productive lives. Tired and satisfied from a day of wholesome work, they take to their beds as the sky begins it dropping cover of darkness.

Thus it was early for me to be upstairs wrapped in home-sewn quilts, lying beside Violet in a large, soft bed. Yet the peace, the rightful feeling of being in the perfect place, spread from my soul to every bit, every speck of who I was, inside and out. It was too perfect to let sleep seep into it. I lay awake so very happy.

Eventually, sleep did come. And, for awhile, it kept me its prisoner. Then turning in my sleep, my face borne to the window, the light from the moon and the stars woke me.

"Mmmm, this is good," I murmured, my body reclined in sweet air-dried sheets and my head sunk luxuriously in a pillow of feathers.

"Cora?"

"Mmmmm," I answered, still wallowing in the sweet nearness of sleep.

"Cora, I need to talk with you."

"You can't," I mumbled, holding my covers tight to me. "I'm shunned."

"I *need* to talk to you."

"Okay." I said, reluctantly switching to my other side. Opening my eyes wide and blinking sleep out of them, I saw across her face a swaying veil of starry lace dropped by moonbeams leaking through the window.

"Give me your hand," she said.

I slid my fingers from my quilted cocoon and lay them on her hand. She pulled them farther from the covers and held them to her cheek. Her skin was sleepy warm and soft.

"Are you staying?" she whispered.

I thought awhile. I had said 'yes' to the bishop. I meant it then. Did I mean it as I spoke in the night with Violet? Probably. In the comfort and simplicity of that bed, that house, that peaceful home ... probably.

"I think so," I said, then paused, thought, spoke again. "If I can. If I can take the Ordnung and live within its confines without compromising what I know to be true in my soul."

"It could be hard. Bishop Herrfort doesn't forgive easily."

"It's not his forgiveness I need. He wasn't hurt by what I did. Maem and Da. You. Lily. Annabelle. You're the ones I hurt."

"He won't think of it that way."

"No, I suppose not," I said, sighing, rubbing my thumb over her knuckles. "But, he's fair. Rigid, but fair. The Ordnung is his tome of truth. and he wants it to be mine."

"Cora, if you're serious and really want to live here as one of us, then you have to *be* one of us. And the Ordnung is who we are. You can't be half Amish. Not in this Order," Violet said, pushing my hand away and turning onto her back.

"And I can't be half English, either. Who does that leave me to be, Violet?"

"I don't know. One or the other. And I guess it's you who has to choose which it will be."

Silence filled the room for a long stretch of time as I pondered the spoken words still hanging in the air. And, I thought, Violet had gone back to sleep.

She had not.

"Weren't you afraid during all that time of shunning? Twenty years ... and even now still under the ban. Weren't you afraid of going to hell? Aren't you afraid now?" Violet asked, awake and flopping back onto her side, facing me. "You broke the rules of the Ordnung. You broke your tie to heaven. *And that's so.* Your soul is dead. Right now it's dead ... until you confess and repent and obey and do the works God meant for you to do. All these years I have prayed you would come back and be saved again. I don't want you to stay dead to me. Please, Cora. Try to obey the Ordnung. Do what the bishop says."

"I will ... as best I can," I said, thoughtfully. "And yes, I was afraid. At first. I thought about you. About all of you. All the time. I worried about you. I dreamed about you. All of you. But mostly Lily. Especially Lily. She was so fragile. And, in my dreams, I'd reach for her. She was like streams of liquid sliding through my fingers. Slipping a mournful keening through them. Slippery. Sad. Sometimes, she would lay her hands on her belly and that essence of sorrow sounded through her body, reaching, searching for what was gone … what I took from her. Yes, I was afraid. But you can't live in fear forever. The edges of the worst nightmares dull and lose their sharp, piercing pain. Eventually they hide, fitfully, in the deep ravines of your soul and there are times, unwanted, uncalled, they surface. But less and less often."

"I guess you toughened up and made a life for yourself," Violet said. I couldn't read beneath the inert covering on her face.

"Are you angry?" I asked.

"A little. It hurts to be forgotten … but I guess we had times when we didn't think of you, too."

"You were never forgotten. Just tucked away." I put my hand on her cheek, again. "And I didn't toughen up; I found a church that taught me truth … and love."

"I love you, too, Cora," she said, answering my unsaid proclamation of love for her.

Smiling, I patted her cheek and bade her turn over and sleep.

"I'll rub your back," I whispered as she rolled onto her back.

"Mmmm," she sighed, when settled and my hands moved over her nightdress. "Feels good."

"Cora?"

I woke to a tapping on my shoulder.

"Violet, go back to sleep," I said, almost there myself.

"I'm awake again. And I've got more to say."

"*No*, you *don't*," I said, wanting to stay in the soft dark place dropped over me.

"I do," she said, tapping me harder.

"Please, dig into your head and find the word *shunned*. And remember what it means!"

"This isn't funny, Cora. I need to talk more."

"No," I sighed, burrowing deeper into my quilts, "it's not funny. And what is it you want to talk about? And can't it wait? Please."

"No, it can't wait. I'm not supposed to be talking to you at all but since I've already messed up tonight, I might as well get everything said and then I can start shunning you for real tomorrow."

Groaning, pulling the covers around me, I turned over and faced her.

"Talk," I said, sighing.

"I've been thinking. About Lily. And I'm puzzled. Are you still going to try to find out what happened to her?"

"She died, Violet. She fell in the water and died. Talking done? Can I sleep?"

"No," Violet whispered. "Don't we need to find out how it happened? Why Lily died? Don't you want to know who the baby's da was?"

"Of course, I do, but I don't know how to get those answers," I said, sadly. "I've tried. I talked with the sheriff. Harriet doesn't know anything. She has a few suspicions. Nothing concrete. You don't know anything about it. Aaron won't talk to me. Not about this. I was lucky to get the few words he did speak earlier today. Herrfort won't help me. Where else can I look?"

"*Bishop* Herrfort, Cora. Be respectful. Don't slip. He's gonna be watching you every minute and he doesn't handle disrespect well. And maybe I can help. With the Lily questions," Violet said, sliding up to sit against her pillow.

"How?"

"Okay, let's think. You said Harriet had some suspicions. What'd she say?" Violet asked, reaching back and punching her pillow. "Miserable pillow. I'll bet Englishers have more than one lumpy mass of feathers to put their heads on."

"That's true," I said, smiling wryly. "And everyone has her own bed, too."

"Even married couples?"

"Sometimes," I said, thinking what an alien thought that must be to my Amish sister.

"Humph ...," Violet said, her face wrinkling in disbelief, "okay, what'd Harriet say."

"She thought the father might be Jacob."

"Jacob Lapp?"

"Uh huh," I agreed, nodding my head.

"Aaron's cousin." It was a statement, not a question, she spoke.

"*Rechts,* right " I said, my tired head falling back to remembered language.

"You're coming back into our world. Sounds good," Violet said, smiling. "Maybe we should ditch the English for always and just talk Pennsylvania Dutch. You'll remember the old words faster that way."

"It's been a long time since I spoke with an Amish tongue," I said, rubbing my hands over my eyes and cheeks. "And you know, Violet," I continued, softly, dropping my hands onto the covers, "English is really a beautiful language ... intricate, so many words that speak magic, flow, twist and redirect, expand thinking. They are as flowers that open slowly, new patterns and colors and textures revealed on their petals with each miniscule spurt of growth..."

"You said Harriet had suspicions," Violet interrupted. "What else did she say?"

"Not too much." I said, hearing impatience in her voice.

"Okay, then let's take what she did say and stretch it out. She said 'Jacob'. Jacob's Aaron's cousin. So, since we know Jacob won't tell us whether he's the father or not, being as he's got a wife and thirteen million children and he wouldn't want them to discover his sin. We've got to get Aaron to talk."

"Jacob was pretty much a little kid when I left," I said, thinking Violet was doing very well with the English tendency to exaggerate.

"He was seventeen, going to Sunday sings and even more significant, enjoying the benefits of Rumspringa. Plus he was cute. Really cute."

"And Lily was beautiful," I said, remembering. "Jacob would have noticed."

"She was innocent and gullible," Violet added, emphatically. "Trusting."

"And sweet. Almost like a mythical, magical nymph."

"Young, frisky Jacob would have been more into the 'innocent and gullible'. Now listen, we've got to find a way to make Aaron talk."

"If he's got anything to tell," I said, hopefully.

"He might. He's not talker, but I'll just bet his head is full of all kinds of information. And you know what, I've got an idea. He lives in that big, old house all by himself. And he's not a real sociable guy so he hasn't let the ladies come in and do any cooking or cleaning for him. So his house must have dust a thousand inches thick. I've tried to get in there, with Maem 'chaperoning', to do some cleaning, but he won't even let us in. Well, maybe once in awhile. But here's the thing ... he's always thought you were pretty hot stuff, so ..."

"Where's all this idiomatic English speech coming from?" I asked, mystified by her verbal abilities.

"You. And it's kind of fun Interesting, at any rate." Violet laughed. "You know, it really is good to have you back. Refreshing. Anyway, he would probably let *you* in and I could come along so the bishop wouldn't get all antsy thinking you two were doing things you shouldn't, and then, I could do some cleaning way far away from the room you two were in. And you could pick his brain. What do you think? Sound pretty good?"

"Maybe. Let's sleep on it, Violet. I'm really tired. We can talk later," I said, surrendering to a weariness sinking heavy on my body."

"What if we can't. Sooner or later my conscious is going to win out over my wants, and I just won't be able to talk to you anymore."

I could see her in the dark space behind my closed eyes and I smiled. I was sure she would find a way to speak her thoughts again ... and again. And I nearly slept. Nearly.

"Cora?"

"No, Violet," I murmured. "No."

"Just one question," she whispered. "It's important."

"Mmmm, okay, I'm listening," I mumbled, neither opening my eyes nor turning to face her.

"Why did you come back now? You've had so many years to seek us out ... to fix things, to belong again, be my sister. To repent. To love us again."

"I've always loved you." And with her words my eyes opened and I was fully awake.

"But you stayed away. I need to know ... why are you here? Why did you really come back?"

A nostalgic melancholy came over me. My back to Violet, I looked out the window. Clouds had covered the moon. The sky seemed hidden, darker. I wondered if there was snow in the clouds. Or rain. Cold, winter rain. I had heard her words, heard the plea in them ... and the sadness ... for years wasted, perhaps from a fear I would not stay and she would lose me again.

Why had I come back? And why not sooner? I could have. After Lily died, there was no reason not to return and confess, repent, rejoin. I don't think it was stubbornness. Or fear ... maybe a little of that. I think the greatest reason was rejection ... not a concern I would not be taken back if I submitted to the rules of the Ordnung, for I knew I would be, but the sorrow of no one seeking me out. I left and no one came to get me, reason with me, take me home. No one seemed to care, to worry, to love me enough to rescue me from the English world. Wasn't God's love, given to be shared, greater than man's rules? And then, I found a compassionate God Who sealed my heart with His salvation and His Holy Spirit and, as time passed, it seemed the English world became my world.

I thought about it. Initially, I told myself I would go back to Wander Lane to discover what had happened to Annabelle. The mixed recipe of guilt and certainty that I done right, laying in my heart, troubled my sense of assurance. My English life was secure; I needed to know my past Amish life was repaired. And, also, of as great import, was the need to resolve the mystery of Lily's venture into a world not approved by Amish edict ... and to discover the circumstances of her untimely death. But the real reason I returned to Amish country? I knew well what it was.

"Cora?"

Tears rose from my soul and trembled behind my eyes. I turned and took Violet's hand in mine.

"I came back to know where I belong. I came to find *me*."

The next morning Da, finished with barn chores, hands and face washed clean, the linger of animal dung and aging hay lingering on his clothing, sat at the breakfast table, looked at Violet and said, "It would be best if you keep your bedroom door open at night."

Then he turned to me, sitting behind him at that separate small table used just by me, and his eyes looking straight into mine, said, "Understood?"

It was the first word he had spoken to me since I'd returned to his house.

Eyes closed, chin down, I nodded.

How could I not understand. Someone heard us talking in the night and had told him. As our father, it was his duty to direct and discipline; as his children, it was out duty to obey. Violet would not dare to speak to me again. And so our plan was stomped deep into oblivion. Shunning is a burning, binding rope which pulls ever tighter and tighter.

Chapter Twenty-Five

After that morning it seemed the days grew colder … outside the wind blew harsh and snow fell thick … inside words were few and smiles were scant. Yet there was a certain quiet, a diminished but evident tranquility, in the house. I walked the rooms, cleaned and sewed and cooked, with a heavy sack of guilt strapped on my back. A joyful return had become a burden of unrepented sin carried by me and, in part, by those I loved.

The Bishop had come to our house the day after Da had admonished Violet and me and gathered us into a room peopled by only the three of us.

"I have been told you have been talking to one another," he had said, his words clipped and distinct. There appeared to be no room for levity in his voice or demeanor.

Neither of us answered.

"Is it true?"

Trembling, Violet nodded. I said nothing.

"The Ordnung is clear. I shouldn't have to tell you," he said, looking at Violet, "and I won't tell you again. This is your warning. Cora is shunned. If you speak to her while she is still under the ban, you will be shunned, too."

"And will she join me in hell then?" I interrupted, unable to control my anger.

The Bishop turned to me, his face imperturbable. "You know the rules, Cora. You could help her obey them, but you don't. It doesn't speak well for you. How can I lift the ban when you test it and mock it and cause others, like Violet, to scorn it by your unwillingness to yield to it?"

"I won't tempt her to speak to me again," I said, reluctantly, gazing on Violet's paled face and drooped shoulders. "There will be no reason to reprimand her."

"I pray not," the Bishop said, glaring one last time at Violet and then looking at me. "She's a good woman. And it's help I'm giving you both in order to bring you back into God grace and to keep Violet out of a state of separation from Him. We slip, Cora, but we can return to His salvation and love. It's choice, Cora. It's choice."

I knew his sincerity and I felt his anguish in my rebellion. He truly believed I was walking a path of damnation. Surely it gave him no pleasure. But he was wrong. My feet were stepping on a God-given, God-guided path to glory. And though they, sometimes, veered off the edge, they quickly stepped back … by the faithful guidance of the Holy Spirit.

It was not until the next day Violet found the courage to speak to Da regarding the Bishop's visit. I was dusting in an adjoining room and heard them speaking. I listened, eavesdropped, an Amish act of disgrace. But, in my mind, justified. Their words were of my concern.

"Da, was it you who told the Bishop?" Violet asked and I listened as her voice dirged soft, a mournful regret.

"I will not lose my last daughter." Stern. Solid.

"Me? You mean me?" Sorrow, unbelief, flowed pleading from her mouth. I raised a hand to cover my lips and willed my body to silence.

"Yes." And I heard his word so sharp it could cut syllables in the air.

"You have me and you will always have me. *Always*," Violet whispered and my ears could barely fathom her speaking.

"Not if you are shunned," he said and I felt the tremble in his declaration.

"I will always be your daughter," she repeated. "And Cora. She will be, too. She *is*. Your daughter. Same as me."

"Not yet."

"*Now*."

"No, not now." And then, it was I trembling. For his words were stone.

I went to the Bishop, and with head high and hands clasped, named my sins of disobedience executed since my return to his boundaries of spiritual leadership. I didn't consider that declaration was offered to him as a confession nor would I accept he had the right to absolve my sins. He was not God.

"Do you understand why you are shunned?" He said, grim faced, his back lined so straight he seemed to me a statue.

"I do," I replied. "You think it will bring me back to the church … to Jesus. But I'm already there."

"A stubborn pride will not bring you there."

"I *am* there. Don't you understand?" I asked, earnestly, leaning toward him, thinking my words could pound against his being and sink into his comprehension.

He sighed and sat, bent his arms upward against his chest and held his chin in his hands, his knuckles pressed against his lip.

"The English concept of the universal church," he stated, sliding his clenched hands under his chin. "That's what you're saying you belong to."

"Not exactly," I said. "God's concept of the catholic church ... the all-embracing unity of believers. All of us who believe the gospel."

"Do want to return to *this* community as an Amish woman?"

"I do," I said, softly. "As an Amish woman who *knows* Christ."

"We've had this discussion before. You know what's required. Decide, Cora Pooler, look into your heart, pray ... let your doubts and arguments go for awhile and live Amish. Remember how it was before you left. Your family. The immediate ones in your house and the far reaching in the homes all around you. The whole brethren. Family. Security. Love. *Salvation.* Live what it is. Then decide."

And that's what I tried to do. But how could do that? How could I, a believer, integrate all the tenets of the Ordnung with the knowing in my heart ... Christ, my savior, my intercessor to the Father was mine; salvation sealed by the Holy Spirit dwelling within me was mine. How could I accept, per Amish doctrine, I walked dead, damned, among my Amish brothers and sisters until I kneeled before them in their church meeting and accepted their Ordnung, their rules, as my only path to salvation?

I tried.

A layer of cold coated the hearts of us all ... of all of us who lived in Da's house, a quiet that was nearly peace, but tainted by my state of shunning. And my struggle to reach what was full in their souls.

It was hard to sit quietly, not saying the words that were aching to spill from my mouth as I watched George's gawky teenaged boys amble about the house laughing, teasing their sisters, glancing awkwardly at me, then quickly looking away. I wanted to say, *here, see me. I can laugh too. And sing. And play. And hug.* But I said nothing. Only smiled. I think that was allowed.

When driving the horses to quilting gatherings, Maem talking with Violet, she huddled so close to our Maem, I, spaced a little apart from them, sat mute in the buggy. They spoke loud enough, clear enough, that I didn't need to strain to hear their words. There are ways to circumvent unwarranted punishments without disobeying. And then as the ladies grouped around the quilting frame, working and chatting, I sat, separated from them, with needle and thread, fashioning a square from colored bits of fabric. Wordless. Listening. Invisible.

It was the same in church; it was same wherever I went. A kind silence. A kind turning away. A loving passing over. Pain for me. For them, hope for my return to community.

It was hard not to hold Alice. My hands, yearning to stroke her soft skin; my fingers, longing to gently tickle her sweet, pink tummy. Yet I was grateful to hear her baby laughter and to see her chubby little fingers stretch and reach and tug and explore. And it was good to hear and watch the older children. My family. Increased. Changed. Mine.

I longed to grab Violet's hand, swing it with mine and run through the snow, roll in it beside her, push my arms under it and spray soft, white, cold snow over the whole of her. Laugh. Play. Share.

And I wanted, so badly, to talk with my brothers. To remember our days growing up together, we so close. To discover whom they had become ... what they liked, what they did, what they thought.

I craved Maem's touch. Her hand on my face. Her arms, strong, holding me close to her bosom, the remembered scent of her body. Holding me with a force that spelled love. Protection. Permanence. Promise. There were moments when she ... accidently? ... brushed against me or stumbled beside me and she would take those moments to lean against me, to hold my arm or put hers around me to gather her balance. And so many times, I would catch her staring at me. Sometimes, her face sad. Sometimes, shining happiness.

And I wanted to see joy in Da's face, too. Again. For me. His firstborn. His lost child, back.

And drifting behind all those desires was the essence of Aaron.

I was hanging sheets in the side yard when I saw Bishop Herrfort's buggy pull into our driveway. My hands were cold and stiff from the flapping wet sheets whipping against my skin; my cheeks, pulled tight from the sting of the mid-March wind. Dropping the sheets and clothespins into the laundry basket, I hurried towards the house.

A second buggy followed the Bishop's. Deacon Lapp was driving that one. Jesse Miller sat beside him. They were a trio of authority. Bishop, Deacon and Minister. I shuddered and stopped. This must be important. And I was sure they were coming to bring news to me. Perhaps the shunning was over. However, they didn't look in my direction, but, tending to business, tethered their horses to the hitching post, collected themselves in a group, and walked, rather strode, to the back porch and the kitchen door. At the same time Violet opened it to them, I saw Da come from the barn and walk swiftly up the driveway.

Moving behind the hanging sheets, I saw them go inside the house. And I saw Da gather speed. Then Violet came out, clutching her cape around her shoulders and, though she couldn't see me, motioned from the porch to where I should be. And I saw Da, behind her, hurry up the steps, pass her without looking her way and go into the kitchen.

There was no avoiding it. I left my hiding place and went to discover my fate.

They were seated at the kitchen table. The trio and Da. Maem was pouring tea in our old white cups, daily scrubbed and free of stain. A stable bit of an unchanging world. Security for those who never left.

As I stood by the kitchen door, concentrating on the black clothed men of power, I felt as from a distance a squeeze on my arm and moving against the edge of my sight line, I saw a wisp of Violet's body slipping out of vision. Across the room I heard the setting thud of the teakettle onto the stove and the swishing rustle of Maem's skirt as she slid out the kitchen. My eyes did not turn to look at her. There was no help to be had. The decision was made. Concrete. Without malice. With desire to see me obedient. With love.

There was a single chair pulled straight away from the table. An empty chair. Waiting to be filled. Waiting for me. I stared at it. Afraid.

Bishop Herrfort looked at me and nodded.

I sat.

"Aaron has told us you go into his house. Is that so?" he asked.

"Aaron would not lie," I said, softly.

"When he's not there. With Violet. The two of you." He kept his voice low and controlled.

"That's so," I agreed, clasping my hands to quell their shaking.

"To clean and to cook."

Pressing my lips together, I looked down at my lap.

"Violet asked for permission," I said. "He gave it, albeit reluctantly." The shaking had invaded my throat and my words quavered.

"He is appreciative," the Bishop said, squinting, leaning towards me. "He said you've made no attempt to speak with him."

"That's true. I have not." I tightened the clasp of my hands so they would not raise and rub my face.

"That's good," he said, the two other men nodding with him. And my father began to look relieved.

"Susanna Beachy tells me you go to her house daily to bathe her infirm *mudda* mother and, she says, you sit by her bed. Sometimes, your stay is lengthy."

"I do. And it is. Sometimes."

"And you sing to her."

I swallowed the hurt in my throat and said nothing.

"Singing is not talking," he said, slowly. "Susanna Beachy says it soothes the old woman."

I held my breath and waited.

"She says you do not speak to the *muddah*, just sing to her."

"That's true," I whispered.

"And you help with the added washing of clothes that comes with the caring of an old, ill lady."

I dipped my head, then raised it, looked into his eyes.

"And the clean-up ... of her body," he said, a slight frown on his face.

My eyes stayed on him. I said nothing.

"And the preparation of special food ... for an old lady's tender stomach."

His eyes had stayed on mine the whole time.

"She is grateful," he said.

I let out my breath.

"You've attended all the meetings we framed for you so that you would know and understand the importance and the charges of the Ordnung," he continued, rubbing his chin, the skin bare above his beard. Fleetingly, a wondering why that part of an Amish face was allowed to be shaved crossed my mind. Odd. "You have learned them, recited them and it appears you have practiced them. We are pleased. At the next Sunday Service we will welcome you back into the church. The ban will be lifted and you will be in a state of grace once more."

I had tried so hard to conform … to obey. Tears welled in my eyes, spilled over. I would be Amish again. Accepted. Welcomed. Visible. But still, they would not see me as saved until that day of public confession and repentance. There was a measure of sorrow, a tinge of regret, in my tears. It would be a day of recognition, but, unacknowledged by them, not a day of salvation for me. That day had come in an English church. Then and evermore, Jesus is my Lord.

It was good to be able to open my mouth and let the words fall out to land on Amish ears. And by the time summer arrived, full blown and wanting grass to be mowed; seeds to raise through the ground with spreading vines, lush leafing, and ripening fare; pastures to produce plentiful nourishment for cattle and horse; fences to be mended; fields to be tended; Sunday nights to belong to young Amish men for the wooing of young Amish women, and by that time, summer, my voicing of words had become common to me.

I had become a visible person within the brethren, an active participant of community. I ate with them, churched with them, quilted and sewed and canned and weeded and laughed and *talked* with them. I was, fresh in my heart, Amish. And I tried, worked at, hiding English from my soul.

And Aaron. We were friends again.

Chapter Twenty-Six

"I think Aaron likes you."

Toting heavy baskets filled with eggs and early tomatoes, Violet and I walked down the hill towards Wander Lane. It was a scorching, skin burning day; the asphalt was sticky under my feet and my Amish dress was heavy. Without shade the sun glared hot on my face. Lifting my right shoulder and arm, I tried to rub the itching trickles of sweat running down my face, but the basket was too heavy and I couldn't lift it high enough to reach beyond the edge of my cheek.

"Did you hear me?" Violet asked.

"You walk too fast. I can't answer and keep my legs moving at your unwarranted pace ... at least not at the same time," I complained.

"You're talking now," Violet said, not slowing, "so you can walk and talk ... all at the same time."

"Look," I said, pointing. "On one side of us is a whole parcel of trees. Shading the road. Why can't we at least walk on that side. In the shade?"

"You can. I'm not going to. The sun's good for you. All kinds of good stuff ... vitamins ... killing germ power ... are in those rays." She looked at me and laughed. "You're just too English still. Lazy habits. Spoiled. Gotta get those muscles tuned up and working. You're an Amish woman now."

"An aging one," I said. "I've been pulling weeds all morning and I think I deserve a spot on that log over there to rest my body so I'm full of vim and vigor when I finally get to see Harriet again."

"Okay, we can stop and take a break just as soon as you answer my question."

"You didn't ask a question," I said, crossing the road, taking a long step and clearing the narrow ditch.

"I said, I think Aaron likes you."

"That's not a question. That's a statement," I said, dropping on the log.

"Well, he does. The real question is, do you like him? And be careful of your eggs. You put them down that hard, you could crack them."

"It's the tomatoes that are so heavy," I said, setting that basket down next to the eggs. "And yes, of course I like him. Don't you?"

"Did you ever love him?" she asked, after settling herself beside me and putting her basket of eggs on her lap.

"Why do you ask?" I said, lifting my skirt and rubbing my face dry with it.

"Modesty. Modesty. The Bishop will put you on the shunned list, again. And I think you might love him now because I think you used to. Before the shunning. And it's logical to think that way. And it's more than I just think he cares a whole lot about you. I know it in my bones. And if I were allowed, I'd bet on that love. And like or not, Cora Pooler, you're no spring chicken. This could be your last chance."

"I'm too old to have children," I said quietly.

"Doesn't have to be a marriage requiring children. Could be just a loving companionship for two lonely people."

"What makes you think I'm lonely?"

"You need a man, somebody who's not a brother or father or friend. You need somebody more … to talk personal to."

"I do that with Aaron. I'm not lonely."

"To touch," she whispered.

I turned and looked at her. Despite the sun, her face was pale. Moving closer to her, I put my hand on her arm and stroked it."

"What about you, Violet?" I murmured, gently. "What about you?"

"I wasn't meant to be loved," she said, dropping her head. "Not by a man. I'm plain, Cora. And I don't speak sweet like other women do. I just say what is. And that's not … girlie."

"What does God say, Violet?" I took her chin into my hand and held it there while I earnestly spoke to the depths of her mind. "God looks at the heart … for that's where beauty is. And you may not believe this, but you should, your heart shines right through your innards onto your face and eyes, and the loving touch of your soul lands on all that you do and say. Do you think the others, even Aaron, can't see that?"

"No man has asked me to marry. And now I'm too old."

"Not too old yet not to have babies." I took my hand from her chin and patted her cheek. "And neither is Aaron."

"He could be a *dawdi* by now," Violet laughed, ruefully.

"But he's not," I said, "… and he looks at you, too."

Discerning my want to see Harriet alone, Violet set her baskets down inside Harriet's restaurant door. She smiled at me and said she would be at Hattie's fabric shop. Maem needed material for a baby quilt she was making for the new Beachy baby.

"It could take me awhile. Hattie's a talker." She winked. "Kind of like Harriet."

After she left, I picked up the baskets, one by one, and put them on the register counter, then, slowly, looked around the room. It was empty. I moved through it, touching tables, chairs, pictures on the walls, skimming my fingers over slippery menu tops, lifting salt and pepper shakers, feeling their ridges. Unbidden tears rose from a place in my heart. I could feel them sliding upward, branching throughout my chest, resting behind my eyes. Tender tears of memories. Of this place. Of Harriet … and Bailey. Of Aaron and his pumpkins. Of lingering emotions and thoughts and words hovering in the space of times passed.

"Come, we can talk in the back room."

I heard the voice behind me. It was Harriet. And at the same time, Bailey came from the kitchen and two couples walked through the front door. Time moved forward.

I looked at Harriet's face. It was the same. Beloved face, it had not changed. She put her arm under mine and led me through the dining room to the place of storage, the room where Maem had held me.

We sat.

"You're not shunned no more," she said, shaking her head. "And it's about time."

"I'm no longer shunned." I agreed staring hard into her face. I could not read it.

"You're an Amish woman now. Whole and for sure." She frowned and folded her arms over her chest. "A black dressed, white capped female."

"Yes." Uncomfortable under her unwavering scrutiny, my eyes left hers and roved the room. I saw a canvas bag on the self across from us.

"My valise," I said.

"Yep. Aaron brought it to me when he brought me the car."

"He drove the car?" I smiled.

"He did," she said and, breaking eye contact, grinned. "Did a right smart job, too."

"How'd he get back home?"

"Walked."

I saw him in my head. Driving too fast down the hill. Knowing if the sheriff saw him, he'd give him a thumbs up. Propelling the car up and down the village streets. Stretching the drive to last longer.

"I used to love him," I said. "A long time ago. When I was young. I think he loved me, too. But it didn't happen. Marriage. His mother didn't like me. Or any other girl. That might like him."

"Do you love him now?" Harriet asked.

"Yes, but different. Just as deep. But different. I'll always love him. He's a memory that will never disappear."

"A memory?"

"A memory," I said and a bit of magical wonder, not solid … whimsical … trembled through me. "A memory and more, better. And now I can see and touch him. Put the new Aaron with the remembered Aaron. Make them one. Join them together."

We were silent, digesting the old, contemplating the new.

"And Daniel?" she said.

"I try not to think of him." And it was if a star struck my body, penetrated it, and sent glaring flames throughout my being.

"He thinks of you," she said.

"How do you know that?"

"He calls."

I leaned back in my chair, closed my eyes and covered my cheeks with my hands.

"What does he say?" I whispered.

"He asks about you."

"What do you tell him?"

"About you? Nothing. I didn't know what was happening to you. There was nothing to tell. No one could talk about you. It was as if you died." Her words rang sorrow. Then she looked at me. "Now, I know. Now I can tell Daniel you're not shunned anymore. And you're happy. Are you, Cora? Are you happy?"

"Is he all right?" I asked, seeing him through my closed eyelids.

"He misses you."

I lifted my head and looked at the valise. There were clothes in there. English clothes. I should tell Harriet to burn them, but I knew I would never say those words.

"Will he call again?" I asked.

"Every month on the fifteenth day."

I bent my head and spread my fingers, pushed them hard under my *kapp*, laced them through my hair. The strings on the *kapp* were loose and it slid from my head onto the floor. I let it lay there.

"Your hair has grown," Harriet said, touching her own straggly strands.

"Amish women don't cut their hair. You know that. At night they let it down. For their men to see." I ran my fingers through my hair, lifted it, let it drop, lifted it again. "I wonder what Amish men think when they look at an English women with their hair exposed, tossed, curled, colored bright, for all the world to see."

"What shall I tell Daniel when he calls?" Harriet asked, bringing me back to sensibility.

"Tell him to forget me."

"No. Not yet. I won't do that. Not yet."

I sighed and stood up.

"Violet will be coming," I said. "I need to go."

"What shall do with your valise?"

I didn't answer.

The walk up the hill was slow. Both of us seemed to be lost in thought.

"I saw Sheriff Parker," Violet said, breaking the silence.

"Lowell Parker," I said with no great joy. "And what did the sheriff have to say?"

"He said," and Violet smiled, "he said, 'so I guess she's talking now.'"

"It would be my guess it was a sarcastic remark."

"Your guess would be right."

We walked for a while without talking. After a bit, Violet stepped off the road and bending into the ditch, pulled some strands of Queen Anne's Lace from the clumps growing there. I kept walking.

"When you were an English girl did you wear blouses as intricately patterned as these?' She asked, catching up to me, swinging the flowers in front of me, laughing.

"Even finer," I said. "Like the sleeves of an Englisher's wedding dress, or the edges of a little girl's socks. So delicate and dainty only a golden haired princess could wear such regalia."

"And your underwear. Was it as slippery and shiny as the pictures in magazines?" she asked and I heard a touch of wistfulness in her voice.

"As silky as the smooth top of water in a quiet stream. As soft as the underside of a rose petal."

"The sheriff asked if you're really going to stay. Are you?" she asked, abruptly.

"Did he mention Lily?" I said, not answering.

"No," she said. "And if he knew who the *Da* was, he wouldn't tell us. Not if it was someone he didn't want it to be. I don't think anyone, including the sheriff, knows why Lily died that night. And maybe that's better. Would you want Maem and Da to know if she had purposely walked into the water and drowned?"

"It's called suicide, Violet," I said, coldly.

"Would you want them to think of her in hell?" Violet said, softly.

And in those words I heard sadness. But a perverseness had come over me. Perhaps, it was the lace, all the beauty I'd left behind in the other world. Perhaps, the question 'would I stay?' The foolishness of it. Why would I have gone through all the months of silence if it was not to stay? Still I could not stop the hard edge of resentment that came unbidden and colored the tone of my words.

"But they're Amish," I finally answered her. "They wouldn't think of her. The dead Amish aren't spoken of. Not by our people. Lily's dead. Forgotten."

"It's true, they are not spoken of. But you also know hearts don't forget, not the ones they love," she said, quietly. "And it seems to me your heart is very hard right now. Why?"

"I don't know," I said, my words clipped crisp, my eyes focused on the road. But I took her hand and held it the rest of the way home.

The next day I found myself alone with Aaron in his kitchen. Violet and I had made a stew for his dinner and while it was simmering we did a quick cleaning of his house. Finished, we checked the stew and realized it needed more salt. But there was none left. We had used it all.

"I'll go run get some," Violet said, and then, winked. "Or maybe I won't run. Maybe, I'll take baby steps. Who knows, Aaron might come in from the barn while I'm gone and you might just find yourself all giddy and pleased to be here alone with him."

"I don't think so," I said. "Just go get the salt and be quick about it. I sure don't want anyone seeing I'm here alone with him and then go running to Herrfort and tell I'm sinning. Big time."

"Might mean a marriage," Violet sing-songed.

"Might mean a shunning," I said, with a touch of anger.

She ran off and, after a bit, Aaron did leave the barn and come to the house. He came through the kitchen door, quietly closed it and stood there watching me stir the stew. I kept my eyes on my hand holding the spoon, stirring, around and around the rich, thick sauce. The aroma was rich and hearty, reaching into the room, spreading, mingling with the smells Aaron brought in with him ... the stench of cow hide and horse sweat, the heavy grainy odor of barley and oats and dried corn, leather, the stink of animal waste... and his own heady scent, a combination of all his work, his day, his life. The smell an Amish man carried, unaware, unashamed.

"Smells good," Aaron said.

I turned. His eyes were on me. I looked away. Concentrated on the stew.

"Saw Violet headed for your house. Didn't see you. You staying for supper?" He said, leaning back against the door.

"She went to get salt." I didn't want to look at him, to think of other times in this kitchen with him, times gone.

"Smells good," he said again and I sensed his movement, inhaled his scent ... closer. He stopped beside me. Bent over the stew. "Looks good, too."

"Violet saw Sheriff Parker in town today." I said, my body stiff, aware.

"He hasn't been around lately. Probably knows there's too much work for me now to stop and talk ... even with him."

I turned and faced him.

"Do ever get tired of it? The sameness of it?" He was nearer than I thought. His body, his stance, his voice, his force ... unchanged since I knew him, young, as a boy, then older. My friend. Pal. Buddy. Near lover. Almost husband. Lost for twenty years. And I ... not the same. Different.

"Tired of what?" he asked.

"Black pants. Suspenders. Straw hats. Buggies. Women who cook and quilt and hide their hair under black *kapps* and white *kapps*. And wear their skirts thirteen inches above the ground. Exactly. Cows and corn cribs and windmills and long leg-cramping sermons. Everything the same. Everybody the same. Don't you dream? Don't you wonder? Don't you want to explore? Fly in a plane? Wear cowboy boots? See a movie? Ride a motorcycle? Shave your face, shave your head … or even let the hair grow on your chin and under your nose? Stick a purple flowered handkerchief in your pocket? Kiss a girl for no other reason than she's just plain pretty? Don't you ever want to look different from everybody else?"

He stepped back, walked to the kitchen window, looked out for some minutes. I stirred and stirred and *stirred* the stew.

"Why would I want to do that, Cora?" He said, finally, still looking through the window, his back to me.

"To be you. Unique. Like nobody else."

"Is that what you want?" he asked.

"It's so peaceful here. Everybody works so hard. Shares. There's enough for everybody here. Security. When I'm old, and even if I'm alone, someone, many someones, will take care of me. I don't have to think. I don't have to make decisions. I don't have to worry about my face wrinkling or my body sagging or my dress being the wrong color for my skin tones or my fingernails breaking. None of that. The body works hard here, but, I think, maybe, the brain grows soggy. I don't have to think," I said again, turning from the stove, looking at him, seeing he had turned and was looking at me. "I just have to be able to read and remember the rules of the Ordnung and obey them and then I am … what Aaron? And then I am what?"

"One of us, Cora. Then you are one of us. Amish." He stared at me. "Is that so bad?"

"No," I said, shaking my head, dropping my head, looking at the ground, then at him. "It's not so bad. It's productive and sure and loving and predictable … and beautiful. But what if your mind is full of dreams and what if you have the talents, the gifts, to soar with those dreams? What if your mind is full of numbers that want to be put together in a way never seen, to form something never before made? What if there are words in your head aching to be put together in a way that brings new thought and beauty to the one who reads or hears them? Don't you see? We don't question here. We all think alike. We all dress alike. Look alike. Wear our hair the same. Keep our faces simple. Hide our feelings, our thoughts. Bury them. From others ... from ourselves."

"It keeps us from being prideful."

"But it doesn't. Not if you race horses to see whose is fastest. Not if one quilt is prettier than another. You can't erase uniqueness, Aaron. You can try to stifle it, but underneath the clothes and the peaceful faces are hearts and minds that are different, no matter how hard they try to be the same. Why should that be punished?"

"We're happy, Cora. We work hard at living good and Godly lives. How can you fault that?"

"I can't, Aaron. I can't. For what you say is true. You are a good people. A kind and loving people."

"But you're not happy?" he said.

"I don't know."

"Why did you come back?"

"I had to."

"Why?"

"I don't know if I can explain it. I don't even know if I want you to know," I said and feeling an army of tears gathering behind my eyes, I bit my lip hard. I didn't know why they were there and I didn't why I didn't want him to see them. Pride?

He stood there, quietly, waiting.

"I remember those days, years ago when we were children ... then older, a young man and a young women," I said, and then, softly, "I'll try to tell you. I'll try to make you see."

He nodded ever so slightly and I could see a want in his eyes to understand, an encouragement, a struggling effort to hear with his heart.

"I loved you then. When we took our free time from school and chores and played together. When we stole extra moments and explored the limits of our world. I loved you then. And later. With a fuller love ... a yearning love. A shy love that wanted to learn the secrets of adult love. I know that time can't be relived, but, I think, there was a need to come back and revisit those feelings, maybe test them. And not just yours and mine. I wanted to know Maem's love again. And Da's. And Violet's, my brother's. To be part of it all again."

Somehow without realizing, I had moved the stew from the heat of the stove and moved myself to stand by Aaron.

"But those were whispering reasons calling from my soul," I continued, putting my hand on his arm, looking out the window with him. "The reasons I allowed my ears to hear were a need to see Annabelle, a need to say 'goodbye' to Lily and, I think, mostly, a need to dig into my roots, the soil of my youth, and see if I was still planted here."

"And you haven't seen Annabelle," he said and I heard his voice, tender.

"I think I did ... one time in Ohio. But I'm not sure. It might have been a want come as truth through desire." I rubbed the sides of my face. Perhaps to hold that hope firm. Then I turned to Aaron. "What do you see? Right now looking through the glass, what do you see?"

"Fields. Pastures. The creek, the barn, the cows gathering to be milked," he said.

"Amish country," I said, moving closer to him, my body touching his ever so slightly. "And if Annabelle is looking out her window at her Amish hills and clouds and flowered ditches, she is seeing with the same eyes as ours. She's Amish, Aaron, and that's what I wanted her to be. I might never see her face or her hair or her body. But I needed to know her heart, her soul, was where it belonged. And I found out. It is."

"And Lily? What do you need to know about Lily?"

"How she died. Why she died. Who raped her. Who Annabelle's Da is."

"She wasn't raped, Cora," he said and I felt his body stiffen.

"What?" I said, stepping away from him.

"She was willing," he said.

"My Lily, you're saying my Lily willingly let a man use her body."

"Not a man. A boy. Just a boy. And her. Losing control. Both of them."

"No. You're wrong. Do really think my Lily would lay down in the dark, lift her skirt and say 'yes' to an act she was sworn to deny until marriage?" My lips could barely shed the words from my mouth. "She would not."

"She did," Aaron said, quietly.

"How do you know?"

"He told me."

"Who?"

Aaron sighed and hung his head.

"*Who?*" I repeated.

"Oh, Cora, it's really so simple. There was no rape. It was Jacob. Lily was just a frightened young woman … she knew nothing of the way of a man and woman joining. But she loved him and he told her it was all right. She believed him … *chose* to believe him. And then she was with child. He didn't know she was pregnant. He didn't know that until it was done … the child born and my uncle, Bishop Herrfort, come looking for the mother who had taken her infant to Wander Lane and left her there. And even then, he didn't really know. He thought it was you that had a child and left it in town. Until Lily told him. So heartbroken she was that she wanted to tell everybody. She wanted you back … and her conscious clear. It didn't happen. Jacob talked her into keeping silent. She couldn't handle it. The secret. The sin. And then she died."

"You think she killed herself," I said, tears running so fast and hard down my face I thought they would cover me with a salty stream of choke-causing water.

"No. I don't know what happened. No one does. Probably never will. But I don't think she killed herself. I think she was a poor, hurting soul walking in the dark, not thinking, not watching where she was going. Just hurting. And she lost her way."

"And drowned," I said.

"And drowned," he agreed.

I rubbed my eyes and shook my head. We would never know why she died, but I was glad she wasn't raped. And then, I smile ruefully, I had never heard Aaron put so many words together all at one time.

Aaron took my hands from my face and looked into my eyes.

"And you, Cora? You. Have you decided who you are?"

"I thought I had. Now I'm not so sure."

Chapter Twenty-Seven

I spent much time in prayer that summer. Seeking. Searching. I sought in the refuge of this unpretentious Amish soil where decisions were simple, uncomplicated, clear. And I searched in the vastness of my heart with a love that beat true and hard for the fields; the pastures; the sky and the creek; the animals, wild and tame; the stark, efficient buildings and their trappings; the people; my family. Why did it seem to be not enough for me? The love. The peace. It was everywhere I looked … nearly everywhere. Yet I had lost something. It was as if I carried a basket of apples and some fell out … and when I stooped to pick them up and held them in my hands, they were shriveled and soiled, their colors dulled. And though I stroked their skin and wept over them, they stayed unpolished and damaged.

On one of my trips into the village with Violet, our buggy filled with produce and baked goods to sell in the village park, I left her on the pretext of finding a bathroom and stretching my legs for a bit. Instead, I went to the library and signed for a card. And there I found a pictured book with the technical names and reported accounts of the behaviors of African animals in their native habitat. I took it, along with a newly released novel by a bestselling author I had always appreciated, to a check-out computer. Pressing the proper spaces against the monitor's screen, a remembered feeling of fingertips moving quickly over slightly hollowed computer keys caused an unexpected pleasure, bade a smile touch my lips.

I slipped the books, one light and the other, heavy, into a thin, yellow bag lying on the counter for patrons to take. Then I asked the librarian if she might have a safety pin I could use.

She gave it to me with a smile and said I could keep it. I thanked her, went into the ladies restroom and pinned the bag with the books inside my skirt. It was awkward and they were heavy. But I didn't care. Books. Close to my body. Waiting to be read. Joy.

Bishop Herrfort discovered I had the books. I didn't know how he knew, but, obviously, someone had seen me going into the library or reading in places I thought no one would see ... the oaks far behind the chicken coop, the corner in the barn where old harnesses were thrown, in my bed snuggled beneath quilted covers. Maybe the bulge in my skirt betrayed me. I didn't know. It didn't matter. The Bishop knew.

He warned me.

"I know, Cora," he said, his voice, stern; his body, unyielding. "I know it's hard to step from the freedoms of the English world. The things we shouldn't do entice. Sometimes, there's a measure of challenge that is hard to resist. But, if you think, Cora, if you consider the reward, it's worth the price of resistance."

"They're books, Bishop. How can they hurt me?"

"They take you away from the work you should be doing. They make you want things, a way of life that is not Godly. They tell of sinful happenings. They're frivolous. Time wasters." He kept his eyes on me as he spoke. "Take them back. Don't get more. Be careful, Cora Pooler. You're walking on slippery ground."

He took my library card and walked away from me.

It was more than a piece of cardboard that I lost. It was a stretching land of learning and connecting that he stole. I tried not to be resentful; this was a life I had chosen. That should make the tie to it stronger than just being birthed there. It should.

Violet knew I was reading books not sanctioned. I had shared with her stories, visions of places never seen by Amish eyes and never fathomed in Amish minds, information gleaned from my treasured and forbidden books. The ventures into those books pleased her. But after the Bishop spoke with me and I told her of his warning, she was frightened ... frightened that I would grow dissatisfied, resentful, stifled, and leave.

"Please," she said, "he means only good. And the rules are there to keep our hearts and minds pointed towards God. You know that and I shouldn't have encouraged you by listening to your stories. It was wrong. Cora, listen to him. Don't let him shun you again. *And don't go away again.*"

I didn't respond. My mind, embroiled; my heart, sad, I had no words of truth. Not then.

I didn't see Aaron often. There aren't many spare moments in an Amish summer. It's a time of unrelenting labor ... for working the fields, mending fences, chopping wood, harvesting ... preparing for harsh winter months.

Violet and I continued to clean his house, do his laundry and cook for him. I would send her, alone, in the heat of the day, to take him water, perhaps, a cookie or a piece of his favorite cake wrapped in a cloth napkin. Her visits took longer and longer.

"You're cheeks are so rosy from the sun," I would ease when she returned.

"You know the sun doesn't burn me," she countered. "My skin absorbs the rays and turns dark."

"Then from what are those circles of red I see on your cheeks?"

Shrugging, she laughed.

"Happiness," I said.

And she laughed some more.

I knew it was time to go when Rebecca Eicher was shunned. She was caught with gloss on her lips and eye shadow on her lids. She was only eighteen and, normally, it would have been overlooked. But her time of Rumspringa was over and she had been baptized.

She was a sweet girl. The shunning was painful for her. Late one afternoon, I found her hiding under the oaks in our far back yard, crying.

"It will pass," I said, softly, "and you will be welcomed again."

"You mustn't talk to me. I'm shunned. You'll get in trouble." Her voice trembled low.

"But I can sit with you," I said, touching her shoulder as I sank beside her onto the grass.

"It won't matter," she said, breaking, again, her own ban of silence. "If I get too sick and die or fall off a wagon or the porch or out of a tree and break my bones or hit my head so hard that it kills me ... don't you see, if I die before my shunning is over, Jesus will not want me. I'll go to hell."

"Do you love Jesus?" I asked, gently placing my hand on her arm.

"Yes," she whispered.

"With all your heart?"

"Yes," she answered, her head down, nodding vigorously.

"Have you surrendered your will to His?"

"I have, oh, I have." She looked at me with pleading eyes. "But even so, I have sinned. I'm shunned. I'm not part of this community anymore. Not now. Not yet. And I know when the shunning's over, though I'll try hard, it'll keep happening. The shunning." She moved her face closer to mine. "Don't you see? I want too much. I like rosy cheeks and lips. And I like pencil around my eyes and shadow on my lids. I really try, but I keep failing. I know I will go to hell for being too worldly. The bishop said if I don't change my ways, that's where I'll go."

"No, you won't. The Bishop shouldn't tell you that. You've confessed your love for Christ before the church. You've given your heart to Him and now God loves you as His child. He doesn't stop loving you because you sin. He is everywhere in your life. And He won't leave you because you've sinned. Ask for forgiveness. *From Him.* He's a good and loving God. And you belong to Him. Even during your time under the ban. Just love Him back. And trust Him."

I'm not sure if she believed me. But I did know she would confess to the Bishop she had sinned again by talking with me. She would tell him what I had said. And then, I would be shunned. Again. And I wouldn't repent. I would speak those same words again and again and again. And my shunning would go on and on and on. Over and over and over again. The truth of my words would never be heard. Not in the heart. Not in Bishop Herrfort's community.

Dear God, I have looked to You, listened to You. Always, always. And always, You have been with me. When I hear Your call, my heart strains to reach into Your Word and soak Your Will into the very core of what is me. Obeying. Giving You glory. And when my faith is too weak and failure touches my words, my actions, still You are there. Touching ... sometimes, gentle; sometimes, firm. Forgiving. Loving. Always. And when I please you, my heart soars. My God ... Father, Son, Holy Spirit. Giver of life. To me. Taking my sin. And, even then, loving me. Always. Holding Your hand out to me. Folding Your arms about me. Always. Telling me I have done my time in the land of my Amish brethren. And now it is finished. Your gift of choice left with them. You say, they will remember.

Dear Lord, I lay my heart at Your feet.

I walked down the hill on the fifteenth of September. I went into *Harriet's Homemade Soups and Hearty Sandwiches.* She looked at my face and a knowing passed over hers. Saying nothing, she got my valise and handed it to me.

I changed my clothes and waited for Daniel's call.

CPSIA information can be obtained at www.ICGtesting.com
Printed in the USA
LVOW13s0334220514

386783LV00002B/2/P